Medium in the Middle

Rob Preece

BooksForABuck.com
June 2010

This is a work of fiction. All characters, events, and locations are fictitious or used fictitiously. Any resemblance to actual events or people is coincidental

ISBN: 978-1-60215-128-4

Chapter 1

Being dead doesn't make you smart. It doesn't make you quiet, either.

Not that any ghost I've met admitted not knowing everything. They get in my face, moon me, demand attention and then they whine about the dumb things living people do, things they'd probably do themselves if they could. Admittedly, they don't have a lot else to do with their time.

Who cares, right? Most people never notice even when the dead shout at them. Ghosts can hear us, but that's *their* problem. At least that's the way it is for most people.

Not for me. I'm Annie Neeter, and I can't help but listen. Because I'm a medium, caught in the middle.

When I watch TV, I see people claim they can talk to the dead—like that's so special. Guess what? Everyone can talk *to* the dead. Most any time you open your mouth, you can bet dead people are listening. Every time you make a fool of yourself, dead people are laughing. The dead hang around in bars, restaurants, golf courses, sports arenas, and even worksites, just like they did when they were alive. A lot of people have died over the years, and they've got to go somewhere. Maybe you can't see them, but chances are you've got a ghost or two watching you, looking over your shoulder, checking out the play list on your iPod, and nagging at you to pay attention.

Like Harry Bitter was doing to me.

"That's the old Arndt place." Harry pointed at the document I'd dragged up after a thirty-minute search. Naturally he'd been no help in finding it. "Olay Arndt, I think his name was. Meanest man you ever met, wasn't getting paid for it."

"That's good to know, Harry," I lied politely. I didn't say anything about his out-of-date suit or the purple look his face had, probably from the heart attack that had killed him.

I was doing my job, researching titles in the basement of the Dallas County Courthouse. Harry was doing his job, too—being annoying.

Unlike Harry, I wouldn't be caught dead in the dreary Dallas County archives room if I could get my job done anywhere else. Its dirty-beige walls, stink of aging paper, and the hum of fluorescent lights forever threatening to go out on strike depressed me. Harry didn't see it that way. The head clerk there, Sam Bert made it even more unpleasant. Harry didn't like Sam, but Sam didn't try to flirt with him all the time either.

Harry hated it when I blew him off. "This Arndt guy, he used to catch kids and eat them."

"Really?" Not that I cared. Olay Arndt, if he really had been the property owner, had been dead even longer than Harry Bitter. And Harry Bitter had died in the 1950s after a frustrated career as a wanna-be property baron. Harry's biggest actual property investment was putting a hotel on Marvin Gardens, but that didn't stop him from going on about his big, long-dead plans.

Since I research titles for a living, you'd think having a live-in (no pun intended) ghost to help out would be a big asset. You'd be right—if Harry's memory hadn't gone on strike before he'd died and maintained the walk-out ever since.

"Yeah." Harry gave a ghostly sigh. "Olay Arndt used to grow apples on that property. He'd set his dogs after the kids who'd come around to nab themselves an apple or two."

If he remembered that much, maybe Olay Arndt really had owned the place. I didn't blame Arndt for setting the dogs on Harry. Harry had probably been as annoying a child as he'd become as a ghost.

A ten-minute search through a thick stack of misfiled documents turned up a property record that showed Harry was on the mark. Olay Arndt *had* owned the property until his death in 1952. At that point, his daughters had inherited and spent the next fifty years subdividing, re-dividing, consolidating, and suing each other until the property was so tied up in legal shenanigans that my computer searches had crashed the system and I'd had to go down to the courthouse to dig up old paper records.

"Good job, dude," I told the ghost. "You called that one exactly right."

"You talking to me, Annie?"

The voice wasn't Harry's. Unfortunately, it wasn't any more welcome than the ghost's.

For the sake of my job, I tried to like Sam Bert. My best sucked. The man had two nasty habits that I knew of—not bathing and coming onto anything female. Either problem alone, I could deal with. The combination, not so much.

I stepped backwards and turned so the stacks of paper I was looking through would be between us. They weren't a perfect shield, but you use what you have.

I gestured to the Bluetooth set I kept fastened to my ear like expensive jewelry. "On the phone, Sam—breaks up the monotony of looking at old records."

My life would have been a lot easier if they'd invented headsets back when I'd been a kid. In those days, everyone thought I was crazy for talking to myself. Now I wear the Bluetooth and people think I'm normal.

Sam sidled closer. "You just need someone to keep you company. That way, nobody will think you've gone off your nut."

"I'm *not* crazy."

"Hey, don't get whiney. I'm just offering my help."

Sam's khaki slacks hadn't seen an iron since they'd rolled off a loom in China, his polyester tie was frayed at the bottom, and his short-sleeved dress shirt displayed a long streak of mustard from a long-ago lunch. Pretty much he looked like he always did, except this time his face showed a slightly furtive look. Maybe because he'd snuck away from his desk.

"Well, what do you say?" he asked when I tried to get back to work. "Want to go out sometime?"

"Uh—well—" I got a brainstorm. "We have to work together. I'm afraid dating wouldn't be professional."

Following by an odor so strong it made my eyes run, Sam took another two steps toward me, walking right through Harry. The clerk carried a pile of microfiche that looked to be crumbling around the edges. Those had to be his excuse for coming into the archives.

Harry squawked when Sam stepped into his space and sidled out of the way, glaring at me as if it were *my* fault he was non-corporal and didn't take up any room.

"I've got tickets to the Mavericks game tonight," Sam said.

"I'm not much of a sports fan."

"Really? Have you tried *betting* on the games? It gives you a stake in the outcome. I think it's pretty exciting." Sam gave his characteristic head-scratch, examined what he'd found, then ate it.

I had to close my eyes. *Eeew.*

When I opened them, Harry was piling on. He stood behind Sam, first grooming Sam like a monkey, eating pretend fleas, then sticking his face near Sam's armpit and managing a pretty good faint. Being noncorporal meant he could flop down hard without actually hurting himself.

I tried to ignore the ghost. Title research isn't the best job in the world, but it paid the bills. I didn't want Sam to think I was laughing at him.

"I know I should get out more," I told Sam. "But I'm really too busy right now."

"You know what they say? The busiest people always have time to do more. It's an organization thing. That's how I manage to both work and keep a social life."

Sam reached a hand toward me.

I shivered. Did he really mean to touch me?

I wracked my brain for some way to keep him away. "Uh, speaking of work, have you ever looked at the Old Arndt Ranch in south Dallas County? There seems to be a missing—"

Sam looked offended and took a step backwards. "The County doesn't pay me to do *your* research, Annie."

"But they do pay him to try to make time with you," Harry said from over Sam's shoulder.

"Sorry." I shoved the dusty stack of old papers toward the head clerk. "Most of these are misfiled and that *is* your job. If you have a couple of minutes—"

"I'd better get back to my office. Closing time in half an hour, remember?"

"I'll be out before then."

"Good. I've got serious money on the Mavericks. I can't miss the game." He headed toward the elevator and I stepped to the other side of one of the big steel bookcases that contain the history of Dallas.

* * * *

The elevator dinged, but I figured it was just Sam leaving until I heard a cheap imitation of Darth Vader's voice. "Sam Bert?"

"Who the heck are you?" Sam retorted to the mystery visitor.

That's when Harry started yelling. "He's got a gun. I think he's reaching for it. He is. Ohmigod, he's going to kill Sam."

Did I say ghosts were useless? I might have exaggerated. They've got no more ability to predict the future than does the Eight Ball my brother gave me when I turned six. Even their versions of the past have to be taken with a boxcar load of salt, but it's hard to hide things from them. If Harry thought the intruder had a gun, he probably did.

Texas is all for concealed weapons, but the Records Department had a strict no-guns policy. Like it or not, there wasn't a hunting season for overweight clerks.

My muscles clenched like I was getting ready to take a punch. In my mind, my non-ghost Sensei reminded me to relax and I thought I did— until I tried to take a step and nearly toppled.

"Petrov sent me," the Darth Vader voice said. "You're late again. You know that's not acceptable."

I was pretty sure I heard the click of a shell being ratcheted into a chamber. Oh, hell, what to do?

"There's got to be a mistake." Sam's voice was always a bit high-pitched, but now it whined like a dentist's drill.

"You're right, Sammy. And you were the one to make it."

"I'll pay. I'm just waiting for my paycheck."

If my brain had been working halfway functionally, I would have stayed hidden. Sam's problems had nothing to do with me. But Harry distracted me by screaming at the top of his non-corporal lungs.

I grabbed the heaviest book I could see off the shelf, stepped from cover, and threw it at the guy doing the voice impression, hitting him in the Darth Maul ski mask that covered his head.

A mask meant criminal activity. It also meant the phony Sith probably hadn't planned on killing Sam. Maybe.

"Are you crazy?" Darth pointed the gun at me.

I hated it when people called me crazy. That word gave me the energy to rush the fake Sith, who looked a bit woozy from his close encounter with literacy.

I have no clue why he didn't send me to join the ghosts. Somehow, though, I closed the distance before he shot me.

I went directly from the run into a jump and I kicked his gun hand with a crescent kick at the top of my leap.

His gun spun across the floor, rebounding when it hit the wall.

I don't know much about guns, but this one was black, solid-looking, heavy as all get-out if my aching foot was anything to go by, and definitely not a toy.

Before Darth reacted, I reversed my foot's direction, popping him in the gonads with a twist kick.

Darth went down and I was on top of him, driving my knees into his ribs. As if a hundred-and-five pounds of woman could keep him down for long.

"Don't just stand there like a lump, Sam," I shouted. "Grab his gun. And call 9-1-1."

"Police," the Darth Vader impersonator said.

Cold rushed through my veins. Oh, shit. I should never have listened to Harry. Still...

"What are you talking about?"

"You've attacked a police officer in the line of duty. Get off me and I'll show you my ID. You're in big trouble, sister."

Now I know that no cop wanders around Dallas dressed like a refugee from a Science Fiction Con, but his confident tone confused me for just a second.

That was one second too long.

* * * *

I relaxed my knees against Darth's ribs slightly when he'd said he was a cop.

The Sith took advantage, bucking his hips and sending me sprawling. He rolled to his feet and barely missed me with his own kick.

Instead of flashing any police ID, he scrambled for his gun.

Sam, naturally, hadn't moved.

"He's lying. He's not a cop. No ID," Harry reported from where he'd stuck his head into Vader's jacket.

"Thanks for the timely call. But I'm not blind, Harry."

The prison tattoo on Vader's biceps was plenty to tell me that Harry was right. This guy definitely wasn't a cop. What he was, though, was on top of his gun.

I shoved Sam into the elevator, jumped in after him, and punched the 'close door' button.

Harry joined us a couple of seconds later, his brown suit blending with the fake wood-paneled elevator as he oozed through the wall.

Darth must have reached his weapon when we were about halfway up to the main floor because he stitched a series of shots through the elevator's floor. The steel construction might have slowed the bullets—it certainly didn't stop them.

Sam grunted. His already stained khakis got darker in one leg and he leaned against the wall, doing his best not to fall and make himself a bigger target.

Harry dithered. "He's hit. Do something, Annie."

I nodded. Stopping the blood was a priority, but I didn't want to save Sam just so we could get plugged again a few moments later. Maybe Darth hadn't been planning on killing anyone before, but he'd changed his plans. And, breathing problems or not, Darth could take the stairs and easily beat us to the main floor.

So I hammered the elevator's emergency stop button.

A loud alarm went off, which seemed like a good idea. It might scare Darth into leaving, and it drowned out Harry's screaming and Sam's sobbing. It's pathetic that I needed a zillion decibels of siren to be able to think, but that was pretty much my life.

As long as the elevator wasn't moving, I at least didn't have to worry about the elevator door opening and seeing Darth in front of me. So, I grabbed my mobile and a wad of Kleenex out of my pocket. Trying to do two things at once, I punched 9-1-1 on the phone, holding it between my ear and shoulder while I peeled Sam's baggy pants up his leg and pressed the Kleenex against what looked like a long scrape just above his knee.

"How come you don't use your headset?" Sam asked.

The 9-1-1 operator answered before I had to respond to Sam's question. I *really* didn't want to tell him the Bluetooth was a fake.

The operator had trouble hearing me over the elevator alarm, but that was her problem. I shouted at her, gave her directions, and remembered everything I could think of about what the fake Sith had looked like, what he'd been wearing, and what he'd been shooting.

* * * *

One good thing about working in downtown Dallas—there are always cops around.

Sirens sounded within two minutes of my call.

An hour later, half the Dallas Police Department was on scene drinking coffee and looking for shells.

Darth, of course, had vanished in the confusion.

You'd think I'd be the hero of the day, right? I mean, this was the first time I'd used my Tae Kwon Do for real, and the bullet holes in the elevator proved that Darth hadn't been making a social call.

I would have thought that, too. Boy was I wrong.

* * * *

Dallas's police headquarters would have been pleasant if I'd been there for a field trip.

As it was, I shivered from the aftereffects of shock and was more than a little queasy.

The two detectives assigned to me, a stud-muffin white guy named Arran Dane and a middle-aged African-American woman named Carly Fineman, were patient as they could be. I didn't need help talking, though. I babbled about Darth Maul, obsessed about Sam's blood, which I'd gotten all over myself, and went through alternate moments of shivering and sweating.

After a while, Fineman got me a blanket to wrap myself in and Dane brought me a cup of coffee.

It wasn't Starbucks, but it was a lot better than I'd guessed it would be, my only knowledge of police coffee having come from hardboiled detective novels where it is universally belittled.

The cops were excited when I remembered Vader saying something about Petrov sending him. They lost interest when I couldn't tell them who Petrov was, or even for sure it was a person rather than a corporation or maybe a brand of earwax. Apparently the name Petrov didn't pop up any red flags in the Dallas Police Department criminal database.

The more questions they asked, the more I, and they, realized I hadn't really noticed as much as I should have. Vader had been dressed in black. Was he in jeans or suit pants? I couldn't remember. Was there a design on his t-shirt? Did his tattoo have words or just a design? I couldn't bring up a mental picture. All I could think about was the way the steel had peeled back as bullets ripped through the elevator, and the way Sam's blood had gushed through my fingers as I'd pressed the Kleenex into his thigh.

The more often I answered, "I don't know," the grimmer the faces on my two cops.

I would have done better if Detective Dane hadn't been completely sexy. His dark blue eyes, black hair, and knife-sharp cheekbones weren't just a little distracting. I couldn't see much of his body beneath the business suit he wore, but what I could see looked good enough to eat.

Which made it harder for me to think about my run-in with the dark side of the force.

Dane's scowl was distracting enough. When a gaggle of ghosts wandered in and started imitating him, overlapping their protoplasmic selves with the detective's body, their lips moving just a fraction behind Dane's speech so the cop looked like a slightly out of focus television tube, I had an even harder time concentrating.

One of the visiting ghosts had holes in his chest and another had his nose adjusted completely to the right side of his face. From their uniforms, I thought I was seeing the ghosts of Dallas Police Past. They didn't fill me with confidence.

The detectives picked up on my distraction. From the way their questioning changed, they thought I was hiding something. Which I was, of course. I didn't want to see that disappointed look on Dane's face when he learned that I was a crazy-woman who talked to ghosts.

After two hours of increasing frustration, Dane's cell rang and he went outside the interview room to take it.

I looked at Fineman and relaxed just a little. She was another female, after all. I was better at dealing with women than with sexy men. "Are we done?"

Fineman blew a cloud of cigarette smoke toward a 'no smoking' sign. "We can be done when you get around to telling us what you're hiding."

"Hiding?" My voice squeaked. The only thing I was hiding was Harry's warning.

"We can't help you if you don't let us."

Dane burst back into the interview room, a big snarl on his face. "All right, we've had a break in the case. This is your last chance to open up, unless you want to be charged as an accessory."

"I've told you everything I can think of."

"Everything?" Dane made sure I heard his skepticism.

"We're going to find out the truth," Fineman added. Dane hadn't let her know what was up, but he didn't have to. The already-chilly room had turned downright icy when he'd exploded back from his phone call. "When we do, you'll wish you'd been straight with us from the start."

I started through my story again, but Dane stopped me almost at once.

"Hang on. You say you heard what sounded like a bullet being chambered?"

"That's right." Surely they wouldn't argue that one with me. I mean, there were a dozen holes in the elevator that told me that Vader was up to no good and had definitely been armed.

"Think real hard. Did you *say* anything then?"

I tried to remember. "I might have been screaming." My throat was still a little sore, but that could have been from inhaling Fineman's second-hand smoke. "But I don't think I said anything in words until I'd knocked away his gun. That's when I told Sam to call 9-1-1."

Dane stuck his too-sexy face within inches of mine.

Irrationally, I noticed that *he* smelled like sunshine and ancient forests. I suspected I smelled like old swamps.

"You didn't call the gunman *Harry?*" he demanded. "You didn't ask him what he thought he was doing? You didn't say you were going to kill him?"

My stomach dropped. I had said something to the ghost. Sam should have been worrying about staying alive but instead he'd been listening to me blather. He could have come clean about his gambling debts but instead he was trying to stick me in the frame—maybe because I'd turned down his date.

I blinked at Dane, torn between wishing I could get away from him and enjoying that kind of scrutiny from a guy who could best be described as steamy. I came up with what I thought was a clever evasion. "Why would I call him hairy? I've given you a description. The guy wore a ski mask. He could have been bald from what I could see."

Dane pounded a fist into his open palm right in front of my nose. The sound, a hard smack, shocked me into silence.

"You're not a very good liar, Miss Neeter," Fineman brought her face so close to mine I could count the pores in her nose. "We know things can get out of control. It's obvious your plan didn't work and it isn't right that you're the only one who has to take the heat for that. If you don't give your side of the story, who will?"

Dane shook his head but at least he stepped away from me when Fineman got close. My brain stopped thinking about a sexy guy and started worrying about going to jail.

"I say we lock her in the tank." Dane stripped off his suit jacket, exposing muscular arms beneath a white linen shirt—and his shoulder holster. "A few hours of that and she'll be begging us for a chance to talk."

"Perhaps you didn't realize that it would get so violent." Fineman faked a smile and I noticed the line of gold around each of her upper front teeth.

One of the ghosts pulled out of Dane and pushed himself between Fineman's enormous breasts, his head poking out like a third boob.

I stifled a completely inappropriate laugh. "I don't know what you're talking about."

"Perhaps they didn't tell you what they had planned." Fineman draped a big hand over mine and offered me a cigarette.

I turned down the cigarette and pulled my hand away. Her sympathy was way too fake. Even if I'd been too stupid to figure it out myself, eighteen separate ghosts all reminded me that the police were playing the good-cop/bad-cop game. Clearly Dane had been tapped as the bad cop. He was convincing, so I suspected this was his usual role.

I wasn't an expert at handling sexy guys, but my years interacting with the psychiatric profession had made me an expert on hostile questions. It was time to go on the offensive rather than just sit back and take their abuse. "I don't like what you're implying."

Fineman shook her head in obviously faked sadness. "Think about this, Annie. This Harry guy is walking around free. You don't think he's going to turn himself in to help you out, do you?"

"They've got you now." Two ghosts high-fived each other.

I'm normally not paranoid but I didn't need ghostly visions to tell me that the cops had decided to build a case against me.

I briefly considered telling the police who Harry really was. It wouldn't convince them, I knew that. I'd been trying to convince people since I learned how to talk and hadn't even persuaded my own brother I was telling the truth. Still, they might decide I was too crazy to be a gun moll, or whatever modern-day female accomplices are called. I felt ashamed when I realized why I was holding back—I was tired of every cute guy I met looking at me like I was a jar of nitroglycerine set to go off.

It was obvious that Arran Dane and I weren't going to have magic moments, but I still didn't want him thinking I was crazy. I'd practically rather have him think I was a criminal than a nut-job.

I decided to put an end to what had become a pointless discussion. "I've got nothing else to say."

"If you don't—"

Dane put a hand on Carly Fineman's shoulder. "We'll leave her here to think about it." He focused on me. If you change your mind," he pointed at a button near the door, "you can ring for me."

"I want a lawyer."

He shrugged. "We all have our problems."

"Come on, I watch TV. I'm entitled to a lawyer, right? One will be appointed, all that stuff. Miranda, remember?"

He narrowed his eyes. "Maybe you should have watched more carefully. You haven't been arrested—you came here voluntarily, remember. Until you're arrested and formally charged with a crime, you don't have a right to squat."

That didn't ring quite true to me. "But—"

"If you're not arrested, you can leave," a semi-friendly ghost said. I think she had a crush on Dane and wanted me out of the way.

I nodded without thinking, then noticed the strange looks from the two detectives.

"If I'm not arrested, then I'm out of here. You've got my phone number. Call me if you want to listen to what I have to say instead of putting words in my mouth."

"On the other hand, we *could* arrest you." Fineman forgot she was supposed to be the good cop here.

"Then I'll get a lawyer and get out of here anyway. You pick, but don't play me."

"Don't leave town," Dane grumbled.

It wasn't as if I had any place to go, but his attitude bugged me.

It was annoying to realize that I still found him sexy. I don't like to think of myself as shallow, but his hard body and deep blue eyes did something to me.

Dane followed me out of the interview room and down the hall. "You think you're being smart walking out of here, Miss Neeter, but you're not. Whoever he his, Harry knows we've been talking to you.

13

When you walk, he'll figure you spilled. If you don't talk to us now, he might silence you for good."

"*Spilled?* Do they *train* you to talk like 1930s gangster, or did you pick this up yourself?"

He clenched his fists so tight his knuckles turned white and I jolted back when one of the ghosts made a punching motion at my head.

Dane gave me a pitying look and I realized he must have come to the same conclusions every other guy in my life had—I was a crazy woman.

I didn't need giggling ghosts to tell me that Dane followed me outside the substation and toward the bus stop. He didn't try to keep it a secret.

Chapter 2

I'm not antisocial. And the rumors that I hate guys were invented by high school kids who didn't get why I wouldn't make out with guys in the back seat of cars. *You* try to get in the mood when a car-full of voyeur-ghosts are peeking down your unbuttoned blouse and checking out the action. If you can, you're better than me.

Good excuses or not, I didn't have a boyfriend to call and pour out my sorrows to.

On my way to the bus stop, I called my brother, Jack.

Unlike my parents and the rest of the world, my brother didn't blow off my stories about ghosts. He didn't believe them, but he listened. You see, he felt responsible for them.

He thought my visions came from when he'd fried my brain back when I'd been a baby. My mother had been running an errand and I'd stopped breathing and turned blue. Jack's four-year-old logic had concluded I needed to be warmed up—and he'd popped me into the microwave oven.

If I could believe my brother's stories, I hadn't actually cooked for more than a couple of seconds. It had happened when I was so young, I don't know if I'd seen ghosts before that—but the zap was as likely an explanation for my talent as anything. I'd never been struck by lightning, abducted by aliens, or bitten by a vampire. Jack was certain microwaves were the culprit for my weirdness, but what did he know?

Jack, like everyone else, wouldn't believe that the ghosts were real.

You'd think I could do the TV psychic gig. The one that goes, *someone whose name starts with 'J' is trying to contact you.* The problem is, ghost-talking isn't like a telephone. I can't just call particular ghosts, and most ghosts don't play parlor games.

Even though he didn't believe in ghosts, Jack believed in taking care of me. Predictably, he invited me over.

I insisted on clearing the invitation with his wife, Lauren. She and I weren't exactly at odds, but she was protective of my brother and their child and thought I was a bad influence. To my surprise, though, she seconded his invitation. So I walked over to the West End rail station, and headed north, into Plano, a suburb of Dallas.

I didn't know if the cops would treat Plano as leaving town so I wasn't going to ask them.

Unlike the rest of Dallas, the rail is usually a ghost-free zone. It was new enough that not many people had died on the trains, and I suspected that the electrical currents running the trail distracted the spirits. No such luck this trip. A flock of ghosts jumped onto the train at my stop—with a couple more standing in front of the speeding train and grabbing a rail as they whipped through the machinery at fifty miles an hour. Ghosts and vehicular traffic both have a tendency to make me seasick, which is one reason I'd never learned how to drive.

Once on board, the ghosts cornered me and persuaded me to help them play a dice game. I was used to this and carried a pair with me most of the time. So I pulled the dice from my handbag, and tried not to look at the ghosts. The woman in the flapper outfit wouldn't have been bad if she hadn't had a syringe hanging from her arm, but the guy with his head in his hand was gross, even for a ghost.

I shook the dice and smiled at the cheers and groans when my first roll was snake eyes.

Lots of people like games, and being dead doesn't change that. It does, however, put a crimp on their ability to get a game going on their own. They sure can't play bridge, which was a game my parents had tried to teach me until they decided I was cheating all the time. I couldn't help it if the ghosts always whispered what cards my opponents had.

Ghosts always cheat, which makes playing poker with them an exercise in frustration. They couldn't manage videogames without messing up the electrical currents so bad the TV would fritz out. That leaves dice games and a few others.

Since they're non-corporal, though, they can't actually throw the dice —they leave that to living people. Pretty much anywhere people are rolling dice, ghosts swarm around.

Needless to say, I didn't spend much time in casinos.

During the ride to Plano, I kept rolling the dice and the ghosts asked me about my day—for them it seemed that one day was pretty much like the other.

They were always interested in my normal, boring days but they really hung onto my account of the Darth Maul attack and the hot-cop run-in with an interest almost as great as my next roll of the dice.

"You need to tell the cops the truth," one of the ghosts said. "Harry saved Sam's life. He should be the hero. Just because he's a ghost, he's not getting any credit."

"Yeah. How come we never get credit for anything?" another demanded.

"Cause we don't do nothing."

"Do to."

"Do not."

"Okay. Maybe we don't do much. But—"

The ticket collector wandered into my car, cutting off a debate that was tragically similar to so many ghost-driven conversations.

The conductor hardly gave my ticket a glance, but he did give *me* a strange look. Part of his job was to call the Transit Police if transients started squatting on the line. He must have seen me talking to myself when he'd been on the other side of the door and wondered if I was a fruitcake. Naturally none of the ghosts bothered warning me he was coming. They seemed to think it was a lot of fun having everyone think I was crazy.

I made a point of taking my Bluetooth out of my ear and then putting it back in. The conductor gave me a relieved look.

When I got off the train, Lauren was waiting in her car—with company. One member of that company, my three-year-old 'Little Jack' in his car seat in the back, was welcome.

The other part, a nasty ghost with no clothes on—sat rubbing his protoplasm over Lauren's body while he stared at me, daring me to do something about it.

Considering that Lauren is pretty enough to be a movie star if she ever gets tired of being a lawyer, she got a lot of ghostly attention wasn't especially unusual. That didn't mean it wasn't disgusting.

I gestured for him to move out, but he grinned pointed at his groin. "Why don't you sit on the big one?"

I pretended to have to squint. "Why don't you take the toy soldier and find a keyhole to put it in?"

"What toy soldier?" Sadly, Little Jack was still working on his voice control.

Lauren winced, then looked concerned. "Having a bad spell of it, Annie?"

"*I'm* fine. It's this pervert who's got problems. Move it, jerk."

"Is it one of the ghosts, Aunt Annie? What's he doing? How come I can't see him?"

"I do see a ghost and he's sitting where I want to sit."

"Oh." Little Jack considered that. "Does he take up a lot of room?"

"I'm just don't want to sit on his lap." True as far as it went.

The ghost finally moved, but did so by crawling over Lauren, rubbing all over her before slithering through the closed driver's side door.

I waited until the ghost completely exited the car before sitting. "Thanks for picking me up, Lauren. I've had a rough day."

"Jack said. Do the police really think you're involved in that uh-incident downtown?"

"What insendent?" Little Jack echoed from the back.

"A bad man tried to hurt someone I work with," I explained.

"Did you stop him? I'll bet you gave him a karate chop." Little Jack made a slapping motion to the side of his car seat. "Hi-yah."

My nephew was the only person I knew who was actually impressed by my green belt in Tae Kwon Do.

I took in a breath to brag on my twist kick, then caught Lauren's warning look. "Uh, no. Sorry. No karate chops."

"Did the ghosts help?" he continued. "Maybe the ghost of Jackie Chan."

"Jackie Chan isn't dead." Lauren didn't believe in my ghosts, didn't like Little Jack talking about them, and thought my martial arts training was way too violent.

Since my brother humored me about my ghosts, Little Jack remained fascinated no matter that his mother disapproved.

I tried to steer a safe course. "The police heard me talking to one of the ghosts named Harry, and they think I was talking to the gun—uh, badguy." I caught myself way too late.

"Did you say gun, Aunt Annie?" Little Jack's face reddened with excitement.

From Lauren's glare, Little Jack wasn't the only one getting excited. I didn't need any ghost whispers to guess this was the last time I'd be invited to visit if I didn't shape up to Lauren's specifications.

"Did you tell the police about your psychological issues?" Lauren spoke carefully as if waiting for an explosion. "If they understand you talk to your little people all the time, I'm sure they'll back off and pursue more fruitful lines of research."

Because she was a lawyer, Lauren sometimes couldn't stop herself from talking like that. I mean, who says things like 'pursue more fruitful lines of research?'

"Of course I didn't tell them. Do you think I *want* people to believe I'm crazy?"

She sighed, but somehow managed not to even wrinkle her perfect face. "Is it better that they think you're a criminal?"

Lauren didn't get it. She hadn't grown up with people shaking their heads when she walked into the room. She hadn't been the one who'd had screaming fits in the girls' locker room because pervert ghosts hung around gazing at semi-undressed teenagers. She hadn't ever discovered that her date to the Senior Prom had only asked her because he'd lost a bet to her brother. Nobody's life is perfect and I was sure Lauren had faced bigger tragedies than discovering that Neiman's didn't have the dress she wanted in size two. I just didn't know what they might have been.

For me, the answer to her question wasn't obvious. Something about sexy Detective Arran Dane put me back in adolescent angst. Maybe I really would prefer that he think I was a dangerous criminal than to know I was a crazy-girl who talked to ghosts nobody else could see.

* * * *

My brother, wearing a big red apron with hot pink lettering that proclaimed: *There's a Charcoal Fire in my Heart,* greeted me as we got out of the car. "I'm grilling steaks, but I'll whip up an omelet if you'd rather."

I could never tell whether my brother was really happy to see me, or was only pretending because of his lifelong guilt over zapping me in the microwave. His effusion whenever we got together seemed simultaneously authentic and completely over the top. Then again, he was over the top with everything. The big wet kiss he gave Lauren when she walked in the door made me want to put my hands over Little Jack's eyes. And she hadn't been gone ten minutes. Although a part of me was grossed out, a bigger part wished I had someone who would be that happy to see me. How pathetic was that?

I waited for things to calm down before I answered him.

"I would love an omelet." There weren't a *lot* of cow ghosts in the city, but there were *some.* Cow ghosts don't talk any better than living cows, and I doubted they'd gotten any smarter for being dead. Still, the look on their faces when they caught me in mid-burger, disapproving and tragic, stuck with me for a long time.

Even eggs were problematic. I checked Lauren's refrigerator to make sure the eggs were free-range. I'd never seen a chicken ghost, but my brother's house was in what had been, until recently, farming country. I didn't want to have to face the ghost of a chicken that had been cooped up in a tiny cage.

Jack finished cooking, helped Lauren cart massive quantities of meat, vegetables, French bread, and wine to the table, and the four of us sat down for a late supper.

For a relaxing change, Jack and Lauren's dining room was blissfully ghost-free.

For the next half-hour, conversation was limited to how the food was coming (well), whether I wanted red wine or white (red), and how Little Jack was doing at the Montessori school he attended (he'd been picked to play a wise man in the school Christmas pageant and was very pleased).

"You'll be spending the night here, of course," Jack announced once we'd rinsed off the dishes and loaded the dishwasher. "Little Jack doesn't get enough time with his only aunt."

"I bought a pair of jeans and some clean underwear in your size," Lauren added. "You can wear one of Jack's t-shirts as a nightshirt. And I got a new toothbrush for you. Because you always use that as an excuse not to stay."

I was torn. I'd made my apartment mostly safe from ghosts, but after the day I'd had, ghost-makers made me more nervous than the already dead. "You're sure?"

"You can come to my t-ball game tomorrow, Aunt Annie," Little Jack proclaimed. "And you can watch my new *Winnie the Pooh* video."

How could I say no to that? "Oh, Jackie, that would be—"

A clanging bell sounded, like an old-fashioned telephone that just kept ringing.

My nerdy brother looked at the oversized wristwatch he always sported. "Intrusion alarm. Probably the neighbor's dog but I'd better take a look."

Jack equipped his home with all of the latest gadgets, including a security system that would have made Fort Knox proud. He tapped at his watch and the TV turned on. Multiple display windows showed various camera angles. In one of them, a dark-clad person was snooping near his garage.

"Human-style dog," Lauren said.

My hormones recognized that shadow slightly before my logical brain did, and flushed a load of adrenalin into my system.

"It's Arran—I mean Detective Dane," I said. "He's the one who thinks I did it. I thought I'd lost him when I got on the train. Guess not."

"We'll fix that," Lauren promised. "Annie, give me a buck."

I'd gotten a couple of Susan B. Anthony dollars in change for my train fare so I pulled one from my pocket and handed it over.

"Okay, I'm representing you. Let's get this detective in here and take care of your problems."

"But—"

"I'm a good lawyer, Annie. Trust me."

"Yeah, but—"

"Oh, he's kind of sexy, isn't he?" Lauren smoothed back her hair. She was fiercely loyal to my brother but that didn't stop her from flirting with anything with a 'Y' chromosome.

Dane seemed to have caught sight of the video camera. He glared at it, his jaw tight and a vertical line going straight up his forehead from between his eyes.

"He's a cop," I warned her.

"You noticed, did you?" Lauren giggled as if we were sharing a girl-bonding moment.

She tossed her head, sending her dark hair swirling everywhere, hitched back her shoulders, making the most of her figure, and instructed her husband to invite the detective in.

Jack had been married to this woman for five years, but he still had to shake his head clear before pushing another button on his wristwatch computer and speaking into it.

Once again, I had to swallow. Nobody would ever look at me that way.

"Detective Arran Dane." Jack's voice sounded like a hell-and-brimstones preacher coming from a dozen speakers spread through his yard. "There is no need for you to lurk. Come on in and ask your questions."

Another push of the button and the garage door opened so Dane could join us in the family room.

"Better go to bed, big guy," Jack told his son. "Brush your teeth and come back to give mommy and me a hug."

Little Jack shook his head violently. "I want to see the policeman. Does he have a gun? Can I touch it? Will he shoot it?"

Sometimes I get depressed that I was twenty-five, single, and, except for a couple of college-era drunken moments, practically a virgin. But then I saw my nephew in action. What would I do if I had a kid? Considering that the world believed me insane and I'd probably be committed if it weren't for the deinstitutionalization movement, I had no business even imagining doing anything that might bring a child into the world.

Moments later, Dane's presence filled the room. He gave Jack a nod, me a quick glance, then Lauren a long and appraising stare.

I gritted my teeth. I *wasn't* jealous, I couldn't be jealous. I wouldn't be jealous. Dane was nothing to me.

"Well, Ms. Neeter, you got what you asked for," Dane announced. "I've got a warrant for your arrest."

* * * *

I have to give her credit, there's more to Lauren than movie star looks. She stared down the detective, told him that she represented me, and that she didn't appreciate his flippant answer to my request for an attorney the last time he'd had me alone.

"We've got an attempted murder of a county employee in a county-owned building, ma'am," he answered. "Being polite and keeping everyone happy is not our highest priority. And no la-di-da lawyer is going to change that. We're going to get to the bottom of this case no matter whose toes get stepped on."

I would have gotten pissed and slugged him, but Lauren must have heard worse slurs all the time. "My client has already told you she heard the gunman declare he was sent by someone named Petrov. Have you questioned this Petrov person? A title researcher wouldn't seem my first choice for an criminal accomplice."

"With what they charge? I've always thought they were highway robbers."

Lauren stiffened. "This is not a joking matter. My client has cooperated fully and will have nothing more to say about this crime if you refuse to treat her respectfully, Detective."

"Is that right?"

She nodded. "What you may not know is that Annie has a well-documented case of schizophrenia. She often talks to people who aren't there. Which is what she was doing during this assault." She turned to me and spoke slowly as if I would be confused by big words. "Annie, was the Harry you mentioned the guy with the gun?"

"Of course not. I don't know *that* guy's name."

"Go ahead and tell the detective who Harry really is. Tell him the truth, as you know it."

I couldn't read Dane's expression. I suspected I wouldn't have any problems reading it once he heard me out. He'd switch back and forth between disbelief and pity. Disbelief I could take, but pity pisses me off.

Jack stepped in to rescue me. "My sister—"

Dane held up a hand. "Let her answer the question."

"I was talking to a ghost," I admitted. "Of course you won't believe me, nobody believes me. Still, that's who Harry is—Harry Bitter. When he was alive, he was a wanna-be developer. He went broke during a 1950s recession and had a heart attack. Now he likes to hang around the County Records building and imagine he's going to buy and develop on different properties. He was the one who told me about the gunman. Which was why I threw the book at him."

"You threw a book at a ghost?"

I sighed. "Don't be ridiculous. I threw a book at the guy with the gun, Darth Maul."

Dane's pen froze on his pad. "Maul? So you did recognize the guy?"

Did I have the hots for a guy with a sub-normal IQ? This time I slowed down, talking to him like Lauren had talked to me.

"I've told you this before. Darth Maul was a character in one of the more forgettable Star Wars movies. The gunman wore a mask that resembled that character."

Dane's eyes narrowed—something he seemed to do a lot, which made sense to me as it made him look even more sexy than usual, but he didn't put on the pitying expression I'd expected.

"You know, Ms. Neeter, this is the biggest load of crap I've ever heard. No offense, Mrs. Neeter, but I can't believe you're naïve enough to believe that either."

"You can call me Lauren," she said, earning a big smile from the detective. "And trust me, Detective Dane, I have ample documentation of my sister-in-law's condition." She turned to her husband. "Sweetie, run and get those files you keep on your sister."

"What files?" I had no idea my brother kept files about me.

"You know how Jack worries about you." Lauren patted me on the arm, keeping up that soft 'talk-to-the-idiot' tone. "He's been trying to figure out how the microwaves could have damaged you ever since he was four—and he's still at it. You know that accident is why he became an electrical engineer, don't you?"

Did I detect the slight hint of bitterness? If so, I couldn't blame her. A husband should be obsessed with making his wife happy, right? And his wife shouldn't have to put up with him fixating on curing his insane sister.

Unfortunately, there was nothing I could do to make Jack give up his guilt. Considering that I probably would have died of SIDS if he hadn't done something, I felt nothing but gratitude. I'd rather *see* ghosts than *be* one.

"I never asked him to worry about me or to try and fix me."

Lauren's face softened and she patted me on the arm again. "I know, sweetie. I get protective of Jack, that's all."

"Very charming." Dane's sarcastic tone cut the air. "You're seriously claiming that your husband cooked your client in a microwave oven and that this makes her not responsible for her crimes?"

"It's pretty clear," I said, "that you're going to believe what you want to, regardless of the evidence."

Lauren made shushing motions, but I was sick of his crap. "I'm not a criminal but I have been able to see and hear ghosts ever since I can remember. If it had anything to do with the famous microwave incident, so be it. If not, then there's another reason."

"Okay," Dane grinned at me. "Prove it. Ask my dead grandmother her favorite perfume."

I sighed. How many times had I gotten that kind of response? No wonder I found it easier to deny everything. "Bring her ghost around, Detective, and I'll ask her for you."

He folded his arms across his chest. Yeah, it was a nice chest. Still, that folded arms thing pissed me off.

"Just what I thought."

I'd heard this all my life. Maybe because Dane was so sexy, or maybe I'd just been pushed too far, but I wanted to show him more than I'd wanted anything in my life. "If you want proof, I'll give you some."

"Annie—"

Maybe I had been raising my voice. Okay, definitely. I thought I was entitled. "No, Lauren, I'm sick of this. I'm going to show this detective something he can't explain without the ghosts, then I'm going to laugh at him when he insists on making up some implausible excuse."

"She doesn't like having her reality attacked," my loyal attorney advised the detective. "She truly believes she sees ghosts. You might consider that before you decide you'd like to put her on the witness stand. And if you think she is connected with the shooter, you'd better have your head examined. Even a criminal is smarter than to hang around with someone who has more imaginary friends than real ones."

I swiped away a tear but belatedly kept my mouth shut. Lauren was defending me as well as she could, but she wasn't sparing my feelings any in her efforts.

My brother bustled in with a stack of cardboard cartons so tall they towered above his head.

He plopped them down on the floor, opened a couple, and then yanked out a worn manila folder from the third, holding it out but not letting go of it. "These are all records of Annie's problems, her discipline issues, and her years of psychiatric and psychological counseling."

He pulled back the manila folder and examined it. "I think you'll find this one most helpful. It's the psychiatric evaluation done by the juvenile court system when she was in high school. I assure you, her symptoms haven't changed since then."

Symptoms? Usually Jack at least pretended to believe me. He should have said *visions*, maybe *manifestations*. *Symptoms* was very much the wrong word.

Dane tugged the folder out of my brother's hands and flipped it open.

I'd asked a ghost to sneak a look at my files when they had been in a locked filing cabinet at Aaron Burr High, where I'd gone to school. Assuming she'd reported back with the truth, I knew what a bunch of lies it contained. The only good news was, it just might persuade Dane what a useless witness I'd make.

Once he'd read it, though, Dane would think of me as a nutjob. I really didn't need that.

"Tell you what, Detective," I said before he could get started on his reading. "There's a Starbucks on Fifteenth Street. Buy me a cup of coffee and I'll show you some ghost tricks."

"Why not here?"

I waved my arms. "Do *you* see any ghosts around?" There were probably a couple of ghosts in the master bedroom waiting for their evening entertainment, but frankly, I didn't trust pervert ghosts. I'd lost count of the number of times I'd been burned by ghosts who agreed to help me out, then thought it was extremely funny to lie. For some reason, ghosts who hang around in coffee shops tend to be good-natured and willing to do a girl a favor. For most of them, anyway, real human interaction was even better than the few whiffs of caffeine they managed to consume from the coffee. If I was going to take another chance of making an idiot out of myself, I wanted to up my odds a bit.

"You stay here with Little Jack," Lauren told her husband. "It's obvious that my client is going to ignore my advice. I have to go along to keep her from digging a deeper hole than she needs to."

"Thanks for the vote of confidence."

"You've earned it," Dane said.

Chapter 3

"Can we get this over with?" Dane had ordered a cup of black coffee. Now he glared at us.

Lauren and I both ordered caramel-mocha-lattes with decaf coffee, and were savoring the thick whipped cream layer swirled with caramel sauce. It wasn't our fault Dane was too macho to get anything yummy.

I looked around and saw a couple of ghosts staring longingly at an abandoned chess game on a table toward the back of the coffee shop.

They were older guys, dressed like farmers, with faded feed caps, and dusty overalls. Both wore mud-spattered lace-up boots that were down at the heels and, in the case of the older of the two, split in front so a pair of un-socked toes poked out. They'd probably started coming here years before Starbucks was invented, back when Plano was a farming town and Dallas had seemed like a distant center of urban iniquity. Lacking anyplace better to go, they still came and loitered now that Plano had become one of the largest cities in the state.

They glanced up when I walked over, but quickly returned to a discussion of which player would have won, had they not headed somewhere else in the middle of the game.

Which gave me an idea.

"Do me a favor, guys, and I'll help you finish that game."

"Oh, so you admit to seeing us?" the older ghost asked. "Most people ignore us."

"Well, yeah. How else could I help you with your game?"

"Finish this game and play one more," the younger ghost said. "Then maybe—"

"Two more," the older one corrected.

I shook my head. "It isn't *that* big a favor. I'll either finish this game or start a whole new one for you, your choice. I don't have time to play a bunch of games, though."

"Finish this one," both agreed.

"I've seen better acting by hopped up junkies." Dane straddled the chair the older ghost had been sitting in. "You really are crazy if you think I'm going to fall for that faked talking to yourself."

The old farmer skedaddled out of Dane's way like a pigeon, squawking angrily about the way people just didn't respect their elders any more.

Treating ghosts like they didn't exist was rude, but at times it was necessary. They don't give up their seats, hog the sidewalks, fill the aisles at the library, and take up every airline seat in first class. And this was in

Texas, which was a barely inhabited part of the world until they'd invented air conditioning and made it possible to survive the brutal summers.

I'd never been to Europe or Africa, but I could imagine how overwhelming the ghosts would be in lands where people had lived huddled close together for thousands of years. Living in a city like London or Paris would be like walking through Times Square on New Years Eve, with zillions of ghosts getting in your way, talking to you in languages like Latin, Gaulic, Celtic, or Pict. I loved history but the idea of all those ghosts scared me.

Ghosts wearing anything older than outdated overalls or 1920s suits were scarce in Dallas. The few Civil War-era ghosts stood out like rare diamonds. Would the ghosts of Roman Legionnaires still battle with Huns or Goths if I visited France or Italy?

"Don't mind him," I told the older farmer, who was busy proving to me that foul language really wasn't a modern invention the way some politicians claim. "He's not so much anti-ghost as just unfriendly. He's a cop."

"Figured it had to be something like that," the younger farmer said. "I'm Joshua by the way."

"Daniel." The older farmer squeezed between a chair and the table— just as Lauren pulled it out and sat. He hopped back to his feet, glared at Lauren for a moment, then his expression shifted to a confused smile. Nobody stayed mad at Lauren. No male, anyway. "So, what's this favor?"

"I'm Annie," I said. "This is my sister-in-law Lauren and the cop is Detective Dane."

"Arran," Dane said.

Lauren shook her head. "I think it would be better if we retained some formality in this."

I didn't mind thinking of him as Arran.

"You can call him Arran but I'll have to remember to call him Dane," I explained.

"Yeah, okay," Daniel said. "But what's the favor and when do we get our chess game?"

"A ghost downtown, Harry Bitter, saw this guy come into the County Records building with a gun and warned me."

"Nothing wrong with a gun," Daniel said. "Carry one myself."

"I'm not interested in a political discussion," I said. "I just want some help with the cop."

"Cops never help, they're always trouble." That was Joshua, echoing what I was discovering.

"You said you were going to show me something. If you were just going to fake talking to yourself, you could have done that down at headquarters. I'm being pretty patient with this arrest, but that isn't going to last."

"Tell me something, Detective. Does annoying people usually get you what you're looking for? Because I'm not really finding myself motivated to be helpful."

I was pleased to see him redden a little, not that it made him look less sexy. The added color just heightened his deep tan. Which wasn't fair at all. When I blush, I get blotchy, like I've broken out in hives.

"You don't have to be helpful," he said. "You have to come with me down to the lockup."

"I'll have you bailed out in no time, Annie," Lauren said. "And I don't appreciate you threatening my client, Detective."

"Spare me from estrogen rage."

"You really are asking for it, Detective." I turned back to my new friends. "So are you willing to help."

"Sure," Joshua said. "Play our game and then we'll do you a favor."

I looked at Arran just in time to see him reaching for the white queen. "Don't touch."

He jerked back his hand as if I'd bitten him. "I beg your pardon."

"I promised the guys I'd play out this game for them. You heard me say that, didn't you?"

Right on cue, that pity-look I'd been dreading showed up on his face. It didn't last long, replaced by anger and frustration, but it would only get worse when I finally persuaded him I wasn't faking it. I didn't know that I'd convince him the ghosts really were there, but I suspected I could persuade him I believed in them.

"Detective Dane is in a hurry, guys. We need to give him some answers before he arrests me. If he does that, I won't be able to finish your game for you."

"Hey, I know," Daniel said, "he's got a gun. That's what that other ghost discovered, right? That enough for you?"

I shook my head. "He's a cop. Of course he has a gun. I wouldn't need to talk to ghosts to guess that."

Daniel stared at Arran as if he were a bug the farmer wondered would be worth his while to stomp.

"How about his drivers license," I suggested. "Can you read his middle name off of it?"

"I never paid much attention in school," Daniel admitted. "Not to the reading part."

"Let me see if I can read it." Joshua stuck his face into Arran's jacket, emerging a moment later with a big smile. "Marie, if you can believe that. Big ugly cop has a pansy name. M-A-R-I-E."

Arran was anything but ugly to me, but I guess tastes vary. "Arran Marie Dane," I repeated out loud. "Sounds like a mix of Welsh, French, and Scandinavian."

Detective Arran Marie Dane stared at me as if I'd grown horns. "Who told you? I never tell anyone—" He glared at Lauren. "You did this, didn't you? Probably thought you'd make fun of the cop with the girlie middle name."

Lauren looked at me, wide eyed. Years before, I'd given up trying to persuade people the ghosts were real. But she hadn't researched Dane for me, had no idea how I could have learned his middle name.

Besides, Daniel as close to her as a cat to a catnip mouse. Maybe just a hint of sensation got through to her. I didn't really believe I was the only person sensitive to the dead. Like most things, it was probably a matter of degree.

"He have any money in there?" I asked Joshua.

"Is this another favor?"

"Sorry. Part of the same one. We haven't persuaded him yet."

The ghost made a face, but he finally coughed up the answer. "Three twenties, a five, and a couple of ones. I didn't look in his pants pocket. Not going to, either."

Feeling more than a little silly, I wrote down the numbers and denominations on a slip of paper, folded it up, and dropped it into the center of the chessboard.

"Open your wallet and count your money, Dane. Then unfold that piece of paper and tell me how Lauren researched that."

Arran had regained his composure when he'd decided to blame Lauren for telling me his middle name. "A cheap magic trick. Aren't you going to have the number show up, written in charcoal on your skin."

"You've been watching too much TV. If I were going to pick your pocket, I wouldn't have put the money back. According to you, I'm going to need it to make my bail."

Arran wasn't just worrying about cheap magic tricks, though. I'd seen that look on his face when I'd discovered his middle name. He'd been spooked and he was reluctant to open himself up to another shock.

"What's the matter, Detective? Afraid of a ghost?" I'd always wanted to use that line.

He reached into his pocket, pulled out his cash and counted it, then picked up the slip of paper.

He looked back and forth a couple of times, then grinned at me. "Only two twenties, see? Guess your ghost was wrong. Or rather, your guess was wrong."

This was the kind of joke the ghosts love to pull, and one of the reasons why I never persuaded anyone they were real. "Joshua? I thought you wanted me to finish your game."

"I do. His wallet got one of those flap things. There's another twenty behind that."

"Look in the secret compartment," I said.

The detective pulled back a leather strip on his wallet and pulled out a wrinkled old-style twenty. It looked like it had been there for a very long time.

The glare he gave me had lost a bit the annoying cockiness. "That's a good trick."

"Don't let them look in my purse." Lauren's eyes grew wide. "Was there really a ghost in my car when I picked you up? How am I supposed to know? What if they watch when I'm in the shower?"

Welcome to my world.

Convincing Lauren had hardly been my goal. Hell, she would have been happier not believing. I needed Arran to leave me alone. As it was, he'd probably just think she was putting on an act on my behalf.

Lauren didn't need to know that male ghosts ignored 'women only' signs on locker rooms. She could ignore them—which made her lucky as far as I could tell.

Dane considered the small pile of money, then shook his head. "You probably saw what was in my wallet when I paid for my coffee. And I'm not going to fall for the reverse psychology trick. Mrs-uh, Lauren's purse is too easy. You could have set that up at any time. How about that guy." He pointed at a scruffy-looking kid ordering a fancy coffee for the teenage girl he was trying to impress. Friday night was still date night for high school kids.

"Can you get his name," I asked Joshua.

"Hell," Daniel said, "I don't have to do anything tricky to get *his* name. He comes in here all the time. Can't play chess to save his life. Can't think how many times I've tried to help him but he just won't listen. Poor kid thinks he's God's gift to—"

"So, what is his name? I don't need his history."

"That there's Zane Balders. Don't recognize the girl, though. Think she's a different one than he brought last night. Busy boy that Zane Balders. Gotta say, his grandpa was pretty much the same so at least he came by it honestly."

"Hey Zane," I shouted. "Zane Balders. Come over here for a second."

The kid looked up from where he'd been counting out his change and glared at me. His expression changed to what he probably considered a sexy grin when it lit on Lauren. He heaved himself away from the counter and sauntered over, leading with his hips as if a woman like Lauren could possibly be interested in a punk like him.

"Your name Zane Balders?" Arran asked.

"Who wants to know?" He didn't even glance away from Lauren. Which was a mistake.

"Police." Arran wrapped one of his big hands around Zane's scrawny biceps and squeezed. "Want to answer a civil question, or should I show your girlfriend what a wimp you are?"

"You and what—oh." Zane yanked his arm, realized it wasn't going anywhere, and let his challenge peter out as he got a good look at the detective's face.

Arran was frustrated and looked like he'd enjoy taking out his frustration on someone else—like Zane.

"All right." The kid's voice went up an octave. "So I'm Zane Balders. But I ain't done nothing wrong and I don't appreciate being harassed by the police."

"You see either of these women before?" Arran demanded.

Zane wasted half a second checking me out, then glued his gaze back on Lauren. "I'd remember if I'd seen this one. The other?" He shrugged. "Who knows? Who cares?"

* * * *

After a few more of my 'ghost tricks,' Arran persuaded Lauren he wasn't going to arrest me after all. She made me promise to call her if he started asking me questions I didn't feel comfortable with, then went home to her family.

Since Zane and his date had headed out as soon as Arran let him go, that left me, the cop, and the ghosts. As much attention as he paid us, the barista might as well have been a ghost himself.

I kept my promise to the guys, though, playing out the chess game for Joshua and Daniel. While I was doing that, Arran got a couple of refills on his coffee, talked into his cell, kibitzed the game, and generally made me uncomfortable.

"Why that move?" he'd demand, just about every time I shifted a pawn or knight.

So I'd shrug, remind Arran I was just following directions, and finally have to ask whatever ghost was making the move to explain it to the cop.

Then I'd serve as interpreter while Arran, Daniel, and Joshua discussed strategy.

At midnight, the barista shooed Arran and me out. The ghosts were welcome to spend the night there and I guessed they would. Since ghosts don't need to sleep, they tend to hang out where there's enough light to see.

Arran fished out his keys. "Want me to take you to your brother's house, or to your apartment?"

That was right—I'd given Arran and his partner Fineman my address back when they'd hauled me in for questioning and I'd been one of the goodguys.

"If you don't mind, you might as well take me home. I don't want to risk waking Little Jack."

"No problem. I have to head that way, anyway."

I called my brother and let him know I wouldn't be spending the night after all, then followed Arran to his car.

It was a sporty thing, but it didn't make a sound when he pulled it down Fifteenth Street and then onto 75 heading south.

"It's my personal car," he admitted. "Plug it in and go. Electric means it's got great pickup. And you don't have to worry, I'm a great driver."

So he'd noticed I'd glued my eyes shut the minute he headed onto the street. He might also have noticed that my name was nowhere in the Department of Public Safety vehicle registration database.

It's not that I have anything against driving, although I am as ecology-minded as the next person. It's that ghosts wander out onto the streets all the time. Getting driven over by a car doesn't hurt them, of course. Still, a lot of them had fun making faces as if in horror when a car ran through the same space they shared. Even worse, from more than about thirty feet away, it's to tell living people from the dead. I have a recurring nightmare that I make a mistake and run a car through someone alive.

A lot more ghosts congregate in the middle of the freeway than living humans, but it would only take one misjudgment to ruin my whole day.

I peeked every once in a while as Arran headed south on 75, and saw that the ghosts were out in force tonight. Maybe they thought it was especially fun to get hit by a silent electric car.

"You really don't trust my driving, do you?"

"It's not that, Detective Dane. I don't want to watch the ghosts get squashed." I really squeezed my eyes shut after I'd said that. Maybe I should give a class on how to make sure no guy will ever, in a million years, think of you romantically.

Arran didn't say anything until he took the Mockingbird exit and headed east toward my apartment.

That's when he surprised me. "You can call me Arran."

I sighed. "Okay. I guess you know I'm Annie."

He nodded. "Have you ever considered that there are a lot of mediums who work with the police?"

I'd be the last person in the world to suggest that any medium is a fake. There's no particular reason why other people couldn't pick up pictures from the air or from touching clothing that belonged to a victim. Back when I'd been a teen, I'd done a lot of research on different types of psychics, visited just about every fortune-teller in Dallas, and hung out at psychic fares as if they might offer a lifeline to sanity. I knew that many police departments worked with psychics. I also knew that few within the police force would admit this dirty secret. And of all the cops who might talk about it, Arran would have been last on my list. He seemed like a 'just the facts, ma'am operator.

"Guess some departments are open-minded," I suggested.

"Yeah, I guess that's so. But what about you? Have you ever thought about how many crimes *you* might be able to clear up?"

He surprised me again. "I've already explained that I can't control what I see. The ghosts have to be there for me to talk to them. Sort of like your grandmother and her perfume."

"But do ghosts just show up randomly? It seemed like those two ghosts in the Starbucks, Daniel and Joshua, were regulars."

I opened my eyes in time to see Arran pull into the Mockingbird Station parking lot near where I lived. "Yeah. And slow down. There's another regular who likes to stand right around this cor—ouch."

"It doesn't hurt them, does it?"

"I think maybe he's recreating how he got killed, which is pretty sick when you think about it."

"The thing is," Arran was beating around the bush, unlike his normal cocky self. "Well, the thing is, there are a lot of cases where we don't have enough witnesses. Including the shooting at the Records Office to —uh-yesterday. We have translators for witnesses who don't speak English. Why shouldn't we have translators for witnesses who are ghosts?"

I laughed out loud. "Go home and get some sleep, Detective. You're still coming to grips with what you saw tonight and it's pretty obvious that some of your gears are slipping. When you wake up in the morning, you'll see how silly that idea is. If you still can't figure it out, consider this. How would you subpoena a ghost? Answer—you can't and you'd never compel one to come to court. Even if I persuaded one to come with me, the defense attorney would laugh any ghost testimony out of court. Which I wouldn't blame her for—why should the jury believe me when nobody else does. That enough, yet? How about this, then. What happens when you go into your boss and tell him what a great idea you've got, getting dead people to testify? The only question is whether they'd force you into psychiatric care before they fired you, or just fire you and suggest you go wander the streets with the rest of the fruitcakes."

He halfway reached out an arm to what? Touch me? Hit me? Apparently he didn't know either because he stopped himself and stuck his hand back on the steering wheel. "That's how they've treated you, isn't it?"

Oh, God. The pity thing. "Actually, I've been lucky. My parents and my brother stood up for me until I learned to stand up for myself."

Arran pulled into an open parking spot, got out, and walked around to let me out while I fumbled for the door, trying to figure out how to open the crazy thing.

He opened the door before I found the latch and offered me a hand out.

"I'm a big girl. I can make it from here."

"You think I want to tell your attorney I took you home and didn't make sure you got in safely?"

Was it completely over the top to wish he'd wanted to see me up for my own sake, rather than to please my beautiful sister-in-law?

"Whatever," I said.

He walked me to the elevator, rode up to the third floor where my apartment was, and kept me company me to the door.

I fumbled for my key. "Want to come in for a cup of coffee?"

He glanced at his watch. "Better not. Got a caffeine overload at Starbucks."

He waited until I opened my door and reset my alarm, then turned to go. "I'll see you around."

"Sure, Detective." I guessed the only place he'd see me would be in his nightmares, though. Only desperate guys hang around with the girl who talks to ghosts. With looks like his, Arran Marie Dane wasn't going to be desperate. Not in woman-intense Dallas.

"Arran," he said.

Chapter 4

I'd intended to get some work done on Saturday morning, but I slept late instead.

At nine o'clock, I rolled out of bed, headed for my bathroom, and turned on my lighting system.

I'd had exactly two, non-protoplasmic guys in my apartment in the three years I'd lived there—and both headed out after quick visits to my bathroom. It might have been just me, but I suspect it was the combination of aluminum foil on the walls and windows and my unique lighting system.

Ghosts didn't mind fluorescent lighting, and they practically ate up incandescent. With a lot of experimentation, though, I'd discovered a combination of light emitting diodes and infrared that seemed to discourage them. I'd put it in my bathroom. I slept in baggy pajamas, and make sure my bedroom stayed so dark the ghosts can't see anything anyway, which means they don't bother me much at night, but I couldn't use those tricks in the bathroom. And I don't think I'm weird to want to be able to use the toilet, take a shower, or pluck my eyebrows without three ghosts looking over my shoulder and trying to second-guess me, or offering to scrub my back.

Usually, I didn't even think about the unusual lighting, but Arran was still very much on my mind when I turned on my system and stepped into the shower.

Watching light reflections chase themselves across steamy reflecting sheets of aluminum foil was a useful reminder to keep my fantasies under control. The ability to see ghosts was just not as romantic as they make it out to be in the movies.

I shaved my legs, put on a dab of a lotion that contains a hint of color so you don't need to wear makeup if you're not going anywhere fancy, and pulled on a clean pair of jeans and sweater.

I'd gotten dressed without any ghosts looking in. For me, that made for a pretty good day already.

Ready to face anything, I headed for the kitchen. There I started the coffee, poured myself a bowl of Cheerios, and sprinkled a bunch of raisins in it. My usual breakfast.

Chantal was waiting in my breakfast nook.

"Sorry I'm late," I muttered. I hadn't had my wake-up cup yet and I was grumpy.

"*En Français*," she said.

In a million years, I'd never be able to afford private language tutoring. But ghosts were, so to speak, dying for someone to talk to. So we'd worked a deal. I helped Chantal with her English and she taught me French.

Chantal had come to America with the La Reunion French Utopian Socialist colony that had settled just west of Dallas in the 1850s, but had died during the harsh winters along with many of the immigrants.

That she was still struggling with English after a century and a half said something about French pride and more, I figured, about how hard it is for ghosts to learn new things. Of course, I was struggling almost as much in French and Spanish and I didn't have the excuse of protoplasmic brain cells.

I had the sound turned off on the TV, but it caught my attention when my face flashed across the screen. Some clever reporter had caught a shot of me being bundled away from the County Records building. The TV displayed my name in big print across the bottom.

My blood froze. They might as well have painted a target on my forehead.

"*Un minute*," I said, and turned up the volume.

Typically, I was in time to catch a commercial for a cleaning product.

"Annie, *regarde*. You are this TV, 'ow you say *étoile*?"

"Star. And no, I'm not a star. I'm a witness. Someone tried to kill Sam where I work."

"*Zhen zhey* are coming for you, no? *Zhey* will desire to leave *le* no witnesses."

I was glad more people couldn't see ghosts. Chantal was too cute for words with her French accent, her pouty mouth, and the low-cut dresses she always wore. This morning, she was also too full of bad news. Maybe the psychiatrists had a point about the ghosts being in my mind, because whatever Chantal had to say was exactly what I didn't want to hear.

"Maybe it was like that back in the nineteenth century," I assured her with as much conviction as I could muster. "Dallas is so big these days that the gunman will just assume I'll never recognize him." I certainly hadn't made any sense of the photo lineups Arran and Carly had showed me on the computer—before I'd become their suspect.

"*Non*. You misunderstand. I mean to say, 'e is coming now, 'ere. To your apartment. 'E has the *arme*. *Le pistolet*. 'E is at the door. *Maintenant*, zees minute."

My heart froze.

At the sound of my doorbell, I jumped from my seat, sending Cheerios, soymilk, and raisins everywhere.

I looked frantically around my kitchen for a weapon and snatched up a marble rolling pin Lauren had given me as a housewarming present when I'd moved into my apartment. It was, she'd explained patiently, the perfect thing for making piecrusts. I still had no idea how well it worked with crusts, but it had the heft to be a pretty effective weapon. My Tae Kwon Do instructor would be proud of me.

The bell sounded again.

Chantal faded through the door and came back with a frightened expression. "'E looks *très* fierce. Per'aps you climb out *le fenêtre*, window, *oui?*"

Yeah, right. Like I could outrun a bullet.

I wasn't brave, but I was tired, pissed, and nobody was going to run me from my house. I walked through the ghost, yanked open the door, closed my eyes, and swung my rolling pin.

He stripped it from my grip as easily as if I'd been handing it over to him. Hey, I was supposed to be a martial artist. This wasn't supposed to happen to me. Then again, I didn't think Master Thibedeaux at the Dragon School of Tae Kwon Do would be very happy when he learned I'd closed my eyes before I struck.

"Is it me, or are you are you always grumpy in the morning?"

I opened my eyes.

The mysterious gunman was Arran, of course.

For just a moment, I wondered if it would have been less painful if it had been the killer at the door instead of the cop. One thing for sure, it would have been less embarrassing. The only good news was, I had hit rock-bottom. I didn't think there was any way I could be more embarrassed.

"I saw myself on TV and Chantal said there was a gunman outside. I guess I panicked."

"Chantal, huh? You didn't tell me you had a roommate."

I sighed. "She's a ghost."

"Right." He paused, possibly to catch a breath but more likely to hold back the patronizing chuckle I suspected he really wanted to give me.

He managed it. "I thought I'd take you to breakfast but my detective skills tell me you've already eaten."

I looked down and learned how mistaken I'd been about reaching the bottom of my embarrassment quotient. Cheerios stuck to my jeans, and beads of soymilk glistening in my not-so-ample cleavage. One raisin clung to my sweater exactly at the end of my left boob, like a sun-dried nipple.

Not that I'd really wanted a chance with Arran, and not that I even really wanted him, other than the obvious and purely physical lust that roared through me every time I looked at him. Still, it would have been nice if he could have seen me as a mature and rational human being. The worst part was, I couldn't even blame the ghosts for scaring Arran away, I was managing to do that perfectly well on my own.

"Come in and have a cup of coffee while I wash up," I said. "Why don't you entertain Chantal with some police stories while I change?"

"Oh, yeah, sure. I'll bring her up to date."

Arran didn't roll his eyes—not quite. But it seemed that he'd had a night to sleep—and to come up with a rational explanation for the 'tricks' I'd pulled on him the previous evening. Maybe I should just push him into my bathroom to let him get the full aluminum foil and lighting system effect right away.

I couldn't make myself do that, though. Some hopelessly optimistic part of me wanted to believe that I could hide that part of myself from him.

Chapter 5

Arran hadn't stopped by my place because of my wit, sexy body, or even because he desperately needed a cup of home-brewed coffee. Once I'd explained that the cereal was on my lap rather than in my stomach, he dragged me to the nearby Café Brasil. Only after we'd ordered and the waitress delivered my pecan waffle, loaded with whipped cream, did he explain why he'd darkened my door.

Chantel's theory hadn't been completely off. Arran was concerned that the gunman, still identified as Harry by the detectives investigating the attack, just might decide he needed to eliminate any witnesses. The primary witness, Sam, had apparently been taken off somewhere for his protection. According to Arran, Sam claimed to know nothing beyond a mysterious stranger and me getting into a fight. He denied that the gunman had spoken to him, let alone come after him for gambling debts.

I thought that suspicious, but Arran shrugged. "People," he explained, "lie to cops."

I was still identified as a suspect rather than as a helpful witness, so the cops hadn't arranged any *official* protection for me. Arran was off for the weekend—and had decided I needed unofficial babysitting.

"Sam bets at hockey and basketball games," I said. "And the gunman said something about paying off his debts. I think this was some sort of mob shakedown. Since he was wearing a mask, he probably didn't intend to kill. Maybe he was going to beat Sam up. Maybe shoot off his toe or something."

Arran looked at me briefly, then turned his attention back to his food, inhaling another cup of coffee and scarfing down eggs and hash browns as if they'd walk away if he gave them half a chance.

I considered asking him if he knew how many calories there were in a cup of hash browns, but decided not to bother. He had one of those perfect bodies, and couldn't gain weight.

Finally, he gave me a look I couldn't quite read. "Do you see any ghosts here?"

I looked around. Two kids played in the glass-fronted cabinet that held Café Brasil merchandise. Although they looked perfectly normal from where I sat, I didn't think the staff would put up with that from visible children. Therefore, they had to be ghosts.

"A couple I think. Kids."

He nodded. "Is it worse seeing children?"

Arran's question hit me like a punch. Nobody had ever asked me *anything* like that before. Psychiatrists had tried to get at what physical or emotional damage had made me delusional. Psychologists had probed to learn what gratification I got from being different from everyone else, or tried to build the case that my ghosts substituted for my lack of friends in the real world. My parents and brother had done their best to pretend I was normal. But nobody had ever accepted the ghosts, wondered about them, and thought to inquire about how they affected me.

I checked the detective out, looking for any hint he was messing with my brain, playing more of the cop-games he'd played on me when I'd been in questioning. If he was, he was playing deep. I saw no hint of anything but sincere interest.

"Kids are the worst," I admitted. "Some of them are too young to understand that they're dead. They think their parents just started ignoring them one day. Older children, like the two playing at the counter, act out their fantasies, but they never seem to get older, never grow up. If J. M. Barrie based his Peter Pan character on anything but his imagination, it was probably a ghost." The boys of Neverland, boys who never grew up, playing out their games with Pirates, Indians, sexless Mermaids, and Fairy Women, were so like the youthful ghosts I saw around that I'd had to stop reading that book on the third chapter and could never force myself to pick it up again.

For me, though, the ghosts of little girls were worse. Boys really don't *want* to grow up. Many ghost-boys played out their dreams, day after day —just as Peter Pan had. Girls, though, fantasize about growing up and look forward to grown-up things. Little girls who died too soon would never get there. Girl-ghosts fantasize of living—and that was one thing they could never do.

Arran nodded as I explained that to him.

"Have you thought of letting grieving parents know, persuade them to pay attention, show the kids they're still loved?"

My skin stood in goosebumps. "Just once."

Arran was a professional question-asker. He read enough into my non-answer to change the subject.

"Assuming that Harry does come gunning—"

"Harry was the ghost. I don't know the gunman's name."

He sighed. "Let's call him Harry, then. It might be his name and all the cops are calling him that."

"Which might explain why they haven't found him. It almost certainly isn't his name and there are probably a thousand guys named Harry in Dallas who are getting harassed right now because of your mistake."

He shrugged. "I can't help that. But I won't call him Harry if it bothers you. My question was, will the ghosts warn you if Ha—the gunman comes looking for you?"

"If they're friendly and they know what's going on, sure. If not, they'll do whatever amuses them. Many ghosts have fairly liberal ideas concerning death, you know. Some would like to keep me alive because I can do things for them, like playing chess with the guys last night. Plenty of others just don't care."

Arran had finished off his breakfast. So he grabbed refills for both of us from the big self-service coffee urns at the counter, and returned to the table.

His eyes seemed to flick across every face in the restaurant, categorizing the customers and staff into whatever buckets his brain used to sort people out. I hoped they all got filed as harmless, because Arran looked capable of dealing out justice to anyone who needed it.

He'd dressed down for the day, in a faded pair of jeans and a leather jacket over a form-fitting black t-shirt. I couldn't see his gun, but I'd have known it was there even if Chantal hadn't told me.

He focused his attention on me when he rejoined me at our table, but I could tell he remained aware of everything going on around us. Everything, that is, in the human plane. He hadn't even noticed when he'd walked through the ghost of one of those kids.

"I can't stick around, watching you forever," he said. "I've got this weekend off but I'll be on another case on Monday."

"You think this one will be solved by then?"

"The Harry case, as they're calling it, isn't mine. Carly and I got called in to help interview witnesses, that's all."

I froze in mid-nod. "Does that mean there's another detective out there who thinks I'm involved? Didn't it occur to you that I needed to know that?"

While I steamed, Arran raised an eye at the waitress who bustled over and brought him a couple of biscuits without him having to even order them. Apparently Café Brasil was the equivalent of a donut-shop to the classier set of cop.

Rather than just give me an answer, he busied himself putting strawberry jam on a biscuit, then took a big bite and chewed.

I waited until his Adam's apple bobbed. "Well?"

He took a sip of his coffee and smiled. "They make the best coffee here, don't they? And in a word, yes. Detective Halsgrove is lead. He suspects you're involved. I—"

"So what are you supposed to be doing? Softening me up?"

"If you'd let me finish?"

He waited for my grudging nod. "I sent Halsgrove the psychiatric file your brother gave me. I explained your sister-in-law's theory that you are delusional and that you frequently talk to people who aren't there. The file is pretty convincing so I'm pretty sure he'll realize that any evidence against you is worthless. I—"

"You're trying to persuade him I'm crazy." I didn't know why I was mad about it. After all, pretty much everyone who knew me thought I was insane. Clearly this was a case of my hormones getting in the way of common sense.

"You promised not to interrupt."

"Sorry." I didn't mean it, though.

* * * *

I think we were both relieved when we finished our coffee and had the excuse to end the suffering. I anticipated Arran dropping me off at home and getting away from me as fast and far as he could. Instead, though, he hesitated at the edge of the café's driveway. "Would you be willing to stop by the scene and see if you could scare up some ghost witnesses?"

"*Scare* up ghosts? Is that supposed to be funny?"

He shook his head. "A poor word choice. But I'm, uh, *deadly* serious about this."

Spare me a guy who thinks he has a sense of humor. "Promise you'll lay off the wretched puns and I'll give it a go."

"Not sure I *can* promise that. Sometimes they just ah-apport."

I groaned. "Whoever said puns were the lowest form of humor was way too kind."

"If we can only see the scene from the vantage of the unseen."

I sighed. "I'm not getting rid of you until I do this, am I? So let's get it over with."

Normally Saturday morning would be thin pickings at the County Records Building, either for the living and the ghosts. Since the County shuts down for the weekend, ghosts went elsewhere. I think Harry flocked to the golf courses along with much of the current real estate crowd. After all, that's what he'd done when he'd been alive and many ghosts continued with something close to their normal routine, not letting a little thing like death get in their way.

What they did when they were actually at the golf course mystified me though. They couldn't swing a club or hit a ball—there being no such thing as a ghost ball. Then again, they didn't have to pay greens fees.

Today was different, though. The cops were there in force and the police presence had attracted ghostly attention. As Arran pulled into a no parking zone, I opened my eyes just in time to see him plow through four of them.

Two ended up on my lap—probably that had been their plan all along. Young boys weren't the only ghosts who saw death as the perfect excuse to act out their fantasies.

"Back off, guys," I said.

Arran yanked up his parking brake. "You see some ghosts?"

"Hang on, Detective. You there, get out of my goddamned lap before I exorcise you."

One of the ghosts giggled. "I told you she was the one who can see us."

"No you didn't," another argued. "You said maybe. But I bet she won't really exorcise us."

"Does it hurt to be exorcised?" a third demanded.

"How the heck would I know?" the second said. "I've never been. Nobody I know has ever been. Exorcism is just a myth."

"Nobody you know *now* has been exorcised," I said, "If they are, they don't come back to report on it. Ever."

I was making this up as I went along, but I mentally catalogued exorcism as something to research. I wouldn't want to hurt a ghost, but it would be handy to have a threat to hold over them.

My words created a bit of a stir.

Abruptly, the four ghosts had their protoplasmic bodies outside of the car, with only their heads sticking through the unbroken glass of the windshield. It was a disturbing look, but they'd gotten out of my lap, which was what I'd asked them to do. I couldn't complain.

"We're looking for anybody who saw what went down yesterday," I told the ghosts. "Anyone who saw the shooting, spotted the gunman when he was on his way in, or noticed what kind of car he used for getaway, we need to talk to them."

The four looked at one another, then simultaneously popped their heads out of the cab.

"I'm feeling left out here," Arran said. "Are there really ghosts, or are you putting on another show for me?"

I glared at the detective. "It's what you brought me here for, isn't it?"

"I just thought it would take a little longer. You know, to wander around muttering, staring at the sky, maybe dousing and picking up ghostly emanations, that kind of thing."

"Like on Ghostbusters, right? Let's make a deal, Arran. I don't make fun of your problems and you don't make fun of mine."

"*My* problems?"

"Oh? So you're perfect?"

That shut him up for long enough for the ghosts to finish their debate and pop their heads back through the windshield. "What's in it for us?" Their designated spokesghost was a scruffy-looking specimen who looked like he'd probably died in the thirties based on the hobo beard, and ragged pants. Maybe it was a sixties hippie reprise, but the floppy shoes definitely looked like the earlier generation.

"For one thing," I said. "I won't exorcise you."

"Hey, let's not—"

The spokesghost stuck his hand through the windshield to join his head, making the universal stop sign. "Exorcism would be nasty. I don't think you'd do that just because we didn't help you."

So much for my ability to hold anything over them. He was right, but I wasn't about to admit that. I also wasn't going to admit I'd been bluffing about exorcism in the first place. I had no idea how I'd go about it, or whether it would work.

"Ask anyone who saw anything if they'd like to help make some art," Arran suggested. "You could translate their descriptions for a police sketch artist."

I took a breath to translate but the spokesghost cut me off.

"Being deaf is *his* problem, not ours. We can hear him fine. But none of *us* saw your killer. We want a payoff that *we* can use if you want us to waste our time looking for witnesses."

I faked a laugh. "Wasting time? That's a big joke. One thing ghosts have plenty of is time."

The spokesghost looked hurt. "When you're one of us, I'll look you up and remind you you said that."

"How about we make them deputy officers for the case?" Arran suggested. "They can tell all the other ghosts that they are on Dallas Police Department official business."

"Can you do that?"

"Don't know why not. He looked out the side window and smiled. "What do you guys say?"

"Does he think he's looking at us?" The spokesghost snickered and the other ghosts laughed.

"He doesn't know that you can float upside down in the air with your heads sticking through the windshield. I think he's promising way too much, though. Making just *one* of you a deputy officer should be plenty."

"Oh, no." The spokesghost might have been intelligent when he'd been alive, but he'd been separated from his physical brain for a long time. He fell for my obvious psychological stunt like a skydiver with parachute failure. "He promised. We're *all* going to be deputy police officers and it's too late for you to back off."

"Maybe two of you. Four is—"

"All four or there's no deal."

"You're taking advantage of the cop just because he's blind to you." I sighed loudly. "Still, he did promise, although he did it without my advice. Okay, he'll make all four of you deputy ghost officers. He'll regret it, though, when you guys get distracted and wander off to do something else."

"No distractions for us. Let's go round up some witnesses."

"Detective Dane isn't going to be happy if he doesn't get reports every fifteen minutes," I said. "And if he's unhappy you'll find out how quickly he can revoke those deputizations."

"He'll get his reports." Although the ghosts were out of ordinary earshot, that didn't really matter much. Ghost speech doesn't move the air the way human speech does. If a ghost wanted me to hear him, I heard him and he heard me—even earplugs didn't help. It was that simple. It was also that unpleasant if you wanted quiet.

"Are they gone?"

I nodded. "Off gathering the witnesses you said you wanted, detective."

"If I find out this is all some big trick, you're going to be really sorry."

"I'd get off by reason of insanity."

He narrowed his eyes. "Whatever punishment I deal out will have nothing to do with the legal system."

"Ooh, now I'm scared." Actually a sexual thrill ran through me like a brain-freeze you get from drinking your Slurpee too fast. But I wasn't about to tell Arran that. I mean, how pathetic would that be?"

"Let's go see what the ordinary human officers have turned up," Arran suggested.

Chapter 6

"What is *she* doing here?"

Reporting life from outside a crime scene had to be boring, especially if it was in the forties outside, with a chill wind from the north.

My arrival, as Arran led me to the makeshift police headquarters in the Records Building foyer, was all it took to create a major stir with the bored reporters. Cameramen exploded from their vehicles, and reporters got in my face with microphones.

"Ms. Neeter, is it true that both Harry and Sam Bert are both your lovers and the shooting the result of a love-triangle gone tragic?"

Eeew. Imagining me with Sam Bert was gross. Being with a ghost was nearly as bad.

"Ms. Neeter, have the police arrested you."

"Detective Dane, is Ms. Neeter cooperating? Is it true that she has been ruled a flight suspect?"

Arran ignored the questions, but I couldn't ignore the cameras pointing in my direction. If the gunman watched TV, he'd know my name and connection with the case. Considering I was with Arran, he wouldn't need to be a rocket scientist to guess I was cooperating with the police. If he could stand to be patient over the weekend, Arran's protection would end. Starting Monday, I'd be on my own if he came looking for me.

Unfortunately, what he might not know was how little I actually had seen.

Arran dragged me into the makeshift case room on the main floor of the County Records building.

Four cops were gathered around a laptop in the center of a table. They looked up when they saw Arran and did doubletakes when they saw me.

"What the hell, Dane. I thought you said she was a nutcase. So why the hell did you bring her around?"

Behind him, a pair of ghosts, wearing police uniforms that probably dated from the fifties, waved their fists at me.

"Good morning to you, Hargrove. Has Sam Bert been any more forthcoming on identifying the assailant?"

"He claims he didn't get a good look at this Harry guy."

"Considering they talked for almost a minute," I said, "that's hard to believe."

"That's your story. Bert's is that Harry came in, argued with you, and started shooting.

Arran had said Hargrove was the detective in charge of the case. He was a lot closer to the police detective stereotype. Bald and maybe fifty, he carried about twenty pounds he didn't need in a beer belly that stretched the buttons on his starched white shirt. He'd draped a suit jacket across the back of his chair so there was nothing to hide the ugly yellow sweat stains that marked his pits and the area around his shoulder holster.

"Have you asked Sam about his gambling?" The words were out of my mouth before I thought about them. Sam hadn't been a bad guy as far as clerks went. Even though he seemed intent on making the cops look my way, I still didn't want to cost him his job.

"I read your transcript, Ms. Neeter. I know you've accused him of gambling. Here's the thing, though. We don't have a lot of organized crime leg-breaking action here in Dallas. If someone asked me, I'd say your story belonged in an old gangster movie rather than in modern Dallas."

"Maybe whoever Sam gambles with has been watching those old videos."

"Yeah? And maybe Harry really did come gunning for you but you don't want to admit it. There's lots more obsessive boyfriends who won't go away than Al Capone wannabes."

"Think about what you said, Detective. If someone was gunning for you, wouldn't you want the police to know about it—so they could stop him?"

He laughed, his belly jiggling like a cartoon Santa Claus. "Easy to tell you're not a cop. 'Cause people lie to us in exactly that situation all the time. You tell her, Dane. Maybe she'll listen to you."

Arran nodded. "Halgrove is right, Annie. Especially if there's a romantic angle. Women don't like to—"

"What romantic angle?"

The police ghost who'd made the threatening gestures at me earlier covered his ears, so I guessed my voice might have screeched up an octave. Still, I couldn't believe Arran suspected there might be something romantic going on between me and the guy who'd tried to kill me for no reason other than that I'd been there. Well, that plus the fact that I'd bopped him in the nose with a property records book.

"We have to investigate all the possibilities." Detective Halgrove stood and walked over to me. "You know, you don't seem all that crazy to me."

How the heck was I supposed to answer that? I decided on the truth.

"I'm not crazy, I see ghosts. One of them warned me."

Halgrove got out of my face in a hurry. "Ah. That explains it."

"Although it's unusual, I believe Ms. Neeter's psychic experience might be able to—"

"Oh, no, Dane," Halgrove said with that half-laughing tone guys like to use. "Get your rocks off on your own time, on your own budget. No way are you going to saddle my case with some wacko looking to get publicity for her palm-reading business."

"I just think—"

"Think on your own cases, then, Dane. And let the grownups gets some work done around here."

"That went well," Arran observed as we stepped back into the north wind and the swarming television crews.

Chapter 7

The reporters following us for a few hundred yards, but we weren't doing anything interesting and they soon abandoned us.

I couldn't blame them. Their heated trucks had to be a lot more comfortable than downtown's gray and chilly outdoors. Not to mention the positively frigid looks Arran sent their way.

We got back in Arran's car, picked up Oren Luker, A.K.A. spokesghost (Luker sat in my lap as Arran didn't have a back seat), and drove a couple of blocks to a Chipotle Mexican Grill. There, Arran ordered one of their monster, thousand calorie, burritos, I got a Diet Coke and some chips. There we set up a makeshift headquarters.

Once we were settled in, Luker went back to tell the ghost-deputies where to send their witnesses and Arran got on the phone.

I listened, but his conversation didn't make a lot of sense to me. My lessons were in French and Spanish, not in police pidgin, especially as modified by big bites of burrito. Listening to Arran talk police reminded me of Newspeak from the book *1984*. Scary.

Rather than trying to make sense of it, I gave up and watched for ghosts.

Apparently nobody had died in the West End Chipotle—yet. Ghosts can go anywhere they want, but they're conservative and tend to stick with familiar territory. I decided I would have to do lunch there more often. A ghost-free zone had a distinct appeal.

The ghost-free situation didn't last, though. Arran was less than halfway through his burrito and still on his first cup of coffee when Luker brought in his first witness.

"Deputy Oren Luker reporting." He snapped a clumsy salute. "Bringing ghost-witness Martin Katt for interrogation."

Arran didn't even look up from his phone, which seemed rude to me.

"I thought you said they could see us." Katt's voice was a high-pitched whine. He'd been a skinny guy, about thirty-five, with sandy-colored hair mostly covered by a Homburg-style hat. Based on the hat, I guessed he'd died in the fifties or early sixties, before President Kennedy single-handedly eliminated the men's hat industry. "They don't look anything special to me."

"The girl can see you, but she forgot he can't," Oren, my hobo-spokesghost correctly read the situation. "She's okay but she's not the brightest bulb."

I would have argued but Luker had a point. "Hey Arran. We're in business."

He looked at me, then at one of the empty chairs at our table—the only one with neither person nor ghost at it. "What have we got?"

"First, our head deputy is named Oren Luker. Second, he's brought someone he says is a witness—one Martin Katt."

Arran snapped his phone shut and smiled at the empty chair. "I've got a police sketch artist on his way over. In the meantime, Luker, do you want to get back to work, or stick around and help with the interrogation?"

Luker swelled with importance. "Tell him I'll help. And tell him to look my way. I'm getting weirded out at the way he talks to that empty chair."

It was interesting to watch Arran try to deal with a reality he couldn't see and still wasn't quite sure he even accepted. I couldn't help wondering if I often looked that way, staring off into nothingness while people talked to me, walked around me, and generally thought I was blowing them off. If so, no wonder everyone thought I was crazy.

"Uh, Arran, Luker is sitting next to me and Martin Katt is next to him."

An expression passed over the detective's face so quickly I wasn't completely sure what it was—annoyance? Embarrassment? Anger? It was something negative, at any rate.

Then he smiled in Katt's direction. "Sorry about that, Mr. Katt. I understand that you can hear me, but that you'll need Ms. Neeter to translate for my benefit. Is that correct?"

"Mighty polite for a copper," Katt said.

"Oh yeah," I lied. "He's a regular sweetheart."

"I'm okay with the translation, though I usually got no use for a doll."

A doll? Women hadn't been 'dolls' since before my mother had been born. "Thanks for your patience, Mr. Katt." I turned to Arran. "Okay, we're ready to go, Detective."

Arran pulled a tiny digital recorder from his pocket and put it on the table. I was absolutely sure of one thing—he'd never play that tape in court—but he still went through the police rigmarole of identifying himself, the time, date and location, and the witness.

Three minutes later, it was obvious Katt was wasting our time. He identified the killer as someone named Harry, described him as a *big black man*, and twice suggested that I show him my tits. "Dolls these days do it all the time," he claimed.

"Toss this guy out, Deputy Luker," I said. "He's wasting our time and preventing you from doing your job."

"How was I supposed to know," my hobo-friend demanded. "He told me he saw the getaway. He promised."

"You're a deputy ghost detective now," I reminded him. "You're supposed to figure these things out. If you do a good job, maybe Detective Dane will hold a class in interviewing just for you ghosts."

"That would be so cool."

"What are you talking about," Arran demanded. "We've hardly started with this witness."

I realized I'd stopped translating, so I brought him up to date. "Katt's lying. So he's out of here and Luker is getting back to work. Right Luker."

"And I'm taking this loser with me."

I'd never seen a ghost actually touch another ghost and I hadn't even known it was possible, but Luker grabbed Katt by the ear and dragged him out of the restaurant.

The ghostly commotion must have sent some ectoplasmic waves through the universe or something, because a new ghost appeared almost before Luker and Katt went through the door—literally.

"Are you the lady who sees ghosts?"

I looked at her. Ghosts can wear whatever they want. Which was cool for the kids who got to wear the perfect cowboy or spaceman suits they'd always coveted. I could sort of understand why ghosts like the farmers we'd met in Plano would stick with their shabby but comfortable work clothes. But why a woman would still dress like a homeless person when she could wear Christian Dior was beyond me.

Still, it was a reality. The ghost wore three coats, one on top of another, and her face was filthy.

"I'm that lady. Did you see something about the shooting?"

"Shooting?" She raised her voice. "Someone's shooting ghosts?"

"Calm down. Nobody got seriously hurt and he wasn't shooting ghosts at all."

"Seems to me that once you're dead, you should be free of that stuff. Seems to me you should move on, go to heaven or whatever. That's what my old preacher said."

If there was ever a time to keep my mouth shut, this was it. But I couldn't help myself. "What's he say now?"

"You got a smart mouth, girl. It's going to get you in trouble."

"Happens all the time."

I'd noticed Chipotle's manager out of the corner of my eye. He'd been doing the bob, moving his body forward, then backward while his feet remained in place. Finally, though, he pushed forward.

"This is a private establishment." He spoke kindly enough, but firmly. "There is a homeless shelter across town where you can go if you need help," he continued.

"You can see her?" I blurted. Then I realized he wasn't looking at the ghost, he was looking at me.

"Told you so." The ghost's cackling sounded like a boy pretending to be a machine gun. "Guys like him don't give me no trouble no more."

The manager cleared his throat and pulled a phone from his pocket. "I don't want to have to call the police on you, ma'am, but you'll have to move along."

I looked for some help from Arran, but he appeared to be engrossed with his phone, his act made slightly less convincing by the twitch in his cheeks as he tried to fight down a grin.

Fortunately, I'd had this happen to me before—and I'd learned the secret. I stood up and pushed my finger against the manager's chest. "I don't know who you are, buster, and I don't know what game you think you're pulling. But if a person can't sit here and talk on the phone without someone getting in their face, I think we *should* call the police."

"Talk on the phone. But—"

"Never hear of Bluetooth? Wireless headsets. Now buzz off. My sister is having problems with her husband again and I'm going to hold your restaurant responsible if I can't talk her out of shooting that lying, cheating bastard."

"Oh." Now it was the manager's turn to look for help. He didn't find it any more than I had. "I beg your pardon. I didn't realize... I'd better get back to the kitchen."

"Get me a refill on Diet Coke on your way, will you?"

He grabbed my glass, practically shoved it at a busboy, and scurried out of sight.

Arran raised an eyebrow. "That was impressive."

"Practice."

"Who's your new friend?"

I turned to the ghost, but she was on her way out, clearly frustrated that I hadn't gotten the bum's rush treatment she'd probably gotten way too often. I resolved to be nicer to homeless people. I could understand why a restaurant manager might not want a bunch of derelicts in his place, but they had to go somewhere and, if this woman was a good example, they didn't even have a positive ghost-life to look forward to.

She was halfway through the door when it opened, creating an interesting effect for me. An effeminate-looking guy in a police uniform brushed past her, spotted Arran and gave him a big smile, and rushed over to our table.

"Detective Dane. Thank you so much for asking for my help." The cop pulled out the chair Luker had vacated and laid what looked like an oversized woman's handbag on the table. "Dispatch was joking about ghosts. What the heck is going on here?"

I wondered how ultra-macho Arran Dane would respond to the over-the-top stereotypical gayness of the police artist. To my surprise, he shook the man's hand, thanked him for coming, and told him that I was a psychic and that he'd asked for my help on the case.

"A psychic? How perfectly exciting, Ms. Neeter. I'm so happy to meet you." He pulled a tablet-style computer the handbag. "I'm Ron Sallot. I've never worked with a psychic before. Oh my, this is going to be so much *fun*."

Luker returned from dumping Martin outside, took one look at Ron sitting in his chair, and made that annoying effeminate wrist movement that should have died out about the same time he did—back in the Depression.

I got pissed. "Shape up or ship out, buddy. If you're going to be bigoted, there's no place for you in the Dallas Police."

Ron had been unpacking computer add-ons, but his head jerked up. "I beg your pardon."

"Sorry. I was talking to Luker."

"Luker?"

I sighed. "Arran just said I was a psychic, remember. I talk to ghosts, it's what I do. And ex-deputy Oren Luker was making fun of you."

"Ex-deputy?" Luker looked like someone had kicked him in the gut —pretty good for a dead guy.

"Ex-deputy if you don't shape up and treat your brother officers with some respect."

"This is the artist?" Luker's face contorted as he sought a way out of the hole he'd dug for himself. "Oh, of course. I had no idea. Artists are always a bit, uh, is it okay if I say, 'flamboyant'?"

"Don't know. I'll ask." I turned to the police artist. "Is it okay if he calls you flamboyant?"

"Flamboyant? Yes I should say so." Ron giggled, then pulled a black beret from his bag and set it on his head. "I am an *artiste*, after all."

"Can he draw me while we wait for the guys to bring in some witnesses?" Luker asked.

"I'll check."

Ron and Arran huddled, Arran wanting Luker to get back to work and Ron wanting the experience of being the first D.P.D. IdentiKit artist to draw a ghost. Since Ron would be doing the drawing, and since Luker refused to get back to work until Ron drew his picture, Ron won that argument.

Luker's portrait turned out to be good practice for me. Ron would ask me questions and I'd check Oren out and pass along what I saw. His questions helped me see things I would never have noticed, which was a bit scary when I thought about ghost witnesses. They didn't have Ron along when they'd been checking out the action.

It only took a couple of minutes before a picture took form on the computer screen.

"That's me," Luker gushed. "Except you've got the chin wrong."

Calling the soft spot halfway between Luker's mouth and neck a chin was putting things kindly. I reminded him that he hadn't seen himself in the past seventy years, so it wouldn't be a big surprise if he'd changed.

"Yeah, but man, that chin. It's worthless. Maybe I'll grow back my beard."

I nodded, then got a brilliant idea. "You ever arrested, Luker."

He puffed up with pride. "Girl, I rode the rails, helped organize the auto workers, and stood against the lynch mobs. Was I ever arrested? I'll bet I spent as much time in jail as I did free."

"So this might be an interesting test," I told Arran. "Check out the records for an Oren Luker and see if you find them, then look for the mug shots. Should be sometime back in the 1930s, depression-era."

He shook his head. "Won't prove a thing. You're a research expert. How hard would it have been for you to dig up some old con's mugshot and feed it back to Ron?"

Typical male reaction. "Well if that's the way—"

He held up a hand, just as Luker had done a couple of hours earlier. "I'm not saying I don't believe you. I'm saying this isn't going to convince anybody."

"Sure would convince me," Ron said. "Because I've been down in the basement at headquarters, I know what a mess those records are in. Unfortunately, it would take months to go through that old paperwork and dig up this guy. And a lot of those old photos are faded out anyway. Check this out, though."

He pushed a button and a tiny portable printer spit out a color version of the picture.

After blowing on it for a few seconds to make sure the ink was dry, Ron handed it to me. "Do you think he'd like to have this?"

Luker puffed up with pride. "Don't know anyone else with their own official police portrait. The guys will be lining up to see my picture."

Uh-oh. That put a horrible picture in my head. Because there was no way Oren was going to be able to carry around a piece of paper. It might not weigh much, but it might as well be a mountain for a ghost. And if he couldn't take it with him, and he wanted all of his ghost-friends to see it, the ghosts would have to line up somewhere else—in a place owned by *someone* else. I suspected I knew what, and whom, Oren had in mind.

"Maybe you could frame it real pretty," Oren continued, right on cue. "We'll hang it on your wall with one of those spotlight things on it all the time so we don't have to turn out the lights. That way I could bring the guys over any time. The light rail runs near your place, right? We could get on at Union Station and take it to Mockingbird."

"How the heck do you know where I live?" I was sputtering, but I got the words out.

"Harry told me."

"How'd he know?"

"He followed you home one day. Didn't you notice?"

During rush hours, the train is generally full. Even with the low levels of ghost traffic, it would have been easy enough for a ghost to follow without me noticing.

I decided to drop that topic and get back to the real issue. "There's no way am I going to open a portrait gallery for ghosts."

"Considering what we're doing for you, that's a narrow-minded attitude."

"What you're doing for us?" I looked around dramatically. "So far, what you've done for us is, uh… nothing."

Unfortunately, the arrival of two more ghosts weakened that my Oscar-winning moment.

* * * *

After debunking a couple more bogus witnesses, Arran and Ron were ready to call the plan a flop.

Although interviewing ghost witnesses had been Arran's plan in the beginning, I couldn't help feeling like I needed to do something to make this work. After all, I'd negotiated the deal with the four ghost 'deputies.' I also hadn't told Arran how desperate some ghosts are to have themselves heard. They'd make up stories if they had to, and we'd heard some real whoppers.

When Luker returned with a goateed ghost wearing a Confederate cavalry cap and thigh-high boots, I was ready to call it quits as well.

"What the heck is that, Luker?"

"This is Colonel James T. Tigerson of the Second Texas Cavalry. He's been around a long time and if he says he saw something, then he saw it."

The Colonel looked like both a fop and a fake to me. If he'd been a Confederate Colonel, I was a Navy Seal.

Still, job inflation wasn't exactly limited to modern resumes. And lying about his war history didn't mean he'd lie about seeing a gunman. It didn't mean he'd tell the truth, either.

"Just what did you see, Colonel?"

"Yeah," Luker urged. "Tell her what you told me."

"May I do this?" Arran demanded, interrupting both of us.

"Sorry." I turned to the ghosts. "Arran wants to—"

"We're not deaf, even if he is," Luker said. "Have him ask his questions. But first, where did that picture of me go. Colonel, you've got to see this. Other than the chin, don't you think—"

"What chin?" the Colonel asked. "You never did have a chin, Oren. And now it's too late for you."

"Considering you've got ghost fleas in your hair, you're a strange one to talk."

"There's no such thing as a ghost flea. And that's a lucky thing for you. Some of the places you slept, you would—"

"Guys," I said. "We're getting off course here. Arran is about to give up and yank your deputizations, so you'd better have something here with the Colonel."

"He made *you* deputies?" the Colonel asked. "You're just hobos, which is another way of saying criminals. I, on the other hand, am an officer in the Confederate States of America armed forces. How come I can't be a deputy?"

"They've been helping us," I reminded the ancient ghost. "So far, you've just been causing trouble."

"I'll answer the questions. You just go ahead and ask, young man."

Once I remembered to tell Arran the ghost was ready, he took us through his now-standard questions, establishing the ghost's location at the beginning of the incident, during the actual shooting, and afterwards.

The Colonel said he'd been in Union Station when he'd felt the vibrations of gunfire. Being curious and immune to firearms, in this life if not in his previous one, he headed for the records building.

He'd gotten there too late to see gunfire, but had seen someone heading out in a hurry. Better yet, that someone was carrying a gun. Best of all, he'd pulled off a ski-mask as he'd emerged.

"What was he wearing?" I asked.

"Black shirt, black pants—like ninja pants or something, ya-know. Wouldn't be my choice."

That much was correct.

"Think this one is for real?" Arran asked me when I repeated the description.

"I don't like it when they talk as if we weren't even here," the Colonel said.

"He just might be." I turned back to the Colonel. "If you'd listened to as many liars as we have today, you'd understand our suspicion. But I think I do believe you. I'm going to let you describe the man you saw to Officer Sallot here. He'll ask you questions and you answer. Does that make sense?"

"I could just describe him. Good-sized guy—"

"That's not how it works," Luker interrupted.

"It'll go better if you answer the questions the police artist asks you," I added. "Ron's got a certain order he does things in. It seems to work. You saw what a good picture it made of Luker."

The colonel doffed his cavalry cap showing off a significantly receding hairline. Ghosts can dress how they want, and they don't show the scars of their final encounter with death, but they don't seem to be able to deal with little things like thinning hair—or chinlessness.

"I'd powerfully like a picture like that of me," the Colonel said. "Who knows, I might have grandkids out there somewhere, who'd like to have a picture of me."

Considering my own grandparents had been born a good eighty years *after* the end of the Civil War, I doubted that the Colonel had surviving grandchildren, let alone kid-aged grandchildren. Great-great grandchildren, maybe. "Did you ever have children?"

"Couldn't exactly do that since I got killed at Glorieta Pass, now could I?"

"In that case, I seriously doubt you have grandchildren."

"Hey. I hadn't thought about—" He tailed off, then started again. "I didn't mean literal grandkids. Nephews and nieces is more like it—and before you ask, I did have a couple of sisters so don't give me a hard time —I know that part is possible. Regardless, I'd still like to have a portrait."

"I'll see what I can do," I promised. "After you help us with the gunman."

"Tell Annie you want it framed on her wall," Luker said. "That's what she's going to do with mine. Once it's up there, we can come look at it any time I want to. Since I have this portrait, it won't bother me much I can't see myself in the mirror."

"Now there's a mighty-fine idea," the Colonel said. "Sure 'nough, that's the way it's got to be. You want me to help you, you're going to hang my portrait in your house. With a really purty frame all around it. I want one of them with gold leaf and all, like in those plantations in Mississippi. None of this cheap plastic stuff, seems to be everywhere these days. Didn't have any use for plastic in my day. Can you believe they even make guns out of plastic? Like the gun this guy we're talking about was carrying."

I put my head in my hands. I really hadn't asked for this. "We're not talking about him at all. We're talking about you and your silly demand to put portraits up in my apartment. Now if we can get to the crime."

"Can't say I see the shooting is nearly as important as my portrait," the Colonel said. "Nobody got hurt bad in that little incident, right? But I got killed fighting for my state and that makes me a hero. A hero should have a portrait."

The mental image of my nice apartment lined, floor to ceiling, with portraits of long-dead people I barely knew was firmly planted in my brain. Just hanging the pictures would have been spooky enough, but having ghosts pop in at all hours to check out their portraits would be a nightmare.

"We're wasting time," Arran said. "Agree to their demands and let's get on with it."

"How about *you* agree to their demands? Turn *your* house into a ghost museum?"

Arran considered, then nodded. "If that's the only hold-up, then that's not a problem. I've got a spare room sitting there empty. You can come over and help me set it up. Let's say tonight."

I stared at him. I was not ready to head over to some sexy guy's house, and if I was going to go over to his house, I didn't want the purpose to be setting up a ghost museum. I saw no end of trouble down that road.

"Deal," Luker said. "Tell the Ron guy he can ask his questions. The Colonel and I are ready."

Chapter 8

The Colonel wasn't just a good observer, he was something of a car fan. He identified the gunman's getaway car as a gold, late 90s, Mercedes sedan with Texas plates.

That kind of car wasn't exactly unique, but the Colonel's description, coupled with my own observations of the gunman's if not his face, gave us a pretty good likeness.

Ron tied his computer in to a program that did image matching with the Texas Department of Transportation drivers' license information, cross-referencing the vehicle registration information for everyone in Dallas County who owned an older model Mercedes sedan.

"This is a real break," Ron said. "The image matching technology we have access to basically sucks. But knowing about the old Mercedes should let us get a reasonable number of hits without narrowing the parameters so much we exclude a lot of positives."

Luker wrinkled his nose. "Whatever that means."

I was glad he'd had said that because I'd been thinking the same thing. It was scary that a twenty-six year old woman was as technologically ignorant as a man who'd been dead for seventy years. Unfortunately, the facts didn't lie.

"It means we have a chance," Ron said.

I hadn't vocalized Luker's question, but I managed not to blurt out anything about Ron hearing Oren. He'd seen the mystification on my face, that was all.

"Any other witnesses?" Arran asked. "What about Harry? Harry the ghost, not Harry the gunman," he added for Ron's benefit. "He's the one who saw the gun first, right?"

Although Harry haunted the records building during the week, the ghost deputies hadn't been able to find him that day. But I didn't think he'd have anything to add. He'd been with Sam and me in the elevator until the gunman had vanished.

Once the Colonel finished his description, Arran sent his ghost deputies out to round up anyone who'd seen an old Mercedes in the area. Meanwhile, Ron whipped up a portrait for the Colonel.

"My hair's a bit blonder," the Colonel insisted once Ron had printed out the sketch. And you've drawn my cheeks too round, as if I had apple-cheeks or something."

"You do have apple-cheeks." I picked up the printout and handed it to Arran. "Guess what, Detective? Here's the start to your portrait gallery. I hope you live somewhere near public transportation because most ghosts don't like to walk very far."

He took the pictures and stacked them together. "Can't they fly? I've always envisioned ghosts flying. Goes back to watching *Ghostbusters* when I was a kid, I guess, or Casper."

People's ignorance continually frustrated me. I couldn't be the only person in the history of the world with my problem. Which meant every other real medium had faced the same suspicion and unwillingness to hear.

"Well, yes, ghosts can fly," I explained. "More like floating, really, since gravity doesn't seem to matter to them. But even when they're levitating, they don't seem to move faster than roughly a walking pace. So it takes them a long time to get anywhere under their own power. A ghost *could* fly from here to London. But they'd spend weeks over the Atlantic and that's no fun for them. So, they generally just stow away on airlines."

"A lot of us are still pretty mad about the way the cities shut down the streetcar lines," the Colonel added. "Busses aren't as convenient and they don't print up the schedules so we can see them. And the electricity on the light rail? Burr—it stings a lot worse than those streetcars did."

"Guess most of you don't have Internet connections," Arran said once I'd repeated Oren's words to him. "I'd think wireless would be perfect for you."

"Now *that* would be *sweet*." The Colonel's expression was probably supposed to be ingratiating but instead made him look like he suffered from a ghostly fit of constipation. "An excellent suggestion. Perhaps you could type in the Earls for us."

"Huh?" That was my contribution.

The Colonel wrinkled his forehead. "I understand web pages are named Earl."

I wrapped my brain around that for a moment, then took a guess at what he was talking about. "Gotcha. I think you mean U.R.L. It's spelled out, not run together."

"You'll type them in for us then? Great." Owen already gave me your address, but he asked me to get the detective's."

After assuring the Colonel I would *not* be in the business of typing in either Earls or U.R.L.s for the ghostly community, I passed his request along to Arran.

To my surprise, the Detective actually gave his address, speaking slowly so the ghost could memorize it. Arran had figured out that the ghosts weren't exactly in a position to take notes and was adjusting his behavior to meet their needs.

It crossed my mind that Arran's job required him to learn to accommodate and take advantage of weaknesses, or just differences, in others. Most people can chose who they spend their time with, but in the cop business, it's criminals who decide. And criminals are not known as the world's most stable types. Arran probably had to deal with argumentative, insane, hopelessly stupid, illiterate, and drug-damaged people if he expected to get anywhere. That just might be a good thing. Certainly he'd need a lot of that skill if he was going to put up with me.

It took me a moment before I realized the wishful thinking aspects of *that* thought process. Arran didn't have to put up with me. Once this case was over, he'd move on and I'd be history. All of the attraction going on certainly seemed to be a one-way street.

"I'll swing by for my first session on the World Wide Web tomorrow," the Colonel said to me. "And I'll get over to check out my portrait ASAP. By the way, I hear they give away free homesites. It's been a long time since I had a site I could call my own."

"Homesites are just spaces on hard drives," I said.

The Colonel nodded, his face sad. "I've never had an easy drive in my life."

He headed for the door before I could figure that one out. "I won't do it," I shouted after him. "If you come to my place, I won't be there for you—I won't even acknowledge you. I'm not dumb enough to fall for that one."

Out of the corner of my eye, I saw the restaurant manager shudder as the crazy-woman in his place started shouting at the empty air again. Sure enough, a couple of people in line gave me a startled look and decided to catch their late afternoon snacks elsewhere.

Arran was smart enough to wait a few minutes for me to calm down before smiling at me. "What do you say we give your deputies another half hour to see what they round up? If they don't find anything by then, we'll head for my house. I can throw a couple of steaks on the grill and I've got a bottle of wine I've been saving for a special occasion."

I wish I could say I was too smart to fall for Arran's line. It wouldn't be true, though. I blamed my susceptibility on my condition, of course. Most girls got plenty of practice saying *no* to guys. Being the crazy-girl meant I'd never needed to because guys ran away first.

"We'd better stop on the way and pick up some frames," I said. "The guys won't be happy if you stick their pictures to your refrigerator with used chewing gum."

"That's a particularly disgusting thought."

If he thought that was disgusting, I shuddered to think what he'd say when he saw the aluminum foil and lighting system in my bathroom. Then again, he wasn't going to see that. I was helping him hang up pictures, that was all. Arran was a cop and I was a witness. I needed to get over boyfriend/girlfriend thoughts.

* * * *

I'm not sure what I'd expected from Arran's house. Whatever it was, though, was wrong.

He lived just south of the Trinity River in a highrise condo.

The building was a beautiful art-deco structure built in the roaring twenties, and he'd decorated a three-bedroom condo on the top floor with vintage pieces from that optimistic era, as well as the obligatory reclining chairs and large screen TV. To my surprise, bookshelves lined a couple of his walls. I hadn't seen Arran as the bookworm type.

After opening a bottle of wine and pouring each of us a glass, he grabbed a hammer and nails from a toolbox and headed into one of the bedrooms.

"You're really going to hang up pictures of dead people?"

He shrugged. "I made a deal."

"They couldn't exactly do anything to you if you reneged."

"It's not about what *they* can do, Annie. It's about what kind of person *I* am. If I start making promises I don't intend to keep, what business do I have being a cop?"

I needed to fire some quip back at him, but I was so surprised by his words I couldn't figure one out in time. So I just nodded and took a sip of my wine while I tried to figure out this guy. If he could just be a jerk all the time, it would be easier for me to deal with the attraction.

As Arran had promised, the wine was good.

I suggested that he hang the portraits close together, partly so they'd take up less room but mostly because I feared he'd end up with a lot more if we didn't solve this case quickly. Ghosts talk to each other—since they generally don't have anyone else to talk to, and the ghost grapevine passes information along at Internet speeds. It wouldn't be long before every ghost in Dallas wanted his portrait in Arran's gallery.

The pictures hung, Arran put away his hammer, washed his hands, and dug a couple of huge steaks out of the refrigerator. "How do you like your steak?"

Uh-oh. Another chance to demonstrate how weird I was. "I should have mentioned this before, but I'm a vegetarian."

His face fell, but only for a moment. "No problem. Do you eat eggs and cheese? Or are you a strict vegan?"

Another chance to show I was the kind of woman he should be running from. "As long as the chicken were free range and the cows weren't mistreated."

"I think I've got that handled. I shop at Whole Foods. I'll make omelets." He opened the refrigerator door, considered, then closed it and put the steaks into the freezer.

I felt guilty. "Don't be ridiculous. You don't have to feed me. Just make your own dinner and I'll take the train home."

He grabbed my arm when I turned away, holding me still while he walked around me to look me in the face.

"You barely ate anything today, Annie. And I don't get many chances to cook for a beautiful woman so why don't you relax and keep me company? I can always eat the steaks another day."

A beautiful woman? I almost looked around to see who else had showed up. My sister-in-law was the beautiful one, I was the weird one.

That's when I noticed the way his hand felt on my arm. Instead of feeling harsh and violent, his grip was like what he might use holding a baby bird—firm enough that I would have to pull away, but gentle enough that I felt the warmth of his touch rather than the pressure of his grip.

I blamed it on my relative inexperience with men, but all of a sudden my core got all slick and my knees got wobbly. I leaned toward the nearest solid object to keep my balance.

Which was my next mistake. Because the nearest solid object wasn't a wall—it was Arran's chest.

I meant to push away—honestly. But my arms ignored that command. My legs had been wobbly enough before, but they turned into complete jelly when my face ran into Arran's hard chest and my breasts pressed into his abdomen.

He wrapped his arms around me to keep me from collapsing to the floor like a deflated balloon.

Fortunately my brain chose that moment to come back on line. "Guess you're right about me needing to eat." My voice sounded throaty, unfamiliar, but at least I could talk. "Must have gotten woozy all of a sudden."

"You must have," Arran agreed. He didn't let me go.

Still, he'd fallen for my lie. I couldn't believe it, but I was simultaneously happy that he hadn't recognized my real weakness and miserable that he wouldn't take advantage of me. I wouldn't perform in front of ghosts, and ghost-free moments happened almost as rarely as the times I was with a guy I was interested in.

Then again, Arran had already proved he was the honorable type. If he took advantage of me when I was weak, he'd probably feel obligated to follow through with a relationship—and he was smart enough to realize that getting stuck with a crazy-woman as a girlfriend would be bad for his career.

Arran picked me up, carried me over to one of his reclining chairs, and gently set me down.

His lips brushed against my cheek as he settled me in the recliner, but that didn't count as a kiss. Not really. It was probably just an accident.

"You've been holding up really well," Arran breathed into my ear, "but you were shot at, accused of having something to do with the shooter, now you have to worry about the gunman coming after you. It's no big surprise that you'd go into shock."

"Yeah, yeah. That's it. Just shock. Give me a minute to breathe and I'll be fine."

I might be in shock, but it didn't have anything to do with the gunman—it had everything to do with being with Arran. Which was weird. I mean, anyone sane would agree that having a killer after you was a lot more dangerous than having a sexy cop touch you. Then again, anyone sane would also agree that ghosts aren't real.

On cue, an elderly female ghost appeared through the door and headed over to me. My desire for Arran didn't go away, but I sucked it up. I didn't believe in pubic displays of affection and I counted ghosts as way too public.

"Are you all right, darling?" the ghost asked.

"Do I know you?"

Arran got between me and the ghost. "What are you talking about, Annie. We've spent most of the past twenty-four hours together. Don't you remember—"

"Sorry, Arran. You've got company."

Relief mixed with irritation on his face.

Well, I could understand the irritation. For a brief period, he'd probably been able to forget he was dealing with a woman with my distinctly unusual issues. Maybe that brush of lips against my cheek hadn't been an accident but could have represented the beginning of something. Except I hadn't been able to keep my mouth shut when the first ghost had showed.

"Come on, Ethyl." I recognized the Colonel's voice before I saw him. The cop promised he'd hang my portrait. You've got to see it, even if the artist did get my cheeks wrong. Which room is it in, Annie?"

I pointed toward Arran's spare bedroom. "I think maybe I'd better go," I told the detective. "I have a feeling it's going to get a little crowded here."

He looked frustrated. "Fine. We'll go out. There's Charco-Broiler, a fun steak house up on Jefferson—oh, right. Never mind about the steak. Got it—there's a Thai place on Bishop. They offer tofu selections for all of their dishes. Unless you're worried about soy or rice ghosts, you'll be safe. We'll go there and let the ghosts check out the gallery."

"I don't need you making fun of my problem," I said. "And no, I'm not worried about the ghosts of long-dead rice plants."

The ghosts in the room hadn't reduced my emotional turmoil, just made sure I wouldn't act out my desire. Arran's slam turned my urges into anger.

He ignored my response. "Drink this first, though. You need your energy."

This turned out to be an entire beermug full of wine. If I hadn't known better, I would have guessed Arran was trying to get me drunk.

Yeah, right. In my dreams. He was probably trying to get me unconscious so I'd shut up.

Chan Thai, the restaurant Arran took me to, turned out to be a funky place with paintings of oversized pumpkins on the wall and food so spicy it brought every one of my taste buds to the edge between pleasure and pain. And that was on the 'medium' level.

I got the broccoli with peanut sauce and tofu. Yum.

"Would it bother you if I eat something with meat?"

I inhaled the scent of cooking beef. "I'd eat it myself if the cow-ghosts didn't bother me. Go for it. And let me know how it tastes."

If cow-ghosts poked their noses into the restaurant, I'd just point them his way—and continue eating my tofu. Thank goodness soybeans didn't have ghosts.

Chapter 9

What do you do on a Saturday night after a guy takes you out to a really fabulous dinner and you've had a little more wine than you're used to?

If you're a normal, healthy girl, and if the guy is just about the sexiest male you've been with, a logical next step is to decide whose place to head to for a nightcap and a makeout session—even if you're not quite ready to jump straight into the sack.

Arran had blown off my offer to pay for my share of the dinner. While the waiter was processing his credit card, Arran asked my permission to make a call and connected with police headquarters to get a status update.

Using the Colonel's description and the FBI's image-matching software, they'd identified a couple of possible candidates for the gunman. They were staking out an apartment in Flower Mound, a part of the Dallas-area suburban sprawl we call the metroplex, but they hadn't made any arrests.

Arran clicked his phone shut and looked across the table at me. "I don't think you should be alone."

"Meaning?"

"We've got a couple of matches but the one that looks best turns out to be a guy named Ritchie Stone. He's been in and out of trouble all his life. He beat up one girlfriend so bad she had to have her jaw wired and spent months in traction so he's dangerous. As far as *he* knows, you and Sam Bert are the only witnesses. If your story about the gambling is right, Bert would have to incriminate himself before he could tell us more, and he doesn't seem anxious to do that. If Bert stays quiet, that leaves just you—and every television station in the city has been showing pictures of you, with your name."

The chill that went through me had nothing to do with the colder temperatures that nightfall had brought to Dallas.

"He was wearing a mask. And that Darth Vader voice had to be fake. I could never identify him, so why would he worry about me?"

"Once the Identikit artwork goes out, he'll know better."

"He'll figure there was some other witness."

Arran shook his head. "The Colonel said there were no living people around. Stone will think you saw more than he knew, that's all. So, I'm taking you home and I'm staying with you."

"You're just going to take me back with you?"

"I've got an extra bedroom. You don't have to worry about my motives."

Screw that—it was his lack of motives that bothered me. Arran joined the long list of guys who'd been grossed out by my talent. Which wouldn't have been so bad if I hadn't been so outrageously attracted to him. I knew the cure to that kind of attraction—getting far away from him and staying away.

Another thought pushed that concern out of my head. I'd seen Arran's spare bedroom.

"You're kidding? You want me to spend the night in the ghosts' portrait gallery? Do you have any idea how much sleep I'd get? They'd want me to be their docent."

He had the grace to look bemused. "I'd sleep there myself, but I need the king-sized bed. Otherwise my feet hang off the end."

That was actually a sort of charming picture. "I'm not going to spend the night at your place, Arran."

Suspicion crossed his face. "What *do* you have in mind?"

If I'd really been the hard-edged martial artist I pretended to be, I would have told him I had in mind taking care of myself. Green belt or not, though, I had few illusions that a man willing to riddle an elevator with a dozen shots or more wouldn't be able to catch me unaware and murder me.

"I'll ask the ghosts to keep an eye out for me."

Given Chan Thai's dim lighting, I couldn't be absolutely sure Arran's face turned purple, but I did see his lips moving and was positive he was counting to ten.

"Great idea," he finally said.

I waited for the second half of the explosion. To my surprise, though, none came. "Why don't I take you home, then? It's been a rough couple of days."

I wasn't as relieved as I should have been that he'd agreed to go along with my plan.

Chapter 10

I'd gotten what I wanted.

I was in my apartment, alone.

I'd rousted out a couple of ghosts who'd been sitting on my sofa watching the powered down television, and asked them to warn me if anyone was hanging around or trying to get in.

They'd agreed to keep an eye out for me and I thought they meant it at the time. Being dead, though, doesn't give people any greater attention span than they'd had when they'd been alive. The ghosts would keep their promise and watch out for me—until something more interesting happened.

It didn't matter, though. I was exhausted and still feeling the wine. I needed to sleep. Besides, the more I thought about it, the more I was convinced that Stone, or Harry, or Darth, or whomever he really was, would be hiding from the cops, not hunting down witnesses. Arran was just another over-protective male trying to take care of the crazy-woman because nobody believed I could take care of myself.

My safety assured by rationalization, I turned on my anti-ghost light show, brushed my teeth, and stood under the shower until the hot water ran out, then pulled on my PJs, ran to my bed, and turned on the electric blanket.

I don't think I even got to sheep number three before I was fast asleep.

It was pitch-dark when I awakened, my heart beating a million beats a minute and adrenaline racing through my system as if it were a NASCAR circuit.

"Hey Annie. Someone's coming." Marissa, one of the ghosts who'd been in my living room when Arran had dropped me off put her ghost-hand through my shoulder in an effort to shake me.

That always grosses me out.

Unfortunately, being grossed out by ghost-human overlap was the least of my worries.

My brilliant plan to use ghosts as security guards had a tiny flaw. The ghosts could warn me that someone was coming—but then what? One thing for sure, they weren't going to be a lot of use defending me.

I fumbled on the nightstand until I'd found my phone and dialed 9-1 —and hung up. For all I knew, Marissa was playing a practical joke on me. Anyway, what was I going to tell police dispatch? That a ghost had warning me that someone was heading toward my apartment?

I sat up in my bead and listened: nothing. "Did you recognize him?"

She shook her head. "Living people all look the same to me."

Oh, great. I was being rescued by an anti-life bigot. "Where is he?"

"When I woke you up he was downstairs. Now he's right outside your front door. He's—he's doing something to the lock."

I decided I'd rather deal with Arran's smug 'I told you so' than with Darth Vader. I punched the speed-dial he'd insisted on programming into my cell and waited.

He picked it up on the second ring. "Problems, babe?"

I filed the 'babe' away for later. "According to Marissa, there's someone outside my door. Should I call 9-1-1, or—"

"Coming."

He disconnected before I could say anything else. Which meant I was hosed. Even if he got in his car immediately, it would take him at least ten minutes to get from his place to mine. I didn't think it would take anywhere near that for Darth Stone to get through my door. Probably the only reason it had taken him as long as it had was because he didn't want to wake me.

Once Stone got in, he'd be hyperaware of the dangers. I decided my best approach would be to take the battle to him.

I rummaged through my nightstand until I found the can of pepper spray I'd bought a year earlier, back when I'd lived in Deep Ellum and had to contend with drunk frat boys and stoned bikers whenever the sun set. For them, just showing the can had done the job. I didn't think Stone would make it that easy.

"You show him, girl." Marissa, jumped up and down—shouting, and making fist signs toward my door.

I put my finger to my lips. "Shhh." As if Stone would hear her even if she shrieked at the top of her lungs.

My stomach threatened to come up my throat, but I swallowed hard. Leaving my shoes next to my bed, I padded to my front door.

Marissa hadn't lied. The click of something metallic fiddling in my deadbolt chilled my blood.

I waited until the cylinder started to rotate, then yanked the door open and sprayed.

I recognized the face from the Colonel's Identikit sketch—right as he stuck his fist into my nose.

I'd been hit a bunch of times when we spar in my Tae Kwon Do class. I'd thought I was pretty tough. Wrong. I'd never felt pain like that before.

I reeled back into my apartment, blood spraying from my nose.

Marissa fluttered over me clucking. "I knew this was a bad idea. You should have gone out the fire escape."

I'd shot so much pepper spray into the air that it clogged my throat and made my eyes weep—in addition to the tears my busted nose was creating. Stone's eyes were red and he hacked out a couple of coughs, but he wasn't incapacitated. Not even close.

His hand reached into his overcoat and he came out with either the same gun he'd used to shoot at me through the elevator floor or a duplicate.

"Should have kept your mouth shut, girlie."

Yep, it was the Vader voice again.

We don't do a lot of groundwork in my Tae Kwon Do class, but a guest instructor had worked with us on some rolls and I tried one. Just in time to miss the shot Stone put through my floor.

The Ellises, who lived downstairs, were supposed to be in Galveston for a vacation. I hoped they hadn't come back early. My floor didn't stop the bullet.

"Say your prayers, girlie." This time he took a more careful aim.

In the distance, I heard the sound of sirens. Either someone had heard the shot and alerted the police or Arran had called for backup. Whichever it was, the sirens were too far away to help me, too far away even to have a chance of catching Vader after he killed me.

A crowd of ghosts gathered around Stone, but none seemed especially interested in interfering, let alone able to do anything to help me.

I watched Stone. The second his finger twitched on his trigger, I rolled again.

He laughed and I saw I'd rolled exactly where he'd aimed.

Then one of the ghosts moved and Stone's gun went sailing.

"On the floor, asshole. You're under arrest."

It took my battered brain a few seconds to recognize Arran's voice and realize the shape that decked Stone hadn't been a ghost after all.

"How'd you get here so quick?" That's what I tried to ask, anyway. What actually came out my mouth was a sputtering and nasal gibbering. Who knew that getting your nose flattened against your face could make it hard to talk?

I must have looked even worse than I thought, because Arran looked completely grossed out.

That's when everything went black.

* * * *

"What the hell were you thinking?"

I couldn't help myself. I smiled toward the angry voice.

I felt better than I could ever remember feeling. My brain seemed to be floating in a warm sea, and beautiful colors swam past me, singing wonderful music.

I looked at Arran, who seemed surrounded by light. Like an angel, I thought.

It was he, of course, who'd chosen to break into my bliss and ask me that rude question.

"Hi, Arran. You're very handsome, you know? I'll bet all the girl-cops *love-love-love* working with you."

Something at the back of my mind promised I'd be sorry for saying that but the thought didn't make sense so I ignored it.

He shook his head. "What on earth motivated you to open your door to Ritchie Stone? If you'd waited thirty more seconds, I could have arrested him with no fuss, no broken nose, and no hole through your neighbors' ceiling."

"Is my nose broken?" I put my hand up to my face, but it felt weird, like it was covered with something. "Nah. Can't be. I'm pretty sure that would hurt."

"You don't feel anything because you're doped out of your skull on pain medicine."

I giggled. "You were using me as a trap, weren't you? You're so clever, Arran." I wouldn't ordinarily think that staking me out like some ancient sacrifice was such a brilliant idea. None of that mattered now, though. I was in love with the world.

A whole phalanx of ghosts peered at me over the edge of what I recognized as a hospital bed. Oddly, though, they left a vacant space between me and where Arran sat, glowering. Generally, ghosts don't worry about that kind of thing. Perhaps his anger was enough to repel them, sort of like the electricity that propels Dallas's light rail.

I giggled at the idea and tried to explain it to Arran.

He listened for a few seconds, then shook his head. "You could have died, Annie. If I'd been two seconds slower, I would have been too late."

"You're such a hero. Come over here. I'll give you a big kiss as a reward, Detective." My lips felt numb, but that was okay. Hell, everything was okay. If this was the result of the pain medication Arran insisted I was stoned on, I guessed I could finally understand why some people chose illegal drugs. I mean, who wouldn't want to live a life where everything was happy and nobody had to suffer?

Back in the days when my parents had been sending me to a new psychiatrist every month to try and 'cure' me of my ghosts, the drugs they'd given me had always made me even more miserable than the ghosts did. I think there'd been a theory in psychiatry back then that you cure psychotics by making their dream worlds even more miserable than the real world they were fleeing. The drugs I'd taken for my 'problem' had made me sick and miserable. The drugs I'd been given for a broken nose made me feel wonderful. Given the choice, I'd take a broken nose and the ghosts over their cure.

My mind was working a bit slowly, but remembering Darth Vader breaking my nose brought a bit of clarity to my thought and encouraged me to explore my situation a bit more carefully. Got it—my face wasn't fuzzy after all, my mouth and nose were covered by some sort of gauze.

No wonder Arran hadn't kissed me. He couldn't get through the bandages. It said something about the drugs that I didn't even consider other possibilities—like he didn't want to kiss me.

"If my face is too messed up for you, sweetie," I said, "you can kiss me somewhere else." I tried to tug down my sheets to expose a bit of my hospital-gown covered chest. "Know what I mean?"

I giggled at my wit, even as I wondered if I might have exaggerated the clarity of my thought. I never threw myself at guys. At the moment I couldn't remember *why* I was usually such a stick-in-the-mud. So what if the ghosts watched Arran kissing my breasts? Maybe they'd learn something. And Arran was sexy. I wanted him in my shirt—and maybe in my pants.

"They gave you too high a dose of morphine. The pain meds are probably interacting with the alcohol you drank."

"You made me drink it, remember." I giggled again. The suspicion that I was going to regret this conversation later was definitely growing.

"I remember everything. Including your promise to get out when the ghosts gave you warning."

"Did I promise that? I forgot."

He shook his head. "Yes, you promised. You're lucky I got there so quickly."

Lucky. My brain was working a little slowly, but it hadn't completely turned off. "I think it wasn't luck at all. You were waiting outside, weren't you? You're so smart."

"I don't remember you inviting me to spend the night inside."

"The aluminum foil would scare you away."

He looked confused. Good. That meant he hadn't explored my house after he'd caught Vader. Which reminded me, "So, what happens with Darth Maul?"

"Ritchie Stone, his name is Ritchie Stone. He's a collector for a gambling ring. Turns out you were right about Sam. He has an addiction and wasn't paying his bills on time."

"I guess you were wrong when you said there was no Mafia here in Dallas."

"Being wrong has happened to me a lot lately."

He got out of the chair, stepped to my side, and kissed me on my forehead—the one spot on my face not covered with gauze. "See you around, Annie."

"Oh, no. You call me babe, remember?"

"That slipped out. You aren't supposed to remember that."

Like Hell. I didn't have a whole lot of memories I wanted to lock away and cherish, but his kiss, and his pet name, were a couple I wanted to keep. I thought.

The pain medicine was starting to wear off a bit and a dull throb from my nose was matched by a dull throb from the back of my brain as I started processing everything I'd said to Arran. Ohmigod, I had just begged him to kiss my boobs.

"Did anyone ever tell you that you've got a nice butt?" I yelled after him as he headed out of my hospital room.

He kept walking.

"Didn't your mother ever tell you not to throw yourself at a guy," Marissa asked. "They value you more if they have to work for you."

I blinked. Where had *she* come from? I'd thought all of the ghosts were strangers. "I'm not responsible for what I'm saying. I'm drugged."

The ghost shook her head sadly. "It's a real shame you chased him away. A man like that is a treasure."

"Make me feel better, why don't you? Can't you see that I'm injured here?"

"That Richie guy hit you hard. You should have seen the way you went down. You looked like a jet engine spurting blood all over. Your house is a wreck, by the way. You need to get back and clean it up before it'll be habitable again. All the ghosts who live there are here waiting."

I looked around. Sure enough, they weren't strangers at all. All the ghosts I normally had to roust from my bathroom, my living room, my dining room and especially my bedroom circled around my hospital bed. I wish I could say they looked concerned. I thought Marissa had it right, though. The only thing they cared about was me cleaning up my apartment so they wouldn't have to deal with the mess.

"Why don't you guys go bother Arran Dane?" I asked. "He's got more room than I do, he's close to the Dallas Zoo train station so it'll be convenient for you. Best of all, he's working on a ghost gallery."

"He doesn't talk to us," Marissa reminded me. "Besides, you're more fun."

I had the sneaking suspicion I'd become a *Sims* game for the ghosts in my life.

Chapter 11

When they found out how bad my health insurance was, the doctors were only too happy to shove me out the hospital doors, based on my assurance that I, indeed, did have someone who could wake me up every few hours and make sure I hadn't gone into a catatonic fit. Neither they, nor I, were real specific about exactly who would do the waking. I figured the ghosts would get a real kick out of the job.

I wasn't going anywhere, though, in a hospital gown open in the back to show my butt to the world. So I called my brother and told him I needed help.

An hour later, he, Lauren, and Little Jack were on the scene. Lauren had stopped by Neiman Marcus and bought a pair of killer slacks and a silky sleeveless blouse in my size that I'd never have had the nerve or the bank account to buy myself.

My face was still up in bandages, but the rest of me was okay, except the oversized Band-Aids in my arm where they'd stuck me with the IV.

Fortunately, I had no problems persuading the male ghosts to get out of the bathroom when I went in to change. Being dead doesn't change guys—they'd rather look at Lauren fully clothed than they would at me naked.

"Why don't you come stay with us for a couple of weeks?" Lauren suggested when I came out of the bathroom wearing my new million dollar outfit that made my two black eyes, bandaged nose, and hair still stiff with dried blood look even more disgraceful. "I don't have anything before a judge now so I could go on half-days. You could help out with Little Jack, and we could have a lot of fun."

My mouth watered as I imagined waking up to my brother's home-squeezed orange juice, Lauren's freshly-ground Kona coffee, and Little Jack's always-animated conversation every morning.

My desire to create an artificial family was a weakness, I knew. My parents had loved me in their own dutiful way, but their primary interest had been getting me cured of my ghosts. They hadn't been willing to accept me as I was. I'd spent enough time talking to psychologists to realize I'd never quite gotten over that sense of rejection, even though my parents had done the best they could for me. But hanging out with my brother wasn't the answer. I wasn't a part of their family: I was an add-on.

"I'll be fine," I insisted. "You guys have already done so much buying me these clothes and driving me home."

Lauren surprised me by wrinkling her forehead. It was just for a moment, but it was still something I'd never seen her do before. "Does a certain hunky detective have anything to do with that?"

"What?" I'd thought she believed Arran was just the cop who'd come out to arrest me.

"Don't kid a kidder, Annie. I'm a lawyer, every day I deal with better liars than you'll ever be. Detective Dane is standing outside your room like a dragon guarding a heap of gold, and I think you're the treasure." She stepped closer and lowered her voice. "That man is a hunk and a half, even if he is a cop."

I didn't need my beautiful sister-in-law to tell me that. I didn't need anyone to tell me that whatever Arran and I might have shared, it was over now. "He thought I was a suspect, then I helped him with the Identi-Kit stuff. Now that they've arrested Darth Ma—I mean Ritchie Stone, he's done with me."

"The look I saw had nothing to do with suspect."

And it almost certainly didn't have anything to do with me. Sure he'd probably looked hot and horny—hell, Lauren got even the ghosts working that way and if protoplasmic equipment worked, I definitely didn't want to know about it.

"Come on." Jack had held back but now he grabbed my arm. "We'll stop for lunch and spend some time together before we drop you back at your place. I'll bring you up to speed on what's going on with mom and dad and you can tell us all what happened to you and how you got hurt."

"Can we go to McDonalds?" Little Jack sat on the floor of my hospital room and clasped his arms around his knees as if preparing for a siege. "I saw one when we were coming down the freeway. We never go to McDonalds. I hate those grownup places."

"Yes, sweetie. And you told us about it at the time." Lauren gave me an apologetic shrug. "It isn't exactly ritzy but would Mac-D be all right, Annie? If we went there, you could tell us all the gory details of what happened to you while Little Jack plays."

The kid in question made a face. "I want some gory details."

Marissa, one of my hospital ghosts nodded along with my nephew. She wanted gory details, too.

Lauren put her hand through Marissa to caress Little Jack's angel-fine blond hair. Then she bent and picked him up as if his forty or so pounds were nothing. I thought of her as being weak and girlie but she definitely had some muscles—which would have made her even more annoying if she hadn't been so good for my brother.

"I know you do, baby," she said. "But some things are grownup talk."

"Like the ghosts?"

"Definitely like the ghosts," I said.

"Hey, I like kids," Marissa claimed. "I'm not like that pervert over there."

Sure enough one of the ghosts who trailed after Lauren had gotten naked. Why was it the guys you *least* wanted to see naked were the ones who always showed it off? I wouldn't complain if Arran got naked. Instead, I got pudgy ghosts who'd been fifty-something when they'd died and hadn't taken care of themselves for years before that.

I helped Little Jack clamber down from his mother and took his hand. "McDonalds sounds great. Considering how my face feels, a milk shake is about all I'm up to anyway. Ritchie's fist was bigger than my nose, which means I've got a couple of loose teeth.

"As well as some beautiful shiners," Jack said. Remember the one you gave me when you found out how I persuaded Fast Freddie to take you to the prom."

"How'd you give daddy a black eye, Aunt Annie?" Little Jack demanded.

"That's on a need-to-know basis, Little Jack," his father said.

"Okay." Little Jack sidestepped around Marissa, then tugged me toward the door. "Can we leave now? There are too many ghosts here."

Prickles shot down my spine like the time I'd plugged in a lamp with both fingers on the electrical tines. How could Little Jack know the room was full of ghosts? After twenty-some years of shame and psychiatric *treatment*, I'd come to terms with my talent. But any terms I'd come to were about me. Lauren and Jack wouldn't forgive me if Little Jack turned up with my ability to see the dead. I wasn't sure I'd forgive myself, either.

"Why do you say that?" I'll give him credit. Jack asked his question in a casual voice, exactly as if they were just carrying on a normal conversation.

Little Jack laughed. "Can't you see the way Aunt Annie's eyes move? Whenever there are ghosts around, she always looks at them and tries to get out of their way. Except there's never anyone for her to get out of the way of. So she just twitches."

My relief in hearing he wasn't afflicted outweighed the downer in learning I twitched—but not by much. Chalk one more line in the long list of why any halfway intelligent guy would run-not-walk away from Annie Neeter.

"I think Little Jack has a brilliant idea." I glared at the naked ghost. "Let's get out of here."

* * * *

Getting out of the hospital was harder than it should have been.

I swear they had me fill out the same form six times.

Finally, Lauren got on her horse and told the administrators to back off. A couple of minutes of lawyer-talk, and they took one last imprint of my battered Visa card, and let me go.

Little Jack navigated us to the nearby McDonalds with the unerring accuracy of a GPS system—or a kid on a mission.

The large game room just outside the main dining room swarmed with kids even though the parking lot and most of the tables were empty. The kid's room held a ball pit, where they jump into a big pile of balls, and a tunnel maze they could crawl through. Dozens of children screamed and laughed as they raced through the maze, jumped into the balls, and played complicated made-up games that no adult could possibly understand.

A part of me wanted to pull off my shoes and jump in myself, even though I was (a little) taller than Ronald McDonald's hand. My parents had never let me play that way—they'd been too busy carting me off to the next miracle doctor or exorcist for a cure.

I suppressed the urge. Some mom would probably call the police if an adult woman who looked like she'd just walked off the set of a slasher film jumped into the pit near her children.

Little Jack had no such restraint. He told his mom he wanted the four-piece Chicken Finger Happy Meal, then raced away into the maze.

It wasn't until he leapt from the top of a platform into the ball pit that I realized what was different. The other kids didn't splash when they hit the balls. The other kids were ghosts. No wonder I didn't see any parents.

I swallowed hard. I was used to seeing ghosts, of course, but I never got used to the children. Watching those once-living kids swarm around my still-alive nephew goosebumped my arm. Creepy.

"What?" Lauren grasped me by the arm.

"Nothing that can hurt him," I said. I didn't like using the 'G' word around her.

She stared after her son, as if glaring hard enough would bring the invisible into focus. "Are there any of the creepy pervert ones around him? Because if there are, I don't want him playing there. And I don't care that they can't hurt him. It's too gross."

My throat choked. Lauren had never believed in my ghosts. Maybe, intellectually she still didn't, but I'd convinced a part of her and I couldn't figure out whether that was good, or whether I'd destroyed a part of her innocence forever. "No perverts. Just kids who died young and who get to spend the rest of their existence being kids."

"You're sure they can't hurt him?"

"Being a ghost isn't catchy."

I watched as the ghosts incorporated Little Jack into their games, playing around him as if he were both a fellow player and an obstacle as he ignored them and writhed through the balls, exploding from them in a shower of colors and laughter.

The ghosts laughed with him, diving through the balls like dolphins through the sea. I realized it was no wonder their game seemed so complicated. These ghost-kids had probably been playing them for years.

"How do you know whether they're real?" Lauren and I were in a booth and my brother was picking up the tray of food. "Couldn't they just be your imagination?"

"They might be. But they tell me things I couldn't otherwise know. How could I have imagined Ritchie would have a gun? How could I have known he was at my door?"

"Subconscious—"

I sighed. "I know. There are always rational explanations. But I really see them, Lauren. And I couldn't imagine all they say. I mean, I'm taking French lessons from a ghost, and I've learned enough that I'm reading Stendhal's *Le Rouge et Le Noir*. How could I learn a language from my imagination?"

"That trick with Detective Dane's wallet was pretty amazing."

My brother set down the tray, slid into the booth, and put his arm around his wife's shoulders. "Whispering girls-only secrets?"

"Talking about the ghosts," I admitted.

He shook his head. "You've got too much going for you to obsess about dead people, Annie. Even if you see them, and I'm not saying you don't, can't you see that they're interfering with your social life? What about that cop? Why not give him a call and see if he'd like to do something with you. Lauren and I can't use our symphony tickets next weekend. How about I give you the pair and you invite him?"

"I started it," Lauren said. "Did you know that ghosts stand around and watch people when they don't know it? I mean, they might be watching when we're in bed together." She wrinkled her nose. "Eeew."

Jack shook his head. "We can't think about that, babe."

"Sorry." I must have started apologizing for seeing ghosts as soon as I'd learned to speak, certainly before I had any conscious memories. Now, though, the word stuck in my craw. The ghosts had come through. They'd saved my life and they'd provided the information needed to identify the suspect for an attempted murder. Why *should* I be sorry about my talents? Why shouldn't I use them? For the first time in my life, I wondered whether my ability might not be a gift, rather than a curse.

I grabbed my chocolate shake and sucked on it hard enough to crush the straw. The sweet rush of chocolate and cold didn't bring any answers. "Tell you what. I've got to get home so why don't I just walk to the train from here?"

Lauren reached across the table and grasped my forearm. "Jack is doing the guy thing, trying to solve problems. I bet Detective Dane will do the same. Here's a trick every girl should know—you just look at them like this." She opened her eyes wide as if she'd heard something wonderful and amazing. "If you can do it without gagging, you might say something like, 'Really? That is so smart.'"

Jack's face was a picture. "You mean all these years, that admiration was just an act?"

She dropped her grip on me and patted him on the head. "Have to humor my little stud-muffin."

"I get the message." He sighed. "I didn't mean to offend you, Annie. I just worry that you spend so much time in the world of the dead that you forget that you're not one of them. You'll have plenty of time to be a ghost after you've died, so why not enjoy life? Why not—"

"Sweetie, you're doing it again."

"Sorry."

I took another sip from the chocolate shake. Still no answers. Still better than nothing. "I know you're still taking care of me, Jack, and I appreciate it. But I can't just ignore my gift."

"You think it's a gift?" Jack's eyes widened.

Was he really surprised, or disappointed? I'd assumed I was a burden to him, never even considered that my brother might get some satisfaction out of caring for his handicapped sister.

"Maybe it's a wonderful gift," I finally answered. "I've just never thought of it that way before."

* * * *

My brother went from reflective mode to protective when he saw my apartment.

The police had removed my deadbolt, cut a chunk out of my floor where Ritchie's gunshot had gone, and left a mess everywhere else.

I yanked down the crime scene tape, swung open the otherwise unsecured door and went in. "I'll be fine."

"With no lock on your door?"

"The condo complex has a maintenance guy. I'll call him and he'll be up here in five minutes to put in another one."

It took both my stubbornness and Lauren's persuasiveness to convince my brother to leave me alone with the ghosts, in my apartment. If Little Jack hadn't been along, I don't know that we'd have succeeded. Finally, though, the three of them headed out. It was time to clean up the mess.

Naturally the ghosts were no help at all. I think people would like them a lot more if they would just pull their weight.

"We don't make the messes, why should we clean them up," was Chantal's observation.

I hadn't made the mess either. But even if she'd wanted to, Chantal couldn't have helped. I knew that, but I was still pissed about it. I had a plan, a mission for my life, and I was wasting time with a vacuum cleaner. There was something definitely wrong with this picture.

Three hours later, I had a lock, had washed my hair and scraped off the gunk they'd put on my arm before sticking in the IV, and I had a livable house.

Finally, I could begin to work on my idea.

My work with Ron Shallot, the police sketch artist, and the ghosts had shown me that the ghosts and I could make a difference. Sure, Ritchie was small potatoes in terms of organized crime in the Dallas area, but he was a start.

Now that the police had arrested my personal Sith, I didn't have to worry about my safety. Arran and Detective Finley had been interested in the name Ritchie had dropped, Petrov, but I hadn't gotten the sense they would follow up. Which meant it was up to me.

Petrov name sounded Russian and I'd read about the Russian mob taking over a lot of the crime networks the Italian Mafia had abandoned as the traditional Mafia moved into respectability. Debt collecting for illegal gambling just might be the kind of crime the Russian mob would be interested in tackling.

Unfortunately, from what I'd read, the cops had a hard time penetrating the Russian mob, made up as they were, of relatively new immigrants who knew and trusted each other.

The ghosts wouldn't have that problem.

I briefly considered sewing up an outfit with tights and a cape, but rejected that idea as silly and probably something dreamed up by a male stuck in perpetual adolescence. Instead, I grabbed my phone and called Arran.

I just knew he'd be as excited as I was about my new crime-fighting ideas.

"Dane."

"It's Annie."

A pause. "Are you all right?"

Why did everyone always ask me that? It wasn't like I couldn't take care of myself. "Of course I'm all right. I've got an idea."

"You make it sound like that doesn't happen often."

"Very funny." I wondered if I should have called Detective Fineman instead. Arran probably thought I was stalking him.

"I assume you called to share your idea with me."

"Yeah, I did. I'll bet the ghosts will help us go after Petrov. And that'll be just the start. I can help you fight crime here."

I listened to the silence for a good thirty seconds. "Hello, are you there, Detective."

"What's the matter, Annie? Can't get those meds out of your system?"

"Think about how well it worked with Ritchie." My voice pitched a bit higher and I knew I was talking fast but I was afraid he'd hang up on me. "We never would have gotten that ID if the Colonel hadn't come through for us. Ghosts can go everywhere. You can scan for bugs, but you can't scan for ghosts. You were the one who suggested it, remember?"

"This is not your job, Annie. Don't even think about messing with it."

"Everyone knows that the cops use snitches for most of their cases. But the problem with snitches is, you never know when they're setting up their enemies. Ghosts don't have personal motives, and ghosts wouldn't lie just to cut some sort of deal with the D.A."

"No."

I decided to apply a bit of pressure. "I wanted to know if you'd like me to report what I find to you, or whether there are some other police channels. Maybe your buddy Detective Halgrove would be interested."

"Halgrove would have you locked up for interfering with a police investigation. And guess what? I wouldn't argue with him. Stay away from this. Ritchie Stone is trouble enough, and he's just a foot soldier. Whoever this Petrov is, he's got a lot more Ritchies. You don't want him gunning for you. Your ghosts can't protect you—you've already proved that."

"You suggested it."

"That was before you got hurt."

I couldn't decide how to take that so I just ignored it. "Tell me where he lives, Detective. I'll take it from there."

I listened to the silence again, but this time it wasn't because Arran was being quiet: he'd hung up on me.

Chapter 12

Neither Fineman nor Halgrove answered my calls, but I didn't let that discourage me. I called Ron Shallot, the police artist, too, and left messages with all three explaining my idea and reminding them how well it had worked with Ritchie Stone.

Surely one of them would want to take advantage of my talent. Considering I'd proved that I really could talk to the ghosts, the rules would have to be changed.

While I waited for the call-back, I booted up my laptop, scrunched down in my couch, and went to work. If I had already found Petrov and had some preliminary information by the time I got the call, I would be that much ahead of the game—and able to impress my new partner, whoever he or she turned out to be.

Yahoo! People Search turned up exactly nobody living in Dallas with a last name of Petrov and stubbornly refused to search for a first name only.

I got up and grabbed a glass of wine and some crackers, stared at the crackers for a minute, then put them back in the cupboard since my jaw was still hurting. If Arran had been right about the drugs, I wouldn't feel the pain. Therefore, a glass of wine would be perfectly safe. With that in hand, it was time for some serious digging.

A Google search turned up two and a half million entries with the name Petrov. That was a bit more than I could handle.

It turned out that Petrov was a common Russian last name, and that it had been held by a number of political leaders over the years.

Narrowing the search to Petrov and 'Rusian Mafia' turned up 'only' twenty-thousand listings. Still too many. Narrowing it to Texas brought up some really weird stories, but nothing that seemed related to a local crimelord.

Apparently Petrov had managed to stay below the radar screen. Now that I thought about it, that wasn't a big surprise. Newspaper investigation of organized crime would be dangerous to a reporter who didn't have access to the ghosts. Which represented another opportunity. Maybe I could freelance for the *Dallas Morning News*. I thought a lot of ghosts would go for that romantic *Front Page* reporter look.

I needed more to go on though, before I started cashing paychecks, or even asking ghosts for assistance. Fortunately, I researched for a living. Whoever Petrov was, he figured to own property somewhere in the North Texas area. I had access to the computer databases for Dallas, Collin, Tarrant, or Denton counties—the four counties that make up the

Dallas-Fort Worth metroplex. If he'd ever purchased property under his own name, I'd have him. If that didn't work, I'd try to hack into the Department of Transportation drivers' license database and see if I could find him there.

I took another sip of wine, then started with the Dallas County records, logging in and entering a search.

I must have been deep in concentration, because I jumped and spilled my wine all over myself when someone knocked on my door.

"Such a comedy," Chantal observed.

"Yeah, right." I walked over and opened the door.

Arran glared at me. "You didn't even ask who it was."

"Don't worry, Arran. Even if I'd known it was you, I would have still opened it." I examined the thunderclouds in his face. "You bring sunshine into my day."

He stared at the wine I'd spilled on myself. "Are you bleeding?"

"Yeah. You've wounded me by refusing to even consider my idea. Don't you think—"

He brought his fingertip to one of the drips on my arm, then tasted it.

The effect was so sexy I shivered.

"Wine."

"You startled me."

"This isn't funny, Annie." He pushed past me, then flopped at my dining room table. "You're putting yourself in danger. Didn't you learn anything from Stone?"

I stared at him. His face was drawn and dark circles surrounded his eyes. Not that he still didn't look good enough to eat. Still, it was worth reminding myself that I wasn't the only person who'd had a rough time lately. While I'd at least managed to catch a dozen or so hours of drugged sleep after my run-in with Ritchie the previous night. Arran had been working nonstop.

I cut him all the slack I could stand, but this was too much. "You were the one who asked for my help, remember?"

He looked at his hands. "I'm not proud of that."

"Meaning?"

"Meaning, who cares about Ritchie Stone? Going after him put you in danger and catching him didn't solve anything. He'll be out on bail in a day or two, so it didn't even get a creep off the street. Then there's—"

The shriek I'd been trying to hold back didn't stay held, nor did my mostly empty wineglass which hit the wall and shattered. "Out on bail? He'll be coming for me again."

"That's my point. You've put yourself in danger and I'm responsible for it. When I make a mistake, I'm not too proud to admit it and change my behavior. Why don't you consider doing the same? Going on chasing after badguys would be adding more mistakes on top of what I've already done."

"Who cares about mistakes if he's going to kill me?"

Arran rubbed his fists into his eyes. "Killing you would be the dumbest thing Ritchie could do. If anything happens to you, he'll be an immediate suspect."

"So I'm safe."

"Safe from Ritchie, maybe. Definitely not safe if you continue making waves."

"How would Petrov even know? It's not like the ghosts would tell him."

"How did I know? You blasted your idea through the entire DPD. Everyone is laughing at me for going with a psychic—or psycho as they call it."

"I proved it, though. That Identi-Kit sketch looked just like him."

"Right. You couldn't have done better if you'd seen the man yourself."

He was agreeing with me, but his voice held an edge I didn't like. "Point?"

"Halgrove has put out the word that you saw Ritchie and you're claiming to be a psychic to get money out of the department. Also, he's still saying you had something to do with the shooting."

I tried to fake a laugh but couldn't actually manage to get any noise out my mouth. "Ridiculous."

"I don't think you're dumb enough to let someone shoot at you through an elevator shaft. Any of those bullets could have ricocheted into you."

"But—"

"If you keep pushing this, it won't be the ghosts who tell Petrov you're hunting for him. He'll learn it from the cops. Not all of us are good at keeping our mouths shut."

That wasn't reassuring. "It would be like Ritchie, though, right? If anything happens to me, you'd suspect Petrov. That should give me some safety."

"He'd rather be a suspect than to have real evidence against him."

I'd need to think about this. So this was why Wonder Woman insisted on a secret identity. It was time to change the subject. "I don't understand how Ritchie could make bail. Two shootings in two days sounds pretty serious to me. And it's Sunday. I would have thought you'd at least hold him for the weekend."

"Yeah, that's a surprise." Arran sounded bitter. "It's amazing what a good lawyer can do. But you're assuming we can connect him to the County Records case. All we have is attempted breaking and entering and carrying without a permit."

"He tried to kill me."

"It would have helped if you'd waited until he'd actually gained entry before you pepper-sprayed him. He's claiming he was just passing by and you attacked. His lawyer is threatening to sue you."

It figured. Why should anything go right?

"If I'd waited, he would have killed me."

Arran nodded.

"The more I think about what you said, the less confident I feel. Considering what we know about Ritchie, just because coming after me would be dumb doesn't mean much. It was dumb to come after me in the first place—the guy just isn't genius material. And what do you mean, you haven't connected him to the shooting. You got his gun, didn't you? Surely you can compare the bullets fired."

"I'm not saying we won't connect it, just we haven't. We're still waiting to hear from the lab. Bottom line, though, we're talking about a flesh wound to Sam Bert and a broken nose to you. Serious, but not murder. He'll be out on bail even if they connect it."

Chantel tried to nudge me with her elbow, and act that sent her elbow right through my ribs. I thought she was going to make a joke about Sam having plenty of flesh to wound—certainly Harry would have made that joke. She fooled me, though.

"Ask if 'zees Richie Stone will be the, 'ow you say, informateur."

"Good idea. Might as well save my skills for where they're needed." I turned to Arran. "Hey Detective. I'll bet Ritchie knows where this Petrov lives. Why don't you convince him to grass-out his boss?"

"Grass out?"

My cheeks burned. I love reading English police procedurals but I hadn't realized the terminology wouldn't make sense to an American. "You know, snitch."

He gripped my hands hard enough that his knuckles went white. "We call them C.I.s, Confidential Informants. And haven't you listened to anything I've said? You need to forget about this. You can't believe what I felt like when first Carly called called to let me know you were asking about Petrov, and then Halgrove blasted an e-mail to the department warning you were trying to wangle money out of the department."

"Poor baby."

"Hey—"

"I never asked for money. Don't you cops pay rewards for arrests and convictions, though?"

"Sometimes. But you're not going to do that. I can't protect—"

"Listen, Detective. I'm twenty-eight years old and I've accomplished exactly nothing in my life. I've got a talent, an ability that, even if it isn't unique, is for sure pretty rare. If I don't use that ability to accomplish something, what does that say about me? If I refuse to do what I can to help make Dallas better and safer, why was I given this ability in the first place?"

He dropped my hands like I'd burned them. "You've got a talent all right, a talent for trouble."

"Why'd you become a cop, Arran? I'm betting you could have gotten other work. I even suspect you could have found a job that paid more and offered better hours. I think you did it because you believed in making a contribution. Right? Why shouldn't I get a chance to make a difference?"

He inhaled, then exhaled slowly. He was a guy counting to ten because some dippy girl wasn't following his rules. "All right, Annie. Get on that computer of yours and submit your application to be a cop. Suffer through the academy, work as a beat cop for five or ten years, and study up for your promotion to detective. Once you've done that, you'll know enough that you can help track down criminals, and you might even have learned something about keeping yourself safe."

My eyes burned. Why couldn't he see what should have been so obvious?

"What are you afraid of, Dane? Do you think my ghosts would put old-fashioned policework out of business? Are you worried—"

His fist slammed into my table. "I'm not *afraid* of jack-shit. But you're right about one thing—I am worried. I'm worried that your do-good attitude will get you killed. Which is, as you point out, your problem. Consider this, though. When your stomping around in the middle of police investigations gets you killed, maybe you won't be the only one hurt. When you mess up a case, maybe some innocent person gets taken hostage, maybe an undercover cop is outed and murdered, maybe you're real lucky and all that happens is that evidence gets suppressed because a defense attorney can argue there's no way it could have been legally gained. So criminals who would have been in jail are back on the streets. Any way I look at it, I can't see anything good coming out of it. We've got hundreds of cops whose job it is to track down criminals. Why not let us do our jobs and stay the hell out of the way?"

* * * *

When I agreed to consider Arran's words, he probably thought I was agreeing to give up on my plan.

He was wrong, of course. I'm not a real religious person, but I believe things are the way they are for a reason. If I was given an ability, it had to be right that I use that ability. Putting together that Identi-Kit on Ritchie Stone was the kind of thing only I, with the help of the ghosts, could do.

If Detective Halgrove spread negative words about me, that might make it harder for me to do what I needed to get done: it wasn't a reason to back off. I believed that kind of negative energy would come back to him.

Since Ritchie was getting out of jail, I had two targets to go after. There was Petrov, of course. And there was Ritchie himself.

As Arran had unkindly pointed out, the police case against Ritchie wasn't especially strong. Unless he'd been dumb enough to use the same gun in both attacks, or unless he'd been carrying the Darth Maul mask in his personal effects, possibilities I regarded as within Ritchie's margin of error, a decent lawyer would make sure the jury never saw the Identi-Kit portrait and would cast enough confusion about what had happened outside my door that he might walk.

While it might be true that he hadn't killed anyone in either of the attacks I'd been involved in, Ritchie had shot a lot of bullets. The odds that a criminal with that quick a trigger-finger hadn't killed someone during his career seemed low.

Just like a videogame player needs to level-up a lot before facing a boss level, it made sense to go after Ritchie before messing with Petrov.

I only wished Arran was helping me rather than getting in the way. With him to handle the physical parts, the ghosts to handle snooping, and me for intelligence, I figured we were a perfect team. Sure Little Jack thought my green belt gave me the kind of mystical power Wonder Woman held, but the past couple of days had opened my eyes to how dangerous the world could be.

An hour after I'd promised Arran I'd consider his words, he still hadn't left.

I was conflicted. A part of me wanted to be on the trail, talking to ghosts, putting together the case against the Petrov crime family. Another part savored hanging out with Arran—almost as if we were a couple.

Except we weren't.

I didn't need any ghost whispers to deduct that Arran was there because he felt responsible for my safety. He believed he'd messed up when he'd let me work with Sallot on Ritchie's picture and now he intended to protect me—from myself as well as from any external enemies.

He headed back into my living room from an extended tour of my apartment, checking out the security features and jotting down a list of things that needed replacement or upgrading. He definitely didn't approve of the new knob provided by the condo's maintenance team. Besides being 'flimsy' and 'cheap,' he believed the maintenance guys just might have made a copy of the key before giving it to me.

I nodded as he went through the list. A new deadbolt wouldn't be too bad, but replacing the windows was out of the question. Lauren and Jack had spent thousands of dollars on new windows the previous year. Title research didn't pay that well.

"You know what cops learn about people?"

I considered, wondering if he'd gone philosophical on me. "That they're all have a dark side?"

"That too. I was going to say we notice when people avoid answering questions. Even after everything I've said, you're going after Petrov, aren't you?"

"Oh, no. I've had enough trouble with Ritchie."

He grasped my chin and pulled it so I was facing him. Chantal got between us, punching at him in some weird effort to protect me that didn't do any good at all. I still felt the warmth of his hands against my face and the hard smoothness where work had left calluses on his palms.

"Let's make a deal, babe."

"What," I squeaked so badly I cleared my throat and started over. "What sort of deal."

"The deal is, you don't lie to me any more. You suck at it."

"What's your side of the deal?"

"I don't kill you."

"That doesn't sound very even."

"How about I don't kill you and I buy you dinner?"

It wasn't the most romantic date request in the world but I wasn't about to look this gift horse in the mouth. "Deal."

"Let's go, then. We can pick up a new deadbolt on the way home."

Chapter 13

I was relaxed and had fun shopping and eating at a funky little deli that served Lebanese food.

It wasn't until we got back to my place that I discovered Arran counted the outing as a real date.

That was when the detective invited himself in, grabbed me by the shoulders, and kissed me.

Not only didn't I complain, I kissed him back—hard.

I'd fantasized about being with him since I'd met him. At least this time I wasn't so drugged up that I'd begged him to strip me naked and kiss me wherever he wanted.

Two seconds after his lips hit mine, I realized my fantasies were due for an upgrade. I was ready to let him strip me naked and kiss me everywhere he could think of. In fact, I would have paid him if he'd suggested it.

Ten seconds after that, I revised my life story.

I'd only *thought* I'd been kissed before. I'd never felt the tingle of awareness that connected my lips directly to my core. I'd never sensed the hot flush spreading from my cheeks to my chest, blood whooshing as my heart raced, or the swollen sensation as my breasts seemed to press for freedom against my bra. All this was new territory, territory I desperately wanted to trail blaze.

I put one hand on his chin, and ran the other down his chest. My brain wasn't working too well but I knew if I didn't occupy my hands elsewhere, they'd get busy stripping my clothes off so I could expose every skin cell to Arran's touch.

The guys I'd slept with at the state school had been boys, really, and the hard muscle of Arran's chest surprised me. Even through his shirt, he radiated heat like the engine of a Nascar racer.

I traced his lips with my tongue, then plunged it into his mouth, tasting coffee, baklava, and Arran.

"You go, girl. You give that man your hot action, just like you're dying to do."

I hadn't thought anything could distract me from Arran's touch. I'd been wrong.

I jerked away from Arran's grip and wheeled toward the voice. "Harry, what the hell are you doing here?"

"Come on, Annie. Take off your shirt. I think the cop will like what he sees. I know I will. You're not big as some, but looks like you've got the right shape."

Somehow a couple of buttons of my top had come undone and one of my cups hung out, my nipple forming a hard point through the satin fabric.

I pulled the rest of the way free from Arran and shoved my boob back into my top, buttoning myself with fumbling fingers. Harry had been joined by half a dozen grinning male ghosts. All were fully clothed, which was something of a blessing, but it wasn't enough.

"Is it too much to ask to have an occasional evening to myself? There've got to be two million women in Dallas. Surely some of them are more interesting than me. So, go do your pervert act with one of them."

Arran cleared his throat. "I hope you're not talking to me."

None of this was Arran's fault, but that didn't mean I wasn't pissed. "What the hell were you thinking, anyway, Detective? You know I've got ghosts around. You know I get distracted when you kiss me. Did you intend to make me lose track of where I am so I'd be completely humiliated? Because you know I don't want to be a ghost-flasher."

"My kisses make you lose track—"

My face burned. "Forget I said that, Dane. I don't need your pity. I don't need you figuring you've got to sex me up to keep me from investigating what's going on with Petrov and Ritchie. I don't need you giving me new fantasies when the old ones were perfectly adequate."

"You're having fantasies about me?"

"Don't let it go to your head. I'd probably have fantasies about any super-sexy cop who saved my life, spent time with me, and took me out to nice restaurants. It has nothing to do with you."

He reached a hand toward me and I backed through Harry, smacking into the wall. "What were you thinking, Arran? Did you really think I wanted you to kiss me?"

He grinned. "I'm a cop, Annie. I examine the evidence and make my findings. I not only *think* you wanted me to kiss you, I *know* it. Further —"

"Ridiculous. Maybe you should just leave." I was being irrational— hell, I knew that. But I had been even more irrational when I'd come so close to hopping into bed with Arran, forgetting about the ghosts who would like nothing better than to watch the whole show. I couldn't really work up a good mad at anyone but myself, but I faked it as hard as I could.

"With Ritchie out there? I'm not going anywhere until I know you're safe."

"And you figured the couch wouldn't be very comfortable so you'd seduce your way into my bed? Well great. You can sleep in my bed. I'll sleep on the couch."

He held his hands toward me, palms out. "Look, Annie. I know you're embarrassed by your feelings, but don't let the ghosts rule your life. Make your own decisions. I enjoyed kissing you and I plan on doing more of it. If you don't want me in your bed yet, that's your decision. But don't make me into the badguy here. We're both adults. There is nothing wrong with exploring the attraction between us."

"Real grownups do it in private."

"I don't see anyone but us."

"That's because you're blind. Right there is my old friend Harry, who couldn't bother showing up when we needed witnesses but is waiting in line when the last thing I want is someone watching. Joining the boys is Chantal, as if it were time for my French lesson. Oh, and look, here's Oren. Hi, Oren. Get tired of looking at your portrait over at Arran's place? Did you bring those three pervert ghosts I don't even recognize, or did they arrive here under their own power?"

"We're not perverts," one of the three insisted. He was an elderly ghost with a wispy beard, pee-colored pants, a white dress shirt that had seen better days, and a pair of ghostly glasses perched down his nose. I didn't think ghosts actually need glasses to see with, but they are big on dramatic effects.

"You were watching, weren't you? If that isn't perverted, what is it?"

"We just happened to be hanging around when you went into your mating ritual with the cop. What did you expect, that we'd avert our eyes?"

Back when Lauren and Jack had been dating, I'd spent a lot of time averting my eyes. It isn't that hard. "Yeah. Or go somewhere else."

"But we like talking to you."

I realized Arran was standing there watching me talk to the ghosts, his eyes flickering back and forth between me and wherever he imagined the ghosts to be as our conversation shifted.

"I'd be happy to give you a running translation if you're interested," I told him.

"Oh, no problem. I think I can pick up both sides of the conversation just by listening to you."

"You do see why that kiss was a mistake, I hope."

"I can see why your brother thought it was a good idea that you got some living human attention. Even if you see ghosts, that's no reason why you should let them control your life."

"My brother suggested I needed you to pay attention to me?" This time the flush on my cheeks had nothing to do with arousal. "That jerk told you I was so desperate I'd be an easy score? I know he tried to pimp me out when I was in high school but—"

"It was just a conversation, nothing like you're implying."

"Oh, no? What was it like, exactly? Did he offer to pay you if you'd take me out and give me a good fucking? If not, definitely hit him up for the bucks, I'm sure he'd be willing to fork over some real money. My brother never has believed I could—"

"Stuff it, Annie. If you're afraid of exploring what's going on between us, fine. Just be honest to yourself about what's going on. Now, do you have a couple of blankets I can borrow, or should I run out to the Walgreens and pick up some emergency supplies?"

Arran's words hit me like a cold wave in the face. Clearly my hormonal reaction to his kiss was still kicking in. I mean, I knew my brother tried to choreograph my life. I knew the ghosts would never let me have any time to myself, especially not time with a guy. I knew I didn't have a legitimate shot at a guy like Arran. I should be happy I'd gotten as much as I had.

"Sit down," I ordered him. "I'll make coffee."

"Decaff if you have it. I need to be back at work tomorrow."

"Right. Decaff." I didn't actually have decaffeinated coffee, but I didn't figure to be getting any sleep after what he'd put me through and figured it would be funny to get Arran wired, too. Even though I knew better, imagining him sleeping on my couch, let along on my bed, sent a tingle straight to my sex.

"You don't have any, huh? I wouldn't mind a glass of water."

I thought I was supposed to be the psychic one. How come he always knew when I was lying?

I got him his water, then turned on some music. I wanted to get into the shower, turn the water on full cold, and stand in it until my body stopped tingling from Arran's touch, until I could recapture that comfortable numbness I'd learned to surround myself with back when my parents had first told me I wasn't really seeing ghosts and that I could never tell anyone about my reality.

Standing naked in my shower while Arran waited only a few yards away would defeat the entire purpose, though. I didn't have a setting cold enough to make me numb when he was around. Instead of being hot and bothered, I'd be cold, uncomfortable, and still horny. That wasn't an improvement.

Instead of retreating to the shower, I bustled around, picking up a couple of books I had lying around and reshelving them, wiping down my kitchen counters, and avoiding Arran's gaze.

I knew I wouldn't, really, combust if I looked at him, but my relationship to reality had always been tenuous and having a six-foot-something mountain of testosterone in my apartment made that relationship even more distant.

Although we'd just eaten, I decided to pretend the ache in the lower part of my torso came from hunger rather than desire and fished out my emergency chocolate—a one-pound bag of almond M&Ms, which I considered the ultimate comfort food.

I poured the entire bag into a bowl and set them on the table in front of Arran, then remembered the way my brother ate and grabbed a handful before the Detective could inhale all of them.

"Thanks. I love that kind."

My heart went lubba-dubba. As if a shared desire for chocolate meant anything at all. Who doesn't love M&Ms?

Rather than dig in, though, Arran set down his water glass and headed deeper into my apartment.

My confusion only lasted a second, but that was enough. "Wait. Don't—"

"Just going to wash my hands. I promise not to look if you've got underwear hanging in your bathroom."

One thing about being psychic, I didn't leave underwear hanging around where the ghosts could ooze their quasi-bodies through the fabric so that wasn't my worry. What was my worry was—

"What the hell?" Arran emerged, blinking from my bathroom. The strobes flashed around him. My ghost-repulsion system seemed even more effective on the fully human male as it had ever been on the ectoplasmic males it had been designed for. Again.

I sighed. "Do you really need me to explain?"

"Ghosts?" He knuckled his eyes. "I wouldn't think they'd get headaches."

"They don't like electrical surges and they don't like flashing lights. I don't know whether it gives them headaches, exactly, but using it means I can sometimes at least go to the bathroom without someone inspecting or making jokes about golden showers."

"I didn't need to hear that."

"Welcome to my life, Arran. In the movies, ghosts seem to swoop around mysteriously, only appearing when you need them. In the real world, they can be a pain in the rear and there are so goddamned many of them.

"More every day, Oren gloomily added. "Seems like a bunch of losers doing the dying these days, too. They're moving into the old neighborhoods and really degrading the places.

"Yeah, right. Like you old dead people are so classy. Anyway," I turned back to Arran, "As I was saying, dead doesn't make them any nobler, less perverted, or more ethical than when they were alive. But it does mean there aren't any consequences if they get caught. So, they act out the fantasies you normal guys suppress. Let me tell you, high school girls locker rooms are so thick with ghosts, you can hardly see in front of you."

"I—"

"And screw that pitying look."

"I was just going to say that I don't blame you for the bathroom display then. I understand where you're coming from."

I doubted he did. Guys aren't raised with the sense of body awareness that girls are. They like to strut their stuff, like the idea of people staring at their naked bodies. If I told him a couple of sexy twenty-something female ghosts slept next to him every night, he'd probably be flattered rather than grossed out. Still, he was trying to understand me and I had to give him credit for that.

"The hall light should give you enough illumination to wash your hands with. So, suck it up, be brave, and go back into the bathroom. Unless you want to just wash in the sink."

"I might as well get used to the lights." Arran flipped the electrical switch, winced as he stepped into the bathroom, and turned on the faucet. Uh, do you have any other surprises waiting?"

"You won't like my bedroom."

"What do you do there, run high-powered death rays?"

"Oh for goodness sake. Just go in there and check it out."

Two seconds later, his laughter rocked my apartment. "Aluminum foil?" He was laughing so hard he could hardly walk as he stumbled out of my bedroom, wiping tears from his eyes. "You've got your entire bedroom papered with aluminum foil. Even the windows and ceiling. I was kidding about the death rays but it must look like something out of Star Wars when you turn on your lights."

I was so glad I hadn't fallen for this guy.

"Lucky thing for you you're spending the night on the couch, huh?"

His laughter stopped suddenly and he stepped closer to me. "I could put up with aluminum foil. If the aluminum foil keeps the ghosts from disturbing us, maybe we could—"

"Enough, already. You've already earned more than my brother paid you. So, back off and give me room to think."

"Nobody paid me anything."

Yeah, right. A sexy guy like Arran was chasing after me because he really wanted to be saddled with a woman who spent her life talking to non-existent beings and who had to keep a fake Bluetooth device in her ear so she could pretend to be on the phone to prevent being committed to a mental institution by everyone who saw her. That was so likely.

Unless, of course, Arran just slept with whatever woman he happened to be nearby.

Normally that idea would have been offensive. But since he'd kissed me, my thought processes were hosed. Wouldn't it be better to have sex with him, even if we both knew it was just convenient because-he-was-around-sex rather than happily-ever-after-sex, than never to have sex at all?

* * * *

Maybe my brother hadn't paid him. Because Arran went to sleep on my couch, along with a couple of female ghosts I hadn't seen before but who must have gotten word that a sexy guy was visiting. I punched my pillow a couple of times, then settled down alone in my twin bed, surrounded by aluminum foil. My electric blanket provided a cheap and inadequate substitute for the warmth I'd felt in Arran's arms.

Dressed in my bulkiest pajamas, with the blanket cranked up to high, I counted sheep.

Sometime around three hundred, I realized the sheep weren't getting the job done. Adrenaline continued rushing through my body, and my breasts and womb reverberated from sensations that Arran's kiss had kicked off.

Considering my track record with men, I was a past-master at taking these matters into my own hands.

I pulled down my pajama bottoms, slid my finger between my legs and—nothing. Even with no ghosts watching, I couldn't let myself go. I was probably worried I'd scream when I came and Arran would come racing in to the rescue. Unfortunately, it was increasingly obvious that it wasn't *my* touch my body was holding out for. It had tasted the real thing and wasn't going to settle for any homespun substitute.

Another two hundred sheep and I decided things couldn't get worse. The help I needed was right outside my bedroom. So what if I humiliated myself with the detective, as long as I got laid. And if he rejected me, at least I'd know for sure where I stood.

I'd been the one who'd backed off when Arran had kissed me, so it was my turn to make the next advance.

I washed my hands, fueled myself with a double-handful of Almond M&Ms, then padded, barefoot, out of my bedroom and into the living room.

Arran looked like an angel, his golden body glinting silver in the reflected glow seeping through my miniblinds from the halogen lights illuminating I-75 outside.

Despite the chill in the February air, he'd tossed off the blanket I'd given him.

Unlike me, Arran hadn't bothered with pajamas. His chest was naked and looked every bit as good as I remembered. His boxer shorts might be baggy, but they didn't hide the fact that he was having *very* pleasant dreams.

He looked like an angel, all right, but a very naughty one. The two ghosts who'd gone to bed with him continually flowed their non-corporal bodies over his, running their spectral hands into that gap in front of his boxers, teasing his nipples with their ghostly tongues, and whispering sexy ghost sounds into his ears. I knew there could be no physical contact between the dead women and the very much living cop, but I wondered if they might have connected with his dreams.

I was used to ghosts talking to me while I was sleeping and didn't think anything of it when their words penetrated into my dreams. Now I wondered if sleep lowered the barriers for ordinary people, let them pick up just a hint of what the ghosts whispered. I'd experimented with that years ago, when I'd persuaded a couple of ghosts to whisper in my parents' ears while they were sleeping. They'd begged my parents to give up on the psychiatrists who were ruining them financially and ruining me with their drugs and so-called therapies. Those dream messages hadn't done any good and I'd given up on the idea.

Looking at the jutting flagpole in Arran's boxers, I suspected I'd given up too soon. There was no doubt what Arran was thinking about.

I was jealous.

"Hey detective."

If someone wakes me up, I make snarfing noises, rub my eyes, and look for coffee. Arran went from sleeping to pointing a gun at me faster than I could see.

"Jeez. You could hurt someone with that."

"Sorry." He put the gun back under his pillow. "I don't advise sneaking up on an ex-soldier. Iraq taught a lot of us bad habits."

I hadn't even known Arran had been a soldier, let alone served in Iraq. Would the ghosts of their enemies taunt American soldiers during the night? One thing I knew from some of the Bible-thumping preachers my father had taken me to when he'd finally despaired on medical treatment and sought divine help for my 'condition.' Iraq had been the center of civilization for thousands of years. Ghosts from Babylon, Assyria, Israel, Persia, the soldiers of Alexander the Great, Rome, and Arabia probably still mingled there, still fought their ancient battles.

Now that I thought of it, though, I'd never actually seen ghosts fight. Maybe that offered a hopeful sign for the future.

"I didn't mean to startle you," I said.

"Not your fault." He shook his head and patted the pillow to make sure the gun was safely stowed. "Guess you're not the only one of us with problems, huh?"

I sat down next to him. "Was the war horrible?"

The two female ghosts squawked and made shooing motions, but I ignored them. He'd scared away my immediate need for sex when he'd pulled that gun on me, but he'd done something even more dangerous— he'd opened up, just a bit, as a person. Before, it had been about weird Annie and the sexy stranger. If the stranger turned out to be human, have a history, issues of his own, I wouldn't be able to just have sex with him and get on with my life. I'd get hooked—and hurt.

"Somehow I don't think you woke me up in the middle of the night to interview me about my military experiences."

"Never mind *why* I woke you up." I certainly wasn't going to tell him I was jealous of his two girl-ghosts. "Right now I want to know about you. You know everything about me—you've even read my psychological profile. The only thing I know about you is that you're a Dallas Police detective." That and that he kissed like a dream. But he didn't need me stroking his ego.

He stared at me for a moment, his eyes shadowed in darkness. "Okay, Arran Dane's history. Born in Pittsburg, but my parents moved to Texas when I was a kid. Never quite picked up the Texas accent, though. High School at Sunset. Joined the National Guard after graduating, and took the classes I needed to be accepted into the DPD at Mountain View and UT Arlington. My Guard unit got called up a couple of times, once to Iraq and once to Afghanistan. Same story as a million or so other guys and gals."

I sat down next to him, shifting his legs out of the way. "You always wanted to be a cop?"

He pulled his blanket up so it partially covered his chest. "My dad runs a print shop but I'm a bit colorblind. Which means I'm pretty worthless when it comes to handling the big printing jobs. I've got a couple of uncles back in PA who are cops and it seemed like a good job —reasonable pay, benefits, and you're not stuck at a desk all day."

I looked at the ghost who'd been whispering in Arran's ear and she shook her head. I agreed with her. Arran was hiding something.

"No lies, remember?"

"Consider who's talking."

"My lies don't count since you see through them as fast as I can say them." I scooted a bit closer to him. Sex was out of the picture, for the time being, at least, but that I found comfort in his warmth, in the touch of his skin against my own. Which made no sense at all. I mean, people had to have hot burning urges for sex—otherwise the species would have died out before it really got started. But finding comfort just by being close, what was that about?

Arran looked startled, then draped an arm over me. "My grandfather was a cop, too. He was killed in action when I was a kid, just a couple of weeks after we'd moved to Texas. I suppose that might have affected my decision."

"I suspect something like that could have influenced you."

"Don't get snarky. It isn't becoming."

"You're talking to the woman with aluminum foil on her walls, remember. 'Becoming' is not where I'm at. If I'm going to amount to anything, it won't be because I'm any sort of sexual diva."

Arran took my hand, raised it to his lips, and kissed my knuckles. "So you want to go after criminals instead? You get it, don't you? People who deal with criminals get killed. That's why you've got to back off. Let me take care of Stone and pretend you never even heard the name Petrov. I've got enough on my conscience without worrying about you."

I sighed. "Okay, Detective. You've convinced me. No more chasing after Petrov, no more chasing after Ritchie. From now on, I'm back to title search and nothing else."

The cop caught my chin, turning my face so his eyes could bore into mine.

"One of these days, I'm going to teach you how to lie, babe. For now, though, don't even try."

So much for trying to make Arran feel better and more secure. I was going to go after the criminals whether he wanted me to or not, though. My gift, such as it was, called to me and I fully intended to answer.

So I settled in next to him on the couch, pulled up the blanket so it covered both of us and so his nearly-naked body touched my pajama-clad self. Savoring his warmth and the sense of safety it provided me I dozed off. I could definitely get used to this.

Chapter 14

Arran growled at me while I made coffee, told me to forget my ridiculous plans, and instructed me to forget anything he might have said during the night.

"Neither of you said anything or did anything worth the wait," Harry complained. "And how come you don't take out that lighting system in the bathroom? Then I could take a shower and we could ride the train to work together."

"We'll be going to work soon enough," I said. "And don't worry, detective. I'm not going to tell anyone that you became a cop because you're looking for revenge for your grandfather."

"That isn't what I meant."

I suspected what he meant was, he wished he hadn't told me anything at all about himself. He'd liked being the sexy mysterious stranger who rode in to rescue the damsel and then headed out of town forever, his work complete. How else, after all, could a guy who looked like him, had a good job, and was obviously straight, have remained single?

Speaking of work being completed, though, mine certainly wasn't.

Batman had it all over Wonder Woman. For one thing, Batman's secret identity was a billionaire who didn't have to work. Wonder Woman was a nurse who had to superhero in her spare time. Sort of like me—I was a title researcher. Without untold billions to support my crime-fighting habit, I had to earn my paycheck if I didn't want to become a homeless superhero.

Arran smiled at me after finishing his second cup of coffee. "Are you going to be careful?"

"I'm always careful."

He shrugged. "Try it, just for a change, then."

"Damn it, Detective. Do you think I *want* to get hurt?"

"Let me think. You opened your door when you knew a known shooter was outside trying to get in at you. I'd have to say the evidence points that way."

I'd had domestic thoughts for a few minutes while Arran had been getting up, shaving in my bathroom and pretending that the flashing lights didn't bother him, then brewing up a big pot of coffee for the two of us to share. He was messing with those memories in a hurry.

"I do the best I can, Detective. So, get out of here and let me go to work."

"Want to give me a key in case I get home before you?"

My mouth moved by itself a couple of times but fortunately I'd already swallowed my Cheerios so I didn't dribble. Finally, I managed a to choke out an answer. "Home? As in, you think you live here now?"

"I told you I'm keeping you safe. Despite what happened at the County Records building last week, I think you should be okay at work. It's here that you'll have problems. Now, will you meet with me after work and run your crazy ideas by me, or do I have to send out a Be-on-the-lookout?"

"Yeah, right. Go to work. And no, I don't have an extra key."

"Oh, no problem. I know where the locksmith put one when he installed your new deadbolt yesterday."

"That... that,"

Arran grabbed the spare key from the bookcase where I'd left it, nodded politely, then headed for the door. When he reached it, he stopped and turned back toward me.

I wondered what he'd forgotten. I'd seen him pick up his gun so that couldn't be it.

Instead, though, he walked straight to me, kissed me on the cheek, and strolled away as if he'd already done a good day's work.

I would have said something but he'd managed to confuse me again and I just stood there with my mouth gaping like a fish.

The two girl-ghosts who'd spent the night with him did what I should have, kissing him at the door and making squealing couple-noises. "Bye darling. Have a nice day at the office."

He turned to close the door and winked at me—almost as if he'd heard them.

Damn. Detective Arran Dane got more complicated by the minute.

"So," Harry said when the sound of Arran's footsteps faded away. "Are you just going to stand there, or are you coming to work?"

"I need another cup of coffee."

"You've already had three."

"Oh." If I drank any more I'd be running for the bathroom all day—something I tried to avoid whenever possible, for obvious, if ghostly reasons.

I made sure my Bluetooth fake was in my ear, caked on some makeup to try to cover my two black eyes, and headed for Mockingbird station. I'd swing by the title company I did freelance work for to pick up the latest projects, and then head back to County Records, which the cops had turned back over to the county.

An hour later, I was downtown, passing a pair of County Sheriff Deputies who installing a metal detector to control access to the Records Building. Talk about closing the barn door.

I stopped by Sam Bert's office before heading down to the archives.

"You doing all right, Sam?"

"What the heck happened to you?" he demanded.

"Huh?"

"You look like you went eighteen rounds with George Foreman."

From Sam's reaction, the makeup job I'd done to tone down the bruising hadn't helped. Then again, the taped up nose might have given me away. It made me wonder exactly what Arran had been thinking when he'd kissed me. I wasn't exactly model material on my best day and I hadn't had many best days lately.

"I, uh, fell down the stairs."

"Right. And the stairs just happened to leave knuckle bruises on you. You really must live in a dangerous neighborhood." He leaned forward across his desk. "Is your nose broken?"

I backed off a bit. He'd had an Egg McMuffin for breakfast, and I didn't need to see the wrapper in his trash to know. The evidence stuck to his cheek and ran over his tie.

"Right the first time, Sam. Your friend Ritchie Stone came looking for me."

Sam looked at the ceiling. "Why couldn't you just leave it alone? You don't want to mess with these guys."

"Are you kidding? You were the one Ritchie shot, remember. If that bullet had hit a couple of inches to the right, you'd be singing soprano."

"At least they know I'm not singing to the cops. Which is why I'm still breathing."

And he didn't know he was talking to a newly minted superhero. Sure I needed to get my research done, but this was too good an opportunity to miss.

I grabbed Sam's coffee mug, poured him a fresh cup and got one for myself, putting a buck in the cash box to pay for the two.

He eyed me suspiciously. "Thanks."

"No problem." I pulled up a chair at his desk. "So, Sam, how much are they into you for?"

* * * *

It took a few minutes to coax out the facts.

Sam's sense of self-preservation battled with his need to talk about what had happened to him. I suspect my being female had something to do with him finally opening up.

"You know I like to put a few dollars on the games," he confided. "Just to make them more interesting. I mean, maybe it's technically illegal but—"

"But lots of people bet on games." I was bonding here. "Heck, the newspapers even print the point spreads."

"Yeah. I mean, they don't print up the current prices for meth, do they. Different type of crime, different type of criminal. Sports gambling is respectable and who's it hurt?"

Considering Sam had taken a bullet in his leg and I'd had my nose broken, I could have mentioned a couple of victims, but that didn't seem to be the way to get Sam to open up. I just nodded and smiled, hoping my busted up face wouldn't persuade him to shut down.

He was on a roll, though. Having justified his behavior, he wanted to tell someone about it.

"A guy who was in the football pool told me about a place you could make bigger bets—with a better payoff than you'd get in Vegas. I figured, hey, I *live* these games. I've got season tickets to the Mavericks and Stars, and I go out to the same bars as the players afterwards. I research the jocks, study the coaches. I probably know as much about who's getting it at home and who's out partying as anybody. I can make some money. It's not like the county pays that much for this job, you know."

I nodded again. Sam probably cleared five times more than I did, but I'd never met anyone who thought they were overpaid so why should Sam be different? "I take it things didn't go so well, though?"

"At first I was okay. Sure I lost some, but I won at least as many. It's just lately, I've been on a bit of a losing streak. I know I'm trying too hard, getting desperate, and that's no way to gamble. Once my luck turns, though, I'll be able to pay the guys back and everything will be fine."

He took a sip of coffee, then dug a napkin from the McDonnalds bag in his garbage and wiped his face with it.

There must have been a chocolate shake in the bag because he left a brown streak down his cheek. If it had been Arran, I might have been tempted to lick it off. As it was, it was just disgusting.

"Ask him where Petrov hangs out," Harry urged. "Even if he makes his bets by phone, he has to pay off in person. I doubt he'd just mail them a check."

I was getting there but I thought Sam would be suspicious if I just blurted out the question so I beat around the bush some more.

"I'm surprised they sent Ritchie Stone here to your office rather than just meeting up with you at the American Airlines Center. You said you were going there after work, right?"

Sam looked uncomfortable. "Well, I've owed them for a couple of weeks now and it's possible they thought I was avoiding them. Maybe they—"

"Maybe they'd already approached you at the center and decided to escalate?"

He searched the McDonnalds bag for something I was pretty sure he wouldn't find, like a good answer. "It's possible."

"I sure hope you figure out a way to pay them back, then. But I doubt you'll be able to do it by what you win gambling. The cops know about the betting ring now and they'll be looking to shut down this Petrov guy."

There was nothing fake about Sam's shudder. It was the real thing, down to the sweat sheen on his pale face and the jiggles that went through his fat. "We'd both better hope you're wrong about that, Annie."

Harry and another ghost who'd wandered in tried to imitate that fat jiggle motion, but they failed miserably. Either ectoplasm doesn't bounce the way fat does, or they were just too skinny.

"We'd better hope they close Petrov down and put him in prison, then."

"Don't say that name anywhere. I sure hope you didn't mention it to the cops."

"Of course I did. Ritchie said it."

He buried his head in his hands. "Ritchie *can* say it. The man is an idiot, but they trust him. Us, they don't trust. If they find out we've been blabbing, we're both dead."

I was pretty sure it was too late to keep this a secret from Petrov. The cops had questioned Ritchie after they'd arrested him. He might not have answered any questions, but I was pretty sure they would ask about Petrov. By now, he would have reported in and he sure would have mentioned that little tidbit.

Since Sam looked about an inch from a heart attack, I decided not to share my guesses with him. "Mum's the word."

"I just wanted to put a little money on the game. Is that so bad?"

"Book him, Dan-o." I hadn't seen Ghost Deputy Oren Luker come in, but there he was dressed, I noted, in what looked like 1930s detective-wear. It was a step up from the hobo clothing he'd worn on Saturday when he'd helped Arran and me.

"That show was on after you died," I said.

Sam squinted at me. "Are you okay, Annie?"

"Sorry. Just distracted for a second." Distracted and weirded out thinking about ghosts sitting in people's media rooms, watching

106

television shows while living humans went on with their business as if they were alone.

"I see. Well, you'd better get to work."

This was a first. Usually Sam did whatever he could to keep me, while I tried to flee from the stench. I decided to try one more thing.

"I suppose I'm like most girls, I've always liked horses. Does this gambling connection handle off-track betting?"

Sam lit up. "You bet it does. If you tell them I introduced you, they'll give me a break on the interest I owe them, too."

"Cool. You have a phone number. Or do I need to visit them in person to set up an account?"

"You can—" he caught himself. "Someone will be in touch with you. It's easier that way."

Easier for them to hurt me, maybe. "Never mind, then. Considering what happened last time one of them paid me a visit, I think I'll do without."

"Look, Annie, I've got a lot of work to get done. Maybe we can talk more some other time."

I nodded, grabbed my coffee, and headed down to the archives.

"What he's so busy with was checking out the Mavericks lineup for tonight's game," Oren said. "I got a look at his computer while you were talking to him."

"Whatever. I didn't learn anything from him, and that's the important thing."

Harry stepped through Sam's office wall. "Maybe you didn't get anything from him, but he got something from you. He's on the phone with the gambling operation now."

I tiptoed back down the hall, stopping just outside Sam's office.

"That's what I'm telling you. She was asking questions about you. I didn't tell her nothing but she knows your boss's name."

He paused. "Nothing doing. I'm already in trouble with the County thanks to Stone's visit on Friday. Anything happens to her, it had better be a long way from here."

"Thanks, Sam," I whispered. "You're a pal."

* * * *

"Seems to me, this is a job for the police." Harry, Oren and I were huddled in the Archives room and Oren had been going on for some time now.

"The police don't know where to start," I reminded him.

He gave an ethereal sigh. "I'm not talking about the living police. The ghost police always get their man."

Considering the ghost police were all of two days long, I didn't think so. "Oh, really? Name one."

Oren looked hurt. "We got Ritchie Stone, didn't we? Without us, there wouldn't be a picture and the cops wouldn't have known where to start."

From what I remembered, Arran had collared Ritchie just in time to save my butt from getting shot. That set a pretty low standard for 'getting their man,' but I decided not to argue the point. They had helped, and if I understood Oren right, they wanted to help again. "I'll bite. How do you suggest that the Ghost Police and I find this Petrov guy? He could be anywhere."

"We just—" he kicked at something that wasn't there. "Hell, I don't know. I'm not much of a cop yet. I mean, a week ago, I was a hobo, on the other side of the line. But you promised you'd have Detective Dane give us some training, right? Why don't you get him in here and have him start training us on those detective techniques. Once we know the cop secrets, we should be able to track Petrov down in no time."

"You'd just type the information you need in the police computer database, would you."

He winced. "I don't think most police work requires actually touching things."

"I bet it does, and I'll also bet you'd better drop any dreams of making me into the ghost police secretary. Della Street I'm not."

"We all have to do what we can, Annie, pitch in with whatever abilities we have. Besides, you're a girl. Girls are supposed to guard the office while the guys are out chasing cops."

"That was seventy years ago, Oren. Things are different now."

"Same sleazebag criminals, seems to me. If only we knew how to catch them."

That wasn't the answer I'd been hoping for.

"Can't help that," Oren said, when I told him I was looking for something more positive. "There are about ten million people within a hundred miles of here. And that's just the living ones. I can't hardly talk to all of them, can I? Especially since you're the only one I've found yet who bothers to answer."

"How about the ghost squad works on finding where Ritchie Stone hangs out and me and Annie find what property Petrov owns?" Harry suggested. "Since you guys already put a collar on Stone, I'll bet you can track him down again."

"Hell yes we can," Oren promised. "That would be a piece of cake. We know what car he was driving and we know the address he's got listed on his driver's license. It's probably a fake address, but most people pick fake addresses within a couple of blocks of their real address. Don't know for sure but I think it's something about making sure the address is believable."

"You'll keep me posted?" Harry demanded.

"Deal." The two ghosts shook and Oren headed out the (closed) door.

I stared at Harry for a moment. "Do you feel each other when you do that?"

"We're guys. Guys don't feel, we just are."

"Yeah, right. Very Zen. I meant when you shake hands. Do your ectoplasmic entities or whatever you ghosts are actually made out of actually touch? Is there a sensation?"

He shrugged. "Not really. Shaking hands is just being polite. Those of us who've been dead for a while were brought up right. Not like the dead people we've gotten over the past twenty years—bunch of rudenecks, they are."

I didn't know how to respond to that, except that I thought things were only going to get worse so Harry and the other old-timers had better get used to it.

Seeing I didn't defend the new ghosts, Harry bustled over to a stack of property documents waiting to be refiled. Only when I had settled down over a microfiche reader did he hit me with his zinger. "I don't think your honey could feel what Tiffany and Cassandra were doing to him, either."

"Tiffany and Cassandra?" My laugh wouldn't have fooled anyone over three. "Oh, you mean the ghosts with Arran last night. He's not my honey and that isn't what I was thinking about when I asked about touching."

"Sure it wasn't. Now, where would you live if you were a mobster? I'm thinking, Highland Park. Nice area, old trees, good schools for the kids. Long as money is no object, of course. Can't believe the prices. In my day, you could buy a nice place for less than ten grand."

I told him I didn't think mobsters looked at neighborhoods that way.

"Why wouldn't they? Everybody cares about those things. I'm surprised you don't know that, you being a real estate professional and all."

* * * *

My job was boring.

At some level I guess I'd always known that. Spending the day determining whether the power company has an easement, detecting covenants, making sure there are no property liens, unpaid taxes, or lawsuits applying to real estate doesn't even *sound* that interesting. But I'd never really worried about that. After all, the job paid the bills and let me work away from people who would be weirded out when I talked to ghosts, I could do most of it from home on the computer, and it didn't require a driver's license the way a lot of jobs did.

Having something I really needed to be spending time on, though, made the boredom a million times worse.

Harry chuckled to himself about old friends, probably mythical gangsters from his days in Dallas, and real estate developments so old not only were the buildings long gone, the developments that had come after them were being torn down too. Having a lot less fun than he, I discovered that nobody had paid Dallas School Taxes for an abandoned strip mall back in the 1970s but the Sheriff hadn't actually auctioned off the property. It was the kind of discovery that could ruin a deal, and I should have felt good about saving my clients a lot of hassle, but I just couldn't get excited.

So I quit work at three and spent the rest of the afternoon searching for anything on Petrov, Petrof, Peterof, and every alternative spelling Harry and I could come up with.

We found nothing.

Oren reported in at five, with pretty much the same news. He'd mobilized the Ghost Deputies, invaded every home within ten blocks of the fake address Ritchie had listed on his driver's license, and kept watch on every street and garage. This massive use of ghostpower had witnessed four extra-marital affairs, two burglaries, more drug deals than Oren could count, and not a sign of Ritchie or his car.

"Okay, we need a plan," I said.

Nobody said anything for a while. It was pretty obvious we needed a plan: nobody was going to argue about that. Unfortunately, nobody seemed to have a plan in their back pocket.

Oren soundlessly paced back and forth across the archive room, his feet appearing to sink an inch or two into the linoleum floors. Finally he turned and pointed a finger at my chest. "If any of us were real policemen, we'd know what to do. But we aren't. I'm doing my best with the Deputy Ghost Police, but we don't have the training we need, the training you promised us."

"I didn't mean to imply that you aren't—"

"It's not about us, it's about you. You need to get that cop on the case."

"You mean Detective Dane?"

"Who else, dummy? J. Edgar Hoover?"

"Arran doesn't want our help, he wants us to keep away and stay safe."

Oren glided over to stand directly in front of me. "Well, we need his help. So I guess it's just up to you to change his mind."

Chapter 15

"Sam Bert has left the office. He's heading out now." Harry stuck his head through the wall of the parking garage where I was hiding, made his report, and vanished to maintain surveillance.

A couple of minutes later, Oren appeared, chuckled to himself. "Oh, this is just too rich. That fat slob just stood there looking around like he's afraid someone might be watching. Guess what, somebody was."

I didn't say anything. Our plan, such as it was, had been to keep an eye on Sam, figuring he'd connect with the gambling ring as quickly as he could. Since closing time at the County Records building, I'd stayed huddled between a couple of cars in the multilevel parking garage, keeping my head ducked so the attendant wouldn't call the cops thinking I was a bag lady.

Oren popped back through the wall and headed out to tag-team with Harry.

"Sam's heading north," Harry said when it was his turn to report. "He pulled a ticket out of his pocket so he's got to be going to the game."

"Who's playing?"

"It's a Stars playoff game. Come on, Annie. Even I know that and I've been dead for seventy years. Haven't you seen everyone driving around with those flags hanging out their windows?"

Had I? I couldn't remember. I was pretty sure Arran and my brother didn't have little flags hanging from their cars.

"Time for me to follow him." I headed out of the garage.

The Stars are Dallas's hockey team and they play in a huge brick structure called the American Airlines Center.

It's really an attractive place, although I'd never understood why Dallas's taxpayers had to pay for a stadium designed to let overpaid sports figures skate around, or run around in their underwear in the case of the Dallas basketball team. I figured both flags and using tax dollars to subsidize sports millionaires must be a guy thing, although there were plenty of women in the crowds heading toward the Center's gates.

"Who needs a ticket?" A slender black man waved a handful of tickets in the air.

Oh, yeah. I wouldn't get far following Sam without one.

"How much?"

"For you, babe, I'll mark it down. Only three hundred dollars."

"Three hundred dollars?"

"Shhh. Not so loud. I don't want my other customers to know I'm giving you such a deal."

"I haven't got three hundred. Besides, those tickets say they're fifty dollars."

"That's what they say, but nobody's going to give you a better deal than me."

"Hurry." Oren looked frustrated. "Sam's getting away. You were supposed to keep up."

"Sorry."

"I'm sorry too, lady. But if you're not buying tickets, get out of my face. Who needs tickets?"

"I can't get in."

I said it to Oren, but the scalper heard me. "We all got problems, lady. I don't tell you mine, don't waste my time with yours."

Another plan had lasted about five minutes before self-destructing. Which seemed to be par for the course.

I followed Oren and arrived outside the Center just in time to see Sam disappear inside. He'd probably contact the gambling mob inside, but that wasn't going to do me much good.

That was when I saw something really weird.

I avoid air travel for the same reason I don't drive, because I get weirded out by all the ghosts. Airline seats are uncomfortable enough when you're by yourself. Sharing one with a talkative ghost is worse. Not to mention the fun of watching ghosts get sucked through the jet engines, which seems to be one of their favorite sports, although they appear none the worse for the experience when they come out the other end.

Of course I'd known that sports events also attract plenty of ghost watchers. I'd never watched them ooze through solid walls by the thousands before, though. It was unnerving.

"Your deputies can continue to monitor Sam," I said to Oren. "Even though I'm out here. Right?"

"No problem. Assuming you don't freeze to death."

February is normally spring in Dallas, but it felt more like winter and I hadn't brought a jacket. "I'll find a place to hang out. You can keep up the relay. Let me know who he meets with and whether he's gambling."

"How are we going to tell?"

"Listen to what he says. You don't think Sam is smart enough to have learned some code you can't figure out, do you?"

"Guess that's true. Although you living folks can be pretty sneaky."

"I'll wait at Dick's Last Resort."

Oren grinned. "If you see Milly, give her my regards."

"Who?"

"He's sweet on a girl who hangs out there," Harry whispered pointlessly since Oren could hear him perfectly well.

"A living girl?"

"What use would I have with a living girl?"

I didn't know the answer to that but clearly Tiffany and Cassandra found some satisfaction in hanging with a living man. Considering how hard I was working not to be jealous of them, though, I just agreed I'd keep my eyes open for Milly.

I had no idea how difficult that would be.

* * * *

Dick's Last Resort was filled with fans and the TVs hanging from the walls blared out the pregame activities. The fans didn't seem to mind the incongruity of traveling for miles to end up half a mile of the stadium just to watch the same show they could have from their own sets. I figured it was really about hanging out with other fans, and being there when after the game, when the players went looking for some fun. Come to think of it, even in the stadium, most people watch the huge monitors hanging from the ceiling rather than the game itself.

Although Dick's was not ancient, it was definitely not a ghost-free zone. Males of both the dead and living sorts panted over a couple of barely post-college girls (living and sexy) who'd decided to let guys lick salt off their hard abdomens as they downed tequila shots. A few female ghosts looked on with disgusted expressions that mirrored those of the still-living women in the crowd. If I'd had a mirror, I suspected I would have seen that same glare. It's hard to compete with twenty-one year-olds who don't have any shame at all. Being dead wouldn't help, of course.

The bar was deliberately tacky, with old signs, knotty wood panels, and dim lighting that nevertheless was plenty for all of us to watch those two young women make fools out of themselves.

A couple of cops sat at the bar, drinking coffee that might or might not have been laced with something alcoholic. I tried to shrink into my skin at first, afraid one of them might recognize me and call Arran to let him know where I was hiding, but then I realized they didn't have any attention to spare for me. Like every other male around, they had eyes only for the two pretty blondes.

Right on cue, though, my phone rang. Sure enough, the ID told me it was Arran. He must have made it to my place and discovered I was a no-show.

I considered picking up the phone, but he'd insist on coming down here and dragging me away. It was nice that he wanted to keep me safe, but I wasn't going to be safe until Petrov and Ritchie were both arrested and in jail. For me, the safest thing was to stick my neck out and hope it didn't get cut off. At least, that's what I told myself.

The crowd stood when the national anthem came over the TV and shouted out the word 'stars' when the barbershop quartet sang that word, then they all sat down for more alcohol. Few of them looked like they were on their first drinks.

After an astoundingly long wait, a waitress finally made her way over to the table I'd found in the corner and took my order. Dick's was known for their spicy chicken wings, but I stuck with vegetarian nachos and a beer. I figured the odds of a vengeful chicken ghost were higher here than they'd be anywhere outside a farm.

Oren reported in a few minutes later. Sure enough, Sam had headed directly for a lower deck seating area, made a phone call, and been joined by a man he'd called Petrov. You couldn't do better than that. My luck was finally changing.

I was a bit surprised that a criminal boss would actually meet up with a common gambler like Sam, especially as he had to know the police had been warned about Sam's gambling problem, but maybe the crime business didn't use IQ testing for its applicants.

Oren gave me a description that would have been good enough for Ron Shallot, our favorite police artist to create a picture from and headed back to the stadium. He and Harry would, he assured me, keep track of Petrov and warn me if the gangster left early. I suspected they just wanted to watch the game. Unlike human fans, after all, ghosts can get as close to the action as they want.

Fortunately, television cameras don't pick up ghosts. I was spared watching big Canadian hockey players skating through hundreds of noncorporal but very real people.

Petrov was either a fan or there was a lot of gambling action. Oren had stopped by a couple of times, and Harry once. I was on nursing my third beer by the time the game headed into overtime, but Sam and Petrov were still inside and watching.

"Is he your boyfriend?"

I looked up to see an attractive woman just a couple of years older than me standing near my table. Like most of the other women there, she had on a pair of tight jeans that showed off her figure, and a Stars jersey —hers ripped out in the neck to show an impressive cleavage.

"I beg your pardon."

"That guy, Oren. What's he to you?"

"You can see him?"

"No. I always walk up to strangers and ask them about people I don't see."

I'll blame my slow uptake on the three beers. "Hey, are you Milly?"

"Who wants to know?"

"I'm Annie Neeter. Oren asked me to say hi if you're Milly."

"Yeah? And he's too busy to do it himself? He's a ghost. One thing he's got is time."

"He's helping me out."

"Oh, so he is something to you."

"I've got a boyfriend," I lied. "A cop. Oren is helping both of us out. My cop made him a ghost deputy."

Lying like that should have made me feel guilty. Instead, I felt pretty good, as if calling Arran my boyfriend really made it so.

She shook her head. "That's the strangest thing I've ever heard. Ghosts don't do crime. We can't hurt each other and we don't have anything to steal. Why would we need police?"

I could have argued with her about the ghost-crime thing. If those naked men in Lauren's bedroom weren't criminal, we needed more laws. Instead, I just answered her question. "Oren is helping us track living criminals."

"They're all going to die anyway, and then they'll just be ghosts."

"Not all of us are in a big rush," I admitted.

She sat on a chair, her torso cutting through the table since the chair hadn't been pulled out. "Guess I can remember feeling that way."

"He's moving out." Oren appeared in a breathless rush. Not that ghosts actually breathed.

"Which exit is he heading toward?"

"West."

"Crap." I'd been hoping for south, which would have been closer.

"So, you wanted this non-ghost to tell me hi, did you?" Milly leaned into the Ghost Deputy. "Couldn't get up the nerve to tell me yourself?"

"Sorry Annie. I gotta go."

I'd told Arran that ghosts don't move any faster than normal people do, but Oren proved me wrong. He was completely out of there in one blink of my eyes.

Well, he'd given me the description and the exit Petrov had used. If I couldn't take it from there, I didn't deserve my honorary membership in the Ghost Deputy League.

I threw a twenty on the table, glanced at the bill and added another ten. Like Harry had said, in real estate, location is everything. I guess the location of Dick's Last Resort was prime.

As I left, though, I took a skeptical look at the two blondes involved in the shooters. Were they really just a pair of girls having fun, or might they actually be a hired part of the ambiance?

That was a question I'd have to worry about later if I hoped to catch Petrov before he vanished into the massive crowds of despondent fans. Sure enough, the Stars pulled defeat from the jaws of victory, blowing a two-goal lead and then getting crushed in the shootout.

Oren had said that Petrov wore a green Stars jersey, was in his forties and balding, and ten pounds overweight. His detailed description included nose shape, jaw, eyebrows and all of the other things Ron had demanded, but I didn't have an Identi-Kit with me and the crowd was too big for me to do more than scan.

Since most of the guys were middle-aged (reflecting the ticket price), and overweight (reflecting that they were fans rather than jocks themselves), I had to look for the one distinctive mark Oren and Harry had both noted—Petrov had an ugly scar that ran from his jawbone across his neck. That, I hoped, would be hard to miss—as long as I managed to get in front of him.

Plenty of hockey fans were already out the gate and dispersing to their cars by the time I got near the west exit. Although I'd jogged the half-mile or so from the bar, my stomach clenched partly from the three beers and partly because I feared I'd waited too long.

Just as I was considering my options and considering cursing myself and the ghosts for carelessness, a man matching the description perfectly strolled through the door.

If it hadn't been for the scar, Petrov could have passed as an accountant. His face was pale, and his glasses hadn't been stylish since I'd been born. His stomach pushed at the too-tight nylon jersey, the pucker of his belly button jiggling with every step he took.

A couple of obvious goon-types kept the gambling boss company, walking close to him like Secret Service agents defending the President.

Petrov chuckled as he walked and told jokes that had a pair of underdressed and apparently underage girls giggling. He slapped the backs of what seemed like dozens of well-dressed types who approached him, wanting to shake his hand, desperate to share his air.

Although the American Airlines Center might have been paid for by our tax dollars, there was nothing democratic about the way they handled parking. A handful of limousines waited in the 'no parking' area while the ordinary fans had to walk a mile or so to where they paid exorbitant fees to store their cars.

I figured Petrov for one of the limos. Sure enough, the girls and all but one of the bodyguards piled into one of the limos. I scribbled down the license number but Petrov surprised me by continuing on past.

I almost dropped my teeth when he and the one remaining bodyguard climbed onto the Trinity Rail Express, the commuter train running between Dallas and Fort Worth.

This was too good to be true. A train, with its huge crowd of semi-drunk fans, on-board security, and anonymity would be the perfect place to observe Petrov close-up and undetected.

That he was boarding a train heading west, away from Dallas, could also explain why I hadn't been able to find any Dallas property registered to Petrov. Sure I'd done computer searches in all of the neighboring counties, including Tarrant, but I'd concentrated on the big city.

The train's whistle blew just as Petrov got on board, causing me a bit of a dilemma. The train was ready to leave and I didn't have a ticket. The penalty for riding without a ticket was high, but the penalty for messing up the investigation just might be my life.

I decided to risk the five hundred dollar fine and made a dash for the train. I had to wrench my foot out when the train's door closed on it but I made it.

"Ah, Miss Neeter." His accent was heavy and sounded Slavic although I didn't know enough to tell a Russian accent from Polish or Serbian or whatever. "I made a bet with Sam Bert that you would track me down," Petrov continued, "and here you are—right on schedule. Poor Sam owes me again."

* * * *

Poor Sam, my ass. Try poor Annie Neeter.

I was struck by the silence and emptiness of the train car.

Plenty of people had climbed into the car Petrov was using, but they'd clearly gone elsewhere. Petrov and his guard sat in comfortable looking seats. A couple of other bodyguards, guards who must have known I'd been coming and set this up long before I'd arrived on the scene, leaned against the connecting doors at the end of what they'd turned into Petrov's private car.

I glanced toward the train's closed doors and saw that the emergency brake had been disconnected. I was stuck. "Neeter? You must have the wrong person."

Petrov chuckled, his belly slopping over his belt like an aging waterbed. "I hardly think that's possible, Ms. Neeter. Not after our mutual friend Sam Bert sent such a charming photo."

He reached into his slacks pocket and my body tensed up like an overwound spring.

Instead of a gun, he pulled out a folded sheet of paper, which he tossed to me.

Sure enough, Sam had taken a cellphone digital picture. It wasn't much as far as composition went. My mouth was open and I was staring at something that wasn't on the screen at all so I looked like a loon, but I was fully recognizable. I was even wearing the same sweater I still had on. There was no denying this one.

"Okay, I *am* Annie Neeter. But you have the advantage on me."

Petrov gave me a grandfatherly smile. His eyes, though, made a lie out of that expression. They were the pale blue of arctic ice, as cold as I imagined the Siberian steppes would be in the middle of the darkest winter. "Has anyone ever told you you're a horrible liar, Ms. Neeter? You know who I am, but I'll tell you again. I'm Ivan Petrov, a—shall we say —friend of Sam's. And you were looking for me. Well, you've found me. What do you intend to do about it?"

About then, I could have used a little help. There were a couple of ghosts handy, but they looked dark and Russian and were muttering to themselves in words I couldn't understand. I thought they were as likely to be on Petrov's side as mine. Besides, even if they wanted to help me, what could they do? Ghosts might be handy if someone wanted to send a message *to me*, but they were useless in getting messages *from me* to someone who might be able to help, like Arran. Assuming Arran could be bothered to help me. Blowing him off that evening might not have been the dumbest thing I'd ever done, but it would certainly make my top ten list.

Still, thinking about Arran gave me an idea.

"Actually my boyfriend, Police Detective Arran Dane, says I'm a pretty good liar." I was getting used to the idea of calling Arran my boyfriend. Imagining it still tingled, though.

"I detect another lie. Which is the lie, though? That Dane says you're a good liar, or that he's your boyfriend." Petrov leaned closer to me, his breath beery and warm on my face. "You know, I think you fabricated both of these. If you lie this often and this badly, it's amazing you're alive."

I would have done better to keep my mouth shut, I realized. I would have done better yet to listen to Arran and gone back to my place and his protection. Not only would I have been safer, I might have stood at least a chance of getting lucky. From the icy stare coming from Petrov's three bodyguards, getting dead was the likely outcome of this meeting. They didn't look like murder would bother their consciences for a moment.

"I told the police your name. If anything happens to me, you'll be the first guy they suspect."

"Sam mentioned you were charming. Won't you have a seat, Ms. Neeter?" He patted the seat cushion right next to him. "I dislike standing while the train is moving."

Sure enough, the train had pulled out of Victory Station and were chugging our way west, toward Fort Worth.

I didn't have a chance to answer him. Instead, the guard who'd gotten onto the train with him grasped me by the shoulders, shoving me downward.

For just an instant, I have visions of using my Tae Kwon Do skills to escape his grip, disarm him, and use his own gun to hold Petrov and the three bodyguards hostage. But reality, and my teacher's warning to use violence as a last resort caught up to me in time. My chances of winning that fight, green belt or not, were about the same as the odds I'd be elected America's next President.

Instead, I went with his shove, directing myself to a seat across the aisle from Petrov. Sitting directly next to him would be too creepy.

The guard looked to Petrov for guidance and the mobster waved his hand, accepting my partial compliance with his order.

"You've been trying to find me for a couple of days now," he said, "and I have to admire your persistence. Perhaps you have something you'd like to ask me? Or perhaps you wish to place a wager. Sam said you spoke to him about betting on quarter-horse races."

"Yeah, sure. I heard you—"

"But if you continue to lie, I'll have my friends escort you off the train—now. Did you know that this train travels in excess of sixty miles an hour? I'm afraid that the drunken escapades of one passenger after a hockey game would be written off as a sad moment, complete with editorials about the need to control alcoholic consumptions."

His threat was completely matter-of-fact. Life and death were subjects as casual to him as they were to Milly the ghost.

Chapter 16

"Killing me would be a bad idea."

He waved a hand. "No need for threats. You've already mentioned dropping my name. It was highly indiscrete for Mr. Stone to mention it in your hearing. I think, though, that Mr. Stone, not myself, would be the subject of most police interest."

I thought he was right. "He may be out on bail for now but he's probably dumb enough to have used the same gun in actual murders. When the lab does it's work, they'll be able to put enough pressure on him to make him squeal like a pig."

"I doubt that Mr. Stone will be squealing, as you so charmingly put it, to anyone."

I laughed. "Well, you know him better than I do, but you were the one who used the word indiscrete."

"You misunderstand me, Ms. Neeter."

Although I didn't hear the door open, Ritchie headed down the aisle toward me.

Oh, shit—had he heard me saying he couldn't be trusted? I thought fast.

"You know, Ritchie, I think we're in this together. Anything bad happens to me, lots of bad things happen to you."

"Too late."

One of the ghosts laughed and I did a doubletake. Petrov was right, Ritchie wasn't a threat to me any more, but he also wouldn't be doing any talking. Not to anyone but me.

"Where's your body, Ritchie?"

"Either you're trying to persuade me you're crazy," Petrov mused, "or the stories I have from my, uh, friends in the Dallas Police Department are true. Do you see the ghost of Mr. Stone?"

"You killed him?"

Petrov's belly jiggled as he laughed. "I? Hardly."

"You had him killed then."

"While I won't admit that, I will say that I'm surprised you're not happier he's no longer a threat. Mr. Stone swore he'd pay you back, and I'm afraid squirting him in the face with pepper spray made him quite angry. Whoever had him killed may have saved your life."

I was glad I was sitting because my legs were trembling so hard I didn't think I could have stayed upright. What had I been thinking when I'd left Arran out of this?

I pulled my purse closer and slid my hand into it, trying to be nonchalant. If I could just set up a call to Arran, he'd be able to track me. It wasn't as if the train would leave the tracks and go into hiding, after all.

"No." Petrov's face lost any hint of the jolly accountant look. For an instant, the man behind the pink face and bulging belly was revealed, the man who'd earned and survived a slit throat at some time in his career. "I'm hoping the two of us can come to an agreement, Ms. Neeter. But if you threaten me, or abuse my patience, I will change the terms of this agreement in ways that are very much not in your favor."

"What sort of agreement."

He smiled. "Excellent. You wish to discuss the terms of our agreement. See how easy that was? We develop a shared understanding, state our needs, and see if there's some way we can help one another— achieve fair exchange and mutual benefit. It's the American Way, no?"

The Russian-looking ghosts nodded along with Petrov and I decided to do the same. The gangster might be smiling again, but the hard cold killer look was still near the surface, barely disguised at all.

"We're going to be such good friends," he said. "Now, I have some ideas of what you need. You'd prefer, I'm certain, not to be prosecuted for hunting down and murdering Mr. Stone."

I couldn't help it, I laughed. "Like I could do that. I don't even drive."

"Perhaps not alone. But you mentioned that Detective Dane was your boyfriend."

"And you told me that was a lie."

"Quite right. Unfortunately for Detective Dane, not everyone is as discerning as I. There are already many in the police force that the two of you are," he paused, "is *involved* the right term?

"That's their mistake."

He nodded. "Of course. Yet, it could become a problem for the two of you, if evidence shows that he killed the man who'd threatened you."

I wasn't laughing any more. "You'd frame Arran?"

He shrugged. "I am a criminal, Ms. Neeter. Do you really think I'd stop short of framing a cop who's too honest for his own good?"

My eyes burned and I didn't seem to be able to see anything other than Petrov's face. "Tell me what you want."

* * * *

The train pulled into Hurst Station and Petrov went silent while his guards hustled the handful of entering customers through the doors and into the cars on either side of his own. Only after the train accelerated did he speak.

"You were wise to keep your mouth shut."

"Enough innocent people are getting hurt."

"Quite so."

"Now, are you going to tell me what you want? If scaring me is your objective, you've succeeded."

"That just might be the first thing you told me that isn't a lie. You are frightened." He reached across the aisle and stroked my cheek with his hand. "Your blood has fled from your hands and has flushed your cheeks. You are an attractive woman, Ms. Neeter. Doubly attractive because you're frightened."

Eeew. His touch wasn't sexual, it was a twisted pantomime of a mother's touch, pretending care, parodying concern. I suppressed a shudder and swallowed hard to resist a strong urge to hurl.

"You see, Ms. Neeter, you have no need to be frightened. I have no wish to be your enemy. In fact, you and I are going to become best friends, business partners in a way. We'll grow rich together, each leaning on one another for our own unique skills."

"Yeah, right. Because I'm such an expert statistician, right? Do you want me to take over the football pool or the basketball gambling ring?"

He shook his head. "I know you Americans make jokes about everything but I'm quite serious. I'm going to give you the money you need to move out of that horrid apartment near Mockingbird Station. With real money, you'll be able to tear down your aluminum foil walls, and buy yourself a place at least as nice as the one your brother owns. Perhaps you can move to his neighborhood and spend more time with the beautiful Lauren and the amusing Smaller Jack, as I believe you call him. You'll be able to afford a driver so you won't have to catch the 7:34 train every morning."

I nodded, trying to look indifferent, but I wasn't. Petrov was showing off, proving he'd done his research, that he could get at the people I cared about. How else could he know about my aluminum foil walls? It wasn't as if I bragged about them. How else would he know exactly what train I took each morning? The veiled threat to my brother and his family, though, was the real kick to the gut.

"Perhaps you're wondering why I would give you so much money, make you my partner," he said, "being as I am, a man of business rather than philanthropy."

"I guess you don't want me to run the drink concessions at your gambling joint."

"You're an intelligent woman, I'm sure you can guess." He leaned back across the aisle, grasping my shoulder in a grip that seemed simultaneously friendly and threatening. "But since you insist on joking,

I'll tell you. You see, Ms. Neeter, you impressed me."

He pulled away and reached into the seat pocket, pulling out the Identi-Kit image of Ritchie Stone. "Your talent was bad news for the late Mr. Stone, of course, but it is a skill that could prove highly useful in my business."

"I'm not sure how police sketch artists—"

"Come, Ms. Neeter. There is no need to be obtuse." He snapped his fingers and the guard handed him a thick document.

It was newly printed but my tongue seemed stuck to the top of my mouth when I recognized the psychiatric hospital seal on the top page.

Petrov beamed at me like a father watching a precocious child.

"My psychological profile. How'd you get that?"

"As you know, Detective Dane sent a copy through police channels to clear you from suspicion in the records building shooting. I have friends in the police department. All it took was a few minutes at a copy machine and a fresh beautiful printout was mine."

"I'm confused. You want to be my partner because you have a psychological profile that classifies me as delusional."

He shook his head sadly. "No, Ms. Neeter, although more than a few of my employees have been judged by your society to be insane, I don't wish to hire you because I believe you're delusional: quite the contrary, in fact."

"That's—"

He patted the thick sheaf of paper. "The police believe this document proves that Detective Dane has fallen for a nut-case. I'm afraid his chances for promotion are slim as long as the two of you are seen to be involved. But I am a Russian. I don't have the ultra-rational mindset of you Americans."

He reached under his jersey and pulled out a silver crucifix, caressing it briefly, then letting it press down on the jersey's nylon fabric. "We Russians are used to sharing the world with things beyond our understanding: Baba Yaga in her forest hut on chicken-legs, shape changers and talking foxes. Why shouldn't ghosts share our world?"

Just my luck. The one man in the entire world who believed in my talents happened to be a criminal mastermind. "But—"

"Of course Americans think you're crazy." He made *American's* sound like a curse word. "Americans think everything is a disease and look for a pill to cure it. *They* laugh at your visions, but I ask whether you might be telling the truth. Now that I have seen what a poor liar you are, I think you must be."

"Meaning?"

He sighed. "Meaning, the ability to talk to ghosts and have them talk back, to give them orders and have them obey, to send them places where no one else can go, where they can see and hear everything. These things could be valuable to me."

He rubbed his hands together and an unpleasant smile lingered a moment on his lips. "Very valuable indeed."

Helping Petrov excited me about as much as being thrown from the train. Considering that was my option, I decided to negotiate. "Can you put a dollar amount on *valuable*?"

He grinned. "Oh, Ms. Neeter, what a question. So American to think everything can be weighed on the scales of the all-mighty dollar. I was thinking of value in terms of human life—your life in particular. You're alive right now only because of what I see as your value."

"Okay, that gives me an idea. But you mentioned cars and houses."

"As the Bible ordains, I don't bind the mouth of the kine who help me harvest."

Clearly Petrov didn't see any contradiction between being devout and being a murdering criminal. I didn't think that would help me, though.

"I'm listening."

Petrov surprised me. He'd learned of my ability to talk with ghosts less than forty-eight hours earlier, yet he had a comprehensive plan to use that talent. I was to employ ghosts to spy on his fellow criminals, gather blackmail material on cops who pried too hard, listen in on players who were being pressured to throw games, and send early warnings if the cops or feds decided to make a move against Petrov and his empire.

I'd never thought of using the ghosts to do any of those things, which might prove I wasn't a natural criminal. Of course, it might also have meant I wasn't as bright as I imagined I was.

"Ghosts talk to me but they don't run errands for me," I explained when he looked up from his notes. "And you can't threaten them. They're already dead and are past pain."

His eyes twinkled. "I understand you came up with suitable bribes when you were working on the portrait of Mr. Stone."

"I don't think—"

Petrov shook his head. "You're going about this quite wrongly, Ms. Neeter. You think you want to persuade me you can't help me. That is a horrible mistake, perhaps a deadly mistake. If you wish to survive, if you want your brother and his beautiful family to remain healthy, if you wish Detective Dane to escape accusations of murdering Mr. Stone, you must convince me that you *can* make this work. I want you to put your mind toward creating suitable rewards for ghosts who cooperate. Some wish portraits of themselves: fine, we can hire artists. Some want titles, to be Deputy Detectives or Confederate Colonels. Some want purpose in their dreary existence. Some, perhaps, wish only for someone to listen to them, hear their tales of lands that are lost, of friendships long sundered." Petrov paused for a moment, as if considering lost lands and friendships. Weirdly, a part of me felt sympathy for the man. But it was a small part, and one quickly put down. He'd threatened my family—he deserved whatever suffering had made him into what he was.

"With my money," he continued, "and your skill, there is no reason they can't have these things. They can have them, and they will earn them."

I'd always liked the idea that being a ghost put people beyond the petty issues of the living. Helping Petrov would be a crime, but perhaps the biggest crime would be turning free spirits into ghostly laborers.

As he had done too often, though, Petrov seemed to read my thoughts, his pale eyes boring into mine. "Is it so horrible to give ghosts what they want, Ms. Neeter? With an infinity of time before them, wouldn't they give up a few moments where someone needs them, where they can have an effect that extends to the world they have left behind, yet cannot really leave?"

No one, not my brother, not even Arran, had asked me that question. Perhaps Petrov was right that Americans were too caught up in rationalizing everything. Even those who were willing to believe in ghosts didn't really think about what it might be like to be one. Petrov had, though. Only his thoughts had exactly one objective—discovering how they could help him.

"I don't know," I finally said.

He nodded as the train pulled into Texas and Pacific station in Fort Worth, the end of the line. "It's ironic, is it not, that I must have honesty from my employees although your society labels my business as a dishonest one? So I appreciate your qualms. I respect you for wishing to protect those who have no one else to protect them. But you must understand something else, before we part ways. You are too dangerous to be loose. If you won't help me, I simply cannot let you help those who would destroy me. So, I suggest you consider my words carefully."

He stood and offered me his arm.

I pretended I didn't see his gesture and stepped down onto the platform.

Although the night was a moonless pit of darkness, the station provided plenty of lighting, the silvery glow making everyone look ghostlike.

As with Dallas's Union Station, the T&P was old Texas, from an era where railroads were king and when Dallas was the hub for cotton trade and Fort Worth for cattle—the beginnings of a rivalry between the two neighboring cities that lingered into the present. Many real ghosts congregated at the station, some in cowboy hats and dusty boots, some looking like gamblers.

I studied them, wondering if their lives were as empty as Petrov believed, if they were looking for purpose, any purpose at all, that would allow them a connection to the world they'd left behind.

Hundreds of fans, mostly still drunk, mostly happy despite the Stars' loss, shoved their way out of the train and lurched toward waiting cars, often walking straight through the ghosts.

At a gesture from Petrov, the two bodyguards who'd watched the doors grasped one of my elbows each and hustled me toward one of several waiting black limos.

"What the—"

"Surely you don't think your new boss would leave you here in the middle of the night. Charles will take you home."

Petrov stepped into the second of the limos, nodded to the driver, and vanished into the darkness.

"Want me to follow him?"

"What? Uh—oh, hi Oren."

I hadn't even noticed the Ghost-Deputy had tagged along. Maybe those grim Russian ghosts had made him keep his distance. Although ghosts didn't seem able to physically interact, there might be rules I didn't know about.

I felt better knowing I had a friend there, even though Oren could do nothing to help me with my all-too-mortal problems.

Come to think of it, maybe nobody could help me with my problems.

"Well?" The ghost waited, his upper torso in the car near me, the rest of his ethereal body hanging out through the limo's hardened steel exterior.

"Can you keep up with his limo?"

The driver lowered the shield. "You talking to me, lady?"

I gestured to my fake earpiece. "On the phone."

"Oh. Sorry to interrupt."

Oren watched Petrov's limo peel out of the parking lot. "Uh, no. I couldn't keep up that pace."

"Just keep me company, then."

The limo driver shot me another look. Unlike Petrov, he didn't have a foreign accent. From his polished cowboy boots and the strong odor of

127

chewing tobacco, as well as his drawl, I guessed he was a local boy.

Oren extruded himself through the car like toothpaste coming out of a tube and nuzzled up next to me. "You sure your boyfriend won't mind."

Despite everything, I had to smile. "I don't think he's the jealous type. I'd better call him, though. He's going to be seriously pissed."

"Not as pissed as he'd be if you were dead."

It was a nice thought—I only wished I believed it.

* * * *

"Did you get the license number?"

I decided I would have been happier if Arran would just yell at me. Over the phone, his voice sounded indifferent, as if he no longer cared that I'd stood him up and avoided his calls. He quickly went into his 'just the facts' detective mode.

"I tried." I gave him what I remembered, but it wasn't as if I'd had time to write things down.

Arran wasn't sympathetic.

"If that's the best you can do, I guess we'll live with it. At least the computer lets us look up partial matches. I'll see what I find."

"Okay. And Arran…"

"Yes, I'll send a squad car to pick you up."

"You don't need to do that. The limo driver is taking me home anyway."

That broke through his indifference. "You want to ride with Petrov's driver? You believed Petrov when he said he'd send you home? Maybe your brother is right and you really are insane."

I knew I'd been in the wrong chasing after Petrov on my own and not even letting Arran know I'd stand him up. Arran had given up his personal life to park his sexy body on my couch, and in return I'd blown him off and ignored his calls. But he kept pushing and I'd done all the groveling I could stand.

"Maybe you should take your little police nightstick and shove it up your rear end."

"Uh-oh. I don't think that was the right thing to say." Oren grinned at me, but he looked distraught.

"We've got a lot to talk about," Arran said.

Three minutes later, flashing lights warned my driver to pull over.

He obeyed, then shifted the oversized auto into park, and glued his hands to the steering wheel in plain sight of the officers. This looked like a drill he'd been through before.

For the next five minutes, we sat still on the side of old Route 80, as more and more cop cars roared onto the scene, lights flashing and sirens blaring.

After finally completing whatever paperwork cops get busy with after pulling someone over, or maybe after just reading his horoscope to make sure it was a good day to pull over limousines, a couple of husky cops knocked on the driver's window. "Come out, slowly."

The driver obeyed, keeping his hands in sight as he stepped from the car.

The second both of his feet were on the ground, the cops shoved him against the side of the car and patted him down.

Cops from other cars gathered around, several of them taking shooting stances, their automatics held in both hands. A couple even dragged their shotguns out of their trunks.

This had all of the earmarks of a classic cluster.

I huddled in the back seat, breathing in the stench of nervous sweat from the anxious cop. Without wishing any harm to the driver, I still hoped the limo was bulletproof. Because if one of those cops heard a car backfire or if the driver sneezed unexpectedly, I suspected that every gun in the place would go off and keep shooting until no one was left standing.

It seemed almost a foregone conclusion that they'd shoot eventually. Surely that much testosterone would have to find a release.

The driver said nothing until one of the cops reached under his jacket and pulled out a jet-black semiautomatic pistol.

"Gun. He's got a gun."

The cop with the shotgun ratcheted a shell into the chamber, the sound cutting through the nervous chatter.

"I have a concealed permit, officer," the chauffeur said just as I was sure all hell was going to break loose. "In the car. If you'd per—"

"You just stand right there, asshole. Franks, you check the car. See what he's got. And be careful. He might have a bomb rigged."

A cop who didn't look old enough to be out of high school climbed into the driver's door. His eyes went wide when he saw me. As if by magic, his gun was in his hand, pointing straight at me.

"There's someone else in here. A woman."

"I thought you were here to pick—"

"Shut up." Franks's weapon hand trembled but we were close enough I didn't see how he could miss if he pulled the trigger, whether on purpose or by accident.

"Seems like old times," Oren observed. "Can't count how often I was rousted from a car by cops looking for alcohol or whatever. Guess police work hasn't changed that much since I was alive, after all. 'Course the good news is, when they start shooting, won't hurt me at all."

I kept my mouth shut. I must have flickered a glance toward where the ghost was sitting, though, because Officer Franks whipped his weapon in that direction.

"Is someone else with you?"

"Just ghosts."

"You criminals all think you have a sense of humor, don't you?"

I decided any answer would land me in deeper trouble, so I kept my mouth shut.

Wrong decision.

He jerked his gun. "I asked you a question and I don't like it when women blow me off."

A pair of big hands attached to hard-muscled arms reached in, grasped Franks by the collar and belt, and lifted him out of the car. "You were assigned to locate the concealed permit, not to harass the woman."

I recognized that voice.

Sure enough, a moment later, Arran's face peered through the door.

I opened my mouth to thank him, but he beat me to the punch.

"You have a special talent, don't you, Annie? I've never met a woman who created so much havoc everywhere she went."

"I know you're going to tell me why this is a good thing, right?"

"You bet I will. As soon as I figure it out."

"The hostage will be leaving the car now." Arran's voice was like a lighthouse lamp cutting through the darkness. "Stand down your weapons. This situation is over."

"There's no hostage," the driver said. "I was asked to drive the woman home. If she'd asked me to drop her off earlier, I would have been happy to do so."

"We'll talk about this down at the station." A bald cop with stripes on his shoulder took control of the situation. "We're going to have to talk to the woman as well, Detective. You're in Arlington jurisdiction here, not Dallas."

"She's been threatened and is in shock," Arran answered.

The Sergeant, if I understood police rank insignia correctly sighed. "Nobody is going to scare your precious girlfriend, Dane. But you know we've gotta talk to her."

"I'm staying with her."

"If she wants you as her legal representative, I guess you can come along. Up to the woman."

Arran nodded, then turned to me. "It's me or we roust your sister-in-law out of bed. I'd prefer for you to trust me. Of course, it's pretty obvious you don't."

I wouldn't trust anyone as angry as he was. From the stare he gave me, I figured he'd throw me to the dogs for a quarter. Still, Lauren would just tell me to stay quiet, which would make the whole thing drag on. I hadn't done anything wrong, after all, so I should be safe, right?

Unless the Arlington cops had found Ritchie's body and connected it to Arran and me.

"Fine, come with me. Let's get this over with." I said.

Arran shook his head. "Don't kid yourself, Annie. It's going to be a long time before this is over."

Chapter 17

"Come on, babe."

I snuggled closer to Arran's chest. "What? Where—"

"You fell asleep in my car. It's almost six in the morning."

"Got to get to work."

"You need to sleep."

My eyes felt glued shut, but I managed an effort of will and forced them open.

Sure enough, we weren't at my place at all. Arran had brought me back to his apartment, again.

He carried me as easily as if I'd been an infant and headed toward the elevator. "Want to tell me what you didn't tell the Arlington police?"

I buried my face in his hard chest. His muscles stuck out from the effort of lugging my hundred and something pounds across his apartment lobby and I liked the feeling. "I told them everything."

"Yeah, right."

"What is it about you guys? Everything I say, I get accused of lying."

He froze in mid-step. "You lied to Petrov?"

"Of course I liked to Petrov. What do you think, I'd just open up to him like he was a long-lost brother?"

"I did some research today. Didn't find much, but from what I did see, lying to Petrov could be a very bad idea. Unfortunately, we don't have much of an organized crime unit in DPD. Most of their energy goes to drugs. It isn't that we don't care about gambling, but it's not exactly at the top of our priority list."

"The Baptist voters would get pissed if you legalized it so you ignore it."

"I don't make the laws."

"Sounds to me like that's exactly what you're doing if you choose to chase after some kinds of criminals and just walk away from others."

He started walking again. "I'll vote for you when you run for State Senate and you can fix the problem, all right? Now what the hell were you hiding from the Arlington Police Department?"

"Heard anything from Ritchie Stone?"

"Changing the subject isn't going to help. But no. Stone has dropped off the radar scope. Probably laying low until the heat drops off."

"Laying low, yes, but for him the heat is permanently off."

Arran froze. "You're saying he's dead? You're sure?"

"I saw his ghost."

"Damn it, honey. You should have told Sergeant Downs."

"Right. He'd believe that, of course. Besides, I don't have a deathwish. Petrov has it rigged. If I don't go along with his crazy ghost-spy plan, he's going to point at you as Ritchie's murderer."

"Ridiculous. Why would I kill that scumbag?"

"Because you've got a crazy girlfriend and you'd do crazy things to make her happy."

"I don't have a girlfriend."

I was surprised that hurt me. I mean, I'd been telling myself the same thing—that Arran was interested in me because I was connected to the shooting, because I was female and around, because he had so much of the male thing going he couldn't help turning the head of any woman and I just happened to be the current target. Still, hearing him come right out and say it made it more real, made it obvious I'd been in denial despite myself.

I put my arms against his chest and shoved. I didn't want him carrying me any more. The arms that had felt comforting and safe around me suddenly seemed confining and dangerous.

"Don't tell me, tell Petrov. But I don't think it's going to help you. He'll be happy to have a little blackmail leverage on one of Dallas's finest no matter what our relationship."

Arran ignored my efforts to escape his grasp as easily as if I'd been a clawless kitten.

"As I was saying, although we don't have much on him, we do have some C.I. reports that a Russian took over some local operations. Over the past six months, there've been at least three unsolved deaths of professional gamblers. Nobody put together those two facts, but I can make some deductions. Your new boss is a dangerous man."

"You cops may not know much about him, but he knows plenty about you. You did hear me tell APD that he got my psychological profile from the police, didn't you? Which cops do you know who gamble?"

"Probably all of them."

"That's a big help."

I gave up pushing at him and demanded that he put me down. He seemed reluctant, but finally did as I asked.

"Anyway," I said, "I know Petrov is dangerous but I don't know what to do about it. Did you learn anything about his neck? Someone cut it hard enough to take his head halfway off. I'm not a doctor, but the scar goes ear-to-ear. Wouldn't that kill someone?"

"Apparently not. Unless he happens to be one of your ghosts."

Arran thought he was making a joke, but I had to consider it. If ghosts existed, why shouldn't other paranormal beings? Could Petrov be a ghoul or vampire? None of the ghosts had mentioned anything like that, but maybe vampires were as invisible to the ghosts as ghosts were to most people.

I liked the idea because then I wouldn't have to admit I was afraid of a mere human. Unfortunately, the more I thought about it, the more reasons I came up with why Petrov was just a man. He'd worn a silver crucifix next to his skin, he'd been warm to the touch, and I'd seen his breath steam against the damp night at Fort Worth's T&P Station.

It added up to Petrov being alive. Horror movies notwithstanding, he seemed a lot more dangerous as a living being than if he'd been dead.

"He's not a ghost and I'm not going to be able to ignore him. Unfortunately, I don't know what I *am* going to do. When I tell him I won't work for him, he'll either kill me, or frame me for Ritchie's murder. And go after you and my family."

"Best thing is to stay away from him for a while," Arran said. "If he can't find you, he can't threaten you."

"You're dreaming. He knows where my brother lives. If he can't find me, he'll hurt them. He made damned sure I knew that."

Arran unlocked his apartment door and ushered me inside. "That is a problem. Let me talk with the Lieutenant and see if we can come up with some suggestions."

"Like what?"

He shook his head. "Like I said, let me talk to the lieutenant. Right now, I've got nothing.

* * * *

Arran urged me to get some sleep. Instead I brewed up a pot of double-strength coffee and went in to chat with the ghosts.

The detective had his usual crowd of girl-ghosts, hoping to pick up a little warmth from his too-hot body. I was hoping for more, though.

I wasn't especially surprised to see the Colonel and Oren in Arran's spare bedroom/gallery. The Colonel had brought a couple of his buddies from the Civil War to see his portrait and was still going on about how the artist had messed up his chin.

My run-in with Petrov had me a bit melancholy. I plopped myself down on a hard wooden chair in the gallery and stared at the small crowd.

They must have picked up on my mood, because they ignored me, joking amongst themselves and pointing out every flaw in the portraits.

It finally dawned on me that they were working too hard at having fun.

"Tell me something," I finally said. "What's life, uh, I mean death, like for you guys?"

They stared at me as if I were speaking in tongues.

"I'm serious, guys. Do you miss living? Do you want to communicate with your relatives or anything like that? Do you even remember having family?"

"I've still got people," the Colonel said. "My sisters. I told you that."

"Yeah, I heard you say that. But do you keep tabs on their descendents? Is there really anything you'd like to tell them?"

He laughed. "Why should I bother? It's not like they'd do anything for me. None of 'em even visit my grave. Besides, they probably know more about what's going on than I do." He shook his head sadly. "Lots of things have changed since my day. When we rode out, we were so sure we'd win the war and come home heroes. Any more, I'm not even so sure I was fighting on the right side, and my ghost is the only part of me that came home."

I'd grown up in Texas, so I knew most of the south *still* considered the southern cause to be noble—the white part of the south, anyway. The Colonel must have done a lot more thinking than I would have guessed a ghost could manage if he'd gotten that far. Still, I was stuck on the first thing he'd said.

I'd never actually seen many ghosts hanging out at graveyards. To me, a ghosts was what was left when the body gave out. Why should they care what happened to that left-behind flesh? Wouldn't that be like me caring about what happened to the hair I left on the floor at the cheap hair salon I went to?

"Would you like it if they went to your grave?"

The Colonel took off his ostentatious cavalry hat and scratched his balding scalp. "It's the thought that counts."

Okay, I could see that. "You like your portrait, of course."

"Hell, yeah!"

"But why does it matter to you? No living humans, other than me and Arran, are likely to see it. And your fellow ghosts can see you as you really are, with your chin the way it really is."

He fingered his deficient feature. "Maybe."

"Seems to me that you're pretty self-sufficient. You don't need anything from us living people. That's probably why most living people can't see you."

"She's got you there, Oren agreed. 'Cept I've got a bad feeling she's talking herself into something I ain't going to like."

"What did that Russian want her to do, anyway?"

Glad to have the attention of the Colonel and his friends, Oren launched into a detailed description of our detecting, the way Petrov had turned the tables on me, and his plan to use the ghosts as spies on his enemies.

Arran came in just as Oren was wrapping things up. "Pretty quiet in here."

"It is for you."

"Ghosts?"

I almost said, *no, Arran. I just like staring at the walls for hours,* but I was afraid he'd believe me. A part of him might be convinced by my ghosts, but being a cop had trained Arran to handle contradictory facts. All the way to his bones, Arran was a skeptic. Part of him would never believe in my reality no matter what proofs I showed him.

"I think Petrov's plan could work."

"You mean—"

"Think how easy it was for us to persuade Oren and the other Ghost Deputies to help out. Remember the way all of those ghosts lied to have a chance to get interviewed, to have their words recorded? If you have eternity ahead of you, and you can't touch anything, can't do anything that makes any difference to anyone, not even other ghosts, you'd do just about anything to be noticed. That was lucky for us when we needed Richie's description. It'll be lucky for Petrov if I cave into his demands."

"You can't do that. He's a killer, remember."

I really didn't need that reminder. I'd been talking with ghosts for over twenty years that I could remember, plus a few more in my early childhood I couldn't remember. In all that time I'd never come up with a plan for using the ghosts for my own good. I'd let myself get roped into doing things for them—playing their chess games, leaving on the TV while I was at school or work so they could watch their favorite shows, chatting with them when they felt lonely. Yet both Arran and Petrov had instantly grasped the potential for turning that relationship around.

Abruptly, I felt sickened by the whole thing. Sure, Arran had meant well and was doing his job. But so what? Just because the ghosts were dead didn't make it right to exploit them.

I'd once read that cops and criminals are a lot alike. I could see a lot of differences between Arran and Petrov, but in one key respects, they were identical—they both believed in manipulating others in order to pursue their own goals. By letting myself be used by Arran, I'd opened the door to being used by Petrov.

If I survived this, I decided I'd move somewhere far away, somewhere that nobody knew me, and where no one could guess my connections to the dead.

Maybe, I realized, my condition wasn't as rare as I'd imagined. Maybe I was just a slow learner, always expecting other people to adjust for me when, in fact, that was really the last thing I needed.

Moving away from Jack, Lauren and Little Jack would be tough. To my surprise, I realized moving away from Arran would be tough as well. Like a splinter, he'd gotten under my skin.

Before I could get on with my life, though, I needed to clean up the mess I'd made here in Dallas. That meant making sure that my vanishing didn't get my family killed, or my non-boyfriend accused of murder.

"Have you called your lieutenant yet? You don't want me to work with Petrov, but I don't want Jack, Little Jack, and Lauren in danger. I don't want you in trouble, either."

"I can take care of myself."

"Somehow I knew you'd say that. But you know what? You're not the only person who can spot a lie when she hears one. You can't handle this."

He shook his head, but he checked his watch. "Let me toast you a bagel so you'll have something solid in your stomach to pour that coffee over. I'll call him at nine when he gets into the office."

"Great. Maybe he'll be able to pull a miracle out of his ass, because that's what it's going to take."

* * * *

Lieutenant Daniels didn't have any miracles. Not unless you consider putting a wire on me a miracle.

I considered it suicide.

Arran was torn. "He didn't search you last time and he admitted to murder. It could work."

"Petrov is a criminal, but he isn't stupid," I said. "The man read me like a book."

"Maybe you're just easy to read." Arran offered me another bagel.

I waved it aside. "I don't need food, my stomach is already feeling sick. I need a plan. But if I had my druthers, the plan would involve me staying alive rather than going out in a blaze of glory."

"You got something against the dead," the Colonel demanded.

"I assume there'll be a nice service when I'm killed in the line of duty, right?" I added.

"Don't get snarky. We'll figure something out."

"Why not just go along with Petrov," Oren suggested. "The cops are bound to catch him sooner or later. When they do, you'll be off the hook."

"We'll call that Plan A," I said.

Arran swallowed. When I'd turned down the bagel, he'd taken a bite of it himself. "I have a bad feeling I'm not going to like Plan A."

"You're going to hate it. Oren says I should just go along with Petrov until you guys catch him."

"Yeah, I hate it. What's Plan B."

"Easy." The Colonel made a halfhearted grab at the bagel, looking disappointed but not surprised when his hand went through the bread—and the table. "They didn't have bagels back when I was alive. Not here in Dallas, anyway. I'd powerfully like to taste one. Looks like a donut."

"They don't taste like donuts," I said. "They're only slightly sweet and they're a lot more solid."

The Colonel sighed. "I can barely remember sweet."

I grabbed my napkin and wiped my eyes. How had I never thought about that before? Ghosts didn't get to eat. I'd go crazy.

"Get used to it," Oren said. "You spend longer dead than you do alive."

"Give me one of those bagels after all," I told Arran. "I'm eating it for the Colonel."

Arran raised an eyebrow. "Bet he'll be grateful."

"Just do it. In the meantime, he says he has a Plan B. Let's hear it, Colonel."

"Kill him."

"I beg your pardon."

"According to young Oren here, your Petrov already has a nice line along his neck. Sort of like the lines on a clothing pattern in a book. Take a knife and cut along the line, but make sure you cut deeper than whoever did it the first time. I'd do it myself, but I'm not much good with knives any more."

"Plan B is that we murder Petrov," I reported to Arran.

My timing was not great. He dropped the bagel he was carrying. I was impressed that he managed to catch it before it hit the floor. With that kind of speed, Arran actually might be able to get the drop on Petrov and his guards.

"That doesn't sound—"

"Yeah. So far I'm still leaning toward Plan A."

Arran grabbed a knife and sliced the bagel, his sharp blade cutting through the firm cooked dough as if it were barely there. Yes, Arran had the strength to kill.

He didn't owe me anything, but I suspected he would kill if he concluded it was the only alternative.

Even if I could morally justify murdering Petrov, asking Arran to do it had some real problems. The most basic was that he'd probably confess to the police and ask for a lethal injection once he'd finished with Petrov. There was no way I was going to have that on my conscience.

If murdering Petrov was the answer, I'd manage it myself. Somehow. I wasn't sure I could kill just to save my own life, but I didn't doubt I could to save Little Jack.

"Let's go back to something rational. Like hiding," Arran suggested.

"I've already told you—"

"I know about the blackmail threats. Your brother and sister-in-law make plenty of money. Maybe it's time for them to take a vacation somewhere far away. In the meantime, I'll get together with some cops I know in Fort Worth and we'll track Petrov down. Once he's locked in jail, everything should come back to normal. Hell, you can even use the ghosts to help us find the evidence we need to lock him up."

"I don't want to use the ghosts any more. It makes me feel dirty."

"Don't worry about us," Oren said. "We can take care of ourselves."

"Not like there's anything you can do to us if we don't want you to," the colonel agreed. "We got over that fear of death thing when we died."

"I'm trying to do what's right here."

"Screw what's right," Oren said. "We're going to take down that Petrov guy and you're going to help us."

That's when my phone rang.

In a macabre moment, I'd picked the jingle about the worms crawling in and out as my ringtone.

The joke was on me, though, when I checked who was calling. It was Petrov.

Chapter 18

"We can get together tonight. Seven o'clock," Petrov said the instant I identified myself. "There's someone I need looking into."

"I'm still thinking."

His grunt sounded like someone who'd taken a punch to the gut. I decided it was his idea of a laugh. "Think as long as you wish, but be ready when my driver swings by. You can wait for him at County Records. I wouldn't want to disturb Detective Dane's peace and quiet."

He knew where I was. Running looked to be an impossible task.

"If I'm there I'm there. If I'm not, it means I had something better to do."

"Charming. But your bravado won't help, and it just might get someone hurt."

"I don't know what you—"

"Have you heard from your family lately. How is the charming Small Jack doing?"

My heart gave a big squeeze, then faltered. "You bastard."

"Not at all. I'm a true believer in family."

Petrov paused a moment to let me consider his words, or maybe to grovel.

I didn't grovel but that was mostly because I was still listening to hear whether my heart was going to start beating again.

Eventually it did, raggedly, but hard. If anything happened to Little Jack, though, I knew I'd wished my heart had stayed stopped. I believed in family too, but obviously not in the same way Petrov did—not to use them to hurt people or get an angle on them.

Finally Petrov continued. "Oh, I'd better get off the phone. I think you're about to get very busy."

The ringtone started the second I punched the *End* button. I was going to have to change that tone but offhand, the only thing that came to my mind was a funeral march.

"Hello."

"Annie, it's Lauren. I just got the strangest call from Little Jack's day care. They said that you'd dropped by and checked him out. I know we gave you permission in that form, but I didn't think you'd do it without telling us. What's going on?"

Oh-shit-oh-shit-oh-shit. "Lauren, I didn't do anything, I swear. But I have a really bad idea I know what's going on and it has to do with that guy who tried to kill me the other day. Let me see what I can find out."

"Do that. In the meantime, I'm getting the cops."

Lauren had talked loudly enough that everyone in Arran's house had heard both sides of the conversation.

"Tell Petrov you'll go along with whatever he wants," Arran said. "Our first priority has to be getting Little Jack to safety."

I nodded. I didn't have any choice.

I pushed my phone's back button to pull up the number Petrov had called from when something buzzed.

I stared at the phone trying to figure out what I'd done wrong until Arran walked over and pressed a button on a little machine near his couch. "Yeah?"

A voice crackled over the machine. It was an intercom, of course.

"We've got a kid down here. He says he's looking for his aunt but he's got your apartment number. Do you know an Annie Neeter or a Jack Neeter?"

"Is he alone?"

"All by himself."

"I'll be down in a second. We've got a situation here so stay on duty. There'll be a cop by to pick up the surveillance tapes and there'd better not be any problems."

I was heading down the hall before Arran finished talking.

He caught up to me at the elevator. "Sounds like he's okay, Annie."

"Of course he's okay. This isn't about hurting anyone, yet. Petrov is showing off. I wouldn't help him if he'd actually hurt Little Jack, but I'd do anything to keep my nephew safe. Anything."

Little Jack enjoyed being the center of attention.

By the time Lauren arrived from Plano, twenty cop cars sat in Arran's apartment parking lot, lights flashing and police radios squawking into the warm air.

A crowd of onlookers and the curious gathered to watch, giving the lot the feeling of a carnival.

It felt like I was the only person not having fun.

The first cops on the scene, not counting Arran, had brought a bag of chocolate-covered donuts, and Little Jack got busy stuffing his face, admiring the uniforms and guns, and feeling very important. The cops let him talk on their radios, headed to the neighborhood 7-11 to get him a carton of milk, and generally made a big deal about the brave kid.

Lauren arrived with the sound of sirens, screeching of tires, then the painful sounds of bending metal, breaking glass, and inflating airbags as she missed a turn and ploughed into one of the parked cop cars.

A pair of motorcycle cops followed behind her. Apparently they weren't just an escort because they were off their bikes with guns drawn before they noticed they'd pulled into a cop convention.

Arran headed toward the traffic cops and I tagged along.

"We clocked her at a hundred and twenty heading down 75," the cop with a mustache reported after Arran showed him his detective badge. "She ignored our efforts to pull her over."

"She's the mother of a kidnap victim. Cut her some slack."

"But—"

Knowing Arran wouldn't let the motorcycle cops shoot me, I ran to the door of Lauren's Mercedes and yanked it open.

"Where is my baby?" She was covered in white powder, her hair a mess, and her business suit completely ruined, but Lauren still looked good.

The ghost in the car with her, the same guy I'd noticed with her days before although he'd dressed himself in the meantime, looked pale even for a ghost. He couldn't be shaken up literally, but he sure looked like Lauren's driving had made him rethink his peeping Tom ways.

"I'm okay," he told me as if I cared. "Don't worry about me. I'm okay."

"Boy that's a relief." Then I tuned him out.

"Little Jack is fine," I told Lauren. "He's become quite the mascot with the cops. You probably managed to find the only cops in town who weren't already here."

Lauren waved her hand. "I'll worry about a ticket when I'm not worried about my baby."

"I'm not a baby."

Little Jack rode on the shoulders of an aging sergeant, both of their hands, and Little Jack's face were smeared with chocolate. Both carried half-eaten chocolate éclairs. The sergeant also a cup of steaming 7-11 coffee and Little Jack a matching cup filled with milk.

I suspected Little Jack might be angling for a police outfit soon, but the resemblance stopped there. His Triceratops t-shirt read 'vegetarians rule,' while the sergeant's jacket read 'SWAT.'

Little Jack might not be a baby, but he sure was a cute kid.

"Of course you're not a baby." Lauren looked around before her eyes settled on me.

"All right, Annie. Let's have it. What the hell have you done and how come you had to involve us?"

She was right to be mad. I should have called her as soon as the Arlington Police had let me go. But I'd never imagined Petrov would do anything before I'd gotten back to him with an answer. I'd assumed we had time to make our plans.

I'd assumed Petrov was so stupid he'd just let us get away from him.

I told her everything.

Lauren interrupted a couple of times with questions, keeping me on track and making sure I didn't leave anything out—the woman was a lawyer, after all. But mostly, she just listened.

When I'd finished, she pursed her lips together and blew a long whistle. "This is all *my* fault. I made Jack dig up those papers for your detective. I was your attorney and I let you persuade him about your psychosis. If I'd just told you to say 'no comment,' none of this would have happened."

"That's ridiculous. First you did tell me to say no comment. And second, nobody could have guessed anyone—"

"Of course someone could have guessed. We're not talking about little ghost-tricks or checking out girls in their underwear here. Do you know how much money is spent on corporate espionage every year? Billions. Not to mention what the government spends spying on people. But most of that money is wasted because people can't get access to the boardroom, to the inner workings of their opponents. Your ghosts get around that. You and your ghosts are probably the most dangerous weapon since the atom bomb. And I was the one who put you in the firing line, like some idiot blabbing about the Manhattan Project back in World War II."

It was nice of her to try and take responsibility, but I knew better. "I ignored your advice to stay quiet because I was too caught up in not looking like a crazy-girl in front of a guy who's too gorgeous to live. But it's too late to do anything about our mistakes or argue about who was dumber. We've got to figure out how to stay safe. I think you and Jack and Little Jack need to get away somewhere where you'll be out of Petrov's reach while I try to work this out."

"So you can take all the responsibility? I don't think so."

"Petrov will use the three of you to control me, Lauren. If you get away, I'll have that much more freedom. There's nothing you can do to help me if you stay."

She stared at me for a moment, then nodded. "I hate to leave you exposed like that, but I guess you have a point. I'm due some vacation and Jack never goes anywhere unless I make him. But we can't stay gone forever. And it doesn't sound like you've got a plan that will make next week be different from this week."

"I'm full of plans. Just all of them suck."

"Well, here's the start of one. Whatever you do, make sure you keep Arran in the loop. Heading off yesterday without telling him was dumb.

Besides, he's 'too gorgeous to live,' remember. Here's something I shouldn't have to tell you but I think I do—guys aren't good at subtle. If you want one, you've got to hunt him down."

"There's no way Arran—"

She grabbed me and kissed me on the cheek. "Don't sell yourself short, kiddo. Between you, your sexy detective, and the billion or so ghosts you talk to, you'll figure out something."

"He's not my detective."

Lauren was on her feet and heading toward her son but she turned back to me.

"You know something, Annie. That's part of the problem, and part of what I was just talking about. He's not yours—yet. Don't just piss around moaning about that, do something about it. I'm not being psychic here, just smart. But one way or the other, I don't think you're coming out of this without his help. Not alive, anyway."

* * * *

It took Lauren less than a minute to con one of the cops into driving her and Little Jack back up to Plano—her own car being undrivable after its run-in with a police cruiser. I didn't know whether it was checking out her sexy, if rumpled, body or learning about Little Jack's abduction, but the motorcycle cops dropped any mention of a ticket and instead tried to persuade her to ride with them.

Once Lauren and the kid were gone, the police evaporated like spit on charcoal, leaving me with *my detective*.

Arran cleared his throat. "So it's back to Plan A."

"Way to be romantic," the Colonel said. "Come on, Detective, you've got a lady who's shaken up, and her sister-in-law gave you the perfect setup. You could have scored if you'd played your dominoes right."

I glanced at my watch. The day had gotten away from me and it was two in the afternoon. Which meant I had five hours before Petrov had me picked up at county records.

I thought about what Lauren had said. Sure, it was easy for someone who looked like her to grab a guy and just tell him what she wanted him to do. For me, it had never been that easy.

"Can I ask you a question, Detective?"

"That sounds serious."

"Would you tell me what do you think about me?"

"Oh. It is serious." He considered me for a moment. "Besides the obvious, as in, you're cute, fun, and a little weird."

"Just a little?"

He grinned at me. "I'm a cop. I've seen people a lot weirder than you

144

are."

"Yeah, but—"

"And that's not even counting the criminals."

I wanted to ask him whether we could have a relationship, but that wouldn't be fair. Even if he'd been willing, a huge stretch, hooking up would be the dumbest thing I could do. I'd already decided I needed to move away from Dallas, leave him and my whole life behind—assuming I managed to get out from under Petrov's claws. I couldn't ask Arran for commitments I wasn't willing to make myself. But I wanted something.

I returned to the first things he'd said.

"Does cute and fun add up to enough to go to bed with?"

Arran's face froze. "Seems to me you were the one who pulled back last time we were heading that direction. You didn't want to put on a display for your friends."

"Just because I can see them doesn't mean they're my friends." I heard my pitch and volume both rising, but Arran had tripped something and I couldn't figure out how to stop my mouth from keeping on going. "My so-called friends are a bunch of perverts is what they are. And at least I do my best to get some privacy. Unlike some people. I can't believe you spend every night sleeping with two dead girls. And you think I'm weird. What's that about?"

He looked at me as if I'd gone crazy, which I guess I had. "I'm spending every night with two ghosts? You didn't mention that before."

"Tiffany and Cassandra. And don't tell me you don't hear them in your dreams. I saw your stiffie when you woke up. I know what—"

"Tiffany and Cassandra, huh? And they're perverts?"

I forced myself to be fair. The two weren't doing anything I didn't want to do myself. "They're actually not so bad, really. Not like the ghosts who ride around naked with Lauren."

"And you're jealous of those two?" The corners of his mouth twitched, as if he were that close to laughing but fighting it down.

"I just think it's disgusting, that's all."

"Hey." I hadn't seen Tiffany, but she'd been listening. "What's disgusting about putting a man and a woman together? Sounds natural to me."

"First of all, you aren't a woman, you're a ghost. Second, natural is one girl and one guy, not that multiples. And third, if *I* ever did anything with him, he'd be a willing participant. What you do to him is closer to rape than love."

"Whoa," Arran said. "I get the idea we aren't having a private conversation any more."

"No wonder they promoted you to detective, the way you pick up on these clues. And I'm sorry I asked about the physical thing. Going to bed with me would be a mistake. I don't think you've got room for me in your bed."

"I don't think it would be a mistake at all." He grasped my hand and tugged me back into his building.

The security guard winked at us as Arran led me through the doors and into the elevator.

To my surprise, Oren guarded the elevator door and gestured away the ghosts who tried to follow. To my even bigger surprise, considering he couldn't touch them any more than I could, they actually listened to him and didn't just stream right through his waving arms.

Once the elevator door closed, we were blessedly alone.

Worry descended on me like a lead-impregnated sheet. "I can't promise anything."

"I haven't asked for anything," Arran said.

"What we have is just a physical attraction. I mean, you're a sexy guy and a cop and all. And I've kept you busy, so you couldn't go out with your usual girlfriends or however you relieve your stress. I'd certainly understand if—"

"You're probably right."

"So, maybe we could just forget we ever had this conversation."

"We're not having a conversation." His fist rammed the elevator's Stop button just as his lips descended on mine.

Damn, that man could kiss.

I couldn't get enough. I opened my mouth to his kiss and yanked at his shirt, pulling it out of his pants so I could slide my hands under it, touch his skin.

He moaned when I brushed my palms against his nipples, but he didn't move quickly enough for me.

I pressed my thigh between his legs, feeling the hardness as his dick swelled, then pulled my hands out from under his shirt and grabbed my own top, yanking it open to give him access to my boobs.

He groaned, then lowered his mouth to kiss one breast through the thin fabric of my bra.

"Finally, we're somewhere where nobody can watch us," I breathed —when I could get the words out through the little moans of pleasure that popped out when he did something clever with his fingers and my bra fell open, spilling my breasts into his warm hands.

"Oh, shit."

"Let me guess. You don't have a condom?"

He pressed his hands to my breasts. "Worse. The elevator has a security camera."

I shrieked and covered my tits with my hands. "Those perverts are watching us? We're the stars of their local porn channel? No wonder the security guard winked at you. Do you put on a show for him with all the girls you bring home?"

"You aren't being fair."

"Guess what, I don't want to be fair. Is it completely unreasonable to want to have sex with just me and one guy, without the whole world watching and giving me a critique? I'm self-conscious enough about my tiny tits without knowing that they're being critiqued by a bunch of peanut-munching sports fans."

"Ghosts eat—"

"You're deliberately missing the point." I pulled my top back on, buttoning it so quickly I ended all wompy jawed, like a kid still learning to dress himself.

"Actually, I think you're over-reacting. Watch." He draped his jacket over the camera. "Now, where were we?"

He didn't give me time to think about an answer before he kissed me again.

The taste of his lips against mine made my knees all wobbly, like Jell-o melting on a hot summer evening.

I didn't care whether Arran had sex in his elevator with ten different girls every day. All that mattered was that I be next.

"Okay, Arran." I took advantage of a rare moment when my brain was working and when he trailed his lips away from mine to nibble on the side of my neck. "The camera's taken care of. Now, did you say you had a condom, or didn't you?"

He did.

⁕ ⁕ ⁕ ⁕

We didn't make any friends in Arran's apartment building that day. Shutting off the elevator for two whole hours is simply good form, and ignoring the buzzer and calls on Arran's cell are worse.

I didn't care, though. For the first time in my life, sex was about getting so drunk I didn't mind being watched.

Arran showed me whole new sides to the ancient activity.

I felt deliciously sore, limp as overcooked macaroni, and even sexy when Arran finally released the Stop button and we ascended to his floor.

I wasn't dumb. I realized that leaving Dallas and starting a new life would be even harder now that I'd know what I was missing, but I wouldn't have traded the experience for a winning lottery number.

A whole phalanx of ghosts cheered as the two of us finally emerged from the elevator. "About time you two got it on," Oren said.

Only Cassandra and Tiffany looked glum, but Cassandra brightened up when she saw me come dragging out of the elevator like something a cat coughed up. "Guess you won't call us perverts any more. Now that you've lined up for the same thing."

"Yeah, whatever."

"The audience is back?" Arran asked.

I looked over the crowd. There had to be fifty ghosts in the hallway between the elevator and Arran's door. "You *really* don't want to know."

He drew me close, which reminded me that I'd somehow lost my bra in the excitement. My unleashed breasts brushed against his muscular side, and lingering memories of orgasm sent their little surges through my entire body.

"Back off, guys," he said.

The fierceness in his voice surprised me, frightened me in a way. I'd known making love with him would change our relationship, but I hadn't really thought about how it would do so, hadn't even considered that he too would be changed.

"They're just ghosts. They do what they do."

"People have to take responsibility for their actions."

That was a nice-enough attitude for a cop in dealing with criminals. But ghosts didn't have to take responsibility for their action. First, who was going to make them take responsibility? And second, as far as most of the world was concerned, they didn't really take action. They can't really touch objects, move things, make sound, anything. It was just me, and anyone else gifted or afflicted with my abilities, who even knew they were there. The old saw about a tree falling in the forest applied.

"You aren't going to get all protective of me, are you?"

He grasped my jaw, turning my face until I met his eyes. "You're being blackmailed by a goon and you've been shot at twice. You're damned right I'm protective."

Acting without thinking things through had bitten me in the butt again. I couldn't afford to have Arran feeling protective, not when I intended to go to work for Petrov.

"Don't worry about me."

"The Hell I won't." His grip tightened on my jaw—not quite painfully, but hard enough that I sensed his strength, his power, and the control he used to restrain that power.

"Come on, honey. I've got to get ready for dinner with Petrov."

He dropped his hand to his side. "I'll be watching you, and looking for a way to get you free of him."

I forced out something like a laugh. "I think that'll only happen when either he, or I, becomes a ghost. And you're a cop, not a vindictive killer."

"When he's in jail, he'll have too much on his mind to worry about you."

I tugged him down the hall, stripped his keys from his hand, and opened the door to his apartment. "He's not in jail and he's not going to jail. You know he'll hurt Little Jack if anything happens to him, and he could make that happen even if you arrested him and put him in solitary confinement. Besides, I already told you he's planted evidence to connect you with Ritchie. If he goes to jail, you just might end up there with him."

"Do you think I give a damn what happens to me?" Arran's glare actually sent a couple of ghosts reeling backwards, which is saying something since they were past being hurt by anything he could do.

"I think you should."

"Well tough crap. I didn't become a cop because I wanted to be safe: I'm a cop to do the right thing.

I would have preferred that our afterglow last longer, but I realized it was better this way. If he was mad at me, he would be less likely to do really stupid things to *help* me. It would also hurt him less when I disappeared from his life.

Not that Arran had much to worry about. Dallas is like most big cities: too many single women chasing too few single (and straight) guys. Men who looked like him only went to bed alone because they were too lazy to ask for company.

Since I hadn't been back home, I was still wearing the same clothes I'd worn to work the previous day. I stank of sweat, fear, and sex. And since I hadn't managed to find my bra, I was also indecent.

"We need a plan," Arran offered, as if I hadn't just done my best to piss him off. "I'll follow Petrov when he takes you to dinner and make sure you're safe."

I got prickles on my arms and back, the kind my grandmother used to say came when someone was walking on your grave. "That's a plan? It sounds like going out of our way to get my nephew killed."

"Petrov's not going to hurt Little Jack just because I'm protecting you."

I poked a finger against his chest. "And if you're wrong, no skin off your nose, right? He isn't your nephew, after all. I've got a little more invested in this than you do. Now, do you want to take me home, or should I take the train?"

Going home was the last thing on my mind, especially after I'd touched him, but I was trying to develop a good mad so I wouldn't have to feel guilty about leaving him. Still, it would have been nice if he didn't make it so easy sometimes.

"I'll take you to your place." He practically growled the words at me. "Why don't you pick up some extra clothes while you're there? I've got an empty closet you can use in my spare bedr—in the ghost gallery. Or I could clear out half of the master bedroom closet if you don't mind sharing."

That suggestion hit me out of the blue, especially given his tone of voice. "What are you talking about?"

He looked at me like I'd grown little purple horns. "We just experienced some of the most mind-blowing sex I can imagine, and you act surprised that we're going to keep doing it. Just because you're in trouble with Petrov doesn't mean we have to screw up our private lives." He grinned. "Maybe *screw* is not exactly the right word choice, though."

He wanted more? My body shivered at the thought and my anger trickled away like a run-down battery. Still, my mind knew better. I was teetering at the edge of an abyss. If I moved in with Arran, even for a little while, like until I figured out a way to keep my family safe, I'd become dependent on him. Even if as I didn't depend on him too much, leaving him would hurt. I could survive the pain, though—I'd survived being drummed out of my own parents' house when I'd turned eighteen. But I wouldn't survive undamaged. Leaving him after committing to him, moving in with him, sharing mind-boggling sex with him over and over would re-open every wound I'd suffered. Leaving him after letting myself pretend I could have a normal life, a boy-girl sex life, would feel like Prometheus's eagle ripping out my guts. Pretending this was something more than an afternoon delight would be like voluntarily stepping off the cliff into the Grand Canyon.

"I'll call you," I lied.

"Oh, no." He ran his calloused down my back, lightly brushing his knuckles on the knobs of my spine. "You're afraid, trying to run away. I'm not going to let you just pretend nothing happened. You already have shadows, Oren and Harry and the Colonel. From now on, think of me as one of the ghosts, because wherever you go, I'm going to be watching."

I stepped away from his distracting hand. "Sounds like you've become a stalker. Do I need to get a court protective order?"

"You could try. I'm a cop. You're a criminal. I don't think even your beautiful sister-in-law could bat her eyes and flash her cleavage enough to persuade a judge to issue one."

"Criminal? I'm not—"

"You're planning on helping Petrov, aren't you? He'll use you to break the law, maybe even kill people. If you knowingly help a criminal break the law, you've broken the law, too. Lawyers call it, 'accessory before the fact.' Us cops call it criminal conspiracy. Either way, you're legally responsible for anything he does with the information you give him."

I'd been fighting tears for hours, ever since Petrov's threatening call. They came spilling out now, in big fat pearls. "That isn't fair. You're blackmailing me, just like Petrov."

"If that's what it takes to keep you safe."

I blew my nose on my shirt. I was going to throw that thing away, anyway after the way Arran had twisted it around me to get access to my body parts. "Just take me home, will you? Or are you going to make me take the train after all, with my tits flopping around and me stinking of sex with you."

He inhaled deeply. "Oh, no. I'm the jealous sort. I'll keep *that* experience to myself. Well, myself and a few thousand ghosts."

Chapter 19

My ringtone played the Beatles *Fool on the Hill* and I jumped about three feet into the air.

"It's just Petrov," Oren said. "He told you he'd call."

We were sitting in Sam Bert's office at the county records building—me, Oren, the Colonel, and Sam. Arran had gone off somewhere. I tried to convince myself he'd given up on his crazy idea to stalk me, but I wasn't sure.

"If that's him, then just go," Sam suggested. "I've already kept this place open an extra couple hours so you won't get cold. You think I don't have anything better to do than hang around keeping you company. Not that I'm not happy to help out with a regular researcher like you."

Oh, please.

I glanced at my phone. Sure enough, Petrov's name was up on the display, so I switched it on.

"Hello."

"Yes. I'm outside."

I glanced at my watch. It said two minutes after seven. I suspected I was a little fast, though, and that Petrov was exactly on time.

"I'll be there in a second." I hung up the phone and turned back to Sam. "I do appreciate you letting me stay, even though I know Petrov is cutting you some slack on the interest you owe him."

"Really, Annie. I have no idea what you're talking about."

"Yeah, right." Sam thought I was wearing a wire. Which wasn't a bad guess since Arran's boss had stopped by my house and tried to persuade me to wear one—until Arran had gotten between us and told the Lieutenant where he could shove his bug.

I wished that Arran would be a consistent jerk, so I could persuade myself he was just my usual bad taste in men. But every time I started to believe that, he'd do something like protect me from Lieutenant Daniels and I'd get all confused.

I gathered up my purse and went out to meet my new boss, holding the door to the records office open for Oren and the Colonel.

I walked slower than I normally did. I was in no hurry and wasn't looking forward to magic moments.

Petrov sat in the back of a Lincoln Town Car. His driver was the same guy who'd taken me halfway home the previous evening, before we'd been stopped by the police.

The driver grinned at me and waved as I approached the car. Petrov said nothing.

By the time I got to the car, the driver was out and holding my door open.

I decided to respond to the friendly gesture. "They didn't keep you in jail?"

"What for? I hadn't done anything other than give you a lift."

"Like they always act completely rationally."

He laughed. "Doesn't hurt to have a decent lawyer. I'm Jarred Sanchez, by the way."

"Call me—"

"Mr. Sanchez." Petrov's deep voice interrupted our get-acquainted.

"Sorry, Boss." Sanchez gestured for me to climb in next to Petrov.

Petrov's tone had been conversational, but Sanchez definitely responded in a hurry. I wondered what he would do if Petrov sounded mad. A moment's reflection persuaded me I didn't want to find out.

"I'm sorry I got your driver in trouble last night, Mr. Petrov. I told the cops he was just taking me home." It didn't hurt to be civil.

"Sit. Let's go."

I ended up sharing the back seat with Petrov, Oren, the Colonel, and Richie Stone.

More ghosts crowded into the front seat. Oren had come up with some story about how they'd get help if anything bad happened to me. I figured they were like racecar fans, waiting to see the crash-and-burn.

After closing the door behind me, Jarrod climbed back into the driver's seat and we pulled away from the curb, gliding into downtown traffic.

"So, you're taking me to dinner? Do we do a movie afterwards, or would that be—"

Petrov interrupted me. "It is not true that Russians lack senses of humor."

"Huh?"

"It is too true," Ritchie's ghost said. "If you look at things right, me shooting up your apartment and you spraying me with that pepper stuff was pretty funny. Petrov didn't laugh once."

"It's just that our senses of humor have a little sophistication," Petrov continued as if Ritchie hadn't interrupted. "Since yours doesn't, perhaps you could keep it to yourself."

"Oooh," Oren said. "That was a nasty one."

"I'm sorry," I said to Petrov, ignoring the ghosts. "I've never been blackmailed into becoming a criminal before. I didn't know exactly how I'm supposed to treat this."

"Like a job, Ms. Neeter. Like a job."

"I know a ghost who was with Al Capone during prohibition," Oren said. "Maybe he could help out. Gangsters really did talk like you see them in the movies, 'cept there was always a lot more swearing than those old movies showed."

"I don't think that's necessary."

Petrov clenched his fists. "I hope and assume you're talking to your invisible friends."

Actually, I was pretty sure he was assuming I was blowing him off. "If it's a job, just tell me what you want me to do."

Petrov nodded. He could deal with giving orders.

"Our reservations are for eight o'clock. We'll be dining at Sofia, have you eaten there?"

Sofia was something of a rage lately, a Bulgarian restaurant, of all things. Before it had set up, I'd never heard of Bulgarian food. With its prices, I hadn't figured on doing more than hearing about it.

"No."

"It will work for our purposes. Each booth is semiprivate. No one will notice you talking to yourself."

"What, exactly, are our purposes?"

"A simple matter. One of my, shall we say, competitors, will be dining with a starting player for the—he named a professional basketball team in town for a series against the Mavericks. This type of negotiation can result in dramatic losses for the honest gambler. I'd very much like to know what he's offering and what the player promises."

"You're kidding. I mean, with the money basketball players make these days, surely they don't have to take payoffs from gamblers."

"Sometimes it's money, sometimes it's other things. Consider yourself, Ms. Neeter."

He had a point since I was working for a professional gambler. Although I hadn't persuaded my bosses that a title researcher is worth as much as a starting NBA basketball player, either.

Sanchez kept on the surface streets, then drove around the block a few times when he got to Turtle Creek, the upscale location of Sofia's.

At exactly seven, he pulled up to the ornate doors of the restaurant and jumped out to open his boss's door. The restaurant's maitre 'd hurried over to greet my boss and I was left playing with the handle of my own door—which didn't work.

Only after Petrov had been greeted did Sanchez bother to swing around and open my door.

Petrov took me by the arm. Although his grip was light, I was

154

surprised at how strong he was. He might hire gunmen like Ritchie Stone to do his dirty work, but all of a sudden I had the feeling that Petrov had done dirty work in his day, and would be willing to pitch in if it ever became necessary again.

Petrov and I were ushered to a private room almost as big as my apartment. A bottle of some fancy vodka, still steaming with cold from the freezer, was ceremoniously placed in the room, its seal cracked, then Petrov ordered for both of us and seated himself.

The Maitre 'd, finally noticing me, hurried around to help me with my chair but I've never gotten that. What is the deal about women supposedly being incompetent to sit down by themselves? Then again, what was with not being able to order for myself? Did Petrov think I couldn't read? I snagged a menu before the Maitre 'd could leave.

Sure enough, I couldn't read it. It was written in those funny Cyrillic characters.

"You have an English translation of this?"

"Trust me," Petrov said. "I'm sure you'll enjoy your meal."

"I'm a vegetarian."

His smile didn't fade. "Yes?"

"You knew that?"

"I know a great deal about you, Ms. Neeter."

That was creepy. "Okay, so you ordered me something vegetarian. Now, can we get this job done? Because I'd just as soon get it over with."

Petrov poured himself a tumbler of vodka, tossed it back, then refilled his glass. Only after that did he look across the table. "We'll get it done when my colleague and his guest arrive. In the meantime, enjoy the evening."

That wasn't going to happen. I wondered if Arran had tracked us down, was somewhere nearby listening. Then I tried not to think about him. Petrov seemed way too capable of reading my mind. But trying not to think about Arran was like trying not to think about the elephant in the corner. The harder I tried, the worse I got.

Petrov reached into his pocket and passed over a battered bronze coin.

"What's this?"

"A Kopek for your thoughts."

I looked at the coin. The face of some Romanoff Emperor stared back at me. "Is this worth anything?"

"Are your thoughts?"

Despite everything, I couldn't help smiling. "Not much."

"Likewise for the coin. You are thinking about your detective, no?"

Just for a second, I wanted to open up, tell someone about my worries. The man was that good, considering he was the cause of most of my worries.

"I'm your employee, Mr. Petrov. You get my time. My thoughts are off-limits."

His smile was the faintest upturn in his lips. Then he poured himself another glass of vodka.

A string of waiters arrived with a plate of antipasto, including cold asparagus, olives, and hunks of strong-smelling cheese, as well as some slices of meat.

Petrov went for the meat and I stuck with the asparagus, looking around to make sure no bovine ghosts were watching us.

The ghost of a pig wandered in, sniffed at the antipasto, and shook its head in disgust when it couldn't manage to eat. I wondered if this was a new ghost, or just a slow learner. I could have asked it, and I suspected it would hear me, but I didn't think I'd understand its answer any more than I'd understand a living pig.

Ritchie made shooing motions and eventually the pig wandered into one of the other rooms, carefully following one of the waiters through the door.

Our dinners, along with a bottle of wine that turned out to be just for me, arrived a bit later.

We hadn't done justice to the antipasto, and I started to tell the waiter to wrap it up in a to-go box, but Petrov waved that off. "They're here."

I looked around. "Any of you guys basketball fans?"

One of the waiters perked up.

I pointed to my Bluetooth.

"Sorry. Is there anything else, Mr. Petrov?"

Petrov studied the table. "Leave."

"Of course, Mr. Petrov."

"So, any answers?"

Ritchie raised his hand.

"You willing to do this, or are you going to backstab me to get your revenge?"

"Are you kidding? Anything happens to you, I've got nobody to talk to. These other ghosts are mostly too snooty."

"I'll go along, watch over him," the Colonel said. "I don't understand basketball, but I've known plenty of losers like Ritchie Stone here."

Like that, it was game time.

* * * *

The Colonel and a ghost named Barbara, who'd died in the seventies and still had that Farah Fawcett wing-hair from the old TV show, ran relays while Ritchie sat down right between the gambler and the basketball star, picking up on every nuance.

They went at it for the better part of an hour. Between polishing off a couple of bottles of Cristal and doing more than a few lines of cocaine, they agreed that the star would ensure that his team won by no more than four points. Since the spread was ten, there was a huge potential for making some gambling bucks.

The deal done, the gambler got on the phone with his associates, assuring them the game was a lock and to bet everything on the Mavericks to cover the point spread.

"Betting against the Mavericks on a big game is easy," Ritchie said. He'd come back to report on the conclusions directly. "They can be depended on to win the easy ones and to fold under pressure. So, a lot of people are going to take a bath on this."

"They're not that bad."

"I lost a hundred bucks on them last year."

That seemed enough answer for him. He insisted on going back, since the gambler had brought in a quartette of professional women, in all different sizes, colors, and probably religious attitude.

I told him I didn't want to hear any of the details.

"Not even whether basketball players are, uh, proportionate?"

"Don't try using big words, Ritchie. And I definitely don't need dong dimensions."

"Your loss." He vanished through the wall. It hadn't taken him long to get handle on the whole ghost thing.

I looked at the table. I'd made a dent in my salad, and Petrov had nearly finished his vodka. Good thing he wasn't driving.

"I think our business is done," I said. "That's what you needed to know, right? So, what are you going to do about it?"

He picked up a skewer of lamb and gnawed on it while I looked around. I was going to be sick if a baby sheep ghost wandered through looking for his legs. Fortunately, that didn't happen.

Petrov swallowed. "What do you think I should do, Ms. Neeter?"

"I guess you'll cut the spread you offer. Maybe even put some bets on the other side. Since you know what they know, they won't have you at a disadvantage."

"I asked what you thought I *should* do, not what you thought I would do. But unfortunately, you are mistaken. I can't change my point spread because the gamblers I deal with all watch the spreads set in Vegas. If I try something different, I lose business and trust."

I shrugged. "You pick spreads so the money is half and half, right. So, who cares? You still get your cut. If these guys put enough money on the game, Vegas will change the odds."

"They won't bet in Las Vegas. They'll bet with me, and men like me, guys who won't report the bets, who take the spreads rather than making them."

"Can you refuse to take their bets?"

He shook his head. "Not unless you have ghosts enough to follow every call his contacts made."

I didn't have that kind of ghostpower. "Okay, I give up."

"No." He shook his head. "Tell me what you think I should do."

Like he was going to take my advice. I didn't know what this was about, but I decided I'd humor him.

"I guess I'd tell the police. Shaving points has got to be against some law."

Petrov poured a refill on my wine. "Exactly. It has to be against the law somehow."

"But we don't have any kind of case. Nobody is going to listen to my evidence, considering it came from a ghost."

"Not nobody."

Call me slow. I finally caught on. "You want me to talk to Arran about it?"

"Detective Dane has reason to trust your judgment. It would be a simple matter for him to call the NBA and let them know he learned of possible point shaving through one of his confidential informants. Considering your relationship, I believe confidential is an appropriate term, no?"

Arran and I had gone to bed together once. I certainly hadn't blogged about it or anything. So, how the devil did Petrov know we were intimate? It wasn't fair, especially since the odds of us being intimate again didn't seem great.

"Why would that be good for you?"

"Although it may not be able to prove a crime, the league will suspend the player. He won't be able to shave points."

"But they'll be missing one of their stars."

"They have others. He was willing to make this deal because he's in the final year of his contract and he knows it isn't going to be renewed."

"So, you're being a good citizen is all? Somehow I have trouble believing this."

Petrov poured the last of his vodka into the tumbler. "I don't like to be cheated, Ms. Neeter. And these men were planning to cheat me. I could send leg-breakers to punish them, but I think losing their money on a sure thing would hurt them even more."

"Okay, deal. If I see Arran, I'll tell him."

"I'm quite certain you will see him."

Something in his tone made the hairs on the back of my neck stand straight out. Petrov was alive, but sometimes his eyes and his voice made him sound even deader than the ghosts.

* * * *

"I couldn't get inside that restaurant, it was like a fortress. What the heck went on in there?"

Arran was waiting inside my apartment when Petrov and Sanchez dropped me off.

I told him and he shook his head. "We can't use this."

"Why not?"

"Don't you want to take Petrov down?"

"I want him to vanish from the face of the earth. Letting him lose a few dollars to cheaters would just make him mad. I don't want him mad at me, Arran. Not until I'm ready to disappear myself. Not until I've figured out a way to keep my family safe. My family and you."

"I can—"

"I heard it already. Sure you can take care of yourself. Petrov is a big enough man that he's willing to ask for help when someone has a talent he can use, but you're too macho, too filled with testosterone, is that right?"

"That's not what I was going to say."

"Really?"

He glared at me. "Okay, maybe it is what I was going to say. But just going along with a criminal like Petrov seems wrong."

I didn't like the Russian any more than he did. Still, although Petrov might be breaking the law by taking bets, he wasn't the one trying to shave points. He intended to make his profit more or less legitimately. In this particular area, it seemed to me that his shade of gray was a bit lighter than the others.

"We'll take Petrov down when we can, but letting gamblers get away with point shaving can't be right. Or are you such a big Maverick fan you'd take a win over the spread even if you knew it came dishonestly."

"I'm not that big a fan."

"So make the call. Tell whoever in the NBA is responsible for this kind of thing that one of your confidential informants says their player is getting paid off to throw a game."

It was a lot more complicated than that. Arran had to run things up the pole at police headquarters to see who'd salute, had to tell some lies about his sources, and had to head off for meetings, leaving me semi-alone.

"Maybe I should have told him in the morning," I said to Harry who was lounging on my sofa.

"You need someone to share your bed, just pull down some of that tin foil and I'm your man."

"I don't need anyone to share my bed that bad."

"Come on, babe. You know you can't take the Detective with you when you run. And you won't be able to take the aluminum-wrapped bedroom, either. You're going to have to get used to spending the night with horny ghosts. Why not start with me?"

With lines like that, I didn't have to wonder why Harry had never become the real estate tycoon he'd wanted to be.

Chapter 20

Petrov didn't call me for three days.

During those three days, I managed to keep Harry and the other ghosts out of my bed. Arran kept himself out of it. I wasn't blaming that last on the aluminum foil. He was pissed because I'd gone along with Petrov's plan, even though I'd told him it had really been my plan in the first place.

Thursday afternoon, Lauren called me from the airport. "I'm so excited. I've been wanting to take a vacation for the longest time, but our work has always kept us so busy. Thanks to you, we're going away to—"

"Don't tell me," I said.

"Someplace romantic and cool," Lauren said as if she'd been planning to say that all along."

"How should I let you know the coast is clear and you can come back?"

I could practically hear Lauren's shrug. "Leave a message on my cell."

"But if you've got your cell, they can track you."

"I'm not bringing the phone. I bought a couple of those disposable ones at Dollar General. I'll just phone into the service and pick up the messages. Trust me, Annie, I don't practice criminal law, but some of the tricks businesses play on each other ought to be illegal. And some of them are."

"Have fun," I said.

"Wish you could be coming with us."

"Yeah, right. Like you need me along for your second honeymoon."

"You're our family, Annie. Never forget that."

I wouldn't forget that. I would get choked up about it, though."

Two seconds after Lauren hung up, my phone rang again. It was Petrov.

"This is Annie."

"Ms. Neeter?"

"Hi, Mr. Petrov." I didn't have a clue what to tell him when he asked about my brother and his family vanishing. He'd catch me if I lied, but I suspected he wouldn't be happy if I told him the truth about getting them out of his reach.

"I have another little task for you."

"I've already saved you a ton of money. Why can't we call it even and just let each other get on with our lives?"

"Ah. Have you checked your mail, Ms. Neeter?"

"No." I'd never gotten much mail as a kid. As an adult, I tended to get bills and political ads. Those weren't the kind of content that made you rush down to check the box every few minutes."

"I neglected to pay you for your efforts the other night. You'll find a small remuneration in the mail."

"Fine. But I still want out."

"I understand you played poker while institutionalized."

"Maybe." That was a part of my life I didn't like to think about. My parents had given up on me, dumped me off at the state home. If my brother hadn't gotten active, had me declared his ward, I might be there still, drugged out and vegetable-like, but still seeing and talking to the ghosts.

"I have need of a poker player tonight."

"Why not play yourself? I'm sure you know the rules."

"I'll be by your apartment at seven. Try to be prompt."

"But—"

"And you might wish to suggest to Detective Dane that following us again would be, shall we say, unhealthy."

"Look. I've got plans. If you want me to work for you—"

"Your first job was not so bad, you see. You make Detective Dane look good and help keep sports honest. The next job is also not so bad. See you at seven."

* * * *

I worked from home that day and Arran swung by at noon and dragged me to the Mexican place downstairs for lunch.

He ordered for himself, letting me order what I wanted, which is pretty ordinary, if you think about it, but a welcome change from Petrov.

The waitress tried to talk us into fancy Margaritas, but Arran was working and I was keyed up about whatever Petrov had in mind.

Once she'd left, Arran dipped a chip in salsa, took a bite, and chewed, his jaw muscles clenching with every bite. Finally he swallowed. "I talked to my boss about putting you in a safe house, but no go. That doesn't mean you couldn't run. Your family is on their vacation now, so they're out of range."

"What about you, Arran? Are you going to run, too? I told you he planted something to frame you for Ritchie's death."

"You know I can't—"

"I'm not running until you're *all* safe. Meaning Lauren and Jack can come back to their normal lives and you're out of whatever frame Petrov put you in. Speaking of which, Petrov knew you followed us the other night. He told me to warn you not to do it tonight."

"He's a killer, Annie. I'm not going to let him take you away without doing my damnedest to keep you safe."

"There was a lot of 'I' in that, Arran. You may not believe it, but just because I'm a woman doesn't mean I'm not a grown-up. Maybe you should trust me to take care of myself."

I thought he'd get mad. Instead he laughed. "Listen to you, babe. You're not trying to keep yourself safe, you're trying to keep me safe. And I'm doing the same for you. This isn't a chauvinism thing—we've got each other's back."

"Well, listen to me. Petrov isn't going to hurt me as long as I'm a useful tool. And so far, I don't mind being used. The only people who got hurt by what I did the other night were some professional gamblers and a has-been basketball player who took bribes. I'm not saying Petrov is a good guy, but he's no worse than the others."

"And he killed Stone—"

"Who had it coming—"

"And he kidnapped and threatened Little Jack."

There was that. "Okay, you win. Petrov is scum and I'd be happier if he stepped in front of a truck. Until then, getting yourself hurt isn't going to help anyone. Now, will you stay away and stay safe."

Arran brushed his knuckles along my jaw line. "It's sort of flattering the way you worry about me."

It could have been a romantic moment. Hell, it should have been a romantic moment and it would have been if Oren and the Colonel hadn't decided they needed to ruin it by making kissy noises.

"Would you guys cut it out?"

Arran's face hardened. "They never leave you alone, do they?"

"Who else do they have to bother?" Still, the magic had drained out of the moment. Which was probably a good thing, although it sure didn't seem like it. I didn't need to get more hooked on Arran than I already was.

For the rest of lunch, we tiptoed around, talking about basketball and gambling, but not really mentioning Petrov. Talking about vacationing without mentioning why Lauren and Jack had to take their long-delayed trip. Talking about some of Arran's cases without asking whether they might relate to a larger criminal underworld. Talking about some of the weird things I'd turned up in my title searches without even thinking that I'd have to get a new job when I ran or someone could track me down through my occupation.

If it hadn't been for all the subtext, all of the things we were so careful not to even hint at, and if it hadn't been for the ever-present crowd of ghosts, each more or less dying for the chance to put in a word of wit, Arran and I would have been like some happily married couple going on about our lives.

When I realized that, it gave me something else not to talk about—or think about.

* * * *

Seven o'clock rolled around before I knew it.

As before, Petrov hadn't told me where we were going. I considered dressing up, in case he took me someplace fancy like Sofia's, but decided on the old standby—jeans and a top. If he wanted me in heels or something, he could damned well tell me in advance.

At seven, my phone rang and Petrov announced he was downstairs. I checked the mail on my way out and found an envelope with no return address. I opened it, and ten hundred dollar bills fluttered to the ground.

There was no note, nothing but the envelope and the money, but I knew what it was. Petrov had promised he'd take care of me if I joined his organization. This was the flip-side of his threats.

I stuffed the money in my pocket, then jammed the rest of the mail, mostly political ads, and the empty envelope back in the mailbox. I'd look at it later, when I could concentrate. Somehow, deciding who was going to be the next City Councilman from my district didn't seem as important as it had been a couple of weeks earlier.

Petrov gave my attire a stare. "You're making money now. You could spend some of it looking more professional."

I wondered what a professional ghost-talker wore. Maybe robes and a crystal pendant dangling in my, highly limited, cleavage.

I didn't think Petrov was interested in me sexually, but talking about my wardrobe was still a direction I didn't want to bother with. "So, going to let me know where we're going, or is it a secret?"

Petrov stared at me for a moment, looking through the ghosts as if they weren't even there.

Naturally Oren, the Colonel, and Chantal had crowded in. Chantal was mad she hadn't made it to the dinner because she was a basketball fan. Harry hadn't been around, probably because I'd worked from home. I figured I had things covered without him. Besides, wherever there are people, there are going to be ghosts handy. Since they can't do anything themselves, they spend their time watching people who can, even thought they know that almost none of those people would take their advice even if they could hear it.

"You did warn Detective Dane that his presence would not be helpful, didn't you?"

I nodded.

"Excellent. And is your phone turned off? The police have ways of tracking. The phone companies aren't supposed to provide this information without a warrant, but phone companies are easy to pressure."

I took out my phone and powered it down. I felt naked without it, partly because my phone was my connection to the world, but mostly because it was my excuse when I was caught talking to the ghosts.

"Let us go and visit Mr. Dumas," Petrov told Sanchez once my phone met with his approval.

"Got it." Sanchez angled through Dallas's rush hour traffic, using a fancy GPS system to avoid a congested spot on I-30, smashing through half a dozen ghosts standing around a wrecked semi-trailer, and generally heading east, away from downtown.

Ten minutes after Petrov had picked me up, we were on US-80, moving along at sixty miles an hour through fields sprouting what looked like a mix of young corn and suburbs.

Since he'd taken me to dinner the time before, and since he'd picked me up around dinner time, I'd assumed we were heading toward a restaurant.

When we left the city limits far behind, I got a bit nervous. I'd helped him with the basketball thing, but maybe I'd scared him, too. Not very many people like thinking about the ghosts always being around, always listening, always watching and vicariously participating in our lives. Maybe he'd had enough of me. East of Dallas is the region of the big pines and, eventually as Texas merges into Louisiana, swamps. There were plenty of places to leave a body out here, places where it would likely never be found. Petrov's insistence that Arran not follow, and on turning my phone off took a sinister feel.

The Russian didn't have much reason to hurt me, but I wasn't sure he'd need much of a reason.

I froze when he reached into a cardboard box on the seat between us —a box that had been obscured by a crowd of ghosts. Could he intend to murder me and dump my body in the country? Was he that angry that I'd called Arran?

Instead of a gun, he pulled out a long sharp-looking knife.

I froze, trying to remember everything I'd learned about knife defense. Unfortunately, they teach knife defense to brown belts in my Tae Kwon Do school and I had a lot to learn before I got that far.

"What are you—"

I shut up when he also pulled out a cutting board, a loaf of french bread, an assortment of cheeses, patés, and fruit, and a bottle of wine.

"We're having a picnic?" I finally retrieved my voice. Surely he wouldn't feed me if he planned on killing me any time soon. Of course, I was just assuming some of that food was for me.

"Tonight is likely to be a long night. You'll need your energy."

I loved the idea of needing my energy. Sort of like needing chocolate. Still, "what sort of long night?"

"I was impressed with your skills the other night. Your ghostly friends," here he actually managed to smile at Chantal, almost as if he really knew where she was, "seem to bend over backwards to be helpful. I realized that you could help me deal with a small problem."

A small problem to Petrov just might be a huge problem to me. "I'm not okay with helping you kill people."

He chuckled. He was wearing a business suit that looked off the rack, the white shirt tight against his belly. "You have an unfortunate misconception about our business, Ms. Neeter. Killing people is rarely necessary. In general, there are other ways to persuade them to help."

If he meant that to reassure me, it didn't do much of a job. "Just so you know."

"I understand." He dabbed a bit of paté on a slice of French bread, then popped the entire thing in his mouth and chewed, washing it down with a big swig of the expensive-looking French wine he'd brought. "So, Ms. Neeter, have you kept up your poker skills?"

I froze. "You never said how you learned I played poker?"

"From your experience with Mr. Stone, you know the consequences when I make a hiring mistake, Ms. Neeter. As a researcher yourself, surely you appreciate the need to investigate before plunging ahead.

I nodded.

"So. You once played a great deal of poker. Have you kept at it?"

I had played a lot of poker, but most of that in places I didn't remember. I'd been institutionalized for three years, after my parents had finally given up on me and before my brother had managed to have himself declared my guardian and baled me out. Those of us in the State School who were at least marginally functional, and some of the orderlies had an ongoing poker game we played for money, chocolate, and purloined drugs. Considering how little else there was to do in the loony bin, we'd often played ten or more hours at a stretch, seven days a week.

But I'd never told anyone about those days. And I'd never touched a card again once I'd gotten out. We inmates didn't have any money, so we'd had to offer other inducements as our ante. We girls had something the orderlies had wanted, and that was what we put on the table.

"I know the rules. Full house beats a flush beats a straight."

"That's like telling me a bishop moves on the diagonal and a rook moves on a file and thinking it means you know how to play chess."

"I don't like poker, don't like to remember it."

"But your invisible friends can help you with it, can't they?"

"You bet I could," Oren volunteered. "I used to play a bit myself. Back in the day, a man with a deck of cards always had friends in the boxcars."

"Thanks, Oren. But I still don't want to do this."

Petrov nodded. "Of all people, I understand the pain of old memories. Still, this is necessary and it is something you can feel comfortable with. Mr. Dumas thinks he stays far enough away that he can put his thumb in the eye of the organization. He is incorrect. If he agrees to my protection, he can stay safe and continue in the occupation he loves. If he does not, he will fall prey to someone else."

It sounded like rationalization to me, but Petrov clearly meant it. He also sounded like he knew about memories.

"You want me to play poker."

"I would be much obliged."

"And that's it? No blackmail, no secrets? Just a game of poker?"

His lips twisted up, exposing his stained teeth. "That's it. Oh, and win, of course. Just as you won those games in the State School."

"And then we're finished, I'm off the hook?"

He laughed. "Oh, no, Ms. Neeter. Our partnership is still at the beginning."

Somehow I'd known it wouldn't be that easy.

Sanchez made the driving look effortless, his hands relaxed on the wheel, his eyes seemingly the only things that moved as he scanned his mirrors, his GPS, and the road ahead. I suspected he was looking for more than possible traffic jams or tricky turns, but I decided I really would rather not know.

Instead, I looked out the car's darkened windows.

Although it was now well after seven, twilight lingered, shining down on the black earth of what had once been cotton land but now showed sprouts of corn. A few barefoot African-Americans walked through one of the fields and I looked closely to see if they were ghosts or living people. I always felt uncomfortable when I couldn't tell, and this time was no different.

"In the future, I wish you could tell me in advance what you require. Ghosts don't just apport, you know. And different ghosts have different skills. Oren played cards, but here in the south, lots of people never learned. It's pure luck that Oren accompanied me on this jaunt."

"I never learned cards myself," the Colonel said. "Preacher always said *spot-cards* were the tool of the devil."

"Preacher thinks everything is the tool of the devil," Chantal observed.

"Maybe because they are," the Colonel fired back.

I interrupted before my ghosts got into a full-fledged donnybrook. "At any rate, you're risking leaving me high and dry, here."

"I did not know that—how very interesting, Ms. Neeter."

I should have smiled and kept my mouth shut but I'm not much good at either of those. "I've got a job and a life," Mr. Petrov. "If you have something you want me to do, then tell me and let me do it." I gestured at the bread and wine in the back seat. "If you just want to make time with a female, you probably have hookers in your employ who'd be a lot better company."

"That's telling him," the Colonel gushed.

"I'm sure many have told you that your attitude is charming and amusing." Petrov narrowed his eyes. "You do know they were lying to you, don't you?"

"I hardly think—"

"Correct, Ms. Neeter. I have already noticed that you frequently speak without thinking. I have treated you as a professional, given you no reason to assume I had any sexual interest in you whatsoever. Indeed, I think you've already found that my financial remuneration can be equitable. Yet you insist on attacking me. It hardly seems like the basis of trust that business partners need in one another."

As if Petrov would ever treat me as a partner rather than another tool in his arsenal, like Ritchie or Sanchez.

"Okay, I was out of line there. I just worry."

"Worry can be healthy. Assuming the worst about me and my motivation is unlikely to be life-prolonging."

I mulled that around, unable to turn it into anything other than a threat. "Got it."

"You'll find tonight's poker game to be interesting, I'm certain."

Petrov proceeded to share psychological details on each of the men likely to be at the poker den. Dumas, the manager and owner, was the particular target, but he'd be joined by some of his most experienced customers—men (all men) who were prepared to back Dumas up.

"Don't bother trying those flirty moves on these guys," he concluded. "I won't say they don't appreciate a female, but they're gamblers first and lovers later. Stick to the game, calculate the odds, explore the benefits of your special knowledge and you should be fine."

I didn't like his use of the word, *should*. "What happens if I lose?"

"If you lose, I'll have to use more physical measures—measures both of us would prefer to avoid. Try not to lose, Ms. Neeter."

Sanchez drove on. He'd upped the pace and now wove past slower traffic like a trick bicyclist weaving past stationary traffic cones.

The car's ride was so smooth and level that the wine hardly sloshed around in the glasses as Petrov poured.

Considering Petrov's warning about talking too much, I put my mouth to an alternate use—eating. Although I did limit myself to a single glass of wine. More than one glass and I'd end up picking a fight with one of the ghosts—that and poker were the two lessons I'd learned in three years of institutionalization.

I was scared enough, both about the poker game Petrov had set up and about working for the criminal that a part of me wanted to get drunk to the point where I passed out. I was smart enough to suspect getting falling-down drunk wasn't going to contribute to my own health or that of my family.

Greenville Texas is an hour and about a hundred years from Dallas. I hadn't guessed Dallas's suburbs stretched that far—not to the east, anyway, and I'd always thought of Greenville as representing the old south—in both its positive and negative aspects. One thing I wouldn't have guessed was that this small town would be a gambling Mecca, or that someone like Petrov would care at all about what happened there. But that was where Sanchez pulled off of I-30 and illegally parked in front of a little diner that looked like it had stood unchanging since being opened in the 1920s.

"I thought we were playing poker, not stopping to eat."

Petrov brushed crumbs off of his suit pants and put away the nearly empty bottle of wine. "Did you?"

I made a note to keep my mouth shut in the future.

Oren didn't wait for the car door to open, extruding through the car's steel and glass door, chatting with a cast of ghosts who looked like they'd been in place since the restaurant's opening day.

Although I knew better, I tried the door again, just in case Sanchez and Petrov were feeling better about not locking me in. No such luck.

While I waited for Sanchez to let me out, I studied the faded diner. A chalkboard out in front advertising the daily special of meatloaf with corn and mashed potatoes for four dollars and ninety-three cents. There weren't many bargains like that in Dallas. Then again, Dallas's ghosts don't wear KKK masks the way some of the locals here in Greenville did. I was fairly sure the contemporary locals had left that history behind them, but it was another reminder that being dead didn't make you better as a person. Not that I needed more reasons to delay becoming a ghost as long as I could.

Sanchez grabbed a laptop case that must have held a really ancient computer because it bulged as if ready to explode. He stepped out of the car, opened Petrov's door and gave the mobster a hand out.

Rather than coming around to my side, he just waited. I was glad I'd worn jeans since I had to slip across the thick leather seat and get out on the same side Petrov had. Doing the trashy-celebrity thing and flashing a bunch of ghosts, plus a pair of gangsters, was not in the plan.

Petrov grasped my arm, dragged me into the restaurant, and then kept going.

The ghosts inside were about what I would have expected, assuming I expected something out of the rural south. Tired farmers and their tired wives reflected the rough life on the land. Too many tired-looking children reminded me that we might romanticize the past but life then meant children worked on the farm as soon as they could walk, and often died on the farm, too, both of diseases and accidents. My experience at McDonalds notwithstanding, there weren't as many children ghosts from modern times, which was lucky for me. I had enough trouble dealing with ghosts who'd at least been able to grow up.

Considering the KKK hoods outside, I shouldn't have been surprised that the ghosts also reflected Texas's segregated history. Interestingly every ghost I saw was white, but the patrons were a mix of races, mixed down to the table level. For an instant, I let myself imagine this was a sign of progress.

Ghosts don't tend to be the happiest of people, but it only took me a moment to realize that this particular group of ghosts was more miserable than usual. Several of them congregated around Oren, asking him frantic questions that had him shrugging. The rest, though, glared at the living guests as if they were an occupying army.

It took me a moment, but once I saw it, it was obvious. While the ghosts were a mix of men, women, and children, every single living customer was an adult male between twenty and mid-forties. How likely was that?

The wait staff didn't look especially happy, either, which surprised me. Guys tend to be bigger tippers than women and a crowded restaurant meant bigger tips.

I wondered if Petrov had loaded the place with hired muscle just to keep me in line. That seemed overkill, considering he was already blackmailing me by threatening my family and Arran. Perhaps Petrov didn't mind overkill, though.

"Looks like we'll have to wait for an empty seat," I said. "Maybe you should have called ahead for a reservation."

Petrov tightened his grasp on my arm and pulled me forward. I made another note to myself: *Next time, pay attention to the notes you make to yourself and keep the mouth shut, idiot.*

Then we were through the restaurant and out the back door and into an alley. The stenches of rotting garbage and dehydrated dog feces battled with smell of mildewed clothing drying on overhead lines.

My fear that Petrov had decided I was too dangerous returned. What better place to dump an unidentified body than here?

Chapter 21

I tried to put my feet down on dry spots of the alley, but it wasn't easy. There was so much trash, I wondered if anyone had come back here in the past decade. It was so disgusting, it almost felt like a stage set —for a horror movie.

Petrov hurried me along, with Sanchez trailing, a hand inside his jacket, presumably on his gun.

"I'm not wearing a bug if that's what you're afraid of, Mr. Petrov. You don't have to do all this cloak and dagger stuff."

"You're completely transparent, Ms. Neeter. I would have known if you carried a wire. I thought we'd kill two birds with one rock, as you Americans say."

Keep your mouth shut, Annie. "It's stone."

"Mr. Stone has already departed, as you know."

There was a reason I told myself to stay quiet.

It chilled me that Petrov would make a joke about murdering one of his own employees. Still, it was a useful reminder, as if I needed one, that the Russian wasn't just a friendly elf who made life easier for guys who wanted to put a few bucks down on the game, devil take puritanical laws against it.

Half a block down the alley, Petrov led us to what looked like an abandoned storefront, its windows covered with heavily graffitied plywood boards and its door blocked by iron bars and a padlock.

Or rather, apparently blocked. The bars and padlock swung open with the door and we stepped inside.

* * * *

Eight tables of poker were in play inside the supposedly boarded-up building: at each table, at least five men glared at their cards, at each other, and at us.

Several more men pushed themselves up from where they'd been leaning against walls and headed toward us. Two, I noticed, discretely tucked their hands into baggy and rumpled suit jackets. Unlike the guys at the restaurant, they didn't look like they were expecting us—more to the point, they didn't look happy to see Petrov at all.

Perhaps, I realized, Petrov's crowd at the diner wasn't really not there to scare me but to be handy if things escalated out of control. If these guys started shooting, it would be a bit late for guys a hundred yards down the to intervene, though.

For the second time in three minutes, I noticed being the only living woman in a testosterone-dominated room. Maybe if they'd been cute guys like Arran, I wouldn't have minded. As it was, it wasn't a comfortable feeling.

Although only a few female ghosts mingled with the crowd, at least as many ghosts as living humans filled the room, whispering strategy and discussing the hands. Like the chess-playing ghosts at that Plano coffee shop, they were simultaneously fascinated and frustrated at being able to see but not do.

"You will play this game of poker, Ms. Neeter."

It didn't look a lot like the friendly game I'd spent so may hours at. "I haven't played in this league."

"Yes, I am counting on that. With the help of your friends, I imagine you are hard to bluff."

"They've been known lie to me."

"Indeed." He paused, studying the faces of the gunmen who had walked up to him and then stopped, clearly uncertain what to do next.

"I hope they don't try such lies this evening. It could be costly—to all of us."

I nodded. I hoped they wouldn't decide lying to me about the cards wasn't a good joke as well—it was the kind of joke that could get me killed.

"I told you I'm not selling." A huge African-American man with a shaved head slammed his poker hand down, waved his gunmen back, and stood. He had to weigh in at close to three hundred pounds, a good bit more than me and Petrov combined. There was plenty of fat there, but it was hard fat, the kind that sits on top of solid muscle.

"Mr. Dumas, we meet again." Petrov smiled and stretched out his hand in greeting.

Dumas stared at Petrov's hand as if concerned it might bite him, then shook it tentatively. "I know you've taken over the Dallas games, but this here is just a friendly little outpost and we're a long way from the big city. I don't mess with your operation and I'd thank you not to mess with mine."

Petrov shook his head in mock sadness. "That's the thing, Mr. Dumas. Greenville is an hour from downtown Dallas, but it's close in to Rockwall and Wylie. You're not so far out in the sticks as you pretend. Recently I've gotten word that your *little* operation plays for some of the highest stakes in the state, and that you've been attracting big players from Dallas and around the country."

"What if I have?"

"I think you'll agree that that means you've been cutting into my territory, after all."

Dumas frowned. "I don't complain when any of the home boys go to Dallas for the weekend. Should go both ways, no?"

Petrov's smile could have been patented. It showed just the right amount of patience and friendly interest to work better than an angry threat. "Should it? Does that seem fair to you, Ms. Neeter?"

"Uh—" I so didn't want to get in the middle of this, but Petrov cranked his grip a bit harder on my arm and eased me between himself and the angry gambler.

"Jeez, man. What'd you bring that banged up slut here for? This here is a poker place, not a whorehouse."

Petrov's smile deepened. "Poker? What a coincidence. Ms. Neeter was just telling me she usually wins at poker. I thought she might like a game."

"Skanks can't play, and we don't want 'em."

I didn't much like Petrov, but I was starting to like Dumas even less. "You afraid of something, Dumas?"

Dumas tensed slightly at my words, but kept his eyes on Petrov, looking through me like I wasn't there. "Give me that skank for a day and I'd learn her to keep her mouth shut, 'cept when I have something to put in it."

Petrov laughed. "Beat her at poker, then. Do that and I will give her to you. But if she beats you, you owe me ten percent."

Dumas glared at me. "I don't want her, I just thought I'd help you out, train your slut for you."

I didn't see Sanchez move, but one moment he'd been leaning against the wall and the next, he had a gun pressed against Dumas's cheek hard enough that half the barrel sunk into Dumas's fleshy skin. "You also get to live, asshole."

Maybe Sanchez wasn't just a driver after all.

The poker den had gotten quiet when we'd entered but it went coffin-still then. At least half of the poker players casually reached into their jackets.

"Looks like you're caught in a crossfire," Oren observed.

Yeah, thanks for that newsflash.

"Take it easy." Dumas waved his gunmen back. "We're all grownups here—no need for threats."

The mood in the room didn't get any happier, but nobody pulled a weapon and started shooting. I took that as progress.

"You're not going to kill me," Dumas told Petrov. "'Cause if I'm dead, don't nobody make any money off this operation. Unless you think you're going to move your Russian ass out here to the boondocks and take over. Folks around her don't got much use for foreigners."

"A point," Petrov agreed. "Now that you mention it, though. I'm not making any money off of you right now anyway. And you said unkind things about Ms. Neeter. Most unkind."

"Yeah, right. Sorry, bitch."

If I opened my mouth, I'd start screaming, so I just nodded.

Dumas stared at me, his dark brown eyes seeming to strip away my clothing. "I never heard of you and I heard of all the players."

I just nodded again.

"She cheats, the deal is off."

Petrov shrugged. "Your cards, your club. How could she cheat?"

"You don't know, you won't last long in this business."

Petrov motioned Sanchez back and got in Dumas's face. "I own this business, Dumas."

To my surprise, the big African-American backed off first. I wasn't the only person Petrov scared.

"What's the upside for me?" Dumas finally asked. "If the skank wins and if she loses."

"You stay alive."

"More."

"You win, I leave you alone and you keep my money. You lose and you're part of my organization. You get my protection."

"I already own the police in this two-bit town."

"You don't own the Feds or DPS."

"And you do?"

Petrov showed a pair of brown-stained canines. "Enough."

Dumas considered. "I beat the bitch and you get nothing from me, I get the bitch, but you still treat me like I'm family—protect me. She wins, you keep the slut and I pay you ten percent of my take for the protection. Net, not gross. That the deal?"

Petrov nodded. "That or you can just die. I think I can find someone who would be happy to take over, happy to pay twenty percent."

"Man over near the wall is twitching to pull his weapon," Oren whispered, as if anyone but me would hear him.

"You there," I said. "In the corner. Your boss Dumas will be dead before you can pull your weapon, and I don't think much of your chances of getting out alive. So, why don't you take your hand out from your jacket nice and slow?"

Petrov's smile at me was every bit as dangerous as the one he'd used on Dumas. "You see how helpful Ms. Neeter can be, Dumas? She might just have saved Steve Sanders's life."

It took me a moment to realize Sanders must be the guy in the corner. Talk about annoying levels of self-confidence.

Chapter 22

The biggest pot I'd ever seen before had about ten dollars in it—along with whatever my virtue would have been worth and that had been years ago.

I wasn't sure what the chip denominations at Dumas's club were, but even if they were only a buck apiece, these guys were playing for bigger stakes than anything I'd ever seen. And I hadn't played in years, partly because after a while nobody would play with me and partly because I knew listening to the ghosts was cheating.

Cheating or not, I was here to play. Petrov made sure I knew that he really would leave me with Dumas if I failed.

"So, what are the stakes?" I asked as Sanchez pulled up a chair for me and I sat at the center table. At the other tables, the players had given up their game to kibitz.

This was now a one-table club.

Dumas and four other guys pulled up chairs, leaving a collapsible card chair for me. Two of the gamblers wore green eyeshades like you'd see in one of those oldtime movies about riverboat gamblers. One of the others looked Chinese and didn't seem to speak any English at all. Another wore a pair of dirty overalls over a flannel shirt that looked like it had been colonized by a sweat-eating fungus that hadn't managed a dent in the stink. Then there was Dumas. His hands were so big, they swallowed the entire deck of cards. The man could have palmed enough decks to stock a bridge club without much effort. I'd have to watch him carefully. No point in knowing your opponent's cards if your opponent deals himself nothing but aces.

"Ante is a Dnote. Minimum raise is a D." Dumas growled. "Hundred thousand buy-in."

My neck felt like it needed a good shot of WD-40 as I looked at Petrov. A 'D' was a thousand. A hundred thousand dollar buy-in for one poker game? Even with a small rake, we were talking about some serious dollars. No wonder the Russian wanted a chunk of this operation.

Petrov gestured to Sanchez who opened his laptop bag. I'd been wrong about it holding an old computer. Instead, it was full of neatly bundled stacks of hundred dollar bills.

Dumas grabbed a couple of the stacks and flipped through them, probably making sure Petrov hadn't padded them out with singles or newsprint. When he was satisfied, he shoved a stack of chips across the table.

"What about the others?" Sanchez gestured at the four men at the table. "I haven't seen their money."

"Don't worry about their money," Dumas said. "Your bitch has any chips left after we're done with her, I'll make them good."

Considering how much money was in the case, he hadn't given me that many chips. Maybe twenty singles, and sixteen fives.

I anted and Dumas announced the deal. Five card stud, Canadian stud rules.

Stud is one of the oldest Poker games. You have a single hole card, with all the other cards dealt face up so everyone can see them. Every time a face-up card is dealt, you have to bet—in our game a thousand dollar bring-in was the minimum.

I stayed in until the second up-card, but had nothing. When Oren reported that Dumas had a club as his hole card and two clubs showing, I folded. Canadian rules meant a four-card flush is a winning combo. It's not hard to get a four-card flush.

Twenty seconds after starting the game, I was down two thousand dollars.

I took a deep breath, then let it out. Winning at poker means picking your hands, and minimizing your losses when the cards don't run your way. It's easy to keep that in mind when you're playing penny ante. At a thousand dollars a pop, it's a bit harder.

Petrov had to know that, but my losing didn't make him happy. He started toward a table where a number of bottles had been set, but the guy who'd almost pulled his gun, Sanders, met him before he'd taken two steps. "Stay behind your player. Tell me what you want and I'll pour."

"Vodka."

"Your man?"

"He's not drinking."

"The skank?"

I didn't like the title, but I had a scratchy feeling at the back of my throat and I wasn't too proud to answer to something that could help me out. "I could use a—"

"She's not drinking either."

So much for my Diet Coke.

The next dealer called for Five Card Draw, jacks or better to open—a much better game for me since I could do the math on all of the hands and have a pretty good idea who had a chance and who didn't.

I picked up jacks and junk as the players checked the bet around to me.

Oren reported that Dumas had a pair of twos and an ace. One of the other gamblers, the Chinese-looking guy had three hearts, ace-high, and might go for a flush. The guy in the ugly flannel shirt had a four, five, seven, and eight and might try for an inside straight.

I felt good about my chances and put in a thousand.

If I'd thought a thousand could bluff anyone, I got a quick lesson. I had to remember that for these guys, a thousand was the minimum bet. Not only did the idiot with the possible straight stay in, which was a sucker-bet, he actually raised me five thousand. Nobody else dropped out, either, even the guys with nothing.

I didn't think any of these gamblers were suckers. Other than Dumas who owned the joint, they were professional gamblers. I didn't need Oren's insights to see the way they calculated their odds, nor the way they barely flicked their cards and then put them down on the table so no one else could have a chance to work the angle. What I hadn't counted on, though, was that they weren't playing to win, they were playing to wipe me out. They'd stay in as long as they had a chance, and figuring to share the pot regardless of who won. I was playing against every single one of them, which meant I was in trouble.

The odds of me winning without my ghostly helpers had to be somewhere below zero.

Still, I had my pair of jacks. I called dirty-shirt's five thousand dollar raise and asked for three cards picking up a pair of eights.

Considering the crap the other players had started with, two pairs figured to be the winning combination. But Oren let me know Dumas had beat the odds and drawn another two.

"Bet, check, or fold," he said.

No way I was going to bluff him with his three of a kind. I folded.

Okay, five minutes into the game and I was down another seven thousand. At this rate, Petrov's hundred thousand wouldn't last long. I wasn't sure his patience would last even as long as his money.

After an unrewarding start, things went downhill. I picked up worthless hand after worthless hand.

By midnight, I'd lost forty thousand, winning just two hands, neither with a significant pot.

I had Ritchie Stone's ghost watching whomever was dealing full time. I hadn't seen any evidence they were cheating, other than playing a combined strategy against me, but I wasn't naive enough to think they wouldn't cheat me if they could. Backing Ritchie up, Petrov's eyes bored holes into the head of whoever touched the decks. Several times an hour, he called for a new deck, handing them to Sanchez to make sure they were still factory sealed and unmarked before allowing them into play.

None of that helped. Nor did knowing what the other guys had—not when I could look at my own hand and see it was a loser.

Other than me, the mood had perked up around the table. Dumas and his gamblers had to sense that my luck sucked, and laughed off my few attempts to bluff, simply calling me and raking in my chips. I *had* to bluff occasionally to keep them honest, but mostly I folded as quickly as I could, and waited for something to turn up. And waited. And waited.

Things were ugly.

"I can't buy a hand," I told Petrov.

"I'll let you know if they're cheating. Other than playing together rather than odd's on, but we expected that."

He might have expected that. It might have been helpful if he'd shared that expectation. Then again, what would I have done but worry? "But—"

"But nothing. Try harder." The scar on his neck had darkened and a pulse on his forehead stood out, and he'd made a major dent in the vodka bottle. Otherwise he seemed calm. Which made one of us.

I was already trying harder. Sweat plastered my shirt to my body and my jeans felt like they were layered in grease.

At around one, I finally got something I could use. Playing seven-card stud, I showed a pair of Queens and Mr. Inside Straight a pair of tens. My hole cards were worthless.

Mr. Inside Straight bet confidently, as if his two hole cards contained all the secrets in the universe. He'd flipped them so quickly, Oren hadn't gotten a good look, but he thought they were the nine of spades and the six of clubs.

After a couple of rounds of betting, the others dropped out, leaving just the two of us, and a big pile of chips at the center of the table.

Sixth street, my last up-card, was the three of clubs. It gave me nothing other than a slight reduction in Mr. Inside Straight's chances for a flush. Still, he was showing three clubs, plus the six in the hole Oren had seen for a possible flush in addition to the pair of tens he'd been betting on.

I wavered. He knew I had a pair of queens. With a pair of tens and nothing, would he be betting so aggressively?

If his second hole card was the ten of spaces and not the nine, I was finished. And if his final card turned out to be a club or another ten, I was as good as another ghost already.

Dumas flicked the cards, waiting to deal and Oren grinned. We'd both noticed the gambler's nervous habit and he'd been waiting for it. "Another queen coming for you, under the burn card. You can't lose."

I sure as hell could lose if Mr. Inside Straight pulled another club, but I had a chance. A chance was better than anything else I'd had all night. I matched his bet.

In seven-card stud, the final card is dealt face down. Dumas slid our cards off the deck and across the table.

Oren had gotten under the table, pushing his face through the wood so his eyes barely broke the surface. It was a fairly disgusting look, but it didn't work. Dumas varied his pattern just enough that Mr. Inside Straight's card didn't cross his vision.

He pulled out of the wood, shaking his head. "Couldn't see it."

Crap. I almost spoke the curse out loud. Gamblers aren't exactly critical of eccentricities, but they are always looking for cheats. Talking to someone who wasn't there would raise all kinds of questions, and someone just might find the right answer.

Professional gamblers believe in luck, and those who believe in luck are often willing to believe in other magical things—witness Mr. Inside Straight's unwashed shirt—and Petrov's quick acceptance of my abilities. I kept my mouth shut and played poker.

Emulating the guys I'd been playing with, I flipped a quick look at *seventh street*. As Oren had promised, Dumas had dealt me a queen. Three of a kind beat what Mr. Inside Straight was showing, and what Oren thought he'd seen in the hole. Depending, of course, on Mr. Inside Straight's final down card.

Without even looking at that all-important final card, dirty-shirt pushed a thick stack of chips in front of him.

"He's bluffing," Oren said.

Well, duh. Everyone within a hundred miles knew he was bluffing. Since he hadn't looked at his last card, the hand he knew about couldn't have gotten better. He couldn't know whether he had been dealt another club but there was a chance it was a club. If I called his bluff and I was wrong, I would be out. If I folded, I'd lose the fifteen thousand I'd already bet on the hand, but I would have enough to play on. Surely sooner or later, Oren's peeks would pay off.

Statistics told me to back out.

But the logic of gambling told me Dumas and his pals already suspected something. That was why Dirty Shirt was betting the way he was. If I caved now, with my pair of queens showing and everyone knowing Dirty Shirt didn't have a clue what card he'd drawn, I'd confirm their suspicions.

Like NASCAR drivers, these were the best at their sport, and they knew I wasn't one of them. If I confirmed their suspicions, they wouldn't just toss me out of the game, they'd start shooting.

A couple of Petrov's guys from the diner had slid in, some of them interestingly banged up, but the only thing sure about a gunfight was there was no way I could win. If I didn't get shot during the fight, whoever won would finish me off.

I sucked it up and matched Mr. Inside Straight's bet. "Call."

"Whatcha got, lady."

I didn't *need* to show him. I'd been the one who called, after all: according to the rules, it was up to him to show me what he had. But I hoped this wouldn't be my last hand. If I won, I would clean out Mr. Inside Straight, but he was the weakest of the five men I was playing against. I needed a psychological edge against the others more than I needed to beat one player.

I showed the pair of queens, then the queen I'd been dealt as my final face-down card. "Three queens, with an ace kicker."

Mr. Inside Straight flipped his top card—the ace of diamonds. "Shit."

I reached for the cards. "I think that makes it my game, gentlemen. Shall we play a round of Texas Hold'em?"

* * * *

I wasn't the only one sweating after that big hand.

Mr. Inside Straight was out, meaning I faced a slightly more manageable number of opponents. On that very next deal, I managed a really sweet bluff, building up and bringing in a nice kitty that I ended up having to share with the Chinese-looking gentleman since both of us were playing the board.

Dumas could have built a full house if he'd stayed in and he knew it. His coffee-colored face darkened like a warning thundercloud when I grinned at him.

They'd sensed my nervousness when Mr. Inside Straight had tried his bluff and tried head-games on me. But it's hard to bluff a player who can see all the cards. They ended up playing into my strengths. The more nervous they got, the more they fingered their cards, and the more chances Oren and Ritchie got to make sure they saw everything.

Petrov finally relented on the Diet Coke and the caffeine helped me stay up although I stopped after two when I realized I wasn't going to get a potty break. I wished I'd had that realization a bit quicker.

Seven hours after I'd called Mr. Inside Straight's bluff, I wiped out Dumas, the last of the five men who'd sat down at the table with me.

The sun peeked through thin spots in the black paint covering the windows as I raked in the final pot.

"Ms. Neeter, that was nicely done." I thought I heard a note of respect in Petrov's voice.

"The whore is cheating," Dumas growled. "You promised me an

honest game."

Oren got in Dumas's face, shouting at him, which would have been funny if I didn't think laughing just might set off a free-fire zone.

Petrov didn't see Oren's antics, and he didn't laugh. I didn't laugh either, because I was afraid I'd pee in my pants if I did.

"I insist," Petrov's voice was back to being completely emotionless, completely scary, "on respect for myself and my employees. You will apologize for calling Ms. Neeter that word and the other words you've used tonight."

"The hell I will."

Petrov shook his head slowly. "I went along with your game rather than simply having you eliminated because I believed you could be an asset. Although I will have my ten percent of your rake, I give fair value in return—you stand to make more money working with me than you could without me. But if you have no control over your emotions, you're worthless to me. I have other men who could run this establishment, or I could simply close it down and handle the traffic in my existing clubs. Now, will you apologize to Ms. Neeter, or do you want to take your chances against me right here, right now?"

Dumas looked ready to take his chances, but the Chinese-looking gambler grabbed him.

"Idiot." The Chinese-looking guy hadn't said two words in the ten hours we'd been playing so I'd assumed he was straight off the boat from China. I'd certainly never have guessed he'd have a deep southern drawl. "You made a bargain. You don't keep it, he'll wipe you out and nobody will back you."

"But she cheated—"

"Show me how? We used your cards, your place, you dealt. I don't see any mirrors, so tell me how she cheated. If you figure that out, you have a case. Until you do, apologize to the woman and stay alive."

Dumas's forehead wrinkled like a mutant bulldog's, and he gripped his fists so tightly the skin turned white at his knuckles. "Sorry if you were offended."

His apology was about as convincing as a politician's, but I didn't want to be the one responsible for provoking a shootout. "Yeah. Thanks."

"I'll send my accountant to give you the details of our new arrangement," Petrov said. "Come along, Ms. Neeter."

I considered sneaking a couple of thousand dollar chips down my shirt, but a quick look at Dumas's face persuaded me that wouldn't be wise. My chances of swinging by and cashing them later were about as good as a turkey's on Thanksgiving.

Petrov gave me a look that said I wasn't the only one who heard things nobody was saying, then nodded at Sanchez, who scooped all of the chips in front of me into his chauffeur's cap and plopped the lot down in front of Dumas.

"Pay up."

"House keeps five percent."

"What your suckers agree to is their business. Consider your missing five percent back taxes."

Dumas looked like he wanted to argue, but the Chinese-looking southerner dissuaded him—that and the rest of Petrov's guys from the café, who trooped in the door in response to some invisible signal Petrov must have sent.

Like the men who'd come in earlier, there were plenty of bandages and bruises on this bunch. A few were still bleeding and one had his arm in a makeshift sling. Apparently I hadn't been the only person battling things out during the night, but they'd made it through so I thought Petrov's team must have won that fight, too.

Dumas took a look at the odds, then counted out stacks of hundred dollar bills.

"I'll let you get back to work, partner," Petrov said.

His grip on my arm was a lot lighter on the way out than it had been on the way in. "You were smart not to throw the game."

"Yeah, it took some real brilliance not to want to get my family killed."

"Have I mentioned I don't appreciate a smart mouth?"

"You might have brought it up."

"I thought so. Odd how unsuccessful I've been on communicating when I think I'm being so clear."

Petrov said nothing else until we got to the car. And I hoped I'd learned not to break the silence.

Sanchez opened the door for his boss, and the two men let me scramble in first, crawling across the wide expanse of leather so Petrov could sit in comfort.

When Sanchez got the car on the road, Petrov opened the bulging case and flipped through the stacks of hundred dollar bills, entering something into a tiny computer he pulled out from one of the compartments behind Sanchez's seat.

I couldn't help staring.

Not only had I never seen that much money, I'd never seen anything close. Not even counting the hundred thousand we'd started with, Petrov had half a million dollars there.

He surprised me when he pulled out five thick stacks. "I believe I told you that working for me could be a nice thing for you, Ms. Neeter. Here is a small token of my appreciation."

I accepted the three inch thick stack of hundred dollar bills. "That's —"

"Ten thousand dollars, Ms. Neeter. Your work tonight was both longer and more dangerous than your work for me at Sophia's restaurant. I believe in rewarding work well done."

"But—"

He touched the silver crucifix around his neck. "I'm a religious man, Ms. Neeter. It says in the good book that the laborer is worthy of his hire. Working for me need not be a burden."

He was religious? I wondered if he'd nussed the part about peacemakers. When Ritchie's ghost crawled up next to me, I decided wondering things like that wasn't healthy.

Instead, I stared at the money. Ten thousand dollars was more cash than I'd ever had in my hands before. I could make a down payment on an condo or send myself to college for a year. With this kind of cash, I really did have a chance to get out of Dallas and start a new life for me under a new identity.

I clutched the money close to myself. "Uh, thanks."

His smile was a million miles from the predatory teeth-showing gesture I'd seen before. Instead he looked like a generous uncle or something. "There will be more, Ms. Neeter. As I've already promised, I intend to make you a very affluent woman."

I'd never considered being affluent. Managing to pay the rent was about as far ahead as I'd gotten in my financial planning.

"Just a heads-up, Mr. Petrov. I'm not much of a gambler. A couple of times, I came close to barfing all over the cards. And now I need to go to the bathroom something fierce."

"I doubt that I'll need you to play much poker, or that you'll be welcome at many establishments. Mr. Dumas was a special case and you were a secret weapon. Dumas believed he was invincible in his life because he was invincible at the card table. Prove him wrong at the table, I didn't have to prove him wrong with a bullet."

He signaled to Sanchez to pull over at a gas station so I could take care of my business.

He didn't even seem to mind when I took my money with me into the bathroom.

I wasn't sure if he thought he'd bought me, that I would be a loyal doobie now that he'd paid me a ton of money and promised me a lot more. I admit I felt a bit better about working for him after that game. If anything, Petrov's just-business approach to gambling was safer than Dumas's hotheaded and obscenity-laden strategy. Nobody had gotten killed that night—not that I knew of, anyway, and I personally thought the laws against letting people play poker when they wanted to were a bit silly. I still wanted to get away from Petrov, but I wasn't in as much of a hurry. I had time to figure out a way to make sure Little Jack and the rest of my family didn't get hurt. I had time to make some serious money that would ease my way into a new life once I was ready.

Besides, I'd need all the time I could get. Because I wasn't sure how the hell I could persuade Arran to stay safe. The detective was more stubborn than any two guys, and I didn't want to leave him exposed to Petrov's anger when I vanished.

I looked around to see the early morning traffic on I-30. There were a lot of cars on the road, which meant I'd probably been wrong about Greenville being a far-out small town rather than a part of the growing exurban sprawl that was Dallas. What there wasn't was any sign of Arran. Which made me happy. I hadn't needed his help and I'd begged him to stay away. Who would have guessed he'd actually be reasonable. Maybe there was hope for persuading him to be reasonable about protecting himself from Petrov, as well.

I was pretty sure that if he'd walked into that poker den, Petrov's guys and Dumas's guys would have become friends.

After I finished with my bathroom business, I glanced at the food aisle in the gas station. They had fresh-looking Krispy Kreme donuts, which would normally appeal to me, but my stomach growled at me when I considered, letting me know I wasn't off the hook. I'd managed not to puke on Dumas's cards, but that didn't mean I wouldn't ralph over Petrov's nice leather seats. I wondered if he'd demand his ten thousand back to pay for upholstery cleaning, but I decided even if he wouldn't, I didn't like that picture.

I must have looked a bit green when I got back into the car because Sanchez asked if I wanted a Sprite.

"I think I need to sleep."

"Be an hour before we get back to Dallas, traffic as heavy as it is. You might try a nap."

If someone had asked me, I would have bet money I couldn't go to sleep in a car with a pair of gangsters, one of whom was threatening my family, and a quartette of ghosts, one of whom had been gunning for me a week before.

I would have lost that bet.

The Colonel, who hadn't been much help during the poker game, offered to guard my sleeping body and wake me up if Sanchez or Petrov decided to molest me. My logical brain didn't think that was likely—either the molestation or the Colonel's ability to guard me—but logic doesn't always have a lot to do with anything. I felt better with the Colonel's offer. Two minutes after I'd gotten back in, I dozed off.

Despite the Colonel on guard, I kept waking up, making little gasping noises that pulled Petrov's attention from his computer and his money.

"We won't let anything happen to you," he assured me the third time that happened.

"Thanks." If he didn't know it was him I was scared of, I wasn't going to be the one who broke the news.

What I needed was Arran.

I was happy he hadn't followed me, really. I knew it was completely irrational that I felt somehow abandoned. Still, that's the way it was. I wanted him and was vaguely pissed at him for not being there, although the only way he could have been there was as a ghost and I certainly didn't want that. I wanted Arran for things no ghost could perform.

During the remainder of the drive, I probably woke up every five minutes. The last few times involved escaping from dreams where I was trying to run but with my feet having no traction at all, like I was caught in a huge pool filled with Jell-O.

Petrov didn't say anything after trying to comfort me that one time, but he made patting gestures at me, almost but not quite touching me.

Despite having finished at least a fifth of vodka during my poker marathon and having stood behind me all night long while I'd at least been sitting, Petrov looked as crisp and fresh as ever, which was not especially crisp, but good enough to pass for a middle manager on his way in to the office.

When I peeked, I saw he had moved beyond the half million we'd won, as if it were just another evening's work, and was entering horserace odds in a spreadsheet.

He noticed me looking and turned the screen so I could see it. "We're partners, Ms. Neeter. I have nothing to hide from you. Not that there would be much point in trying to keep secrets from you. You'll just ask your invisible friends."

I really didn't want to be a partner with a mobster. I'd feel a lot better about myself if I could manage to hold onto the whole victim of blackmail thing. Still, I couldn't deny the small surge of pleasure his words brought me. My parents had abandoned me, my brother had rescued me, Arran had made love to me and wanted to protect me, but Petrov was the first person who'd ever made me feel a part of something. He wasn't humoring or taking care of me, he saw me as an asset, something of value. Admittedly something of so much value he'd threatened my precious nephew to get to me, but still. I'd never been valuable before and I liked the feeling.

Not enough that I wanted to learn more about Petrov's business than I had to, though. "Oh, no. I really don't need to learn about horseracing, and I really-really-really don't want to learn about the knee-breaking side. The less I know, the better."

"Not much to know about knee-breaking," Ritchie said. "First, we don't break knees. That's just a movie thing. Second, the job is—"

Petrov interrupted Ritchie. He didn't know the ghost was talking, of course, but I doubted he would have let it bother him if he had. "I'm a Russian, you know?"

I didn't say anything until it became obvious he was waiting for a reply.

"I sort of picked that up."

"We Russians have a long history in dealing with spies. The first lesson is to assume that someone is spying. Always."

"That doesn't sound like a very happy lesson."

He nodded gravely. "There are very few happy Russians."

That was a sad commentary. Although we were already inside 635 and not that far from my place, I resolved to work harder on getting to sleep.

"The second lesson," he said as I drifted between worlds, "is that nobody can ever know who a spy works for."

Since that didn't make much sense to me, I decided it had to be a part of a dream.

My dreams sifted from Jell-o to Arran.

We were making love again. He told me he hadn't deserted me, left me to Petrov's devices. Even in the dream, I knew I was dreaming because he said ridiculous things about wanting to take care of me.

Then he started shaking me.

I didn't take that from anyone, not even a sexy cop. I drew on everything I'd learned for my green belt test in Tae Kwon Do and gave him with my best tiger-strike to his throat, simultaneously shouting, "What the hell—"

"We're here, Ms. Neeter." It wasn't Arran touching me at all, it was Sanchez waking me up. "Back at your place."

While I'd slept, Sanchez had negotiated Dallas's annoying morning rush hour. I'd missed every five-mile-an-hour moment of it. I still felt like death warmed over when I saw Sanchez had pulled into the Mockingbird Station parking lot, but at least it was now warmed over.

"Oh." I saw that Sanchez had neatly deflected my tiger-strike. I might be proud of my green belt, but there was a lot I didn't know, and from the way Sanchez made me miss, I suspected he had spent a lot more time studying the fighting arts than I had. "Thanks for driving."

"It's what I can do for Mr. Petrov."

Something about the way he said that puzzled me. He could have said, *it's my job*, but he hadn't. His tone held just a trace of regret. Considering how Petrov had blackmailed me into working for him, I didn't doubt that a lot of the others in his employ were similarly there against their will. I wondered if Sanchez might be counted in that number. Not that it mattered. It wouldn't stop them from killing me if they saw me putting him in danger. Blackmail can buy a lot more loyalty than money.

"I don't have anything for you tonight," Petrov said to me as Sanchez gave me a hand out of the car.

Okay, my door did open. So, how come I always had to slide across the seat.

I grunted at him. I was still tired.

"I will pick you up tomorrow evening. Nine o'clock."

"Don't bother feeding me this time," I said. "I can manage."

"Mr. Dumas was not the most generous of hosts, was he? How wise I was to bring our little picnic." He turned back to his computer, then shook his head as if reminding something. "I have something else for you. A present, of sorts."

"You've already given me more money than I know what to do with." Although I suspected it would vanish pretty quickly when I had to create a fake identity for myself that would let me escape both from Petrov and from the cops who would come looking for me, wanting to learn the details I didn't want to know about the way Petrov's business worked.

"This is not money. Something more, personal. Perhaps more valuable."

I didn't like the look Sanchez gave me. It smacked of pity. But I couldn't imagine anything personal Petrov might want to give me. He didn't seem the kind who'd get turned on by sexy underwear and even if he was, I didn't think I was his type.

Sanchez said nothing, though, but walked around to the back of the car and pushed a button on his key fob.

The Town Car's big trunk popped open.

I waited. "Well?"

"*Mon dieu.* Zhat is zo horrible." Chantal's accent came out most strongly when she was emotionally distraught.

Sanchez gestured for me to walk around so I could see.

I don't know what I expected—a dozen machine-gun toting prohibition-era gangsters, perhaps.

I didn't think I'd see Arran.

Chapter 23

I'd told Arran not to follow me. I'd explained to him that Petrov knew he'd followed me to Sophia's. I'd begged him to let me handle the Russian myself.

Sure I was conflicted about it, but I still wished someone would listen to me once in a while. Listening to me could have saved Arran a whole lot of grief.

Blood drenched his shirt, and his nose looked like it had been translated into a Picasso painting, leaning way over to the right side of his face. One of his eyes was swollen shut, and his shirt was ripped open to display an ugly purple row of bruises that extended down his ribs from his armpit to his hip.

"Oh, baby."

He glanced at me, then glared at Sanchez. "You want to finish what they started."

Sanchez backed away from the trunk. "Mr. Petrov warned you not to follow her. Next time, think about listening."

"I always listen."

Why do men always have to play games? "Arran, shut up. And Sanchez, what the hell were you thinking putting him in the trunk. He needs a hospital. He's been injured."

Sanchez shook his head. "No permanent damage was done. Mr. Petrov was very particular about this—he respects his half of the deal. As long as you cooperate, and as long as Detective Dane doesn't pull a weapon and force a response, this will continue and he won't be badly hurt. As it is, he's just a bit bruised."

"Bruised? Are you crazy? What about his nose. That's no bruise."

Sanchez shrugged. "Noses get broken when they poke where they don't belong. Besides, it gives you something in common. Now, Detective, do you want me to close the trunk and drive you to the hospital, or do you want to get out and spend some quality time with your girlfriend?"

"Screw yourself, Sanchez."

"Arran, shut up and get out of the car." I knew I was responsible for what had happened to him, but I'd also be responsible if I let anything worse happen to him.

I could tell he wasn't happy with me, but he did shut up and he did get out of Petrov's trunk.

I winced with every motion he took. The guys who'd beaten Arran had been intent on sending a message.

"Detective, let me give you some advice." Petrov had lowered his window. "Listen to your woman. Next time she tells you to keep clear, do it. She's smart, that one."

Arran had to lean against a tree to keep himself standing, but he met the Russian mobster's glare with one of his own. "You know, Petrov, you can stick your advice where the sun doesn't shine."

"Such a way with language."

"You might want this." Sanchez set Arran's weapon on the grass a few feet away from the detective. "I took the liberty of unloading it, so don't get any foolish ideas."

"Nothing *foolish* comes to mind."

Then Sanchez and Petrov drove off leaving the two of us alone in the Mockingbird Station parking lot.

I looked at my messed up semi-boyfriend. Since we'd gone to bed together, it seemed fair to call him that, at least to myself. I was going to wait to hear what he called our relationship before describing it to anyone out loud—to him. "You complete idiot. I *told* you not to follow me."

I wasn't being fair since I'd been pissed at him for not following me half an hour earlier. But so what?

"And let him just take you wherever he wants with nobody knowing? I don't trust him that much. I'm not sure I trust anyone that much."

That tore at my guts. Arran had gotten hurt because he'd been trying to take care of me—admittedly against my specific instructions and in a particularly stupid way, but he was a guy. What else should I expect?

I felt myself getting weepy inside, so I decided to go back on the attack. "I know this will come as a surprise to you, babe, but I'm a grownup. I've been taking care of myself for years now," ever since they let me out of the State School, although I sure wasn't going to tell Arran about that. "Besides, Why would Petrov hurt me? He likes me. I'm his clever new tool. And he's using me to make himself richer."

"For right now."

"Meaning?"

"Meaning, how long before he starts thinking you could be doing the same spying for me that you are for him? How long before he decides you're more dangerous to him alive than you would be dead? He knows your boyfriend is a cop."

His mouth kept moving, but my brain fritzed and I stopped listening sometime around the word *boyfriend*. Thinking the word to myself was one thing. Hearing Arran call himself that was something else. Admittedly it was a silly word for people in their mid twenties for me, late twenties for him, but I'd missed all of that stuff in high school. Even my pre-Arran sexual encounters, such as they were, hadn't involved boyfriends, just guys I'd known or lost poker games to.

I'd already known that it would be tough to walk away from Arran. Once he described himself as my boyfriend, though, everything changed. I wouldn't be walking away from a cop I'd happened to have sex with, I'd be walking away from the only guy who'd ever known my secret and still wanted to be romantic. Even in the State School, where everyone was weird, none of the guys had wanted to be my boyfriend. Although, in retrospect, I had to grant the possibility that was because they were messed up, not just because I was messed up.

Anyway, his calling himself my boyfriend changed everything. I couldn't pretend any more. When I vanished from his life, he'd think I betrayed him. Even if I never saw him again, knowing I'd earned his anger and caused his pain would hurt.

I followed that thought process as long as I had to. Arran was still talking when I came out of my away-state and I tuned back in.

"He knows," Arran continued, "that the only reason you're doing anything for him is because he threatened your family. If he doesn't know it already, he soon will know that Jack, Lauren and Little Jack have dropped off his radarscope. What happens then? Will he still think you're his best friend? Or will he decide that you're as much of a danger to him as you are to his enemies?"

"That's not true at all. We talked about spies and things." At least it seemed that we'd talked about that. I was a bit vague on what we'd said and what I'd dreamed. "Anyway, I'm pretty sure he's thought about the danger I can be and has decided not to worry about it. He even let me look at his computer where he was working on odds for the horses. He's making me like a partner, involving me. Petrov is trying to get my willing cooperation because he's smart enough that he knows that would help him the most."

Arran might be leaning against a tree, might still be bleeding from the scrapes he'd picked up in the fight, and might not be able to breathe out of his busted nose, but he still sounded like he was some sort of king. "You sound like that is such an honor."

Well, in a way it was. "I know he's a criminal, Arran. I'm sorry his guys beat you up. But he's the first person who's ever treated my skills like they were a gift, something precious, rather than like he had to walk carefully around me or else I might explode. He likes it that I can talk to the ghosts. His first thought isn't that I must have forgotten my medication, it's that we can work together as a team. And he's being careful to use me on projects I can feel okay about. Like that basketball player the other day or Dumas's gambling operation."

"*He's* the first person. What about me?"

"Come on, babe. Tell me you didn't look at that paperwork my brother gave you and decide I was one sick puppy who needed being taken care of."

"That was a long time ago. And speaking of Dumas, I wondered if that was why you were going to Greenville. There isn't a lot else out there."

"I spent the night playing poker."

"While I spent the night in the trunk of Petrov's car."

"I think we already had this conversation, Arran, do we need to have it again? I begged you not to follow me. I passed along Petrov's warning. I feel guilty about it, but it isn't completely my fault."

"I didn't say it was your fault."

"I sure heard it."

He sighed. "Look, do we have to stand outside in your parking lot all day?"

I opened my mouth, then shut it. Arran was still bleeding, barely holding himself up, and I was blathering at him. That was not in the dictionary under 'good girlfriend.' "Come on in. You can lay down while I call an ambulance to get you to the hospital."

"I don't—"

"No macho stuff, Arran. If you don't have your nose fixed, you're going to be a mouth-breather for the rest of your life, which will definitely cut down on your romantic life."

"Eeew," was the consensus thought from Arran's all-girl fan club.

I hadn't seen Tiffany and Cassandra arrive, but they were there. I wondered if maybe they'd been in the trunk with Arran the whole time, then decided I didn't want to think about that.

"See? Even your ghost-girlfriends agree."

"*They* aren't my girlfriends."

"Poor baby. Those mean men hurt you so bad." Cassandra ran her invisible hands along Arran's bruised ribs, ending up a little lower and more central than I thought the wounds warranted.

"Get your hands off my boyfriend, Cassandra."

"I saw him first."

"Tough."

"How about you get to work fixing me up." Without waiting, he turned and hobbled toward my apartment. Not before I got a look at his grin. He thought my squabble with his girls was funny, did he?

Right. I was going to fix him up. He needed the hospital, but apparently he needed some encouragement, too. "I think I've got some peroxide I can put on those cuts. That'll feel good."

"Oh, peroxide. My favorite."

"If you give me trouble I'll put it on your hair and you can get that streaked look that was so big with the kids a few years ago."

He held up his hands. "No trouble."

"Good."

When we got to the building, he leaned against it for a moment, gathering his strength. He must have been hurt more than he was letting on.

"We're almost there, babe."

"One thing I'm certain of," he said. "They knew I was coming."

"I told Petrov I'd—"

"They were waiting for me. It was an ambush."

I'd seen that Petrov's goons were waiting for something in the café, but I'd assumed they were there to help out if Dumas caused problems. I had no idea putting the hurt on Arran was part of the plan.

He regained enough strength to climb into my elevator and then led me down the hall to my apartment.

"If you're implying I told them, you can stick your implication where the sun doesn't shine." I held open my apartment door and let him in.

"I'm stating the facts." He sagged down on my couch.

I thought about the ten thousand dollars in my bag and the thousand bucks in my pocket from earlier. Then I thought about what Petrov had said about spies. He couldn't trust me. He knew I was helping him because he was blackmailing me. But he'd acted like he didn't have a fear in the world. Clearly having his guys beat the snot out of poor Arran had been a part of his calculation.

I couldn't help grinning, though, when I thought about how many of Petrov's guys were bruised and battered. They'd caught Arran by surprise, ambushed him with a whole herd of gangsters, and he'd put a hurt on at least eight of them.

But the grin didn't last. Petrov had plenty of guys to handle that kind of stuff and I only had one Arran.

The Russian understood the mix of carrot and stick. The money he'd given me was part of the carrot, and so was the way he treated me—like a respected colleague rather than a crazy freak. The threats had been a part of the stick, but he'd have known I'd managed to send my brother and his family out of town, out of reach. Clearly he'd decided he needed to show me that my little games couldn't protect the people I loved.

So he'd used Arran to send me a message. He'd left Arran alive when he could have done worse, but he'd made sure I knew Arran's fate was in his hands. Just as he'd done when he'd had Little Jack kidnapped.

"Let's take a look at you, babe."

But Arran was done talking. He'd exhausted whatever reserves of energy had kept him going and lay, unmoving except for slow, pained breathing, on my couch.

I looked at that long line of bruises down his side. If it had been just the nose, I would have called a taxi, but I knew from my Tae Kwon Do that a beating could result in internal injuries. Arran needed an ambulance.

I dug my phone out of my purse and dialed 9-1-1.

* * * *

"What the hell?" Arran thrashed in his hospital bed.

"Stay still, Arran. You've got an I.V."

"What time is it?"

I looked at my phone. "Seven thirty."

"I'm dead. I was supposed to be on a stakeout."

"I don't think you would have been much use. You've been drifting in and out of consciousness ever since the ambulance brought you here." At least for that part of the time I'd been able to spend with him. I'd spent a couple of very uncomfortable hours being questioned at the local police substation until Arran's partner, Detective Fineman, had rescued me and given me a note that had gotten me past the uniformed guard outside Arran's hospital room.

"Where's my phone? I need to call the lieutenant."

"Detective Fineman took care of that."

"But—"

"But nothing, partner." As if on cue, Fineman strolled into the room, a bunch of flowers that looked like she'd just pulled them from the side of the road in one hand and a stack of x-rays in the other. "Check this out, buddy. You've got six cracked ribs. You're lucky nothing busted loose in there, cause if it had, you'd be dead."

"I sure as hell don't feel lucky."

"Maybe that's because you got your eyes stuck up your rear end. Lieutenant is not happy."

"That makes at least two of us."

"He told me he assigns the cases and he don't remember assigning you anything last night."

"What case? I got jumped when I walked into a diner."

"I'd love to hear the story." She held up a hand when he looked like he was going to give her one. "When you're ready to tell the truth, that is. I got a part of it from girlfriend here, but she's being awful quiet."

Arran turned his glare back on me. "What's the matter, babe? Afraid you'll mess up your new career?"

I guessed I deserved that. "Don't you see that was a warning, Arran? They could have killed you. They could have dumped you in some swamp out there in the country."

"I'd love to see the way you two work this out," Fineman said, "but I'm supposed to deliver the rest of the message from the Lieutenant. He says to back off from Petrov. I heard Neeter talk about Petrov but I haven't heard we're on his case."

"Petrov was Ritchie Stone's boss."

"Was?"

"Stone is dead."

Fineman dropped her flowers in a clean chamberpot and sat down. "You know this how?"

"Oh, jeez. You really aren't going to believe this. Annie saw Stone's ghost. He told her."

Fineman rolled her eyes at her partner. "When was the last time you took a vacation, friend?"

"I told you you wouldn't believe it."

"I'm not saying I don't believe it. I'm saying it's a funny thing for you to be ruining your career over. You're the rational one, remember? I'm a chick. I'm allowed to believe in intuition and all that stuff."

"I never said *I* saw the ghost. Annie saw it."

"Lucky Annie. So, you decided to open a homicide investigation on the basis of hearsay evidence from an unregistered psychic and you didn't bother telling your partner?"

"Put that way, would *you* tell your partner? Petrov is blackmailing Annie to help him. I was trying to protect her."

Fineman looked me up and down. "Looks like you did one hell of a job of it. Annie's recovering from what happened with Stone. You're getting worse. Seems like you protected the shit out of her."

"You're right. I got—"

Except I couldn't choke back my words any more. "What do you mean, losing his job?" I'd assumed cops were pretty much set unless they take bribes or something. They have a union and all.

"Lieutenant was real insistent that my partner keep his nose out of cases not assigned to him." Fineman shook her head slowly. "Way I see it, Dane won't be able to manage that."

"Point. He sure didn't manage to stay away from trouble after I'd warned him."

Arran thrashed on his bed but managed not to pull out his I.V. "I'm not sure my girlfriend and my partner should be allowed to conspire together."

I flushed. He'd called me his girlfriend before, but this was in front of someone important to him. It made a difference.

"Get used to it, Dane," Fineman said. "Annie here and me going to have to conspire a bunch if you're going to save your tired ass."

Abruptly, though, I knew the answer and it had nothing to do with conspiring. I'd deluded myself when I'd imagined I could magically put Arran and my brother's family out of danger and then safely vanish to some other city. Sure, I could vanish, but they couldn't. My brother and Lauren had their jobs. Little Jack had his school. Arran was always out there on the streets of Dallas, always exposed. As long as they were exposed, Petrov could use them to send me a message—no matter where I ran.

The only way I could protect them was to be beyond Petrov's reach. And the only way that could happen was for me to become a ghost, myself.

Which wouldn't be as scary for me as it was for most people. After all, most people don't know what comes afterward. I mean, lots of people *hope* that they'll go to heaven or whatever. But they also *fear* they might go to the other place, or, even worse, simply vanish from existence. I *knew* that wasn't going to happen to me because I knew where you go when you're dead—wherever you want. Plus, I already had friends on the other side. I could keep up with my French lessons with Chantal. I could hang out with Harry at the County Records building. I could jump boxcars and ride the rails with Oren. More realistically, I could join Cassandra and Tiffany in the Arran Dane Ghostly Admiration Society.

All in all, it wouldn't be so bad.

Arran growled. "Oh, for God's sake."

"What?" Fineman leaned toward her partner.

"Don't look at me, look at her. Annie is getting another of her bad ideas."

If I was supposed to be the one with psychic powers, how come Arran and Petrov seemed to read me like a book? If I was so easy, how'd I manage to bluff a roomful of professional gamblers?

"She looks pretty much normal to me."

"That's because," Arran explained with overworked patience, "bad ideas are normal for her. What is it this time, Annie?"

I decided that a lie wasn't enough—I needed to break our ties now. That would cause him less pain when I crossed over to the other side. Not having ridiculous hopes that Arran and I could make a life together would make it easier for me, too.

"Look, Arran. Fineman is right. You're risking your job for nothing. I don't want your protection." I dug into my bag and pulled out big piles of hundred dollar bills. "Check this out. This is money I earned for one night's work for Petrov. One night, ten thousand dollars—not bad, huh? At this rate, if I work one job a week for him, by the end of the year I'll clear half a million—tax free. So why would I want to rock this boat?"

"Annie—"

I pushed ahead. "And *he* actually needs me, unlike you or my brother. Working this job is the first time I've really felt like I belonged somewhere in my life." Not counting feeling like I belonged in Arran's arms. But I could have that, sort of, once I was a ghost. I was quicker than Tiffany and Cassandra. I could shove them out of the way if they tried to keep me from him.

Arran's eyes narrowed as his gaze went from me to the money, then back to me. "You're being—"

"I'm being sensible. Petrov is my friend. So, leave him alone. Do your job and don't get fired."

I stomped out before I could change my mind.

Chapter 24

I wouldn't think of it as suicide. I was just passing to the other side, becoming a ghost. I wouldn't be weird any more, wouldn't have to worry about I'd remembered to attach my Bluetooth phone, wouldn't have to live in an aluminum foil bedroom. Since ghosts had been my most frequent conversation partners for years, I wouldn't even have to switch friends.

All in all, I assured myself, I was making the obvious choice.

Only becoming a ghost wasn't as easy as it sounded.

You'd think, seeing as I was in Texas, getting a gun would be a piece of cake.

Unlike a lot of people, I'd never had a gun. Understandably, considering they thought I was crazy, my parents had never allowed one in the house and this was one of their few habits both my brother and I had stuck with. Arran had one, but I didn't think he'd let me borrow it—along with just one bullet.

I could buy one, but I wasn't sure how to go about that. And this seemed to be one of the rare weeks there wasn't a gun show in the Dallas Convention Center.

So I put off the gun idea and considered other approaches.

My oven was gas, which was a good thing—I sure couldn't see myself putting my head in an electric oven. I turned it on and watched the flames whosh to life.

No problem, right. Just blow out the pilot. I tried that, but there wasn't one. It had an electronic ignition system.

I went after it with a screwdriver.

"You be careful with that," Chantal said. "Electricity can be dangerous, you know."

I knew that. I didn't know how she did it considering she'd died in the 1850s. "I'll definitely be careful." Like it would be such a shame to get accidentally electrocuted when I was trying to asphyxiate myself.

"You're planning something silly, aren't you?"

"For once in my life, I'm planning something smart."

Planning was one thing. Actually delivering was something else. Who knew they built ovens so solidly?

Half an hour later, I gave it up—but only because I'd shorted out the electricity for my entire apartment complex.

"I tell you ziss is dangerouse."

"You were right, Chantal. Do you have any other suggestions?"

"Shopping. Ziss always makes me feel better."

I couldn't remember ever having the kind of spare cash I had now, thanks to Petrov, yet recreational shopping didn't hold any appeal for me. Whatever I looked at, I'd end up wondering whether Arran would like it. Besides, why buy things when the only time I'd be able to wear them would be to my own funeral?

By the time the apartment manager restored electricity, complete with a lecture to me to be more careful, I had a crowd of ghosts. Harry clued Chantal in on what I was doing and she got snippy with me—whether for trying to pass over or for not telling her, she wouldn't say.

I was more careful this time, and finally managed to disconnect the electronic ignition system, just as Harry launched into a shaggy dog story about someone who'd committed suicide by turning on the gas—and blown up his entire apartment building after he was dead, killing fourteen others.

I didn't want to cross over with an entourage, so gassing myself was out. "Why didn't you tell me this before I had the oven in pieces?"

"Watching you was fun."

"All you guys are going to have to find some other entertainment once I've passed over," I said. "You won't have the twenty-four hour Annie show any more."

"Oh, boo-hoo. We'll all be sorry we weren't nicer to you."

That stung. "I'm not feeling sorry for myself. This is the only way out of the mess I've gotten myself in. As long as I'm alive, Petrov won't give up, and he'll end up hurting everyone I care about.

"Hey, I know." Chantal sounded as excited as if she'd discovered a chocolate mine. What about the old running the car in a closed garage trick?"

"Cause she don't drive, idiot," Oren answered. "Think she can find a taxi driver dumb enough to do it for her?"

I wasn't going to kill a taxi driver, either.

"This is more complicated than I thought it would be."

"Pills are best for a woman," Tiffany suggested. "They won't make you turn blue or anything the way gas could."

"I don't think I can overdose on Tums, and that's all I've got around here."

"What about hanging," the Colonel said. "We used to do that when soldiers got out of hand. You know, raping respectable women, stuff like that."

"Where did all you guys come from?" I demanded. "I'm trying to do something serious and you aren't making it easy."

"We're helping," Tiffany said. "How was I supposed to know you don't keep pills around? Everyone keeps pills around."

Everyone, maybe, except people who'd been medicated out of their minds for the first half of their lives. Surviving those years had given me a deep fear of drugs.

"Can't anyone suggest something better than hanging?"

I didn't recognize the ghost who raised his hand. He wore a torn pair of jeans and a leather vest over his naked chest, and had at least eighteen piercings through his ears, not to mention one each through his nipples —I mean, *ouch*. "How about you go with the hanging, but make it look like one of those autoerotica things, AEA, we call them. Go ahead and act it out, you know, with being naked and everything. That way nobody's going to feel guilty about you killing yourself. They'll think you just made a mistake. Happens all the time.

I'd heard something about that and hadn't understood it at all. Why someone would want to get it off while strangling themselves was the kind of mystery I was pretty sure I'd never understand.

"I thought that was just for guys."

The ghost shrugged. "I've heard about it with guys, mostly, but I think chicks do it, too. Biologically, guys and girls aren't that different, right? Besides, they think you're crazy anyway. They'd just assume you'd read about it somewhere and decided to try it out, not knowing it was just for guys."

I suspected my leather-vested buddy was more interested in getting me naked than in helping with my problems, but nobody offered any better suggestions.

AEA here I came. No pun intended.

Next up, finding some rope.

I suppose I could have caught the light rail and ridden out to Plano where there's one of the big box hardware stores. But I wanted to get this over with. None of the stores in Mockingbird station carried rope. I considered an extension cord, but decided that would confuse the autoerotic accident message.

Finally I found a shop that still carried silk ties. Since the only people I knew who still wore ties were ghosts, cops, or politicians, I wasn't sure why this place sold them, but maybe that's why I got such a grateful look from the clerk when I plunked down my hundred-dollar bill.

I felt like the guy in that Golden Goose story about everyone getting stuck to a goose as I returned to my apartment.

My own little clique of ghosts must have spread the news to everyone they met. There had to be three hundred ghosts gathered everywhere in my house. They didn't even leave me alone when I went into my aluminum-foil-lined bedroom although I several looked like they were fighting off migraines.

"Why not do it in the living room?" the guy with the leather shirt suggested. "You can hook it around your ceiling fan, there. Make sure you get naked first, though. Otherwise there wouldn't be a lot of point."

"Nobody self-asphyxiates in their living rooms. You just want to watch."

"Well, duh. Cause you can talk to us, you're sort of like a ghost already, but you can actually do stuff. That makes you interesting."

Right. It had nothing to do with getting me naked.

"I'm doing it in the bedroom." It would have been a lot easier if they'd all leave, though.

"You don't have to do this. You could just keep working with Petrov," Harry suggested when my hesitation became completely obvious. "As long as you're doing what he says, why would he hurt any of your friends?"

"That isn't the way he works," Ritchie said. "He needs to show his power. He'll keep doing little things to let you know he can. Like he did to Dane."

If anyone should know what Petrov might do, it was Ritchie Stone. And if beating Arran half to death counted as a little thing, I definitely didn't want to encourage him. "I'm going to do this thing. I just need to get myself psyched up."

"If you insist on doing it in your bedroom, you might start, uh, loosening up on the bed first, before you do the tie thing," leather-shirt said. "You know, with getting naked and inserting those toys girls use."

"That isn't going to happen. I'm going to do this, but I'm not giving you a free sex show. So, if that's what you're all waiting for, you can just go somewhere else to find it."

Nobody moved. I might be disappointing them, but even so, I was apparently the best show in town. Every second, a couple more ghosts popped through the aluminum walls and crowded around me.

"Are you going to do it soon?" Leather shirt asked. "Because it's not real comfortable here. If you're going to be a while, maybe you could turn on the TV and we could all hang out in the living room until you're ready."

"Far be it from me to cause you guys discomfort." I climbed up on my bed and looped the tie around the fan. I actually didn't care too much about the ghosts being uncomfortable—all they needed to do was leave my bedroom if they wanted to feel better. But leather shirt's words had reminded me that other people were hurting, and going to continue to be hurt, as long as I was alive.

Making a noose wasn't especially difficult, but my fingers seemed clumsy and I had to retie it three times before I got it right.

"Okay, time to get naked," Leather shirt crowed.

Right. So the emergency response people could look at my scrawny body. Still, nobody would be fooled if I didn't do something to set up the act. I calculated the minimum I could get away with, then dropped my jeans to my ankles, put one hand inside my underwear, and draped the loop around my neck with the other hand.

"Hey, you're cheating us," leather shirt protested. "You aren't showing anything. And don't you at least have a thong you can wear? Those panties look like something Laurence of Arabia might have camped under."

"At least I have a shirt. Where did you get that disgusting vest thing?"

"I'll show mine if you show yours."

I was already showing more than I wanted to. And yeah, the EMT guys would probably be grossed out by my grandmother underwear.

That couldn't be helped, though.

I made sure the tie was looped securely, took a deep breath and stepped over to the side of my bed. My plan was to jump off, let the noose tighten around me, and tough it out for the few seconds it would take to cut off the blood flow in the big carotid artery leading to my brain —something else I knew about from my Tae Kwon Do.

"At least pull your panties down to your knees," leather shirt whined. "We can't see anything."

"You do it," I said, and jumped.

* * * *

You know those stories about a bright light or an endless hallway? I didn't see any of that stuff. What I saw was Arran, looking pissed as hell.

A sense of loss swept over me. We'd never be able to talk again, at least not until he became a ghost.

But Arran evidently didn't see the logic of my decision. He burst through my door, pulled out a pocket knife, and cut me down just as the ceiling fan gave way and crashed onto the bed.

"What the hell do you think you're doing, woman?"

"You're supposed to be in the hospital getting better." My voice was raspy and I self-consciously pulled up my jeans even before I unwrapped the end of the noose on my neck.

"You think I'd just let you make an idiot out of yourself?"

"It's not idiotic, it's the sensible thing. Petrov can't hurt me if I'm a ghost, and he'll have no reason to hurt you."

"She's got a point, Ritchie said. "But if the show is over, why don't you guys come out to the living room where we can thrash out the issues in a bit of comfort.

I sighed. "Sure, why not."

Arran looked baffled for a moment, then realized I was talking to my ghosts. "We got here in time," he shouted over his shoulder.

Fineman came into my bedroom, with her weapon drawn. She looked around and saw how I was done up with the tie around my neck, and that I was still trying to button my jeans. That look earned me a laugh. "The old faked autoerotic thing to cover suicide so we wouldn't feel guilty trick, eh?"

"How'd they figure that out?" leather shirt demanded. "I thought it was a damned good plan."

"For cops," I said, "they're pretty smart. Come on. Let's go out to the living room. All this aluminum foil is giving me a headache."

"Dang. And she's not even a ghost," Harry said.

Still feeling like the fairy tale goose boy, I led a procession of two cops and hundreds of ghosts out of my bedroom, down the hall, and into the living room. It would have taken longer if the ghosts hadn't taken shortcuts through the walls.

"I told you she had a bad idea." Arran was talking to Fineman, not to me at all.

"Look, Arran," I said. "Spare me the macho stuff. Detective Fineman says you're the logical one, so use your logic. As long as I'm alive, Petrov is going to hurt people I care about. What happened to you was just an example. Once I become a ghost I put both myself and you out of his reach."

Arran inhaled, in obvious preparation for interrupting me.

I held out a hand and barged ahead, not letting him get a word in. "Before you say you don't care what happens to you, I know that. But I care—and I also care what happens to Jack, Lauren, and Little Jack."

"Did you ever think about sitting down and talking things over?"

"Isn't that what we've been doing for the past week? We sit, we talk, we plan, we try to reason things out. The only problem is, it doesn't work. The only idea we came up with was to have me play along. But playing along with Petrov didn't keep you safe. Oh, or wear a wire, which would have been even dumber."

"Me getting beat up was my fault. You warned me not to follow you. You weren't responsible."

"I know I wasn't responsible. But it wasn't your fault, it was Petrov's plan. That guy knows psychology stuff. He wanted you to follow because he wanted to hurt you."

"Then why did he tell—"

"He knew that telling you not to follow would be waving a red flag. He figured you'd respond just like you did and he had his goons waiting to hurt you. I'm not going to let him play you any more."

"Maybe we should play him," Fineman said.

"Like the Beatles said, 'we'd all like to see the plan.' The thing is, he's smarter than we are. He's pretty much proved that, hasn't he?"

"He's a criminal," Fineman reminded me. "He can't be that smart."

That was logical. The only problem was, I didn't think it was true.

"I've said from the beginning," Arran's voice was reflective, "that if Petrov's in jail, he won't be able to hurt us. He's not one of the old-time crime bosses with a whole family behind him. He won't have a succession plan that will let him keep control on the outside."

"One problem with that. He's not in jail."

"Another problem," Fineman broke in, "or maybe part of the same problem. Lieutenant says you're to back off of Petrov. You go on some one-cop crusade against him, Petrov is *still* going to be out on the streets and you're going to be a blackballed ex-cop."

"He got my psychological profile from the police," I reminded them. "Clearly he's got connections in the department. And if your lieutenant is telling you to back off, Petrov's reach must be pretty high."

Fineman licked her lips. "This Petrov guy seems like bad news. Maybe we should take him out."

"Good idea," Ritchie Stone's ghost said. "He did it to me, so we do it to him."

"Shut up, Ritchie. This is exactly the kind of thing I was trying to prevent when I decided to cross over." I rubbed the skin on my neck. I was going to have a bruise.

"No assassination," Arran agreed. "But you know the saying about sauce for the goose?"

It took me a second to figure out what he was talking about, but only because I was still caught up in my goose-boy fairy tale. "You mean, we get the ghosts to do to him what he's using them to do to other people?"

Arran smiled. "Exactly."

He was so self-satisfied I hated to burst his bubble. But it had to be done. "Petrov will be looking for that. The second something bad happens to him, something where inside information pays off, he'll be onto us. When that happens, the gloves will come off and he'll come after us. Or come after my brother and his family."

"Guess we'd better get to work, then. We've got to nail Petrov before

Jack and Lauren come back from their vacation."

"Tell the black girl-cop I'll help out if she'll get naked for me," leather shirt suggested.

"Hey, yeah. She's hot," Ritchie agreed.

I shook my head. "Nobody is going to get naked any more, you guys. Your chance to see the scrawny chick with her pants down is over. You want to see naked women, head down to the titty bars on Northwest Highway. This show is a rainout. You'll get your refunds in the mail."

The ghosts milled around. Gradually, some of them faded through the walls or floated up through the ceiling, but more of them than I'd guessed hung around. Life as a ghost must be awful boring if my life could be a highlight.

"You seem just right to me." Arran brushed his long fingers over the marks the silk tie had left on my neck.

I shivered with desire. I wasn't used to being this needy. For the first time, I understood the desperation felt by some of the girls from the State School. They'd craved sex so strongly they'd throw the poker games to get it. At the time, I'd thought they were weak, damaged. I wasn't sure I'd been wrong, but when it came to Arran, I wasn't any better. If it hadn't been for the crowd of a hundred or more ghosts and Fineman, I would have thrown myself on him right there. Which would have been a disaster considering he should still be in the hospital recovering from his wounds.

"Okay," I said. "I'll see if I can get the ghosts to go along on a hunting expedition. I have a bad feeling about this, though. It isn't like Petrov actually trusts me—he doesn't trust anyone."

"He doesn't have to trust you." Fineman showed her teeth. "He just needs to keep breaking the law. Sooner or later, he'll do something we can hook to him. When that happens, he goes to jail same as any other criminal."

"Considering how much my brother hates vacations, we'd better hope for sooner rather than later."

Chapter 25

"We can't get in there."

With what I'd learned of Petrov's habits, finally locating Petrov's home in White Settlement, on the outskirts of Fort Worth, had been no trouble.

Hanging around without being noticed or bringing in the local police was a bigger challenge. So we'd dropped the Colonel and Oren off at his house and set up our camp in a Cici's Pizza a couple of blocks away.

The Colonel and Oren almost beat us to the pizza place.

"What are you talking about?" I demanded. "Ghosts can go everywhere."

"I always thought that," the Colonel agreed. "Even your aluminum foil bedroom won't keep us out although it assuredly gives me a headache. But Petrov has done one better. His whole house is lined with lead and he's got some kind of Russian religious chants playing on his sound system. We bounce off when we try to go through his walls."

"So, use the do—"

I waited until his cook opened the door to carry out some trash and tried. Even with the door open, I can't get through."

"Petrov didn't have nothing like that when I was working for him," Ritchie said. "Must have done some research after he killed me."

"What?" Arran demanded. As usual, he was getting impatient only getting half the conversation.

"The guys can't get in."

"Sure. That would have been too easy."

"Generally," Fineman said, "criminals make it easy."

"You've got to stop underestimating Petrov. He isn't a normal criminal." He'd even halfway convinced me to go along with him, help him out because it was the easiest thing to do. In general, I didn't have a problem with gambling—I'd always seen gambling laws as pandering to religious nuts. But Petrov had burned his bridges with me when he'd had Arran beaten. The only explanation for his behavior was sadism. The only solution, unless I wanted to try the tie thing again, was to get him off the streets.

"So," Arran said, "Plan A bites the dust. We can't get into Petrov's place to find out what he's up to."

I shook my head. "That's where you're wrong, babe. The ghosts can't get in. Thanks to your quick work with a jackknife, I'm not a ghost yet. And lead linings and Russian chants won't keep me out."

"How about servants, electronic motion sensors, and armed guards?"

I almost growled at Arran. I hated it that he was always right. "Okay, I guess those might cause some problems. How about thinking of something positive rather than just coming up with problems."

"Cops always look at problems first," Fineman said. "We need to figure out the worst things that can happen and make sure we've got plans to deal with them. We didn't think that way, we'd all be dead."

That wasn't the kind of attitude Oprah would approve of, but I didn't guess you'd be much of a cop if you went around with an *everything's fine* world view.

"We've already learned the worst thing that can happen—our secret weapon, the ghosts, have just misfired. Now it's up to us and the longer we wait, the more likely it is that Petrov will realize we're after him. We've got to act now, before he finds out."

"We'll act when we know what to do." Arran's voice wasn't patronizing, but I heard that anyway.

"We've got to—"

I knew we had to do something but I didn't know what, so I was just as happy when my phone rang, taking me off the hook for delivering an immediate solution to my problems.

Just as happy, that is, until I saw who was calling.

"Mr. Petrov? I thought you said you had nothing for me for a few days."

"You're making a mistake, Ms. Neeter. May I suggest that you and your friends back off?"

"I don't know what you're talking about."

"Don't you? I suppose you just felt like driving an hour to buy pizza a few blocks from my home."

Oh, shit, he knew where we were—and what we'd been doing. "What, precisely, do you want, Mr. Petrov?"

"Precision—I appreciate that. What I want, and what I expect is you to instruct Detective Dane and Detective Fineman to follow their orders and leave me alone."

The better part of wisdom was to agree, buy some time. "Maybe you should have thought of what you needed and expected before you had Arran beat up, then, Petrov. I was going along with you, helping you out, giving you everything you needed to make you the biggest godfather in the history of Dallas, but you couldn't resist showing me who was boss. You had to—" I brushed off Arran's attempt to hush me and kept going, "you had to send me a message. Well, I'm sending a message back. And that message is, you've stepped over the line. From now on, it's war. And it's a war that won't end until you're in jail."

"There's a saying, Ms. Neeter, that those who start wars don't necessarily get to predict how they end."

My phone gave a click and I saw he'd disconnected.

"Well." I made my voice as bright as I could, "I guess we know where we stand now."

"Yeah, that was real tough," the Colonel effused. "I wonder, though, if this war you're talking about might not end up as badly as the one *I* fought in. You know, when we were outgunned and outmanned and morally in the wrong."

Arran's phone rang before I had a chance to answer the Colonel but I'd wised up enough not to think anybody was being saved by the bell.

"Suspended? Without pay? But sir—"

Arran looked sick. "No, sir. Detective Fineman is not involved in this, sir. It's completely my—"

He hung up the phone. "Sorry, Fineman. We're both on unpaid administrative leave until the department can figure out some excuse to fire us. You'll probably be notified next."

"Ignoring orders comes up as one possibility," Fineman said.

I couldn't help butting in. "If you'd let me finish what I started, none of this would be—"

"Shut. Up. Annie." Arran made each word a complete sentence. "My job is not worth anybody dying for."

"On the other hand," Fineman pointed out, "a regular paycheck sure does come in handy. Especially since Bobbie can't seem to get off his butt and keep a job for more than two days."

"If you call your lieutenant and tell him you're backing off," I said, "maybe he'll let you keep your job. Petrov doesn't care about you, he just cares about himself."

I could practically see the cogs in Fineman's brain, but she finally shook her head. "Got no use for a job where criminals are calling the shots. You're right, Annie. We're in a war. Petrov just Pearl Harbored us, but getting the first shot doesn't mean you get the last. We'll take him down."

Both Fineman and Arran stared at me. I stared back for a moment, until I realized what they were doing. I'd been on the verge of giving them a plan when the phone had rang. Except where a plan should be was a big empty space in my brain.

"I'm out of ideas." A part of me wanted to look away so I wouldn't see the disappointment in their eyes. I'd seen that disappointment so many times before—with my parents, my teachers, my psychiatrists and councilors. But I couldn't look away. I'd gotten them into this. The least

I could do was stick with them and share the pain.

Arran just shrugged. "It's not up to you to come up with all the plans. And don't you dare say anything else about killing yourself or crossing over or whatever you call it."

I shook my head. "I told Petrov it was war. I'm here for the duration."

"Problem is, some wars you lose," the Colonel reminded us. "All of us, when we joined up, thought war was some patriotic romp."

"I thought I was in for the duration, too," Ritchie added. "Except, Petrov didn't let me stick around."

"I want to get discouraged, I'll look in the mirror," I said. "I want a plan, not discouragement. So, who's got ideas on how we're going to put Petrov behind bars for good?"

I'd shaken off most of my crowd of ghosts, but a dozen or so had jammed into Fineman's big pickup truck for the drive over to Fort Forth. Now, they filled the pizza place. All stared at me with blank looks on their faces.

Oh, yeah. They were ghosts. I already knew that ghosts were better at following up on other people's plans than making their own. Considering how bad they were at following up on anything, that said a lot.

Finally Ritchie shuffled forward. "Tell you what, Annie. You persuade that detective to get naked and I'll give you some ideas."

"You want to see Arran naked?" I'd thought Cassandra, Tiffany and I were the only ones with that particular bent. Ritchie was from a class of people who tended to get caught up in anti-gay propaganda. Admitting he'd like to see a naked man was a big step for him.

"Not him—don't make me puke. That other ghost, the one with the nipple rings and cool vest, he gave me the idea. I'm talking about that M.I.L.F. detective. Carly Fineman."

I didn't know what a Milf was, and I didn't think I wanted to. "You want to see Detective Fineman naked?" I checked her out. For an overweight woman in her forties, she was pretty hot. But she was an overweight woman in her forties, which definitely meant she wasn't going to be hired a cover model for *Playboy Magazine* any time soon.

"Are you kidding. She makes my blood steam."

"You don't have blood."

"That's a metaphor. I might not have graduated from high school, but I went for a while."

I didn't know about metaphors, but I decided I should take this as a positive lesson. If Ritchie thought Fineman was hot, maybe that had to prove there really was someone for everyone.

"I don't think Detective Fineman is interested, Ritchie. She's a cop, not a stripper."

"At least ask her, at least. Huh?"

I pondered that. Then I thought about all the Tae Kwon Do classes I'd missed and how, I wished I'd gone so I'd be better at blocking and avoiding punches—something I'd need if I suggested Fineman strip down for a ghost.

Unfortunately, I didn't have any better ideas. "Uh, Ritchie says he's got some suggestions but he wants to see you, well, naked, Detective Fineman."

"He does, does he? Not sure my husband would approve of that."

"No. I wouldn't guess he would be happy about that." I turned back to Ritchie. How about you give us your ideas and we decide how to reward you?" If I'd been willing to die for this, I could strip for it too. "Maybe I'll let you see *me* naked. Does that sound fair?"

"Sounds fair to me," Harry put in. "I want to see you naked."

"No." That was from Arran.

"What's the matter, Arran? Afraid I'll scare away the ghosts?"

"We don't need help from a pervert killer."

"Here I was thinking we need all the help we can get."

"I don't want you—"

"You don't own me, Arran. I'll get naked for whoever I want."

Ritchie shook his head. "I've seen you naked. No offense, Annie, but there's not enough of you to do much for me. Detective Fineman, though, she's hot. Besides, I don't trust you. You said you'd let us watch you, you know, jack off with the rope thing and you didn't."

"I never said I'd jack off with the tie. Besides, girls don't jack off."

"TMI," Fineman said. "Come to think of it, though, Robbie spends more time at tittie-bars than I approve of. I guess I can let this Ritchie creep have a peek if he gives us something useful. Something *really* useful."

"No." That was Arran again.

Fineman cupped a hand to her ear and looked around. "I'm starting to hear an echo. Well, guess what, Dane? You're not the boss of me, either."

"But—"

"Hey, they're ghosts, right? It's not like they can't look any time they want to. Besides, when you get to my age, you're looking for some appreciation."

I was pretty sure I'd never want scumbags like Ritchie sneaking peeks at me and didn't think Fineman was either. But she was willing to make the deal.

"You may not trust me, but you trust Detective Fineman, don't you, Ritchie. She says—"

"I heard what she says. Tell her she's got a deal."

I passed along the message. "All right, Ritchie. Tell us what you've got. If we agree it's worth something, I'll pass along any special requests you have for Detective Fineman."

"You'd better."

"I will."

"Okay. I know where my body hidden. He had me killed. So, get him on murder."

"Petrov said he salted your body with clues that will point to Arran. If we dig it up, we'll be cutting our own throats. Come on, Ritchie. You want to see Fineman in her skivvies, you're going to have to do better."

"If you find my body before the cops get there, you could switch things out, get rid of anything that implicates Dane and make sure the clues point to Petrov."

I wasn't just a title researcher, I was also a fan of crime shows. I knew how hard it could be to cover up all of the evidence. Ritchie might be onto something. "Did he kill you personally?"

"Of course not. Petrov never does his own dirty work."

That wasn't what I wanted to hear. The more steps between the criminal and the crime, the harder it would be for the police to prove anything, and the more likely Petrov would be walking around free a long time after he'd finished off my family and myself.

"We're not going to violate a crime scene," Arran said when I'd passed along Ritchie's suggestion.

"How about just a quick look anyway?" Ritchie asked.

I didn't even pass that request to Fineman. "Forget it."

"But you promised—"

This time it was Fineman's phone that rang. She looked grim when she disconnected. "Too late to take Ritchie's deal. A couple of minutes ago, a supposed jogger spotted a body in the Trinity floodway. Police have already identified it as Ritchie Stone. He's got your business card pinned to the outside of his jacket, Dane. Guess Petrov wanted to make sure nobody missed that clue."

"What do you want to bet that the jogger happens to do some gambling with Petrov?" Arran said.

I looked around. All of a sudden, the walls of Cici's Pizza felt like they were crowding me. "Considering Petrov knows we're here, I'm betting the local P.D. is already on their way."

* * * *

We turned the corner onto Sherry off of Las Vegas Trail just as a herd of White Settlement and Fort Worth police cars converged, lights flashing but sirens ominously silent.

"We need to dump my pickup." Fineman sounded matter-of-fact. "You sure you're not ready to end that guy?"

Arran shook his head.

"Your buddy Ritchie have any other ideas?"

Ritchie and most of the other ghosts were riding in the pickup's bed but he stuck his head through the back window when I signaled to him. "Fineman wants to know what else you have?"

"I've shaken down a lot of guys. Could give you names and addresses."

"Anything connect it back to Petrov?"

"Just me."

"No offense, but no court is going to take your word for it."

Fineman pulled her truck into a junkyard, jogged off, and returned a few minutes later with a set of keys. "Okay, kiddos. We've got new wheels."

Wheels was stretching it, and *new* was not even close. Fineman's keys started an old Buick Regal that poured out blue smoke, but that showed a surprising amount of power.

"Supercharged," Fineman said. "Might not be Detroit's best, but not bad. It sure don't look anything like my pickup."

Said pickup was now draped with a tarp and abandoned in the middle of the junkyard.

"You sure they won't turn you in to the cops?" I asked.

"My brother can be a jerk—I don't think he's that big a jerk."

"I never knew you had a brother," Dane said.

"Let's hope the cops don't figure that out, either. My father had eight women around the metroplex. But blood is thicker and Ty is okay. Oh, you'd better turn off your phones. I don't want to get tracked that way."

We drove around Fort Worth for a while. We hadn't been caught, yet, but we were just putting off the inevitable. Petrov and the police looking for us and we couldn't go home. Sooner or later, we'd make a mistake and that would be it.

"We need to go on the offensive," I said.

"That's what the generals always told us," the Colonel said. "Problem was, every time we went on the offensive, the Union soldiers shot us up."

"I don't care about the Civil War. I know for sure that Petrov will win if we don't do something."

214

"I've never been in a woman's prison shower room," Ritchie said. "Bet that would be pretty interesting."

It didn't sound very interesting to me, and I was increasingly uninterested in hearing from the pervert section.

"How about we wait until we know he's not there and raid his house," I suggested. "Surely he'll have something incriminating there. I mean, if he didn't, why would he have ghost-proofed it?"

Both Fineman and Arran shook their heads. "Cops will have staked it out," Arran explained. We go anywhere near it and game over."

I thought about the time I'd spent with Petrov. He seemed to do a lot of his work from the car. Since cars move, and since Petrov was still a criminal, I hoped the cops wouldn't be watching it as closely.

"Petrov's driver, Jarred Sanchez, seems all right. He could give us access to Petrov's car—and to the computer he keeps in it."

"Any idea where he stays?" Fineman asked.

"No. But the Arlington P.D. pulled him over when he was bringing me home. They'd know."

"We got friends in A.P.D.," Fineman said.

Arran's eyes narrowed. "We're wanted for murder. Nobody's that good friends."

"I know where Sanchez lives." Ritchie leered at Fineman.

"Where?"

"Come on, Annie. No show, no tell. Tell the sexy detective it's her move."

I explained.

Fineman pulled into the parking lot of an abandoned strip shopping center. "Dane, close your eyes."

"You're really going to do this?" I asked.

"Shut up, Annie." She unbuttoned her top and unhooked her bra.

Okay, I'd been wrong about her being fat. She was just built— megabuilt. No wonder Ritchie had been interested.

"Satisfied, Ritchie?"

"Oh, baby."

I don't know where they came from but the neighborhood was suddenly full of ghosts craning for a good look.

"Hey, no touching," I said when Ritchie got a little too close.

"Yeah, but—"

"No buts. That wasn't the deal."

"So," Fineman pulled herself back together, "where's this Sanchez live?"

I think Ritchie's tongue was swollen because he had trouble talking, but we finally managed to get the address out of him.

I wasn't sure how I felt about Fineman's topless moment, but I felt good about tracking down Sanchez. There was no way the cops could guess we'd found Sanchez, so they wouldn't be watching, couldn't be staking us out. This was going to be easy. Right?

Chapter 26

Sanchez lived in a 1970s tract home that hadn't gotten the upkeep or updates it desperately needed. A Big-Wheel and a deflated soccer ball outside his front door told me something I hadn't known but had guessed. Sanchez had a family. As Petrov had taught me, the more connections we have, the easier we are to blackmail.

The ghosts deployed as Fineman pulled in front of the house, some going to the back where they could notify us in the event Sanchez beat a quick retreat, the others burrowing through the fiberglass siding to investigate inside.

A couple of minutes later, the Colonel reported that Petrov's Town Car was in Sanchez's garage, and Oren confirmed that Sanchez was at home watching TV. Better yet, Petrov hadn't extended his ghostproofing to his employee's place. They'd been able to go everywhere and there wasn't a cop or Russian gunman in sight.

Before he let me knock on the door, Arran insisted on cutting Sanchez's phone line, although I thought that was a waste of time since I was sure he had a cell.

Sanchez goggled at me. "What the devil are you doing here, Annie? Mr. Petrov will kill both of us."

"Petrov already wants me dead and you know your family isn't safe no matter what you do. So I'm going to turn the tables on him before he has a chance."

Sanchez looked around as if afraid someone would be listening. Well, someone was listening—specifically, me, two police detectives, and about twenty ghosts. The detectives and I wouldn't talk, and the ghosts didn't have anyone but me to talk to.

"Prison doesn't matter," he said. "He can report my family, have them sent back to Columbia. It is too dangerous there."

I looked at Arran but he shrugged. "Local cops can't control immigration. That's federal."

"We can tie you up," Fineman suggested. "Make it look like you wouldn't help us. Maybe even beat you up some."

Sanchez considered, then shook his head. "Doesn't matter. He won't believe anything. You're going to try to check out his computer, right? Not sure it'll work. He's got it set up so if anyone breaks into the car, the hard drive goes away, empty. And you saw how it's connected? If anyone takes it out of the car, poof."

"But you have the code." I put on my most pleading smile. "He'll kill me, Sanchez. You know he likes to hurt people, so he won't kill me easy like he did Ritchie. He'll—"

"*He* killed Ritchie Stone? He told me he'd set Ritchie up with his own business in Atlanta. I was wondering why that punk never got in touch with me to pay me the hundred he borrowed."

"I forgot about that hundred," Ritchie said. "Damn."

"Petrov killed him. And he's going to kill me too if you won't help us."

Sanchez shook his head. "You're lying, Annie. Mr. Petrov is a hard man, but he wouldn't kill anyone who was loyal to him. Ritchie is loyal. Not very smart, but he's about as loyal as you can get."

"I'm smarter than you are," Ritchie shouted.

"He's alive and you're dead," I reminded the ghost. "So I wouldn't argue the point too hard."

Fineman fingered her semi-automatic. "We could beat the shit out of you until you told us the entry code."

"Come on, Fineman. Sanchez is going to help us without that."

"Unlikely," he said. "And if you beat me, the evidence would be inadmissible.

"How about if I can prove Ritchie is dead and that Petrov killed him."

"How the heck you going to do that? You got Petrov's confession on tape?"

If I'd let the cops fit me with a wire, I might have exactly that. More likely, though, my body would be floating under a bridge in the middle of the Trinity River.

But I had a better idea. "Hey Ritchie, when was the last time you got together with Sanchez?"

It took a couple of minutes, but Sanchez had seen me playing poker. He knew the ghosts talked to me. And he didn't believe Ritchie would give me the details if I'd been lying about Petrov.

"Okay," he finally said. "But what about my family? We need to run, but I only have Petrov's Town Car. And if I take that, he'll have me arrested."

Fineman pulled the keys to the Buick out of her bag. "Take the Regal. You'll need to add oil every time you fill the tank, but it's a good car. And don't tell us where you're going."

"Oh, Sanchez." I reached into my pocket and pulled out the money Petrov had given me. "You'll need this."

"But that's your money."

"You think I want blood money from Petrov? You've got a family to worry about, so you take it."

Sanchez took the money, snatched the keys from Fineman, then led us out to the garage and coded the Town Car open. "His computer is in the back." He backed away. "Good luck."

"You, too," I said. Sanchez wasn't exactly a friend, but he'd been a friend to Ritchie. For once, being the medium in the middle had paid off rather than leaving me stuck.

Arran booted up Petrov's computer, then passed it to Fineman. "You know how these things work better than I do."

"Oh, for Pete's sake, give me that." As a researcher, I spent more time on the computer than I'd want to count.

Most of the files were encrypted and I couldn't begin to guess Petrov's passwords, but the Russian had snoozed the system the last time he'd used it rather than shutting it down altogether. Since he hadn't shut down the system, the last spreadsheet he'd worked on was still open. Not only did it show the point spreads for hundreds of games, which I didn't think was illegal, it also showed the volume of betting he'd taken in—which was a pretty good indication that he'd been breaking the law.

"That, together with what you can testify, should be enough to swear out an arrest warrant." Dane slid his fingers through my hair—an oddly sexy gesture.

"Guess it's time to call in the cavalry," Fineman said. "Except they're looking for you for murder and just might come in shooting."

"Maybe we should be somewhere else," Arran said.

I pulled myself out of the sexual haze Arran's touch had put us in. "If we leave, nobody's going to make odds that this computer won't *accidentally* get damaged before it gets to police headquarters. We know Petrov has moles in the department. They'll protect him. We've got to watch this computer until we're sure it goes to the right place."

"Which would be what?" Fineman asked. "The police are the right place, but we don't trust them."

"Texas Rangers," the Colonel said.

Incredibly, he was right. And he didn't even ask to see Fineman's tits in return for the solution, although he certainly had stared at them when she'd opened up her top earlier.

"Aren't the Rangers supposed to investigate cases where there are suspicions of police corruption?" As a kid, I'd watched *Walker, Texas Ranger* so I knew something, although it was possible that parts of that show were fictionalized.

Arran looked like he'd bit a lemon. "We call the Texas Rangers on our own department, we can kiss our jobs good-bye."

"As opposed to what? Your great chances of being promoted now?"

"Your lady has a point," Fineman said. "We need to call in the cavalry."

"Which would be me." The colonel brought himself to full attention.

"She means the Texas Rangers. Your idea."

"Oh. All right, then."

Fineman got out her phone and pressed the power button. Before her cell finished booting, the phone inside Sanchez's home started ringing.

"Could be a telemarketer," Ritchie suggested.

"I don't think we have much time." I looked at the others. "Something tells me that Petrov is on his way."

* * * *

Fineman completed her call to the local office of the Texas Rangers, explained that we thought we were under threat, and then pulled her gun and clicked off the safety. "They're busy. Probably be an hour before they get here."

"If I was alive, me and my unit could hold them off," the Colonel offered.

He hadn't been alive in a century and a half, but maybe— "Hey Colonel, how about you start a new unit."

"Your detective got fired. He can't make me a ghost deputy any more."

"No, he can't. But you could create a special forces unit from the other ghosts around here. You could send out scouts, keep track of where the enemy is deploying, warn us when they were creeping up on us, and listen in on any plans."

I wasn't sure it would be enough to keep us alive, but these were ghosts, after all. They couldn't do too much.

"Special forces, nothing. Those are scouting functions, and that's what cavalry is for," the Colonel said. "So, that's what we'll be—The New Texas Volunteer Cavalry. Now we need to get us some horses."

"If you don't mind, I'd rather walk," Oren said. "But I'd be happy to help out with scouting."

"You need horses if you're going to be cavalry."

"We'd like horses." Tiffany and Cassandra spoke together.

Good. Let them go play with horses and leave Arran alone.

"You don't have enough time to track down a bunch of ghost horses," I said. "Don't cavalry scouts ever dismount for better, uh, what's the word? Exfoliation?"

"I think you mean infiltration," Fineman said.

"Oh, yeah."

The Colonel shook his head. Reality was busting into his fantasy again. "All right. We'll find horses later. Cassandra, go around and see if you can scare up some more volunteers. Oren, get up on the roof of the garage and keep an eye out. Tiffany, I want you to head south to the corner and watch for any incoming vehicles." He continued shouting out orders to the remainder of the ghosts who'd gathered to check out Fineman's rack.

"Which way is south?" Tiffany barely whispered in my ear.

I pointed.

"Oh, thanks."

"I know you cops all have backup guns and throwdown guns," I said, showing off what I'd learned from watching crime shows. "So, why don't you give one to me and show me how to work it. I'll help defend us when Petrov and his guys head in."

Arran looked at me like I'd sprung a second head. "No way are you putting yourself in the firing line."

"What? Because you're a macho man. If you're willing to fight for me, why can't I fight for you?"

"Because you don't know how." Fineman sounded like she was holding onto her patience with a pair of loose tweezers. "If you've never shot before, a gun would make you more dangerous to us than to Petrov's guys. Arran isn't being a sexist bigot—not about this, anyway. You can help us more by passing on what the ghosts have to say."

I nodded, but then it hit me. Arran and Carly Fineman weren't treating me like a damaged and crazy girl who thought she saw things. They had finally gotten to the point where they could take my ghosts as matter-of-fact reality. More than even my brother and Lauren, they accepted who I was.

God, it was going to hurt when I left town. Assuming any of us lived long enough for that to happen. Because nothing that was going on changed the fact that too many people knew about my secret, there were too many chances for another Petrov to come along and pressure me through my family, or through Arran and Carly.

All my life, I'd wanted human friends—and failed in making them. Now I actually had friends, and everything I did put them in danger.

A steady trickle of ghosts appeared, rousted out by Cassandra or attracted by some voyeuristic interest in the coming violence. I supposed that ghosts were like any other people—they couldn't not look at an oncoming train wreck.

The Colonel put them to work. I repeatedly had to remind him that we needed scouts, he wanted them to hold their ground and not let anyone past.

In the meantime, Fineman and Arran argued firing lines, moved around junk furniture in the garage to create both cover and to fake anyone coming in. It wasn't much, but they did what they could to get ready for an assault.

Ten minutes after we'd organized, the sounds of at least four high-powered oversized vehicles practically drowned out Tiffany's squawk. "They're here. A bunch of guys with guns are getting out of some cars."

"Private, that report is inadequate," the Colonel said. "Type of vehicles, count of invaders, and nature of their weapons."

"Huh?"

"What are they driving?" I was so used to intermediating between ghosts and people, I didn't mind doing ghost-ghost translation.

"Oh. Well, three SUVs are full of guys. Then there's a big Town Car with black windows. It's weird but I sort of bounced off when I tried to get inside so don't know who's in there."

I had a pretty good idea. "How many guys—"

Oren dropped through the garage's roof to answer that one. "Twelve men, in three groups of four, have entered the property. Two of the groups are heading toward Sanchez's home. One is coming straight for the garage. They're armed with what looks like a fancy Tommy Gun."

"What's a Tommy Gun?" I asked Fineman. "Oren says they've got those."

"A Tommy Gun is a Thompson Submachine Gun," Fineman explained. "Used in the twenties up until the Korean War. I suspect Petrov's guys have Uzis, though. They're a nasty little weapon, lighter and more accurate than the old Tommy, and are a lot easier to find outside of antique gun collections."

Submachine guns sounded bad, especially since Arran and Fineman only had pistols.

A boom from the direction of Sanchez's front door indicated they carried more than Uzis. Not that I was a gun expert, but that sounded like a shotgun.

"They just took out Sanchez's front door," the Colonel reported. "Don't know what kind of load they had in that sawed-off, but it just blasted that door right off its hinges. Six enemy troopers are going inside. The rest have stayed outside. They've divided their forces. Now would be a good time to attack."

"It's still six to two," Fineman said. She was inside Sanchez's heavy town car.

"Better than twelve to two," Arran whispered from the ceiling joists where he was hiding.

The first of the group approaching the garage stuck his nose inside.

I hunkered down behind a saggy couch, ignoring the odor that proved a number of cats had used it for sanitary purposes since it had been moved out to the garage.

"Don't see anybody." The gunman spoke with a strong Russian accent. Petrov had called out his homeboys.

Per instructions, I waited until Oren told me all four of those approaching had entered the garage—I'd been told *not* to peek. Still huddling as close to the ground as I could get, I raised my voice. "Police. You're under arrest. Lay down your weapons."

The Uzi's firing sounded like a jackhammer, but it cut off after a second.

A crunch was immediately followed by a sigh, then by what could only be fist against face.

Instead of waiting for Oren to report, I disobeyed orders and peeked around the couch.

Two of the Russians were down, and Arran had his weapon trained on two others as Fineman cuffed their wrists and strapped duct tape over their mouths.

"Badguys are coming at a run," the Colonel shouted. "Had to hear that gunshot. Two more got out of the Town Car, so that makes four coming up the driveway. All six in the house are heading for the interior door.

"Ten coming," I reported, sharing the details.

"Couldn't get him before he fired." Arran massaged his knuckles. "Carly, take the driveway. Shoot to freeze them. I'll try holding off the guys from the house. And Annie?"

"Yeah?"

"Get under the cushions. What part of staying hidden didn't you get?"

"But—"

"But nothing. You're to be heard and not seen. Is that clear?"

"Clear." I went back to my couch.

"Hey, you could get into the middle of it," Oren said. "This used to be a sleeper but the mattress is gone. You're smaller than a mattress."

I wasn't sure how that would help, but if Arran felt better with me hidden, I might as well go the distance. I burrowed under the cat-stained cushions and climbed into the rusty steel of bedframe.

Harry got in with me. "Cozy."

"Don't gag me, Harry. I want to know what's going on so get out

223

there and report."

"Yes, Sergeant."

I guess the Colonel had promoted me.

Harry vanished, poking his head in from time to time to let me know what was going on.

What went on didn't go on for very long.

The Russian with the shotgun blew out the door between the house and the garage while Petrov, his driver, and the other two Russians laid a barrage down.

A few bullets tore through the couch, none, fortunately, hitting me. Sanchez's car wasn't so lucky. The sound of shattering glass performed counterpoint to that of jacketed slugs smashing sheet steel. I thought I heard a human grunt, too.

"Oh, shit. Fineman took a bullet," Harry reported. "Can't see where, but she's down and bleeding. It's just Arran now. And—oh, shit."

"What?"

"One of the guys our team had tied up rolled over and tripped Arran. They're all over him."

"Detective Dane." Petrov's deep voice sounded paternal. "How discouraging to see you again. You just aren't much good at taking instructions, are you."

"Not—" Arran's reply was cut off by the crunch of a Russian boot on already damaged ribs.

I clenched my teeth to keep from screaming at him. That jerk had known he and Fineman didn't have a chance. He hadn't wanted me hidden so I could help, he'd wanted me hidden so I would be safe even if he wasn't.

"Make sure they're disarmed."

"Done, boss."

"Well, Detective. Suppose we cut to the chase. Where is Ms. Neeter?"

"Sent her away with Sanchez."

"I find that unlikely."

"Good. Spend some time looking for her. The Rangers will be here soon enough."

"Believe me, I'm timing their arrival, Detective." He paused a moment. "Mr. Valik, did you search the house?"

"Da. Nobody inside." His accent was a bit stronger than Petrov's. "That's why we took so long—had to check out the attic crawl space."

The click of leather shoes on concrete would have told me Petrov was walking around the garage looking even if Ritchie hadn't told me.

"Perhaps Detective Dane is telling the truth, then. Throw both detectives in my trunk. We'll arrange a suitable site for their final disposal. And Valik?"

"Da?"

"Find Sanchez. He can't have gone too far. Make sure his family dies before he does. It's only fair."

"They're leaving now," Harry reported a few moments later. "Fineman don't look so good. Arran don't look good neither."

I pushed against the bedframe, but the Colonel stuck his head through the cushions. "Hang on, Sergeant. No point in putting yourself in danger."

Right. I'd be safe and Arran and Fineman would take the fall for me.

I'd known leaving Arran would be hard. Making love to him had changed everything. But I'd at least promised myself that he'd be all right. Still, jumping out and surrendering wasn't going to help anyone—it would just mean one more body in Petrov's trunk.

"Sorry the Volunteer Cavalry couldn't come through for you." The Colonel hung his head. "We were brave enough, but we were outgunned. Sort of like during the war."

It was odd that 'the war' meant different things to different ghosts. If I ever got to Italy, maybe I'd meet ghosts who thought 'the war' referred to the recent troubles with Hannibal. "You did your best."

"Well you did, too. Don't knock yourself, Annie."

"Thanks." Doing my best hadn't saved Arran or Fineman, though. And I suspected it wouldn't save my brother and his family, either. Petrov had proved how thorough he was when he'd told Valik what to do with Sanchez.

"Did they take the computer?"

The Colonel vanished for a second, then stuck his head back in. "Yep, it's gone."

My heart dropped. "After all that, we have nothing. We might as well have stayed safe."

I pushed my way out of the couch.

The garage was a disaster. Sanchez's Town Car squatted over three flat tires, with only one rear side window intact. The smell of expensive vodka mingled uneasily with the stench of gasoline, but what dripped from the car was tinged red—from Fineman's blood.

"Unless the cavalry wants to get caught in an explosion, we'd better evacuate," I said. "It's over. We lost."

We'd lost more than just the fight. Everything I'd tried to prevent was coming undone. I just hoped Sanchez got away.

Chapter 27

"Texas Rangers. Put your hands in the air."

I'd been so surrounded by ghosts, I hadn't even noticed the black Ford Explorer that pulled up outside Sanchez's home.

"Ten minutes earlier and you'd actually have done some good," I said.

Two Ranger types, both red-faced guys in their early fifties with big white cowboy hats, pointed huge pistols at me. The only way I could tell them apart was that one wore sunglasses and the other didn't.

"Who are you and what happened here?"

I sighed. I wouldn't have minded talking to the Rangers if I'd thought it would do any good. But without the computer, Petrov was free and clear. "I'm Annie Neeter."

"The ghost-talker?"

I was sick of denying it. "That's right. I talk to ghosts."

The Ranger without sunglasses, trotted off to the garage. "Jeez. Looks like Iraq in here."

"Like I said, we could have used you a while ago."

The Ranger with the sunglasses got in my face. "I understand you're distraught, Ms. Neeter, but we need your attention and assistance. We're responding to an emergency call from Detective Fineman formerly of the Dallas Police Department. Can you tell us what happened to her?"

"She and her partner, Detective Arran Dane, were kidnapped by Ivan Petrov." I pointed to Sanchez's car. "That blood is hers but she was alive when they left."

"You saw this happen?"

"I was hiding in the couch. I heard it happen, and had it described to me by the ghosts."

"The Texas Volunteer Ghost Cavalry," the Colonel corrected.

I passed along that update.

"Ghost-cavalry, huh?" the no-sunglasses one scoffed. "That's a good-un."

Screw you and the horse you rode in on. I thought it, but I managed not to say it. Barely.

"We have several reports that Ms. Neeter can communicate with ghosts." Sunglasses turned to me. "Perhaps you'd like the chance to prove that?"

"I don't have time to play games."

If anything, Sunglasses's face got redder. "I don't have time for games, either. Two police detectives are missing, victims of an apparent kidnapping. If you can help track them down, I'm interested. If you've got messages from my dead mother, I'll take a rain check. Now what is it going to be, Ms. Neeter?"

"The Texas Volunteer Ghost Cavalry is ready to assist," the Colonel reported. "A number of our soldiers retained contact with the enemy. One should drop off every couple of miles to maintain contact.

I met the Ranger's black sunglass-blocked stare. "I'll do what I can."

* * * *

Petrov and his guys had split up. Two SUVs full of gunmen went looking for Sanchez while Petrov himself, along with another SUV full of Russian mobsters headed west, toward the open country.

Ranger Stevens, which turned out to be Sunglasses' name, accepted my demand that we follow Petrov, and browbeat the Fort Worth chief of police to put out an emergency warning about Valik and the SUVs.

To my surprise, Stevens treated me and the ghosts like we were a GPS system, making the turns we suggested, even backtracking without complaint.

Until, that is, we ended up on a stretch of 171. Then he got on the phone and mobilized the DPS, the Cleeburn police, and the Johnson County Sheriff's office to man a roadblock.

"He'll kill Arran and Carly when he sees that," I protested.

"I don't tell you how to talk to ghosts, so don't tell me how to do my job," Ranger Stevens said. "Fineman and Dane are professionals. They knew the risks."

Somehow that didn't make me feel better about getting them killed.

Two minutes later, the Colonel rode a huge white horse up next to the Explorer. Since we were bombing along at close to ninety miles an hour, I was impressed.

The Colonel grinned at me. "I didn't know they could go so fast, either. They must have gotten word about the roadblock," he continued. "Petrov and the guys with him pulled off the road."

"Where?"

He gave me coordinates as best he could, which was not especially great. No wonder Civil War armies sometimes missed each other. I passed his directions on to Stevens, though, who nodded and radioed out a bunch of commands to the cops and sheriff's deputies he'd drafted.

"He can't take the town car off the road," Stevens said. "Have the Volunteer Cavalry watch and see what they do with their captives."

The Colonel drew himself straight. "The Texas Volunteer Cavalry are up to the job, sir."

I think his horse was traveling twice as fast as our car when he vanished down the road.

Two minutes later, Oren popped in. "He's dumping them."

"What?"

"He's dumping Carly and Dane. Hiding them behind a tree. Probably plans on bluffing his way through the roadblock and doubling back. The guys in the SUV have turned around and are heading this way."

I reported this to Stevens.

His teeth had to have been artificially whitened, but I welcomed his smile anyway. "He won't be talking his way out of anything."

"But we don't have his computer."

"We have his car—with blood in the trunk. We have your evidence, and if Fineman and Dane survive, we'll have their word. Besides, Russian Mafia or not, we'll crack this gang. Someone will talk. With luck, Petrov is heading toward death row."

"Great," Oren grumbled. "So, *we* get to deal with him. How come you living people treat death like some sort of toxic dumping ground?"

"Can we argue about rehabilitation versus punishment later?" I turned my attention to Stevens. "You know, Ranger, I'm happy that Petrov isn't going to get away, but I'm really more concerned about Detective Dane. And Carly Fineman, of course."

"Me too. They're good officers. Pull over."

The last was directed to Davis, AKA no-sunglasses.

"But—"

"Car's too slow," Stevens explained. "Hop out."

"I've always wanted to ride in one of these," Oren explained as a helicopter settled on the highway about a hundred feet from where Davis waited in the car.

"Load in," I said.

And they did. Ghosts crowded into the cab with Davis and me, Ghosts grabbed onto the skids and hung on for the ride, and a couple of thrill-seeking ghosts even clung to the chopper blades, spinning around at a million or so revolutions per minute.

"Nice thing about not having any inertia, Oren said. "Still, you don't want to see a ghost puke."

No I didn't. "I want to see Arran and Carly alive."

"Yeah. Sorry about the untimely levity."

I directed the chopper to where a crowd of ghosts congregated. By the time Stevens had given me a hand down, a medivac helicopter had joined ours and paramedics scrambled.

I ignored Stevens, ignored the ghosts, and ignored the paramedics, running full tilt toward the bodies.

Petrov had plenty of reason to want them dead. I feared the worst, but wouldn't give up hope until I saw proof. At least they'd both been alive when they'd been taken into the trunk, the Texas Volunteer Ghost Cavalry had assured me of that.

* * * *

"About time you got here."

The call had come in just before the helicopter landed that the Rangers had caught Petrov trying to cross the roadblock. I was glad, but cared a lot more about Arran.

It turned out, Arran was plenty alive. Alive enough to be cranky. He was also bent over his partner trying to apply pressure.

"I hurried. Uh, is Fineman—"

"She's bleeding pretty bad."

"Let us through." The paramedics shoved their way forward.

"Take Detective Fineman first," Arran commanded. "I think she took a hunk of shrapnel in her, uh, chest region."

Ouch. That would hurt.

"You're both going with us, Detective. Now lie still and let us get you in the stretcher."

"Not unless Annie can come with me."

"It's okay, Arran. I'll see you later."

He sighed. "I'm beat up and I'm cranky, Annie. I don't have time to play games."

"Well good for you. I'm not much in the game-playing mood either."

"You're pissed because I didn't let you get killed, aren't you?"

"You knew you'd lose. You could have just surrendered and not gotten hurt."

"I thought we'd lose. There's a difference. And I kept you safe."

"That's my point. It's not fair that you get yourself killed and I'm okay."

"First, I'd be a ghost so we could still talk. And second—"

"That's the stupidest thing I ever heard."

"And second," he continued as if I hadn't said anything, "I couldn't talk to the Ghost Cavalry. If Petrov had taken you, we would have been sunk. We needed you hidden if any of us were going to survive."

"Look, lady," a female paramedic who looked like she could moonlight on the Dallas Cowboys defensive line shot me an elbow in the ribs. "If this guy is going to survive, we need to get him some medical attention. So back off, will you?"

"I've got—"

"Carly and I had a nice chat while we were rolling around in the

229

trunk of Petrov's Town Car. How many of those things do you think he has, by the way? I think I'm making the tour."

"I have no idea."

"Anyway, since we're not going to get our jobs back at DPD, we thought maybe we'd go into business for ourselves."

"Okay."

"The thing is, detective agencies are a dime a dozen. We know a lot of ex-cops who've done it and it's tough to make a living."

"Why are you telling me this?

"The thing is, we need an edge. We figured, if you'd go in with us, we would have something. Assuming your buddies would play along, anyway. Even if not, your research skills would be useful and we want you. But the Volunteer Ghost Cavalry is hard to top."

"I always liked Nick Charles," Oren said.

"Can you guys back off," I shouted. "I'm talking to Arran, not having a town meeting."

"Come on, lady, move," the paramedic insisted.

"Let the Detective have a few minutes with the Ghost-Lady," Ranger Stevens said. "They've got some shit to work through."

Shit was a good word for it. "Arran. I—"

"So, any interest in going partners with us?"

A month before, an offer like that would have been a dream. I could hardly imagine working with people who not only accepted my differences, but who saw them as positive, as an asset to the team. But a month had passed. "I don't—"

"Don't tell me you're still thinking about vanishing somewhere. You don't have to worry about Petrov any more."

"It's not just Pet—"

"And anyone who looks at what happened to Petrov when he messed with us will catch on that you're more dangerous than you look."

"But—" I cut myself off. Arran was right. Alone, I was a target, but as part of a team that included a tough woman like Fineman, the hard-edged Arran, I wasn't so easy. Especially since I had my Blue Belt test coming up, assuming I didn't miss any more Tae Kwon Do classes.

"You see, you have no good reason not to join us, and plenty of reasons to sign up for the team."

I was tempted. It would be fun to work with Fineman and Arran. These past weeks working with the ghosts had been great. I'd gone from seeing them as ever-harassing troublemakers to helpers and, to be honest, friends.

But working meant spending time together. And spending time

together meant I'd see Arran getting ready to go out on dates with other women, or dragging in in the mornings after a big night out. That would drive me crazy.

"Arran, I can't—"

"Then there would be fringe benefits."

"You're doing a lot of interrupting, you know."

Arran smiled. "Only when I don't like where you're going."

"Distracting me isn't going to work. I can't come to work for you, Arran. It wouldn't—"

"I did mention the fringe benefits, didn't I? We won't have much money at the start, so I thought maybe we could combine resources."

"What the—"

"I thought your aluminum foil and my bedroom walls would be a good start."

I took a deep breath. "What are you trying to say?"

He sighed. "Okay, you win. If you don't want to go into business with us, that's your decision. But I'm not going to take a no on the other. I want aluminum foil in my apartment. And weird flashing lights, too."

"I think you're making fun of me."

His face grew deadly serious. "I'm not really good at the words, babe, but I'm definitely not trying to make fun of you. Since we've been together, I've changed how I've seen the world, and I want more. I'll understand if you want to take it slow, but I want you to be part of my life."

"Friends with benefits?"

He grinned. "I like benefits."

I made myself consider. Arran wasn't promising forever, but he wasn't talking about casual sex, either. He wanted me as a partner in his business and he wanted me sharing his apartment—and his bed. That sounded pretty serious to me.

"Do I need to make a decision right now?"

"I'm not going anywhere."

"The hell you're not," the paramedic said. "You're going to the hospital and you're going now. And don't give me any more sass, Ranger Stevens. Or I'll have the Sheriff arrest you for interfering with a medical emergency."

"Of course I'd heal a lot faster if I knew I had something to some home to." A whole herd of paramedics were bundling Arran onto a stretcher, fitting him with an IV, and doing medical things like temperature and blood pressure, but he kept looking at me as if I knew the answers.

"Oh, hell, Arran. Let's give it a try."

"That's so romantic." Tiffany clasped her arms around Cassandra. "We'll take good care of him until he gets back to you."

"The hell you will. Colonel, arrest these two ghosts. I don't want them anywhere near Arran at least until I've had my way with him."

"I don't know about arresting." The Colonel took off his hat and shuffled his booted feet on the ground. "But if you'd like to come out dancing with me tonight, Tiffany, I surely would appreciate it. And Cassy, I'm thinking Richie has been trying to get up the—"

"I can ask her myself," the ex-knee-breaker put in. "'Course if you don't like dancing, we can do a movie. No popcorn, though."

Cassandra smiled and merged her hand with Ritchie's arm. "If Annie's going to take the foil out of her bedroom, we could try out a horizontal dance. I think I'd like that."

"Can ghosts do that?" I demanded.

The Colonel shrugged. "I'll let you know."

"Please don't," I begged. "I think that's a detail I can wait to figure out."